NORTH

Owen is the pseudonym for two authors – Diane Awerbuck and
Latimer. Diane Awerbuck's debut novel GARDENING AT
T won the 2004 Commonwealth Writers Prize and Diane was
sted for the Caine Prize in 2014. She has long been regarded
of South Africa's most talented writers. Alex Latimer is an
-winning writer and illustrator, whose books have been trans-
nto several languages.

Also by Frank Owen

SOUTH

NORTH

Frank Owen

First published in trade paperback in Great Britain in 2018 by
Corvus Books, an imprint of Atlantic Books Ltd.

Copyright © Frank Owen, 2018

1 3 5 7 9 8 6 4 2

A CIP catalogue record for this book
is available from the British Library.

Trade Paperback ISBN: 9781782399001
EBook ISBN: 9781782399018

Corvus Books
An Imprint of Atlantic Books Ltd
Ormond House
26–27 Boswell Street
London
WC1N 3JZ

www.corvus-books.co.uk

Printed & Bound by MBM Print SCS Ltd Glasgow

MIX
Paper from
responsible sources
FSC® C117931

A single virus permeating a membrane is all it takes for a full-blown infection to take place. A single virus, tiny as it is, can bring death to systems infinitely larger than it. And yet, death in this instance is not the end. It is a pruning so that systems much larger than that individual might be healthier as a result.

DIDIER RENARD

1

You're not even born yet, but if I don't set this down, I'm afraid that I'll forget exactly how it was. Ma had her recipe book, but you're going to have your own history written plain and clear.

Baby, I want you to understand some things about the people you came from, how they fought and struggled so that you could be alive and here and with me. The world is going to be different by the time you're grown up in it, and for that I can only be grateful.

It was bad. And the War was only the beginning.

After it ended, and Renard built his wall between the North and South, the wind still blew the sicknesses from above. And it wasn't like bird flu or Ebola or the plague or something where you knew how it worked, even if it was terrible. The viruses took everyone differently. The worst were the brain viruses, because there wasn't a whole lot you could tell from the outside: no peeling flesh or blackened toes. Mama – that's your grandma Ruth, and don't you forget her – said it was like they were burrowing into the soft meat and chewing through the wiring that made us kind to one another. The men always had it the worst, because they had more juices to turn sour. Testosterone makes you brave and adventurous, but when the worms get in it also makes you want to rip other creatures limb from limb.

We learnt that the hard way.

So when the wind blew, Ma and I would camp in the sitting room and tell each other stories to pass the time. Ma was real keen on passing on her baby-birthing know-how, but sometimes she also told me bits of her life. The details would change between tellings, and she'd get to a point I'd recognize and then change tack completely so I could never tell what was true and what was wishing.

Baby, there are times when you can feel change coming. I mean, actually feel it, like history is being made and you're right in the middle of it. My moment like that came when I first saw your daddy. I felt something when I looked him in the eyes that wasn't romance and moonlight, but some other thing, unpretty as a weed, and just as tough. Love can be like that.

That was my first moment. The next one came not long after that, when he'd gone away and left us. He said he'd be back. The rest of us from the ghost colony – Ma and me, but also Sam and Pete and a whole bunch of the other Southern survivors – were resting against a rock face on the bank of the North Platte, trying to keep the brewing storm at our backs, deciding what to do next now that we'd arrived. I was tired, baby, in a way that I hope you will never be. It's not only about the body, and one day you'll understand that too. A person on a horse gets just as tired from looking back over their shoulder, and I was, for sure, worn down with sorrow and with hoping that Dyce would show. I remember the white lightning in the distance, and how it made the horses restless. They were just as hungry and frightened as we all were, and they were tiptoeing on their hooves that had gone soft as rubber from the time spent wading in the water.

That lightning gave me another moment. It showed us the Northern border wall, and the strange orange of electric street lights beyond it, and after that the glow of high-rise apartment blocks, now and again hidden by sheets of water. Baby, none of it seemed real. It was like looking across onto another planet, or back through time to how things once were.

We were really going to cross into the North! It was unbelievable. It made everything I knew seem wrong. The Wall had always been part of us. When Renard had set up the concrete and the border guards after the War, he had in mind to stop anyone crossing one way or the other. He knew that it would strangle the South. And it worked. We got poorer. And angrier.

But it was the winds that killed most people. We were trapped in the heart of the South, hiding and watching as people took ill and wasted away. No two corpses that I ever saw died from the same disease. You could tell by the way the eyes bulged or sank, were milky or bloodshot, the red trickling like jewelry down to their ears.

For a long time those winds, loaded with their viruses, whittled us down. Millions of people died, I guess. Our immune systems were weak – but there was something else too. You have to *want* to survive. That's the most important thing. You have to believe there is a future you want to be in. Not everyone does.

Some folk headed for the coast, hoping to find boats to take them across the Pacific or the Atlantic: anywhere, like the slave ships all those years ago, but going the other way. Dyce's brother Garrett – your uncle Garrett, he would have been, and your aunt Bethie too – had that grand plan. But the thing was, the sea air was worse. It was wet, and so it actually nurtured the viruses, kept them living for longer, suspended in the air like poisonous pollen. It wasn't fair.

But if Dyce had made it to the coast with Garrett, he would

have died before we had even met, and then you wouldn't have happened. It was fate that your parents met in that world carved down to the bone. Do you believe that, baby? Fate that two people, so different, could fall in love in a time when love was a useless thing?

But love always leads somewhere else.

Now your daddy, Dyce, was only alive because of the hard work *his* daddy did. Your grandpa was no fool: he saw what was coming, clear as day, and when their mama died, he got to spending a whole lot of time teaching his boys survival. Just like the scouts. No one survived by chance, do you understand what I'm saying? We were there and we were there for a reason, and that reason is you. There were the books and there was the teaching – same as what I'm doing here, writing all of this down for you. We can't ever forget. We *are* our stories, and when you're all grown, maybe you'll have a better handle on what I mean by that, but in the meantime, let's go back a bit. There's something real important about this part.

When I first met him, your daddy had caught a terrible virus, which made him blind and weak, like an old-time vampire in the daylight. I carried him – *carried* him – and I cared for him when I got him to a cabin we found. Belonged to an old guy named Felix. (You know what, baby? The Weatherman'll probably still be around when you're grown. He's like a piece of beef jerky. Tell him I say hi.)

It turned out that I had got myself into more trouble than I knew. Dyce and his brother Garrett were trying to outrun some folk who fancied themselves lawmakers. The Callahans. Maybe they'd been lawmen once upon a time; now the laws were whatever they figured might serve them best. I saved Dyce's skinny ass that day.

We all decided to travel together, your grandmama too, and we ended up in the ghost colony, a lazaretto where the sick were gathered to die. Except that here at Horse Head they seemed pretty healthy. Mama got right in there and started organizing everyone, and we found out – guilt makes you lucky – that a lot of viruses had opposite numbers. It sounds weird, but it makes sense: hair of the dog. The alchemists used to think it, and those guys believed in mathematics. You could, in theory, find someone who was living with the cure for your disease in their own body. Sometimes, when the viruses combined in the right way, you could heal yourself. A bit like falling in love.

Because another thing happened at Horse Head too. When you spend a lot of time with a person, you get to know them. They can rub you up the wrong way, like me and your grandma, or it can turn the other way. As your daddy got healthy, he grew on me, baby. It was those eyes. He had the longest, darkest eyelashes, and one day he kissed me until I cried.

We set out to find a life for ourselves – and to lead the Callahans away from the good folk of that colony who'd taken us in. We found ourselves in the bowels of a town called the Mouth. We had heard it was the Promised Land: no one was sick there.

Instead, we found ourselves hunted deep under the earth and into the old mines where they were growing medicine mushrooms. But, baby, these mushrooms were different. They grew from the corpses of men and women who were being sacrificed. Can you believe that? We saw things there and after that turn a person bitter. But you've got to fight against the bitterness. What else is there?

Dyce saved us that time: he could see in the dark. And we took some of those mushrooms with us when we got out, baby.

We packed them up like a picnic and took them back to Ma, to Horse Head, and la-la, happy ending, we survived the winds that should have ended the South. We lived because he and I met and were kind to one another.

But there's never an ending, not as long as there's someone there to tell it, and we had no idea what was in store for us beyond the Wall. Whether we'd be shot dead as we climbed out of that river, North-side, we didn't know.

I got the rest of the story that afternoon, curled up and resting against the rock, when Ma finally told me her side. She was a hard woman, your grandma Ruth, but I guess she thought she owed me. Besides, we never knew just how it was going to pan out: every time we said goodbye might have been for keeps. So that day she spoke for a long time about her life before Renard, back in South Africa, about how she'd escaped apartheid with her man, Wilson, who ended up sacrificing himself so that she could get on the last boat they let dock at Ellis Island. And she always kept her book of remedies with her. You'll know it, baby: it's the one with the pages that are swollen and warped, because they're packed with writing, along with all her seeds and dried cuttings and petals.

But that recipe book was *all* your grandma had. She was alone and foreign in a country where black people weren't high on the list. Renard sure wasn't the first president to have some funny ideas about the equality of human beings; being from South Africa prepared her.

And she was a smart cookie, your grandma Ruth. She found work in a hospital and then trained as a nurse, and when she wasn't emptying bedpans and holding dying hands, she was adding to her recipe book. Adding American herbs and recipes to her African ones, trying – and often failing – to match local ingredients to the ones back home so that her past and her present sat side by side. And being in the hospital helped: they weren't as careful with the dispensary keys back then.

One day she met the man himself – Didier Renard. You know what she told me, baby? She said he wasn't the monster then that he is now. He seemed so ordinary – sympathetic, even, and of course a brilliant doctor. But he was also a cheater, and they had an affair. She was flattered, she said, though at least she looked ashamed when she told me. His wife was blown up in a bomb, you know that? His people say now that's what turned him bad. But it takes more than that, baby. We all have to decide what to forgive and what to forget.

After she told me all that, we hugged for the first time in forever. I remember the hot iron smell of the horses, the rain stinging our faces and the thunder vibrating in my chest. Soon our little gang of Southern survivors would get back up on those poor, tired horses, and then we would wade into the Platte and try to find an entrance point in the barbed wire and the concrete. The same water that was rushing toward us now came from up North. It was right there. Surely we could pass over.

But that wasn't the whole story, or even the end of my part. That was only the bit that I knew then.

2

There were dead bodies caught in the barbed wire under that churning brown water, Ruth knew, but the only person she cared about was Vida. Through the pelting rain she was sure she could see her daughter from here – trapped near the other side of the river.

It *was* Vida. It had to be.

Ruth breathed. Everything hurt. The burning in her bony chest wouldn't go away, but she sucked in as much air as she could. That burn meant her bruised lungs were still working, and it meant that she had a chance to save her daughter – and she would, by God, busted rib or no busted rib.

She screwed up her eyes. The body on the far side of the North Platte rolled and bobbed, helpless under the churning floodwaters, a dark shape riding the current.

'Vida!' Ruth screamed, but the storm stole her voice.

Someone was trying to hold her back, to keep her from wading into the water again, but she pulled loose from their grip, driven by the red maternal urge. She staggered forward, one step, then another, and now the river was all around her. In she went: deeper, and deeper still, like a baptism, and then the chill stink of the water was rising to her neck.

Ruth felt her feet freed from the riverbed as she was upended, and the branches of the smashed cottonwoods – old growth, too hard to bend – caught and tore at her arms as they rushed on with the floodwater. She tried a few strokes, but she was too slow and the current was too strong. Of course it was! Her exhausted limbs against the might of the Hundred-Year Storm. When it took her along with the jumbled mess of horses and branches and bodies, she let it. She felt the air rushing from her lungs.

She fought against blacking out, replacing the panic with insistent pictures like an old-time movie reel: Vida, tiny and bloodied and screaming, newborn in the back of a rusted minivan, the one place that Ruth had felt safe after her escape from Renard and the North.

Then Vida at ten, fierce and chubby-cheeked, checking her traps or bagging the last of the locust swarms, chasing them with a pillowcase that loomed white against her skin.

And then a couple of months ago, from her sweaty sickbed cocoon, Ruth watching her grown daughter set off on her daily foraging round, her hair braided like a warrior's. The everlasting satchel was slung over her shoulder, and her legs were long and strong with muscle. That time she had come back with Dyce and his brother Garrett, and things had never been the same after that.

But she always came back, didn't she? She couldn't be dead.

Ruth wiped her eyes, coughing out a mouthful of cold water that tried to choke her. Surely that shape – right there, within reach – was Vida. She *felt* it. Let it be her, Ruth told the universe. Please let that be my child. Let her live. She was no stranger to begging. Before she had met the people from the ghost colony and found the Resistance, Ruth was long used to praying and bargaining away everything she could think of – her house, her beloved recipe book, her memories, her life – to the bored and faceless gods.

The reply now was the same: only the water that roiled and pounded in her ears, and the knowledge that God helped those who were quick enough to help themselves.

3

Kurt Callahan, thin with teenage hunger, lifted himself out of the foaming water of the North Platte and heaved himself, panting, onto the lip of a concrete pylon that had once supported the railway bridge. There was just enough room around the pillar for him to keep out of the floodwater that surged and sucked at his ankles. He could feel his toes, wrinkled like prunes, inside his shoes – soft and ready to blister. He took off his water-heavy shoes and socks, and hung them above his head on spikes of wire to dry. Then he sat, slicked his straw-blond hair out of his face and wriggled his ghost-pale toes.

Under his spread fingers the rusted rebar held the failing structure together like the bones of a dead bird. Above, at the very tops of the pylons, he could see where the vanished arches had once upon a time been connected. Exhausted, he rested his back against the pillar and stared up at the sky with its rising thunderheads thick with rain, trying to trace the path of the winds that tormented the clouds. Kurt no longer had to fear the poison those winds carried. He raised his fist.

'The last surviving Callahan on the fucking continent, and the first to make it to the North,' he told the sky.

That made him special, didn't it?

But then he'd always known he was special. Growing up, he was taller than most kids his age. Faster and quieter too. Those were the two most important things when it came to trapping. But there was something else about himself that he'd known but hadn't let on about, especially not to his mother. Perspective, he called it.

The end of last summer had come and the snares were empty, day after day. Everyone had eaten the herbs and bark and ants till they were sick of the sight. Kurt saw the men side-eyeing his dog – a mixed-breed mutt with the snout of a borzoi and a bulldog's underbite. Mason was the undisputed canine king of Glenvale, mongrel that he was: the king and only dog. Like horses, dogs had gotten rare – extinct, in most parts. This one had seen too many years of illness and not nearly enough food. One of his eyes had milked over and the other was on its way; his ears were fraying at the edges, bitten down by the mites. His ribs showed through skin pulled so tight that Kurt saw the lumpy surfaces of his organs and thought: Worms. That was where his food was going.

On the first warm and windless day, when the men had judged it safe to forage far from camp, Kurt had stripped the cord from a kettle and set the old wire around Mason's neck. Whistling, he led the dog out of camp, and no one stopped to question him. Kurt, even at fifteen, had been no man's servant. Sometimes Mason went along for company – Kurt could spend hours crouched, watching his snares – but this time he had not taken his bag of sticks and string, nor the knotted fishing line.

Downstream of the river that ran past the Glenvale camp was a small waterfall. It pounded into the pool below, settling into the color of rust. It had something to do with the alders overhead: they leant down and dropped their leaves, staining the water like tea.

Poor Mason, said Kurt, when he got back to camp with the

dog's limp body in his arms. When that cougar had come charg-
ing out of the underbrush, it was foaming pink at the mouth
– blood mixed with saliva – the way all the animals did when
they caught what Renard had spread in the air. Mason took
on the cougar, Kurt said, making his blue Callahan eyes round
with grief. The big cat, rare to the point of imagining, crazy
with disease, had smashed the dog into a tree stump. Kurt had
been too late to save him, but Mason had certainly saved his
life, hadn't he?

Kurt had held out the body, flopped in his arms but starting to stiffen, the animal's tongue swollen and dark, lips drawn
back in a rictus. The women looked at him, their hands over
their mouths. He shoved the body at Bethie, but he should have
known better. She had only looked away, nauseated.

It was a shame to let all that good meat go to waste.

No one had liked eating Mason, exactly, but no one ever
liked what they were surviving on lately. Kurt couldn't decide
what the low point was – the boiled leather tongues cut out
of every pair of shoes, or the dry-bone soup, or the millipedes,
bitter as gall, that had to be wrapped in river weed so they slid
past the tongue without making contact with the buds. Maybe,
if the women had not been so hungry, so eager to skin the dog,
they'd have noticed the burn line around Mason's neck, thin as
cord, the healthy eye spidered with burst blood vessels.

Perspective. Kurt hadn't killed a dog. He had saved a community.

He'd watched Bethie eat her portion of Mason – three vertebrae, with the meat and sinews that joined them. Watching
her pick her careful way, teeth and tongue, through his provi-
sion gave him a strange feeling, a friendly fire in his stomach
that stripped him of his appetite and hardened his dick. He'd

hidden it with his hunting bag slung in front of him. When it subsided, he had gathered his courage and gone to offer her his own plateful so that the feeling wouldn't stop. At first she resisted, saying he should eat, but in the end she took it, didn't she? She was starving by degrees. They all were. The tendons in her neck flexed as she swallowed, and the ivory pendant she wore moved with the motion. It would be warm from her skin. Kurt longed to hold it between his fingers.

It was goddam perspective that got him North-side too. Seeing the Callahan clan for what they were – weak-minded men too shit-scared of old man Tye to think for themselves. No way he was hightailing it back to Glenvale with that chicken-shit posse. It was Tye who could teach him something, Tye the only one who wasn't afraid to stand up for himself.

So he'd made sure Tye had caught sight of him in the treeline, hadn't he? And then, just to make sure, he'd thrashed home-ward as loud as he could without it seeming deliberate. The old man had fallen for it too – hook, line, sinker and swivel. There he was, giving himself a pat on the back for still being a step ahead of the cubs, unaware that Kurt had crept back, silent as a shadow. The old man had gone about his business, which was where things got real interesting. Northern scouts: goddam! Kurt had wanted to step out of the bushes and cut those motherfuck-ers down, but he knew that as soon as he was front and center, he'd lose any advantage he had. He told himself that over and over as he lay beneath the sumac, and he'd been rewarded. Tye had met with the Northern army, bold as you please.

And that wasn't the end, neither. Kurt had also seen what happened next: that whole army poisoned by Garrett's brother and that mouthy girl of his; seen Tye's trophy – the syringe with its antidote – and seen where it had dropped too, still with a quarter-inch left in the plunger. By the time it was over, the slopes were empty – just the needle sticking into the dirt like a stray arrow. He'd cleaned that needle off on his sleeve, then washed it in the river and let it rest for a few seconds on the dying embers of a campfire. It burnt when he jammed it into his arm and he wasn't sure he'd hit a vein, but he'd gotten his dose of antivirals – enough, anyway, to have kept him alive this long.

Yup. It was all down to perspective, for sure. There was more to life than surviving so you could obey orders and hold Tye Callahan's dick while he peed.

Now Kurt rubbed his hand through his wet hair. Bethie was dead and that was that. So was the old man, though he felt no particular pang. Kurt got gingerly to his feet and shook the last of the Platte River water out of his ears and the thoughts of those two doomed Callahans from his head. He needed a plan.

It didn't look good from over here. There was no way he was getting back into the water as it was, with its sticks and logs and guttering, the flotsam a hail of knives as the floodwaters rushed them onward, and so he would have to wait on his concrete island. He needed to rest. He could shelter on the leeward side when the rain got too hard.

The luck of the Callahans was on his side. The next day, near midday, a gold pickup came by, an old couple sitting high inside, propped like puppets. Kurt noted the peeling sticker of the wrench and faucet across the driver's door: DRAIN SURGEON, it said. Natural disasters sure put money in some men's pockets.

Kurt raised his arms and hollered until the driver caught sight of him. The old man got out and stood beside the pickup, thumbs hooked in the straps of his dungarees like Uncle Remus, judging the situation – a fair-headed white boy stranded on some pilings in the middle of the river.

He made up his mind and went back to the pickup, conferring with his wife on the passenger side. She had been knitting something in dark green wool, as far as Kurt could make out, but now she set her handiwork down and got out of the car. The old man began wrangling a battered toolbox from the flatbed, then they both came sliding down the riverbank like Jack and Jill, the mud leaving grayish-brown smears on their clothes. The man waved to Kurt, but the water was too loud to hear what he was saying. He handed one end of the coiled rope to the woman and walked upriver, away from her, looking around, searching for something. He bent to reach into the reeds and emerged with a plastic milk bottle. He half filled it with water and tied the rope through the handle. Then he threw the bottle as far as he could into the water. The woman held onto her end, and the river swept the bottle to Kurt.

The boy grabbed the weighted rope. The man, slipping in his mud-caked boots, went back to where the woman stood. They signaled for Kurt to tie the rope around his waist. When they were set and the river was clear of debris as far as they could see, the man raised a hand and counted to three by raising his fingers – thumb, index, middle.

Kurt slipped into the water and felt the sharp yanking of the rope as the couple reeled him in, hand over hand. When he could stand, the man waded in and helped him out of the water.

'Are you all right?' yelled the woman, but Kurt didn't answer. He raised a rock from the riverbed as big as his fist and crunched it into the old man's face. He fell forward into the water, terminally surprised. The woman started screaming, her mouth a purple O, the way they always did. She turned to run up the slope but slipped. Kurt caught her by the ankle and dragged her backward. She was kicking and shrieking; all he had to do was wait for the current and just let her go. He watched both the good Samaritans tumbling over and over in the water until they vanished beneath the foam.

'Drain surgeon, huh? How about first Southerner to kill a Northerner since the War?' said Kurt. He untied the rescue rope from his waist.

4

Felix woke wet and numb and stuck between two inbred hack-berry saplings, like a shred of meat between a man's molars. But at least he was out of the water and under the struggling low-lying sun, praise the Little White Baby Jesus. He couldn't feel his fingers. He didn't remember hauling himself out of the river, or stumbling up this slope. He did remember falling end-lessly forward into the rivulets of rain that wiggled over each other, the watery knots making mermaids' hair of the drowned grasses. He turned his wrists over, the flesh puffed and bruised from the impact, as if he'd been cuffed in the night, or doing push-ups in the mud.

The portion of the Platte River he could see was curved and unpredictable, still foaming brown from the storm. The near bank was littered with logs, their ends straw-pale and raw in the early light. They lay stiff as the sorry corpses of the stray dogs that had been too terrified by the thunder to be rounded up. Their bodies bobbed by every now and again, bloated bladders with sticks for legs.

'Coulda been me,' Felix told the last one. 'Could, woulda, shoulda. Wasn't.' He coughed out a chuckle and went back to assessing the damage.

Further along the river he could make out the wind-torn shapes of demolished structures – old or new damage, he couldn't tell. If he turned his stiff neck and looked south, out near the horizon, he could see the concrete slabs of the fortress Wall – and beyond that the ragged clouds, still coming in fast with the last of the rain. As he looked back North-side, there were jagged splinters of cladding sweeping past in the river, tumbling over and over in the swell like the teeth of a circular saw.

Felix patted himself down slowly, amazed that he was not worse off from his time in the water. He lay back between the saplings and pieced the sequence together – the rolling over, how he had at least remembered to turn his face sideways so he could breathe through the rain without choking, like a rebirth on a couch or at a church. But still – he would have been fucked. The water had washed him back down the oily slope toward the river again, undoing all his precious progress, until he'd been snagged hip and neck by the twin saplings.

He couldn't say when the rain had let up. It was even now speckling the patches of his clothes dry enough to show it; he had been too dazed to notice. The river still thundered in his skull like a hangover, an ache like pneumonia. The shivering hadn't quit, either, and the dimpled scar on his thigh from the long-ago bullet ached worse than the day he got it. He rubbed the place through his pants leg, thinking about the shiny purple tissue, the X where his knife had dug for the lead like a terrible treasure. He shook his head. It was still weird to think about. Shot in the leg by a moron: ole Tye Wrong-Toilet McKenzie! But that fucker had got his just deserts, as they say in the classics. Yes indeedy. Crushed under a horse, and then his own harrier stripping the flesh from his dead face. It gave Felix the heebie-jeebies. He peered into the sky as if he might see the speckled bird circling overhead, waiting for its chance, like a buzzard.

That made him get up, slow and sore, from between the

saplings. He had to struggle against the outline of his own body in the mud where the streams had washed around his arms and legs. Now, upright, he regarded the depression in the muck, his ghost limbs caught by the spindly trunks. His arms were spidery; his head had been severed from his body.

'Fuck that,' he told the river and the mud. 'That's the Platte for you: too thick to drink, too thin to plow.' He scuffed at the alien imprint with his damp boot. 'So fuck you. I'm alive.'

He turned and limped up the slope away from the river – any place but here – squelching as he went. As he retreated, the water's threats faded, and he could feel the squeeze of his stubborn old lungs and the clench of his shrunken stomach, measuring their workings against the weak morning sun.

Dripping, he passed over the jagged edge of a road, the verge washed loose in black clumps of asphalt, and suddenly there it was, squatting in the wet, the first sign that the previous night – the last forty years – hadn't been a dream. A diner, by God, a low-roofed mirage, the gutter hanging drunk.

It stopped him in his tracks, but the idea of what might be inside got him going again, double time, his eyes pinned to the building in case it disappeared on him. Now he had to pick his way around the storm debris like a crash-site investigator – clothes stripped from washing lines, terracotta potsherds dashed down from balconies, Styrofoam balls like white ticks clinging to whatever brushed against them, and always the leaves and twigs and branches, green to their innocent cores. Every time he thought he was used to it, there was a sudden rust-free razor, a doll's head, a defunct water cooler from an absent office.

Along with every able body in the South, Felix had got used to decay up close, but this looked like fresh damage. Back home after the first virus, when people gave up on maintaining things, there'd been a gradual kind of decline. Folks held on a long time, and buildings were slow to age, but in every house someone was dying, like a plague newsflash or a medieval woodcut; no one gave too many fucks about peeling fascia boards or a few loose shingles or a patch of blistering damp. No, sir. Fucks are in short supply when you're puking your guts out, thought Felix. No time for neighborly niceties.

This, though, was simple storm damage, he was pretty sure. The gutter had been fine maybe yesterday and it'd be propped up and working again tomorrow. The screen door that had blown off its hinge and sagged against the flagstones – that sort of shit would be straightened and reinforced tout suite, good as new. The rest would be swept up and dumped somewhere out of sight. Some things could be fixed so that you didn't remember they'd been broken in the first place. But you had to start on the fixing before too long or you'd never get a handle on a decent repair. And of course, every single thing he'd left behind south of the Wall was beyond that point. If it was working, then that was all you could rightly hope for. Count your blessings and say your thanks before bed.

There was a rectangle of bare wood above the broken door, where the name of the diner had been, Felix reckoned. It didn't make much difference. SAM'S or JEAN'S or BOB'S. They were all the same. There'd be a sweaty cook inside there, Felix thought as he marched, a man with a faceful of stubble and a disappointed past, even now slicing and sizzling a haunch of bacon against his arrival, shoveling flapjacks onto a couple of clean white plates.

As he got closer, Felix saw that there was an animal hunched in the window: a grubby tabby cat. As he paused to peer in at the plate glass, the cat lifted a leg and began to lick its balls. Felix cracked a grin. He could feel the pale sun warm on the back of his neck, and there was a sign just above the cat that made the saliva spring under his tongue and his stomach flip over with delight: HOT COFFEE HOT COFFEE HOT COFFEE.

'Fuck everybody in the North, cat,' he said. 'Fuck 'em sideways to Sunday. But if there's coffee behind that counter, I reckon I can put aside my grievance for fifteen minutes. A half-hour, tops.'

The screen door of the diner lolled against his grip but lifted easily enough. Felix opened it wide and rested it flush against the wall. He had to lean hard against the glass of the door to get it open. The water had swollen the frame against the jamb, but it gave, and the mechanical chime jangled. He had a sudden vision of everyone in this town a robot, like some science-fiction story, but the big white woman with her back to him was real enough. More than real: the vast pink of her flesh in the tented house dress made her blood seem too near to the surface. Felix blinked. Fat people were scarce in the South.

The woman still hadn't seen him. She clicked her tongue in annoyance as she squinted into the lard-speckled lid of the grill behind the gas plates. He stood dumbly in the doorway and looked at the rolls her bra made on her back, like sausages. Then he cleared his throat.

'Don't listen to what the cat says,' she said. 'We're closed.' She was still examining her reflection in the grill lid, fiddling with her hair in its bun. The flesh on her arms jiggled. 'I just come in to sweep the place out. Mind the buckets.'

Felix looked down at the dirty puddle squares of the linoleum and then up at the ceiling. It looked like the joint between two gypsum boards had burst open. The water was still dripping sulkily into a row of empty buckets beside the cash register.

Their sides were scratched. Some had CLEANER written on them in black marker. Maybe there was a war on buckets too.

'No coffee, then?' he asked.

'Nope.' She shook a couple of loose hairs from her fingers and Felix watched them float gently to the linoleum. She finally turned around and got a good look at him leaning there, wet through and still shivering, his paper-thin skin bluish in the daylight, a resurrection man. She gaped at him.

'Jesus Henry Christ! You don't need coffee! You need a defibrillator!'

Felix tried on a friendly smile. 'Yup. It's coffee or I die right in your diner.'

She hefted herself around the counter and picked her way across the linoleum. She was wearing oversized rain boots, and there was something funny about that, but Felix knew better than to laugh.

'First things first, cowboy. We're going to get you to sit right down, okay?' She jutted her chin at a booth near the window. He nodded.

She worked a shoulder under his armpit, and they began to make their way over there. Like war wounded, thought Felix. The woman smelt of bleach and a heavy floral scent that didn't hide the sweat.

He sighed as she slid him into the cracked vinyl of the booth. 'Thank you.'

She stood in front of him, hands on her hips, deciding what to make of him. 'You just stay here, and I'll see if I can rustle something up for you in the back. And listen. You see a light, you stay the heck away from it. Right?'

'Lady,' said Felix, and this time his smile was real. 'I'm too tired to die.'

The woman snorted and sloshed back behind the counter. When she came back a while later with a tray, it was stocked with a pot of coffee, two cups, paper towels and about a dozen donuts. They probably weren't fresh, but then neither was he, Felix told himself.

'But what are you going to have?' he said.

She twisted her lips and he added, fast, 'Just kidding. This looks great. More than great. Heaven on earth.'

She was pouring him a cup. 'Made fresh with today's water, and I don't care how you usually take it. You need the sugar,' she said, and added three heaped spoonfuls. Then she poured coffee for herself.

'Now you just back up and tell me what's going on here,' she said.

Felix thought: Keep it simple, asshole. Whatever you tell her now has to stand the telling to everyone else who comes after.

She was staring hard at him. 'I'm Norma. Where you from, anyway?'

'I don't rightly know,' said Felix. He took his first cautious sip, and it was true, that stuff was HOT COFFEE, and goddam if it wasn't the best thing he'd ever tasted.

'What's that mean?'

He drank again, not caring that his mouth cried out in protest, and leant forward to get a donut, wondering if she could be trusted with the truth.

'What if I told you I was from south of the border? That the storm washed me all the way up the North Platte?'

He selected a donut and took a bite, dusty with sugar and slick with oil, and it made him want to cry. He tried to swallow, coughed, and chased it with more coffee.

Norma's eyes had narrowed. 'Then I'd go into the kitchen

and come back with the biggest knife I could find.' She looked at the tray, then picked up a teaspoon. 'Wouldn't even have to go to the kitchen. I could cut you down with this.' She waved it at him. 'But then, why dirty a spoon? I reckon a rolled-up paper towel would do it. I could just about beat your brains out with a feather.'

Felix held up the hand without the donut in it. 'I get it. I get it.'

'Fuck the South,' Norma said softly, and the color rose from her throat, a blotchy red that might have been pretty on a thinner woman. 'Pardon my French, but fuck them for all of this.' She waved a hand out of the window.

He chewed and swallowed. 'Good thing I'm from New York, then.'

'Big city boy, huh?'

'Back in the day. Spent a little time in Des Moines too.'

'So what you doing here, then?'

'Heard about these donuts.'

For the first time, Norma laughed, her gullet pink and vast. Felix looked away and kept chewing. He concentrated on the empty car park with its littering of sticks and leaves and debris. Far off, way on the other side of the road, he could see an animal moving. He swallowed, the dough dry and catching in his throat. Something out there was walking slowly, loping and tall. He squinted his eyes in disbelief and leant in against the glass.

'What the fuck's that?' He let go of his coffee to point.

'What?'

'There.'

'What do you think it is?'

'Norma, I think it's a giraffe.'

'Well, then, mister. Welcome to Saratoga.'

5

While Felix had lain half dead in his sapling sling, a vehicle was motoring north along the highway. The two passengers in the back of the pickup were quiet, mostly – shell-shocked – listening as the radio fuzzed in and out of tune and the rain clattered on the roof. Every now and again Dyce kept leaning in to get the words of a song, or the plinking of a riff that he recognized from his long-ago life. Why couldn't he sleep, the way Vida was trying to do? The pickup was warm and dry, but he was antsy. He slid his hand into his jacket pocket and fingered the machine heads off the old mandolin. They were still there. He turned them over between his fingertips, until they grew warm as blood. How long had they been driving? Forty minutes? An hour? Things seemed different here in the North. He was having a hard time getting his bearings.

He remembered Ears McCreedy, and unhooked the stuffed squirrel from his belt and set the creature on the seat beside him. Ears stared blankly ahead at the new world, blackened and sodden but as much himself as he had ever been. The water that seeped out of his stuffing and onto the leather seat was stained red by the Colorado dirt packed inside him, but Vida paid him no mind. She was pretty cut up herself, especially around the thighs, any fool could see that: the razor wire at the Wall had done its job. She half lay in the back seat beside him with her eyes closed, and Dyce felt something hurt in his chest as he watched her fighting for sleep. If she hadn't made it here with him, he would have given up. He owed her his life – and also his love. Vida was all he had left now that Garrett and Bethie were dead. Him and Vida and Ears McCreedy: the Holy Trinity.

He reached over, feeling for her hand, then knotted his fingers gently with hers. She squeezed him hard and let her hand go slack. Dyce moved closer to her and slid his arm under her back. She nuzzled against him.

'You smell good,' she said, her voice slow and muffled in his armpit. 'How come you still smell so good?'

'I told you I was magic.'

He knew she was smiling, but it was only a moment. She drew her breath in sharply as the pickup jolted. Dyce looked out the window: they were rolling into a gas station.

'Just need some dinosaur juice,' said Buddy in his high voice. He spoke loudly; overhead, the forecourt roof creaked and groaned, and the wind buffeted the car on its suspension, trying to roll it over onto its back like a beetle.

The little man adjusted his baseball cap – looked like Buddy still loved his HASH HOUSE HARRIERS – and then pawed through his wallet. 'I'll pump if you pay inside. Here's my card. Get whatever else you need – toothpaste, lady things . . . just not the lobster.' He sucked his teeth and smiled, and Vida ducked her head in return. 'That okay with you guys?'

'That's great. Real kind of you,' mumbled Dyce. He took the card between his index and middle fingers, like a cigarette, then turned to Vida. 'You want to come?' He knew the answer.

'Same as always,' she told him.

Dyce waited a moment to gather himself, and then forced open the door against the wild weather. He ducked his head back into the car and Vida scooted over and settled her arm around his shoulders.

'Better you sit tight, little lady,' offered Buddy, but his words were lost in the wind as the door slammed shut again.

The shop front was a fluorescent window into the past, and Vida felt her pulse thrumming. It was like that corner store where she had once bought her comics, back when the shelves were full and you could still choose. She felt her head swim, but pulled back in time. There was no going back there. This was the present, and it would be their future too if she had anything to do with it. There was no way she would let Dyce see all that food and warmth and wealth by himself. He'd never come back!

The shop swam in electric light and it made the South seem long ago and far away, as though the division had happened hundreds of years ago. What was it now? How long had that wall been up? Jesus. Vida didn't know. It hadn't been her whole life: that was all the sense she could make of it. But the years didn't pass the same without the notches to mark them by, did they? People needed celebrations to tell them where they were, to anchor them in the present – Thanksgivings, Christmases, New Years; and the other, secret ones her mama celebrated, half defiant, the ones that went all the way back to when humans first wrung ceremony from a hunt or a birth or the dying of someone they loved. Vida had no cowries or flowers or bodies shrouded in springbok skin; 'as long as I can remember' was her calendar. That and her monthlies, though they had been sparse and unreliable. The Weatherman – he knew the exact answer: their real history was lodged like dirt in his wrinkles.

Now Vida and Dyce paused at the doors, which blasted open at their approach, like a rocket ship. They leant there, acclimatizing in the weightlessness of the false stillness while the air freshener spritzed them. Outside in the wind Buddy's pickup rocked on its suspension.

And then – the other smells! Vida's nose wrinkled. How could the pale girl at the counter live with the oily stink of the corndogs and pies, lined in rows under the hot lights? Beside the teller someone had set a plastic bin, and drops from the ceiling plinked into it. She took no notice, perched on her stool at the till. Dyce looked up at the brown stain on the roof and thought: That would be easy to fix. So why don't they fix it? As they watched, the girl opened another packet of Fritos, and the nitrogen hissed out from the packet, like space rations. She ate at a steady, determined pace, hardly noticing what went into her mouth.

'Help you?' She was looking at them with interest while her hand did its work. Not suspicious yet, but close. Vida tried to stand with her slashed leg behind the less damaged one. No need to freak anyone out. Yet.

'Jesus.' Dyce was breathing at the shelves, packed tight and neat with a hundred things he had never thought to see again. 'Jesus.' He kept trying to catch himself. Don't stare, you stupid fuck, he thought. Try not to look like the village idiot here.

'Not exactly Jesus,' said the girl, and grinned. There were bits of red potato chip lodged between her teeth. Her hand was dipping, hypnotic, into the packet, and then moving to the Styrofoam cup beside her.

Heaven, thought Vida. One, two, three Fritos, and then a sip of coffee. Her mouth was watering.

'This is Old Testament weather,' said the girl. Crunch, crunch, crunch. Slurp. 'And Jay See calmed the storms, didn't he? Pacifist. That out there is his daddy's work. When last you see a rainbow?'

They gawped at her.

'Exactly.' The disaster was satisfying. She knew she was safe. 'Hope you folks've been taking your vitamins, drinking the tap water and all that. After the storms everyone seems to get sick. Low immune systems, you know?' She kept on eating as she talked, sucking the spice off the top of every chip, spitting tiny crumbs on the counter. 'Now how can I help you?'

'We're good, thanks,' said Dyce finally. 'Just looking for a couple of basics.'

She waved a hand. The tips of her thumb and first two fingers were stained too.

'That's all we do. Milk, bread, smokes. Just don't come looking for a combine harvester.' She laughed at her own joke and Dyce tried a smile. 'No offence, but your eyes look like shit, dude. If you want to stay baked, I guess now is the time, right? But there's drops for that round the side aisle, near the mouthwash.'

'Thanks.'

They split up and moved slowly up and down the shelves, Vida making automatically for the sign spelling out FEMININE HYGIENE. She'd thought to do it because of the trickle of blood she'd had to hide from Dyce in the locomotive museum. But standing in front of the shelves with their flowered boxes and rustling pads like decks of cards, she realized that whatever it was, it was gone. One-off. Freak occurrence, like the weather, right? Her mama always said that stress could jam up your insides even if you were regular as clockwork, but she had also said that it only took a moment of pleasure to jog a woman's ovaries into doing their job. Vida took a pack of maxi pads anyway: they were good for all sorts of things. You never could tell, and besides, Buddy was picking up the tab.

She made sure she was out of sight and turned to get a good look at her hurt leg under the store lights. There weren't a lot of slashes but there were a couple of deep ones. She could feel the muscle complaining underneath it, and that was a bad sign. She leant in closer and saw the flesh peeling back in clean strips, like an undone zipper. Fuck. It wasn't bleeding too badly – the cold of the night air had seen to that, and she was no fool, neither. All that staunching on the drive was doing its work. But still. She needed stitches. How long did she have before the true extent was noticed? She limped behind a Gatorade display to get to Dyce and hurry him up before the counter girl saw the whole sorry mess and called the hospital or the cops.

He was still studying the cotton swabs and the condoms and the blister packs of antacid, and when he saw her coming he waved something at her. When she got to him, Vida caught his hand so she could see what it was: a traveler's sewing kit, complete with tiny scissors. Christ, she thought. He was serious about the stitches.

'What do you think?'

'About what?'

'I wasn't getting in close back there just to hear Billy Ray Cyrus.' He jerked his head outside, where Buddy had finished pumping gas and was back in the cab, arms folded, staring into space. 'I was watching how he drove. It's easy – same as my dad taught me and Garrett. You see any bigger scissors any-where?'

Vida felt her heart sink. 'Scissors? Dyce, what for?' She tried to keep her voice down. The counter girl would think they were having a fight.

'Looks like you two gonna need a basket,' called the girl, on cue.

'Thanks,' Dyce called back. He wandered to the front of the shop and back again with a beat-up wire basket.

'Dyce!' Vida hissed. 'What the fuck?'

He made jabbing motions at her neck with the little packaged sewing scissors, their blades dull under the lights.

'Are you serious?'

'We're not here on vacation, Vida. It's Fuck Renard time, remember? We got no business further north. We got to see who came through the border, try to find the others, regroup – and then we need to visit a little Southern justice on these assholes. For that we need a car. And we got one, right here.'

'Are you insane?' She slapped the thigh of her damaged leg, and instantly regretted it. 'You've seen this, right? You know it's going to get gangrene or something? And what? You're just going to slash Buddy? The guy who rescued us? The guy whose card we're using right now? And then what? Are you planning to take over the whole fucking *continent?*'

He stared at her, mute, his eyes black with anger, and her heart jogged with fright. You don't know all of him, Ruth's voice said. Watch your step here, baby girl.

She tried again, calmer this time. 'Look. How about we start small? Like one decent night's sleep, for starters? Something to eat? And then plan this . . . this . . . whatever we're going to do properly.'

Dyce looked sulky, but closed his hand over the sewing scissors and dropped them into the basket. 'Okay.'

'Okay is right, you asshole. What is wrong with you? Now get me out of here before I fall down.'

Dyce deflated. Her face was an earnest oval in the shop light, the cheeks still childishly chubby. There was an old scar in the middle of her top lip that he'd not noticed before, as though the whole of the South was more dimly lit than this lone fluorescent one-stop.

'You know,' he said, and the humor crept back into his voice, 'you're cute when you're upset.'

'Really? You want a spade or you just gonna keeping digging with your hands?'

'I'm being serious.'

'Well, it's a match made in heaven. I've been upset twenty-four-seven since I met you.'

'Guess I got my work cut out, then.'

'Guess you do. Now give your arm to the lady.'

They went, casual and slow, to the counter and mooned over the corndogs.

'I haven't had one of these in years,' Vida told the till girl.

'Heart attack on a stick. But you go ahead and take one. It's on the house, because I like the look of you.' Vida grinned and the girl passed her a brown paper bag, her oily reddish fingerprints on it. Dyce paid for the gas and their purchases with the card, scrawling a signature that the girl didn't check. She kept looking out, suddenly gloomy and resigned.

'You folks do me a favor,' she said. 'If this flood comes any higher, I want you to remember there's a girl at this here gas station, right? Tell them to send a boat. And tell them to be quick, 'cause I'm real pretty.' She smiled, and they saw that it wasn't only the potato chips: her teeth were streaked with fine lines from all the coffee she must have drunk over the years she had been sitting behind the till. She was hoping that it was the real-deal, true-blue Hundred-Year Storm, wasn't she? Because then she wouldn't have to finish her shift. Vida felt sorry for her.

The doors sealed behind them again and they stood under the

lip of the roof, watching the rain turned into a yellow curtain by the gas-station lights, like they were on stage.

When they climbed back into the car, Buddy hailed them and gave Dyce a jovial slap on the shoulder. 'Junior! Where's my change?' He took his card back and stowed it in his wallet. 'Got what you needed?'

'Sure did,' said Vida, and tried to smile at him. 'Buddy, you're an angel.'

'A saint,' said Dyce. 'Thanks, man.'

Buddy grinned and stuck his hand inside the neck of his shirt. When he pulled it out again, he was holding a silver crucifix on a chain. 'Gotta do what the man said, right? Love your neighbor and all that?'

Dyce grimaced. There was nothing for free. He shifted forward in his seat again as Buddy put the car into drive and pulled off into the pelting rain, swiveling his neck to talk as the vehicle leapt forward. Vida watched Dyce's face side-on. He was memorizing every movement Buddy was making – the undersized feet shifting from accelerator to brake; the small hands flicking the indicators and the paddles that dimmed the brights for the lone truck that passed in the opposite direction.

'Some vacation, huh? You two must be kaput. So, I was thinking, there's one of those shelter points about an hour from here – old hotel. That sound good? They'll fix you up and then you can get back home, take your own sweet time.'

Buddy was no idiot, thought Vida. He could smell the trouble on his passengers, and he wanted to get rid of them, saint or no saint. She clutched the bag tighter, feeling first for the plastic sewing kit, then for the scissors inside.

Panic bloomed in her throat. The blades were gone.

She turned, and in the glow of the dash lights she saw the

silver blades glinting in Dyce's hand, half hidden by his sleeve.

'Hey, Buddy. Could you turn this up? I haven't heard this song in forever,' said Dyce. He leant in close.

6

Norma was asking whether Felix needed to phone someone, her pink face scrunched up in concern. Instead of saying, No, everyone I know is floating face-down in the North Platte, he took the coin she gave him and sloshed over to the payphone in the alcove between the men's and the ladies'. The plastic pod smelt like turds and burnt wiring, but he wasn't there to picnic.

He turned the coin over in his hand, like treasure. It was an old twenty-five-cent piece with a picture of the Lincoln Memorial on the back. The year and the slogan had worn off with all the handling over the years, but Felix knew what it would have said: IN GOD WE TRUST. That hadn't worked out too well, now, had it? It was strange to see what had endured, with or without the help of the Lord. They were using these coins before the War started, and that was a good forty years back.

He picked up the receiver, not expecting a dial tone. But there it was, like magic. He dropped the coin into the slot and then dialed the only number he could remember. He'd dialed the damn thing about a thousand times from his parents' phone in those tense few days before the War.

It rang. He half expected his old landlady, Mrs Bishop, to pick up and he'd finally get to ask the questions he'd wanted to ask all along. How's my shop, Mrs B? The stock still there? And Dallas? You seen my baby cat?

He shook his head. It was like he still had water in his ears. All that was a lifetime ago. Mrs Bishop, the cat, the shop with the big-ass, eighty-pound TV sets – they were all gone to dust.

The phone rang and then clicked off. Coin didn't come back, neither. Wasn't that always the way?

'No answer,' said Felix when he got back to the table.

Norma held her head on one side, and her chins bunched together. She came to a decision.

'Now, I don't normally do this sort of thing. But you look like you could use some help, mister. Isn't that what the Good Book tells us? Help your neighbor?'

It was love your neighbor, Felix was pretty sure, but he didn't want to interrupt Norma in full flow.

'Well, I reckon you could use a little neighborly help.'

He waited, trying to look unthreatening.

'I don't usually invite strange gentlemen back to my place, but you can have a shower and get yourself cleaned up, and then we can decide what we're going to do with you.'

'Ma'am, I could do with both of those things.'

'Well, saddle up, cowboy. I can sweep this place out later. It's not like the customers are exactly beating down the door.' She pulled a face at him.

Norma's car was parked around the back of the diner, between two dumpsters and under a sign that said STAFF ONLY. It was a rust-colored Muntz, though the badge had long since fallen off, another pre-War relic, patched and maintained meticulously, but not new. But Jesus Christ! A real car! It was the old stuff that kept on working if you treated it right, Felix thought.

The giraffe was still there, standing on a front lawn, undisturbed, chewing the high leaves of a cottonwood. The creature paused as if it felt his stare, and turned its bumpy spotted head toward the road, jaws masticating all the while, slow and unblinking. Fuck me, thought Felix. Damn thing looks like it belongs here!

'You never seen a giraffe before? Don't they have them in New York?'

'Not when I was a boy, though I can't say what-all is going on up there now,' said Felix. 'Too cold for them there, I always thought.'

Norma sighed. 'Oh, my husband used to love this thing – called it Gemma. Used to leave fruit on the roof for her, can you believe it? She's partial to oranges.'

'What changed his mind?'

'Oh, nothing.' Her mouth jerked at the corners. 'He passed over.'

'Oh,' said Felix. Part of him wanted to say he was sorry, but he wasn't – not about the death of a Northerner, one death among the hundreds of thousands.

'They don't usually come into town like this, but Gemma's half tame, plus everyone's been evacuated.'

'What about you? You also free-range?'

'I'm stubborn. And I'm two hundred and fifty pounds. They couldn't make me leave if they tried. Get in.'

He did, trying not to look as if it was unusual, but inside he felt like a kid at a funfair. A car!

She eased the vehicle back and then began a practiced slalom out of the parking lot to avoid the largest bits of the storm debris. The tires crunched over glass and sticks and Perspex. The heater began warming up as the revs climbed, and the hot blast of spicy potpourri and diesel tickled Felix's nose and made his skin ache. He located the source – a sticky little bottle she had dangling from the rear-view mirror like a fetish.

He wasn't prepared for when she wound down her window

and let a gust of storm-clean air into the car. It circulated high up, and for a moment he sat motionless, fighting the urge to hold his breath, or to tell her to close the goddam window.

Fresh air!

He would have to reprogram himself after the years of hiding from the wind and the sicknesses it brought. He closed his eyes and took in the air in tiny sips, picturing the mushroom spores in his system doing their hopeful work. The antivirals were working so far: if the pneumonia hadn't taken him in the night, then something was on his side. Maybe old dogs learnt new tricks if they had enough to lose.

Or if they had a mission – and a limited time to do it.

As the houses began to flash past, Felix relaxed against the upholstery. He felt as though nothing had changed, that the War hadn't happened at all. He imagined Norma as his ageing trophy wife, fattened up on the money from his TV empire; they were off to a grandkid's birthday party where he could find a corner to drink Wild Turkey until the screaming got too much and he could blame incontinence and escape. And it would all be normal. That was all normal here.

The engine thrummed under the backs of his thighs. They passed house after house, still standing but marked by the storm. Felix expected homeowners to be out and about, moving around, taking off the storm shutters, or standing with their hands on their hips, surveying the destruction. The town was empty – not even a man bent over the remains of a garden shed dispersed like matchsticks.

Norma said, 'It wasn't as bad as we were expecting. They were calling it the Hundred-Year Storm. Thousand-Year, more like. Lucky, huh?'

Felix nodded. 'No looters,' he said, and the disappointment

swelled in his chest. The carnage had been a chance to get rid of everything – the whole stinking mess that they called the First World, the ragged South but also the glorious North, the world and his wife. Start over like the Garden of Eden, without the snake Renard.

And now that chance was lost. The man upstairs had missed a trick there, Felix told himself.

'Not a lot of people left to do the looting. We may be poor, but we have learnt to work together, mister. Crime is down in Saratoga, would you believe it. And that's down from hardly any at all since the War ended. You got to look on the bright side.'

Felix sniffed and Norma shot him a sideways look. His nose was streaming at the chemical smell of the expired freshener, but he was too embarrassed to wipe it. Don't look like a hobo, he told himself. He concentrated instead on the houses that hadn't fared well. An old honey locust had lost its biggest branches when it came down on the roof of one house across the street. The yellow leaves were fluttering like tape at a crime scene, and the wooden attic struts poked at the sky. Norma slowed, and he saw the pale tiles scattered like teeth on the swampy grass. She sucked the air in through her own dentition.

'Didn't see that on the way in. Hope the Schermbruckers got out safe.'

'Where is everyone living? Are there collection points? Refugee camps, I guess?'

'Sure. Churches, schools, the town hall. Further north, outta harm's way. How come you don't know this stuff?'

Felix shrugged and stared out of his window. 'I been busy. And you can't always trust the news.'

Stop asking so many questions, you old fart! You'll give yourself away.

Norma was pulling into the muddied driveway of a peeling house, which had been sky blue when it was new. Below the dermis was the dirty white undercoat – and below that Felix could see the red bricks like open flesh, pockmarked by storm shrapnel. But the bones of the house itself looked okay. It would take more than a natural disaster to wipe out places like Saratoga. Towns were made up of their buildings, thought Felix, but there were other things that kept settlements functioning, things both older and newer – the land on which the buildings stood, and the people who lived in them.

The front door before them had also swollen from the pooling rain and Norma had to lean her shoulder against it to force it open. It was dark inside, mildewed with the history of the family who had lived there. Felix thought of spores, of the breeding they could do in these perfect conditions. Maybe the flood could do some good work for him after all.

Norma showed him to a bathroom, outfitted in tiles they used to call avocado. She gave him a towel and then set out some of her dead husband's clothes on the lid of the green toilet – boxers, chinos, a Brooks Brothers shirt, a sweater.

'He wouldn't mind,' she said, and winked. The clothes looked like a decent fit: Mister Norma must have been Jack Sprat. 'And now I got to go and sweep that diner out. If you're still here when I get back, I can make you some dinner. Make yourself at home.'

'This is mighty kind of you, Norma,' said Felix, and he found tears prickling at the corners of his tired eyes. 'Mighty kind.'

He watched her leave the house. He was alone again, but this time it felt good.

When he turned on the shower, the water sputtered through the nozzle, and for a moment he expected it to be a dribble, or else the color of blood, like a haunted house in a horror movie. But then it came down in a hot blast, and he stripped and stood under it and cried. He'd spent his life cursing the North for taking all the big things away – family, purpose, dignity, health – but as he stood in the warm, deliberate water, with the sugary oil of the donuts still coating his blistered mouth, all the million small comforts he'd missed over the years began to leak back, pattering down on him.

'Fuckers!' he shouted, and thumped at the shower glass with his palm. His own voice startled him, wet and hoarse and croaking with age, and it made him come back to himself. When he assessed the damage, he saw that his violence had barely left a mark in the streaks of soap scales.

Ashamed, he got out of the shower and dried off. He found a pink razor and shaved. Then he looked in the mirrored cabinet for a first-aid kit and patched up the grazes on his neck and hip.

'You bony fuck,' he told his yellowed reflection. He took two painkillers, bright red capsules that were hard to swallow, but he had forced down worse things in his time.

He held the clothes up against his body: they looked like they'd fit okay – better than his own, anyway – and they were, by Jesus, dry. He tucked them under his arm and stepped out of the bathroom.

At first he didn't see the man who had been standing in the passage, dark and tall.

Felix looked up. He fell backward, by instinct, catching his sore hip on the bathroom door handle.

'You Felix Callahan?' the man asked. 'I'm asking for a friend.'

7

Dyce aimed the scissors and did the calculation. He'd need to be quick – one stab at the base of the brain. Stab hard. Then the really dangerous bit, which would be getting hold of the steering wheel before Buddy pulled the whole speeding wagon off the road. He braced himself for the act, willing himself to be more like Garrett. Buddy kept talking, telling him about blues and country, and how they were both the same thing, two sides of a sad coin.

He couldn't do it. He slumped back, his heart beating fast. Vida shifted across the seat of the truck and rested her head on his shoulder, her hand holding his – for comfort and for restraint, to keep it from finishing what he'd almost done. If he'd really wanted to murder Buddy, there would have been no way she could stop him. She was hurt, and he was too strong for her.

But he'd stopped, hadn't he? And that was Vida's doing. They both waited, the knowledge silting down inside them.

What if there was a better plan?

Dyce took a deep breath. It was Garrett's voice he sometimes heard in his head. He closed his eyes and there was his brother, smiling like a dick, Bethie's ghost there too, leaning up against him with her arm twisted around his waist, three fingers tucked into the top of his jeans. What if there's a better way, little brother? *Was* there a way to turn Renard's viruses against his own people? Give him a taste of his own medicine? Dyce forced the image of Garrett and Bethie away and pictured himself, legs dangling from a hillside water tower, looking down on a nameless city as the people below coughed and faltered and stank of the death that hung over the place.

Not revenge, not really. Justice.

That vision, of the necropolis, was no exaggeration. The first time it had happened, he and Garrett and their mom and dad had watched in terror and disbelief. Then, over time, as the post-War negotiations failed, they'd been forced to hide away for good, like gophers or earthworms or the spores of a terrible blight. Even as kids they had been taught to cover their mouths and noses until it was second nature. There were some days when they only lifted the flap of a breath-moist neckerchief to eat or drink. Or vomit. He felt the road smooth beneath him as the pickup raced along. Had they really lived that way for so long? Constantly washing their hands and boiling their water. Climbing trees, scanning horizons, reading the winds and their hundred ways to die.

Dyce couldn't say if the memory of the beginning was his own. He had been two years old: he didn't know how much of it really had happened. It was an inherited familial flashback, a coagulation of all the conversations and condolences, the things about that day that had been said, and the things that no one could say because there weren't the right words.

The family was staying the weekend with Gracie, who was an old friend of their mother's. Gracie was a War widow already, getting paler as she got older, the deep blue rings around her eyes making them stones thrown in a well. Garrett and Dyce could not imagine her having any other life before they knew her.

Their mom wanted to see Gracie to make sure she was okay. 'You don't know how long anyone's got, and she's lonely there,' she told their dad when he huffed about the gas and the wear on their Dodge Dart. They'd driven down from Leadville – Mom, Dad, Garrett and himself – an hour's drive, the furthest they'd ever been, through landscapes they didn't recognize. A mission of mercy, she told their father, but what she meant was that they would have some respite from his moods.

At first they had all been real grateful that Dad had escaped conscription, but then the months turned into years, and he began to understand that he had been excluded from the most important thing that was going to happen in his lifetime. 'Boys, history is being written,' he told them, over and over, his breath beery and his grip too hard, 'and I am watching it from the sidelines.'

Gracie was going to make them meatloaf the night they arrived. It was a celebration, and spirits were high with the end of the War in sight. The South had been making good progress, pushing the Northern soldiers back. Southerners knew not to celebrate a victory before it was signed and sealed, but they'd fought for so long that even the rumors were good enough. Only an act of God could stop their progress. The bottle of wine Gracie kept high on a shelf was opened, the extra few dollars forked out for ground beef. Real meat! Gracie had paid for it the day before, but without a fridge in her apartment, she'd asked to leave it at the store until they arrived.

When they got there, she slipped out while their mom was bathing Dyce and Garrett and their dad was showering, cleaning themselves up from the drive. Gracie had planned to be back at the apartment and frying an onion by the time they all emerged from the faded guest room, smelling of precious soap.

The onion was chopped – Mom found its pale diamonds sweating on the plate beside the scratched-up frying pan – and Gracie had opened the wine to let it breathe, a red-striped cloth resting over the top to stop the bugs. They sat on Gracie's sofa, the kids squeaky-clean and grinning, their dad between them, scowling at Gracie's verses on the walls. THEY WHO SOW THE WIND REAP THE WHIRLWIND, said Hosea 8:7. FEAR NOT, FOR I AM WITH YOU. That was Isaiah 41:10. Mom had sat down too for a while, across from them in Gracie's slanting wicker chair, but when her friend hadn't come back after half an hour, she grew anxious and got up to look for little chores in the kitchen. She chopped the onion finer, unsure of what else might be helpful. She wiped down the counters. It was only when she was rinsing the cloth at the sink that she looked up out of the window and saw what was happening to the people outside.

One woman who has dropped her shopping bags in a coughing fit is nothing to write home about, and two is a coincidence – but as she watched, everyone in the scene began spluttering and holding their chests.

She held her elbows and said, 'Carson.'

'What?' He was scratching at his stubble.

She was trying to speak quietly, but the tension in her voice made them all pay extra attention instead, like the time when Dyce had nearly drowned in the bath when he was a baby.

'Carson, come over here quick.'

He moved fast then, and they stood flash-frozen at the sink, watching as pedestrians bled from their mouths and ears and noses, as if they had eaten rat poison. As the wind rustled the salvia, the passers-by stopped and doubled over, retching their guts onto the sidewalk. He took hold of the window to open it for a better look, but then drew his hand back.

'There's something in the air,' he said, and his mouth pulled funny. 'We got to seal this place up, Tammy. Right now.'

'I'll check the bathroom,' she said. Dyce and Garrett watched her run. She never ran.

Their dad found a jar of Vaseline next to Gracie's ruffled bed, and he began to work it into the seals around the kitchen windows. Garrett was old enough to follow instructions, and he was set to stuff wads of toilet paper into the old steel air vent beside the front door. Their mom slotted towels under the interleading doors: Dyce remembered her kicking at them to compress the fabric, her lips pressed tight together.

When the Vaseline gave out, their dad used stale margarine to seal the bedroom windows. Their mom moved on to covering the taps and drains with cling film. She was crying, but trying to do that silently too.

When next they looked, the street was lined with bodies – some writhing, most still. 'All fall down,' said Dyce, and then flinched away from his mother: he was sure she was going to slap him.

Garrett, years later, said he could see Gracie's pale knees jutting up beside the park, halfway off the sidewalk, her dress soaked in vomit and the bag of ground beef leaking blood into the gutter, first red and then gray.

They were too afraid to open the door, or to check that she really was dead. 'We're just going to sit tight,' their dad told them. 'Right, boys? Like camping.' He almost looked like he was enjoying it.

Oxygen was precious. They couldn't use the gas stove or the hot water, which relied on a pilot flame to heat the pipes. According to Garrett, they spent the week listening to static on the radio and eating Cap'n Crunch and stale multivitamins that said 'For Women' on the box. Then they ate the raw onion.

Since all the toilets were covered with cling film, they shat in the poky little study, using cooking pots lined up on the mottled carpet. They sealed off the stink and tried to limit toilet time to once a day, except for Dyce, who was too little to hold it in. Dad went first each time, then the kids, and Mom last of all. She prayed secretly that they would get out of there before it was her time of the month, the stale air already heavy with headaches. FEAR NOT, she kept reading. FEAR NOT, FOR I AM WITH YOU. The four of them stared out at the flies swarming over the bodies in the street, or sitting fat and bristly on the windows, mercifully obscuring the world outside.

On the fourth day, their dad saw a man and woman with cloths over their faces making a run for his car. They turned the old Dodge Dart south.

'Headed for the coast,' said their dad, with some satisfaction. 'Gas in the tank won't get them far.'

On the sixth day, the kitchen radio came to life and announced that the air was safe to breathe. The national emergency measures had been lifted. The War was over. Hallelujah!

Garrett and Dyce watched their mom huddle against their dad, crying, her shoulders jolting. He said nothing. They'd lost.

The announcer, his voice deep with professional concern, explained that concession talks were being set up. Those who'd survived had nothing more to fear. 'Unfortunately, there have been casualties,' he went on, reading from his script. 'Some civilians have paid the price for peace. We pray for the families of those fallen heroes who contracted the virus. Our sympathies are with them.'

Their dad seemed to draw energy from the news. He was up early the next morning to siphon gas from abandoned cars to pour into Gracie's tiny Lark. They packed up their few things and waited while their mom slowly rigged a blanket across the back seat, the corners wedged into the rolled-up windows to make a tent for the kids – and to keep them from seeing the carnage outside. She said nothing at all on the return journey: Carson had forbidden her to say her last goodbyes to Gracie's body on the sidewalk. She knew he was right, but it was some kind of betrayal. Dyce felt as though he really did remember that part, the miasma between their parents, the dark thrill of their cocoon as the car wove around the bodies on the road. They headed back home thinking that they'd seen the worst and survived it.

If they'd only known, he thought now. He felt the point of the scissors, still tucked away in his sleeve. The sun had risen and Vida was asleep on his shoulder, her arm limp across his lap.

Something beeped near the driver's footwell and Buddy leant forward and picked up a device that looked like one of those pre-War medical pagers. It had been through the wars: it was wrapped in gray tape and the back casing was cracked. He held it up to his ear and closed one eye, to hear the tiny speaker better. Then he set it down. After a slow mile he reached his arm over to the passenger seat backrest and turned around to look at Dyce.

'Hey,' he said. Vida stirred and opened one eye. 'There's no easy way to ask this, but do you guys know a Felix Callahan?'

8

The man in the passage stepped forward and helped Felix to his feet, examining his naked body as he lifted him up, eyeing every pockmark and scar. In the shaft of light from the bathroom, Felix repaid the inspection, sizing up the man who stood over him: the old habit, to look for the weak point that would mean the bloody end of a fist fight. He knew what the man was seeing. It was safe to say there'd be no more hand-to-hand combat for Felix Callahan: those days were long gone. A stiff breeze would do him in, he thought, never mind Renard's invisible critters along for the ride.

But this fellow, this Northerner, didn't seem much better off. Twenty years younger, maybe, but ravaged in the way Felix had gotten used to seeing. On his cheek the man wore a sticking plaster that ran from the bridge of his nose and then down in a square from the hinge of his jaw to the corner of his mouth. Sometime earlier in his life – and it wasn't over yet, even if he did look like the walking dead – welts and blisters had erupted and scarred his skin like constellations. And just like constellations, the spaces between the big-daddy blemishes were littered with the signs of older pustules and boils. And even then between those there were still more signs of suffering. Felix could read the whole history of illness over his face, from plague to pestilence and back again.

The man winked. Felix felt himself relax just a little – his stomach unclenched and the knot of his fist loosened. He stared at the fabric plaster. Whatever was behind it was leaking. Yup. The odds were evening out.

'We been looking a long time for you, Felix. 'Bout seven years now. Whaddaya make of that?' There was something about the way he said his words: they sounded mushy. Damage to the palate, maybe.

The man winced – something hurt, Felix bet – and unscrewed the lid from a water bottle, taking a long swallow. Goddam! Even in the low light of the house, that stain on the plaster seemed to spread a little with each rise and fall of his Adam's apple.

'Now, I hate to rush your first shower in, what, a hundred years?' The man smiled, then stopped when it stretched his crusted skin. 'But we got to get you out of here. Pretty sure I'm not the only one looking for you.'

Felix tried to nail down one question that would make sense of the whole shebang, but he just kept thinking of that damn giraffe, placid as you like, foraging in the trees of suburbia.

Before he could speak, they heard the sound of an engine slowing. As they listened, it sidled up into the driveway, where the fan belt shrieked and the engine died. A door opened and there was the sound of two men talking, though Felix couldn't make out the words.

The man in the passage pushed past Felix and grabbed the fallen clothes that Norma had left for him. Then he reached one arm into the shower and turned the faucet on full blast. It hissed at first, then gushed again, the sound covering their talk.

'Let's get going. We can get you covered up in a minute if you're still breathing then.'

The man nodded toward the street and Felix followed him, feeling the cold.

Fuck me sideways, he told himself. I been more naked these last few days than I ever been before in my life!

The man led the way to the kitchen and out through the back door. They crept around the front of the house, Felix all the while thinking of that game his brothers used to play – keeping low and out of sight so they could scare the shit out of him. He was prey from the day he could walk till their mother told them to quit it. 'Brown streaks in the laundry,' his brothers said, when he asked them why they stopped.

The two men had paused, bemused, trying to figure out how to get in. As Felix watched, the one standing on the welcome mat shoved his shoulder forward at the door, trying to force it open with his weight. He had set his pack down to do it, and he was really putting his back into the break-in. Skinny, both of them, one with a moustache, the other with a few days' stubble and a murderous look. The pissed-off one began pulling the storm boarding off the front window, but the water-damaged door gave way first. The men disappeared inside.

'Car,' said Felix's kidnapper, and he grabbed Felix's arm like a gentleman helping a lady over a puddle. They dashed to it, a silver Ford De Luxe, which had once been a soft-top. Someone had since hammered some plyboard together to enclose it, then painted it white to keep the water out. And praise Jesus and the stupidity of mortal men! The key was right in the ignition. Some people never learn, Felix thought. The man only just waited for him to round the vehicle and get in before he turned the key. The engine coughed once, then sputtered out.

'Come on,' he hissed through his teeth. 'Come on, you bitch.'

Felix leant over. 'Cain't force it,' he said, and then he turned the key himself. 'Gotta be gentle with the old ones, even when you're in a hurry.'

With a bang, the grateful engine took and the man wrenched it into reverse. The car leapt backward into the street, tires spinning. Felix craned back to see the two men come running out of the house. One had his hand shoved in a backpack and Felix understood he was feeling for his gun.

'You gonna tell me who those guys are?' he asked.

'Border patrol. Police, basically – keeping an eye out for folks just like you. And now they know you're here, they're not gonna let up.'

'Just when you think you've outrun the Callahans.'

'What you say?'

'Nothing.'

There was a thunder crack. Felix ducked but the bullet missed, as it had all his life except for that once. The car jerked again as the driver flung his arm up to shield his face.

'Jesus!'

It was the giraffe, galloping beside them, terrified, its hooves thudding along the asphalt.

Felix expected another shot, but it didn't come. The driver righted himself and the giraffe veered off the road, then pulled up, wide-eyed and frothing, as the De Luxe gathered speed like a tank and headed north. The rain started again. Felix rubbed his stinging eyes. It took him a moment to work out where it was coming from – a tiny vanilla-scented basketball hanging from the rear-view. What was with Northerners and their car fresheners? Didn't they know cars smelt great just because of what they were? The musty fabric and the plastic, the rubber and gas: Felix took a big sniff of it all again. Why ruin a good thing?

The man reached to the back seat where he'd thrown Felix's new clothes and tossed them in the old man's lap.

'Gonna catch your death,' he said. 'And then the boys'll hang me as soon as look at me. But I am also tired of looking at your weenie, I gotta tell you.'

Felix pulled a face. 'Not my idea of a first date neither, pal.'

The man grinned, and then touched one finger gingerly to his cheek. 'Aw, shit, this hurts.' He looked sideways at Felix and said, 'Name's Adams, by the way.'

Felix sorted through the pile of clothes. 'Guess you all know who I am. There better be coffee wherever we're going.'

Adams laughed, then coughed, nodding, and covered his mouth. Felix pulled the shirt carefully over his head, then held up a cable-knit sweater, pea green and musty as last year's Christmas baubles. An appliquéd reindeer leapt from one armpit to the other.

When Norma heard the De Luxe coming she looked out the diner window. The car raced northward on the highway. She ran outside into the gathering rain just in time to see the ghost of her dead husband in the passenger seat, pulling on his favorite sweater.

9

Buddy was talking, a squeaky jumble of words.

'The Resistance sent me down to drive the border roads in the worst of the storm. I was looking out for folks like you, anyone washed up over the Wall and still alive. Chances were pretty slim. Then when I picked you up, I couldn't be sure you folks weren't what you said you were – a couple of out-of-luck Montanans. I was trying to figure out a way of asking you without giving the game away, until I got the message here saying to look out for a Felix Callahan.'

Dyce felt his sore shoulders relax. This man was no threat, and that was a bigger relief than he'd reckoned. The days of combat and panic and flight piled up now that he had had a chance to sit tight and think on it all, and he let the heaviness take hold of him. Every damn thing he had done until now was resistance, as if the world was packed tightly over his head in layers and he had to dig himself out. Himself, and Vida now as well. She wouldn't say but he knew that her leg wasn't getting any better. It was starting to smell weird too, or maybe that was just the bloodied cloth around it. Every dumb beat of his stubborn heart felt like work and he missed Garrett like a limb. Now Buddy was telling them where they were headed – something about Des Moines – but in the end Dyce gave up and felt his head nodding.

Buddy eyed him in the rear-view mirror, slumped against Vida, his sore eyes flickering closed.

'Just so you know, we're not going to stay on this road for long,' he said. 'The storm's given us a free pass, but soon as the sun's up we'll be sore thumbs out here in the open, just begging to be pulled over for questioning. So take a nap if you like, but I'm gonna have to wake you in ten. I won't be able to haul your asses out the car all by myself, skinny as they are.'

Vida had stayed awake. She knew better than to close her eyes too. If she surrendered to the yawn that threatened to unhinge her jaws, it would just keep going until the top of her head was sawn clean off. And what a relief that would be! She thought of her mama, keeping her midwife's watch over her young mothers all those days – and nights too, because babies don't wait for you to tell them when to be born. How had she done it and not lost her mind? Someone always had to keep watch, and that was the hardest job because it was never-ending. Dyce could drop away into nothingness – a sleep so deep, his daddy used to say, that he could see Saint Peter – but Vida had to be on guard. The pain throbbed up through the bones of her leg to keep her company.

But it wasn't Saint Peter that Dyce saw when he fell into sleep – no early-pearly gates or goose-down clouds. It was a pure dark. In his state he thought it was the halfway place people get to when they're too tired to dream. But the place he was in had the soft, ominous smell of the cellar – and he knew he was back in the mines below the Mouth, stumbling in the dark ripeness of the killing tunnels under the town.

With the realization came the wet walls pressing in on either side, the greenish glow of the mushrooms like St Elmo's fire. Dyce felt his fists clench as his feet were set on a path that endlessly angled away from him. With each in-breath the air was thicker and hung with spores, until he felt the water in his struggling lungs. He coughed, his hand in front of his mouth. When he took his hand away, he knew the palm would be stained with black mucus, brought up from the slick chambers of his own rotting body.

There was no way back. He knew the passage led only to the catacomb laboratory, where the useful dead lay with their faces upturned in fruitfulness, the mushrooms springing from the holes in their bodies. Dyce pressed himself against the clammy walls of the passageway and fought the scream. He tried to grip with his feet to slow his progress but they sank anyway, further and further in, until he was sure the caverns would swallow him.

From the death vault the spores began to leak faster, like flies. Dyce watched, hypnotized. The two cold hands punched through the wall and clamped his head on either side. In his dream a thick tongue probed his ear and he half sobbed, 'Ester!' She was part of the water table now too, wasn't she? Biding her time, the mindless, vicious clots of her reassembling like DNA, flowing under the cool earth to surprise him again with her violence and desire. He would never be able to kill her. Somehow she would always come back.

The smell was choking him; Dyce felt his lungs sticky with panic. Then those hands with their superhuman strength began slowly to lift him off the passage floor. His feet kicked as if he was treading water, desperate to keep his head above the tide of spores that kept spilling from the room. Garrett had lifted him the same way when they were kids, making Dyce feel he was blind with rage and helplessness, sure that his head would be ripped from his skinny shoulders. Now there were more hands, then more, grabbing at his exposed flesh, groping and pinching his soft parts, searching for the signs of his rich human life: his blood, tears, semen, sweat.

He kept struggling, hoarse with outrage and screaming, but it was no use. The bony, punishing hands wouldn't relent, and at last Dyce understood that brute strength was no help. He went limp, and in the seconds it took for Ester's undead kin to relax in surprise, he drew up his battered knees and shoved against the wall with both feet.

The hands flopped, blind and furious, and Dyce stumbled forward, forward and into the death room.

There was nowhere else to go.

The hungry sisters knew not to follow. The hands grabbed hold of one another, soothing and stroking. If Dyce had been closer, he would have heard the whispering of wet flesh sliding over flesh.

But he was alone. He stood panting, and the curse of his night vision showed him all the old terrors. Would it never be over? The bodies lay quiet, as he remembered them, in all their states of decay. From each face – wrinkled, or freckled, or dimpled, their differences come to nothing – grew the mush-rooms, fat and ripe. Clumps sprouted from lipless mouths and ruptured noses. Fungi grew in bony eye sockets, neat and white as the eyeballs they replaced; in clean-picked ribcages they had made their own gardens, spotted and reddish as kidneys, domed and blue as bruises, hung all around in strings and fronds like fairy lights.

Dyce found that he was crying, as if his body was testing each function to see if it still worked. In his terrible dream he could not stop himself from reaching out to pick the mushrooms, as many as he could gather, from the wrecked faces and the nests of the ruptured, ragged lungs – just as he'd done before. Each time was the same. Even in the dream he knew he was not awake, and even in the dream he suffered and wept and told the dead that he was sorry.

But he had been wrong to think that the bodies were lying quietly. With each mushroom he picked, the robbed corpses groaned. As he reached to harvest that hard-earned fruit, the fingers of the dead stirred to protect their precious trophies. The bones squeaked and flaked and feebly roused themselves to swat his human hands away, but now it was he who was relentless: old and young, newly dead and long gone – Dyce took a mushroom from every single body.

It could have been me lying there, he told himself. Work faster! Make those lives worth something. Don't let it all have been for nothing!

In his dream he coughed again, and this time he felt something hard in his throat, a nub rising in his gullet. It slithered over his tongue and then bloomed from his open mouth. He reached up to feel its soft horror. He ran his fingers under the skirting gills of it and then, with a tug, he pulled the mushroom-tongue out of his mouth. The pain ripped through him and he woke.

He opened his eyes and stared at the roof of the pickup, but he couldn't move. His head lay rigid on Vida's lap; her hand was cupping his cheek. The shudder worked through him.

'Looks like you won't need to wake him,' said Buddy. 'He always have nightmares this bad?'

Vida shrugged. 'Wouldn't you?'

The car slowed and then turned off the road, making for the steel hull of some giant wrecked machine resting in the water-logged prairie. A tractor? Vida squinted into the filtered gray morning. Too small. This was huge.

The pickup rocked and trundled across the soggy grass, and as they got closer she saw the wreck for what it was: the fuselage of a downed jet, one of the relics from the War. Across the outside, someone had painted a word, but they weren't close enough for her to read it. She tapped Buddy on the shoulder.

'That what it looks like?'

'If it looks like your home for the next few hours, then yes. We're sleeping inside that baby tonight,' said Buddy.

'What does it say there? In white?'

'REMEMBER.'

She snorted.

'I know. But it's big enough to hide my truck round back. And I stashed some supplies inside a couple of months ago. Thought, better safe than sorry, and it seems I was right. It's pretty comfortable, actually. Dry. And bigger than it looks from the outside.'

'I've had worse,' said Vida, and Buddy thought as he glanced back at her that it was the first time he had seen her smile.

10

Kurt Callahan kicked at a rock as he walked back along the river toward Saratoga.

'Send the old man down the river with the keys in his pocket. Just great. Fucking genius.'

He balled his fist and punched himself in the leg so hard that he stumbled, then hobbled on. The pickup had turned out to be useless. After he'd killed the old couple, he'd scrambled up the slope, all the while trying to figure out whether he knew how to drive. Stick-shift would be tricky, but he was sure he could figure out automatic. He'd never seen an actual working car, but he'd played plenty in the rusted wrecks of them, tugging on the steering and honking the horn until his uncle Gus had come out and shown him how to drive: a way for the old guy to relive the past. Kurt had soaked in the details – how to use the pedals, the flickers, the mirrors, the gauges – while sifting the instructions for utility. He couldn't help himself: anyone who'd grown up the way he had – strong mind, weak kin – would be the same.

'Now see here. Some kids have smashed in the glass. No sense in that. But you can see where the needle was. Used to point at the numbers.'

Kurt hadn't told his uncle that it was him who'd bashed out all the glass – every bit of it, meticulous and deliberate. Some of the tiny dials he'd had to hammer at with small stones before they had cracked.

But none of the long-ago lessons mattered without the keys. Kurt had searched the cab for a spare set and then resigned himself to stealing what he could.

'Reduce, re-use, recycle,' he said to himself. 'My civic duty.'

In the glovebox was a state map, a rusted multi-tool and a roll of toilet paper bent out of true. Kurt fingered Bethie's swan pendant at his neck as he tried to orient himself. Looked like the small town he'd been swept past was Saratoga, and that it was the closest town by half. He slammed his hand against the steering wheel in frustration. There had been a bridge there too, that he'd tried to hang onto, but the water had smashed his legs against the supports and wrenched him onward. Those muscles would ache now with each step he took on the long walk to civilization.

'Serves you right for letting those keys go,' he told himself. The multi-tool was small consolation.

It was late afternoon when the little town came into view. A diner was perched on the outskirts, right beside the highway, like a hitchhiker leaning into traffic. It made business sense, Kurt figured, risk and reward, but on a busy day it must have been chaos.

He rounded the building, looking for the front door. At the front of the diner he saw a fat woman closing the place up. As he watched, she picked up a tabby cat and settled it under one arm; she fought a set of keys with the other. He took a moment just to look. People were tall in the South, even with all the sickness, but they weren't chubby, and hadn't been in his life-time. He didn't think he'd ever seen anyone as well fed as this woman. He wanted to poke a finger through her floral blouse and into her stomach just to see if it sank in, if the flesh would stay dimpled, like Play-Doh.

Now she had turned back to the counter. He moved fast, his legs complaining, and pressed his nose against the glass of the door, cupping his hand around his face.

'Any food in there?' he called.

The woman shrieked and dropped her keys. She clutched the cat to her enormous bosom like a shield, and it squirmed silently. She frowned at Kurt through the glass, then relaxed a little when she saw he was white, boy-sized, even if he was still damp in places and a little cut up. He could feel the river water sticky on his skin, a film of filth.

Norma came slowly to the door and opened it a crack. 'This ain't the Salvation Army, kid. I'm just on my way out too.' The cat winked lazily at Kurt. He stared back. She sighed and shifted the tabby so that it sat more comfortably. 'All right, sunshine. Don't give me those boo-boo eyes. I get enough of that from Linus here.' She held the door wider, and he caught a reek of cheap perfume. 'That's a pretty pendant. Your girlfriend give it to you? Where you from, anyway?'

'Down South.' Kurt looked around inside. There were half-eaten donuts on one table, some cups with the dregs in them like river mud; Norma hadn't got around to clearing.

She snorted. 'You also got swept up by the river?'

'What do you mean "also"?'

'You're not the first to try that line on me today, sonny. It wasn't hell of a funny the first time, neither.'

Kurt let his shoulders drop a little. Softly, softly.

'Who else?'

'Who else what?'

'Who else was from the South?'

Norma clucked her tongue and thought of the old man in the passenger seat of the De Luxe, working her husband's reindeer sweater over his head. It had taken a minute for her to get over the sight of him – thinking it was her dead husband not only back from the grave, but still eager to escape little Saratoga, just as he always had been.

'Old guy. Had a gimpy leg. Looked like he'd been rode hard and put away wet.'

'He have a name?'

'Not that I got.'

'He happen to say where he was headed?'

'Mentioned New York and Des Moines. Can't say what his plans were, though. We didn't exactly swap diaries and braid each other's hair.'

'Which one's closer?' Kurt asked.

'Which one? You mean New York or Des Moines?'

Kurt nodded. Norma pursed her lips and stared hard at him, all humor vanished. Shit.

'Are you kidding me?'

Kurt shrugged.

'Des Moines,' she said slowly. Her eyes narrowed even further. 'And now I really do have to get going. Enough mopping up for one day, and this mess ain't going anywhere, now, is it? You want some donuts? That's the best I can do.'

'Sure,' said Kurt, and watched her bend to pick up the keys with a groan, the tires of fat squeezing across her back. As she straightened up with glacial slowness, he slipped the old multi-tool from his pocket. He flipped out a long one – an emery board, streaked with rust – and stabbed her in her vast neck, aiming between two moist, rubbery folds of flesh. He felt the tool bend as it met vertebrae. Her skeleton was the same size as everyone else's.

Still, she fell over, top-heavy, her tiny feet unable to support the change of weight. The cat was caught under the woman's arm, wedged against her boobs. It began yowling and clawing and biting to free itself, and it was only then that Norma understood that she was dying, and she screamed too. Kurt stabbed her again, and then once more, for luck. Then he stood back, panting, and saw the tabby work itself loose and dash for the doorway, but he was quick to slam it closed.

'You don't mind if Linus tags along with me, do you?' he asked Norma, but she was past hearing him, the bloody froth already settling on her lips.

That night Kurt slept curled up in one of the booths, holding tight onto Linus, his clothes drying over the grill and his stomach stretched tight with stale donuts and coffee, while Norma's blood pooled on the lino, undoing her long day's work.

11

Felix would have to struggle into the trousers. The back of the car was spacious, but the passenger seat had been pulled all the way forward and had rusted in place; it was too intimate for him to slip each pants leg on gracefully. And he didn't like the idea of climbing naked into the back seat, past Adams. Wasn't there that old story – about the fool who tried to put both legs into his pants at once?

'Close your eyes,' he said. 'This ain't gonna be pretty.'

Adams snorted. 'Sure. I'm driving over here, just so's you know. Watch that bottle on the floor, there. Guard it with your life.'

Felix laid the cuffs over his feet, then unrolled the wadded pants up to his knees. Next he wedged a knee against the dash, lifted his saggy buttocks off the vinyl and pulled the trousers up. Finally. He lay back, panting. He felt like he'd been doing nothing these past few hours but staring at the scrubby gray bush where his penis shrank like a snail.

'Next time you buy me dinner first,' he said. Adams smiled and said nothing. Every now and again he would finger the plaster on his face.

Felix held his hands still in his lap and tried to get his breath back. Jesus, but the sweater stank of mothballs, though that was a relief compared to the vanilla basketball. He couldn't breathe with that thing in his face. He reached up and yanked it off the mirror and tossed it to the back of the car – then immediately regretted not throwing it out the window. Shaking it seemed to have stirred something in it and the smell circulated around the car in waves. Adams didn't seem to mind, so Felix left it. First stop, he'd ditch that fucking thing. He cracked his window further and stared out at the new world: the North.

It still looked rich, even with the storm damage. There had been more to ruin in the first place. There was a row of office blocks at the edge of town, each window boarded over against the storm, and it set Felix to thinking about work. A job! The luxury of it. He had spent the last decade working harder than he ever had before, but it wasn't the kind of life where one man only made signs and another just fixed watches. And you know what? He didn't miss it. Okay. Maybe the TV shop back in New York. But he was younger then, and what he really missed was the idea that you had options. Since then he had made a bunch of KEEP OUT signs and fixed barometers and harvested honey and measured the weather and repaired a gun and drawn maps and plumbed his shack. That was what folk were meant for – the learning and the figuring out. That was what kept you young. The mistakes made you more glad when you didn't fuck up, because you knew how bad it could be.

As they left the city limits now, there were houses on hills flanked by carports, and road signs with clean edges – and not a bullet hole anywhere among them. Somehow there were fences too, as the houses became sparser and the land gave itself over to farming. The wire ran in neat lines, edge to edge, around new-planted crops, the furrows washed flat, the seeds gone down to the sea.

But this didn't happen by itself. Somewhere Renard's people were watching, guards set along the way at likely entry points, paranoid state protectors.

Enough wondering. Time for some answers. 'You ready to talk?' asked Felix. "Cause I got a million and one questions for you, buddy.'

Adams nodded. 'We'll go one, one.'

'We'll do what?'

'You ask a question, then I ask a question.'

'As long as it ain't English lit or calculus. How about we start with this one: who the hell are you?'

Adams adjusted his spine, settling against the seat. 'I'm part of an organization.'

'Christ. Freemasons really are everywhere.'

Adams side-eyed him. 'Better watch that language, friend. Ever heard of the Resistance?'

He didn't wait for a response. Of course Felix hadn't. No one had heard of the Resistance, even North-side of the Wall. Or if they had, it was in the way of a rumor or a myth: here and there an earnest man went missing in the night, or a deranged daughter was sent to a state asylum. And why should it have been otherwise? Renard was still the man – and America was the giant fuck-up it was always going to be.

'Anyway, since the War ended and the Wall went up, there've been people this side that think Renard's regime was basically a military coup. A lot of us lost a parent or a grand-parent or a sibling, you know. A missing generation. Sometimes two. My daddy went back South for the polling before the fight-ing started, and – poof! – it was like he dropped right out of sight. No phone calls, no word – from him or of him. Nothing. The War never made sense. And it's not just me. There's a few of us who never bought into the government Kool-Aid. We know when we're being lied to.'

'I hear you,' said Felix. He reached forward and adjusted the heater, turning a vent toward him. The air came out dry and hot and he rubbed his hands in it. 'That's better. But what's any of that got to do with my scrawny ass?'

'One, one, remember? My turn. What's it like in the South?'

Felix laughed. 'Are you serious?'

'Deadly.'

'You know nothing about your own country?'

'I've never been there myself. And you're the first person I ever met who's made it across the Wall.'

'Jesus.'

'So? I'd like to know.'

Felix sighed. 'How do I know you're not one of them Secret Service guys? Maybe all this' – he waved his woolly green arm around the car – 'is a trap.'

Adams shook his ruined head. 'I just saved you from whatever those two army guys wanted to do to you, and this is how you pay me back?'

Felix regarded him steadily. Adams traded him a hard glance in return, then slammed a hand on the wheel. 'For fuck's sake!'

'Okay, okay. Just keep your eyes on the road.'

'Deal. Now start talking.'

'Where to begin? The South is dead. Wasteland. Fucked.'

'For real?'

'Not to put too fine a point on it, that Wall back there' – Felix thumbed over his shoulder – 'divides this continent into the living and the dead. You know about the wind, right?'

'Some – but pretend I don't.'

Felix nodded, then continued, 'The wind blows a new disease

over those states most every day – and if you're dumb enough or unlucky enough to get caught out in it, you're fucked. I've seen some crazy shit – skin peeling off, eyes going blind, guts falling out. People losing their minds too. Just from breathing the air! Sounds plain weird when you say it out loud, don't it? Never had to explain it to someone before.' He tried to gauge the reaction: he stared at Adams's lumpy skin, his bloodshot eyes, the hair in clumps. Adams was undeterred.

'I know. It looks worse than it is, believe me. But let's talk about you. You've seen a bit of that action yourself, old man. That about the sum of it?'

Felix shrugged. 'You win some, you lose some.'

'Losing is not an option up here, my friend. Official word from Renard's propaganda people is that the plagues are coming in on the wind from the big, bad, dirty South – and they're getting a bit of help on their way. Know what I mean?'

Felix said nothing, the dormant rage he thought he had damped down flickering in his chest. Incredible! Renard was painting the defeated wasteland of the South as the enemy, strong enough to be afraid of, and strong enough to bring to heel.

'Thirsty yet?'

'Why do you ask?'

'There's the deal with the tap water.' Adams reached down into the footwell for the bottle of water. 'Doesn't look different, does it? But it's chock-full of antivirals. New one every day, or so they say. To combat what you bad-ass Southerners are sending over in the air.' He took a sip. ''Course, I know that's horseshit.'

He offered the bottle to Felix. The old man held up a hand. 'No offense, but I don't exactly know where that's been.'

Adams grinned, and he looked almost normal.

'Can we skip a turn?' he asked. Felix nodded. 'Long odds here, but are you one of the Des Moines Callahans? You know, the ones who managed to blow up Renard's wife? You look plenty old enough.'

'You know how to ask them, don'tcha?'

'That a yes?'

'It's a sure-am-but-it-wasn't-like-that. Truth is, Renard blew his own wife up just so that he could justify what he was about to do to the South. What do you think of that?'

'You're shitting me.'

'You'd smell it, pal,' said Felix. 'Now I've answered, so it's your turn. Why were you looking for me?'

Adams spoke slowly, still processing what Felix had told him. 'Well, not you specifically. Anyone from the South. Just got lucky, I guess. I happened to find you.'

'How did you know my name?'

'We monitor the phone lines – specially the numbers that belonged to people who were sent South for the census. The thinking was whoever comes back might just give their old lives a ring-a-ding-ding. Turns out we were right. You tried to call your apartment in New York. Bingo!'

Felix thought back to the diner, to the phone booth that smelt like a sewer, and the smooth-worn, time-traveling coin. That was where sentiment had got him. Goddam cat! he thought. Always more trouble than a creature was worth. But it was love, wasn't it? And that counted.

'We been monitoring those numbers close on a decade now with fuck-all to show for it. But then that storm! Man! That storm! Call from Sara-fucking-toga right on the border line? And right when that big-ass hurricane ripped through? It had to mean something. We got a fair few folk out looking, some of my best men plus some of my worst, even a Santee name of Otis who can track a locust across a prairie. But a call like yours! That was something I had to investigate my very own self. So I came racing, your knight in shining armor, and here you are. My turn.'

'Hell, no! I want the whole story. Why are you looking for Southerners anyway? I woulda thought you'd want to see the back of us, considering the lies you been told.'

'Ah! The best bit!'

'It better be. My back is killing me.'

'Well, listen close. We can't make any sort of attack on Renard while he has the water, right? Can you imagine? Guys dropping like flies. Ghost towns. And the absolute end of any real resistance. So we've been looking for, ah, alternatives for some time now. We need a cure-all. Something antiviral, at least, strong enough to knock out whatever comes in on the wind.'

'That going well?'

Adams grimaced. 'I've volunteered three times to test some prototypes. I survived all three – but only just.' He pointed a thick finger at his own face. 'Not the ladies' man I used to be. So for now, I drink the water like it comes outta the Holy Grail. Let some other young buck take one for the team. You wanna know what's under this plaster?'

Felix shook his head, but Adams plowed on.

'My tongue! The hole goes right through! The plaster's on so I can drink without getting my shirt wet!'

'That's too bad. I mean that.'

'Not as bad as some others I've seen.'

'So you're looking for Southerners for what? More guinea pigs?'

'We figured that any Southerner who's survived without Renard's magic water for as long as this – and then this storm stirring up all the old viruses we ever had – well, that man might know a thing or two.'

'Such as?'

'Such as how to get the old immune system going into a higher gear. And if that's the case, then Renard better get his baseball cup on, 'cause we're going to hit him where it hurts.'

'You talking about them mushrooms?'

'What mushrooms?'

'Those two travelers got them: black girl named Vida and her white boy, Dyce. I warned them the storm was on its way; then we bumped into each other again at the ghost colony. They had a stash of mushrooms with them, last time I saw – some dried, and a whole bunch of spores tucked away inside, I reckon. And some funny ideas about them too. She told me those things are antiviral. But I can't say for sure that either one of them's North-side. Might even be that they're dead by now. Sickness ain't the only thing you got to worry about up here, right?'

Adams was quiet at last, his disappointment thick between them. Felix looked out of the window. Here and there, scattershot as they drove, were the wrecks of old wartime aircraft, Southern fighters and gunships, he was sure, downed in dogfights with their exact replicas. Or were these the Northern aircraft graveyards? They were going fast, and he couldn't tell. On one fuselage someone had sprayed in white: REMEMBER. Felix hiccuped a laugh when he saw it.

'Don't mean shit to remember, if you're remembering it wrong,' he said. Adams didn't respond. They both had a lot to think about.

At an intersection, Adams turned right, so that the mid-morning sun shone in their eyes.

'We going east now?' asked Felix.

'Land where the sun rises, old man,' replied Adams.

12

With the rising sun came the cars. The night before, the storm-draggled North had been desolate: not so different from the wasteland of the South, Vida had thought – and then a pang of longing for Ruth had shot through her. She tamped it back down. Later. There was time for all that later. But as she rubbed at the dull exhaustion at the back of her eyes and peered out of the window of the ruined cockpit, she saw that people had begun the long run home, cars growling and farting carbon monoxide into the moist air, their passengers' prayers just as thick; not all of them would get home to find their houses still standing. Vida guessed that these were the lucky ones who had come from the huge governed spaces that were always thrown into emergency use: football stadiums, church halls, schools. And their journey wasn't over yet, either. Progress was slow.

Dyce came to stand behind her, resting his chin on the top of her head. He whistled.

'Damn! Those guys aren't going anywhere, are they?'

'You said it, brother.'

The traffic was backed up for miles. The cars closest to them lining the highway were piled high and covered with tarps, bulbous and deformed. So many people! With so many things! It made Vida think of the locust swarms that had moved in their rustling mandibled clouds back South.

When the drivers realized that the traffic had stopped altogether, doors began opening. Vida kept expecting something
miraculous to tumble out, like clowns out of a circus car, but it
turned out to be men and children needing to pee. They stood
on the verges, hands on hips, looking for a close and private
place, or just surveying the changed landscape. Around them
some of the kids were hunting for stones in the grass and then
taking turns to aim at the decrepit phone poles. A couple of
guys stepped gingerly onto the marshy slope, shaking out their
stiff muscles. The women stayed at the cars, shading their eyes
or shouting at the children or divvying up the sandwiches they'd
packed in some other life on top of the ticking hoods.

Dyce went to lie down and pulled the dusty blanket up to
his armpits, leaving his arms free so he could eat. Buddy's first-
aid kit had come in pretty handy. His ration stash wasn't too
bad either – almonds and jerky and boiled sweets, like a sulky
picnic. Loaves and fishes, baby, thought Dyce. He didn't care
where they came from. He just wanted to get something down
him before he slept and before they checked the bandages on
Vida's wound again. He was pretty sure it was worse. Soon she
wouldn't be able to walk. He didn't know how she had lasted
as long as she had; inside Vida was a cruel engine that kept
running even as it ate her frame.

Buddy appeared at the door. He was holding some things
from his truck. Now he jutted his pointy little chin at Dyce,
who was trying not to choke. 'Hope you're going to eat that
slow, son. Pardon my saying so, but it doesn't look like your
body knows exactly what to do with it.'

He was right. Dyce had learnt to eat deliberately, but even
so his stomach was cramping and he kept coughing, a dog with
a toad lodged in its throat.

Vida knew Dyce was okay – he'd be asleep soon enough, and he had youth on his side. It was just easier to travel in the dark, and they would have to get used to it. She turned back to the window and nearly shrieked: there was a man so close to the jet that he could touch its rusted side. Most of the men had stopped to pee a little way from the cars, aiming their dicks at the wreck like it was magnetic north, but this one had kept coming, hadn't he? She drew back, shocked, though he'd probably find it difficult to see through the smeared windows. The man looked like trouble – those husky Dutch genes still going strong. He kept glancing back at a cream-colored Lincoln – it wasn't moving in the gridlock any time soon – and then stepping from tuft to tuft so that his boots didn't sink in the mud. Now he moved around the jet, closer and closer, deciding something. Then he unbuckled his trousers and squatted, and Vida had to look away.

She waved a hand at Buddy. 'Hey,' she mouthed. 'Someone's here.'

'Shit.' He pulled his cap on and got down low and crawled toward Vida's window.

'What now?' asked Dyce, sitting up.

'Nothing,' Vida replied. 'We're not doing anything wrong. Just poor Northerners caught without shelter, same as anyone.'

'Stay here, both of you,' Buddy whispered and disappeared again.

The man had straightened up and fastened his pants again, but he had left a steaming turd on the ground next to the plane.

Buddy stepped carefully around it. The man was making his way to the other side now, his hand on the fractured wing, cool as you please. He was bending to look through the engine mounting when Buddy rounded the plane and coughed.

'Morning,' he began.

'Hey there,' replied the man. He was a full head taller than Buddy. They wouldn't stand a chance, even three against one. You never knew what had got inside people since the War, what unseen damage was doing a tour of their private insides. Vida strained to hear them.

'Where you headed, friend?' Buddy was saying.

'Back home. Laramie. You?'

'Nowhere right now,' said Buddy. 'Me and the missus were caught in the storm. Wanted to get home early and misjudged the weather. Sitting tight for a while and now there's all this.' He waved at the traffic jam.

'You sleeping in this baby?' The man slapped a giant hand against the side of the wreck.

'Beggars can't be choosers.'

'Guess so. You need any, ah, assistance?' The man smiled, his teeth square and white, cartoonish.

At the window, Vida shivered. There was something weird about him, voracious. I will eat you up, those teeth said.

'That's okay. I'm all set. If you got a cigarette, though . . .'

'All out. Smoked about a year's worth just thinking about my little house being blown to kingdom come.'

Liar, thought Vida, and her armpits prickled. Those aren't smoker's teeth. No, siree.

'Amen,' said Buddy.

The man put his hands in his pockets. He's touching himself, thought Vida, wondering which little piggy he'd fuck. Why was it always the one thing men wanted when they turned? To hurt something? It was like the viruses tweaked a brain switch like a nipple, and when they went crazy it was all they could think about. But that was in the South, and she knew how they got that way: Renard. So why were they this fucked up in the North, the old land of Canaan?

The man was looking the aircraft up and down.

'Say, I had an uncle who used to fly one of these things. You mind if I take a look inside?'

Buddy shifted from foot to foot. 'The little woman ain't decent.'

The man side-eyed him, then winked. 'I don't mind.'

He brought his wide face up close, breathing fog onto the glass, and Vida ducked down fast, her leg screaming. The man rubbed her window clean with the ball of his palm.

'Oh, hey now . . .' Buddy began, but then trailed off. The man ignored him, cupping his hands around his eyes to help them adjust to the dim interior.

Please don't cough. Please don't cough.

'Can't see shit!'

There was honking from the road.

'Traffic's moving,' said Buddy.

'Yeah, I can hear that,' replied the man, backing away from the plane. 'Looks like you and me and the missus will have to take a rain-check. See you again soon.'

He turned and sauntered back, unashamed of the erection pitched against his trousers. He made it all the way across the soggy prairie grass, not hurrying, and back up to the road even as the horns rose in a chorus of protest at the car holding up the homecoming queue. Buddy, Vida and Dyce watched him turn around to look at the plane one last time. He rubbed at his troublesome crotch and then slid back into the bucket seat of the Lincoln. The engine revved.

'Jesus,' said Vida as Buddy crawled back into the fuselage, his silver cross dangling outside of his shirt. 'What the fuck was that?'

'Don't take the Lord's name in vain, if you don't mind. And side effects, most likely.'

'Sorry. Side effects of what?'

'The antidotes. They do different things to different people.' Buddy's mouth turned down. 'How do you think Renard managed to boost numbers after the War?'

13

The southbound traffic was getting heavier by the minute, and it slowed as it went. Cars loaded down with lifetimes of possessions crawled by.

'Engine's hot,' muttered Adams. He had his arm out of the window, and now he rapped a quick drum roll on the body of the car. 'Plus, any cars heading away from the evacuation zone are likely to get pulled over. Only looters got any business heading north right now. Looters and us. Cops won't know what to do with you – nothing about you says you're from the South exactly – but it's just better to stay off the radar. Once the southbound traffic's eased up a little, we'll be in the clear. You don't mind sitting tight for a bit?'

'Just about all I been doing my entire life,' Felix told him. 'I got no problem with that.'

Adams nodded and turned off the highway onto the gravel of a roadside picnic spot – a rotted bench beside a wall. There'd been a stone memorial here once, for some long-loved wife killed in a car crash, but her rocks had been rearranged in rings and blackened by campfires. Adams parked the De Luxe beneath the lone green ash, and they both got out and watched the line of cars creep past, yard by yard.

'We done with a question for a question?' Felix asked.

'Yup. Practically related now,' said Adams, and grinned stiffly until the plaster on his face pulled too hard at the skin again. He leant back against the bonnet.

Felix went on. 'Right. So. Back in Saratoga, right, I'm sure I saw a giraffe. First out by the diner and then running alongside the car while we were being used for target practice. I'm hoping you saw it too. Unless it's dementia setting in – and that's an option – I'm pretty sure I still got eyes. What's the deal with the animals?'

Adams searched his pockets for a couple of cigarettes, put one in his mouth and offered the other to Felix.

The old man held up a hand. 'Got to keep my baby-soft skin, don't I?'

'You know it,' said Adams. He found a lighter in his shirt pocket, then lit the cigarette between words. He puffed it a couple of times to make sure it had taken, and then hoisted himself onto the bonnet of the De Luxe. 'It's kind of weird to think that you don't know any of this stuff. I mean, we just take it for granted. Anyhoo. There always were a ton of preserves about in the old US of A. Africa's always had the big hitters. We just shipped in the megafauna. You can't supersize a bison, my farmer friend used to tell me, but dollars can buy an elephant. Then the War came and most preserves got blown wide open. No one left to do the upkeep or feed the animals, or else the fences were destroyed. There were all kinds of animals roaming the place, wandering into town. Looking for food, right? Guy I knew said his wife was bringing in the washing one evening and walked right into a goddam rhinoceros munching on her dahlias. And not just the safari-zoo types, either – weird bears and goats from Asia, a couple of kangaroos. But none of those lasted free-range too long. Climate's wrong, there's nothing to eat. Different plants here than they're used to. A whole bunch ate milkweed or pokeweed or something, saw it in the paper. They lined up the bodies and took a photo. Like Noah's ark got into a high-speed crash.' Adams sucked in a lungful of smoke and when he let it out, a thin stream leaked through the plaster. Felix shivered. It wasn't right.

'Giraffes were different, though,' Adams was saying. 'Adaptable. Found their niche. They don't graze low down, see – never ate the real deadly stuff. Then word comes from Renard that they're protected. Like a national symbol.'

'Like the eagle,' said Felix. He thought of Tye Callahan and the way he'd loved that harrier of his. Vicious fucking thing. Hadn't helped in the end, though, had it?

'You got it. You don't touch a giraffe. Lucky they don't turn rogue, the way elephants do.'

Felix shook his head. 'You think you've heard everything.'

The men sat together listening to the idling of the convoy of cars on the road, and looking up at the sky – lighter now than it had been for weeks. High up, swifts were swooping and diving after the flying ants thrown up by the change in pressure.

Adams pinched out his cigarette and then cleared his throat. 'Been meaning to tell you where we're headed.'

'Resistance HQ. You already said. Iowa, right?'

'Yeah, but more specific than that – Des Moines,' Adams said slowly. He paused. 'Capitol Building, to be even more exact.'

Felix tilted his head in disbelief. 'What? That's Renard's home base. Why the fuck would you want to head there?'

'Correction: it used to be Renard's home base – till you Callahans fucked it up. Place got sealed overnight. Official word was that Renard was saying he couldn't work somewhere his wife had died, and who could blame the guy? But if what you told me is right, it was more like he didn't want anyone snooping round and figuring out he killed her himself. His slogan wasn't exactly "Women and children first". It's the last place anyone would expect the Resistance to set up HQ. So . . .'

'So that's where you set it up. Jesus please us!'

'Man, it's perfect. It's still sealed. Not even Renard's men are allowed in. I gotta pee,' Adams suddenly said, real quick, and then he slid down from the bonnet. Felix watched him hurdle the stone wall and vanish into the dogwoods. He hadn't expected him to be able to move that swiftly, but when nature called, a man had to answer. Felix sat up.

'Back to Des Moines,' he said, just to hear the words. He shook his head.

He looked at the line of cars. A white sedan was driving in the wrong lane, determined, lapping the stationary traffic. At the picnic turnoff, it rumbled onto the gravel and came to a stop beside Felix, rattling as it idled. A tiny woman with a silver crew cut leant her head out of the window.

Shit, thought Felix. Police!

He felt a flush of heat rising in his throat – here he was, a fucking Southerner, sitting on the side of a Northern highway in a stolen patrol car! He tried to remember whether there was any indication that this car was a service vehicle rather than a regular car. He couldn't recall a badge or siren rack or anything. Maybe it'd be okay. Maybe she'd look him over and move along. Her door swing wide open. She stepped out onto the dirt.

'Everything all right here?' She had a mole near her top lip, like Marilyn Monroe. Felix watched it bob up and down as she spoke.

'Yes, ma'am,' he said, and tipped three fingers at his forehead in a scout's salute. 'Just waiting out the traffic in a less, ah, unpleasant spot. No use sitting up there breathing exhaust fumes with a bladder as old as mine.'

The officer gave him a sideways glance. 'And where are you headed, sir?'

Shit. Shit. Shit. She's going to ask me to get out of the car. Then I'm fucked.

'Same as everyone.' He waved at the traffic. 'Home. Saratoga. Hope the old house is still standing, but rushing back ain't going to change it one way or the other.'

'Too true.' She made a circuit of the car before she stood at Felix's window and leant over. 'Can I ask you to get out of the car, sir,' she said, and Felix could smell her perfume mingling with the vanilla freshener.

'Ma'am, I don't mean to be funny or disrespectful or nothing of the sort – but before you pulled up just now, I was busting for a pee. Right now my finger's in the dyke, so to speak. Sorry for the indiscretion, truly, but if I get up out of this car, that's the first thing I'm going to have to do. And heaven help whoever's standing in my way.'

The woman stepped back quickly and Felix opened his door and stood, creakily.

'You mind if I take a look in your vehicle?'

Felix knew how it was with cops. Saying 'No way, Jose' when they asked your permission was an admission of guilt. Simple as that.

'Absolutely. And if you find a stinky basketball-shaped air freshener in the back there, please do us all a favor and toss it out the window.'

Felix turned and waddled toward the edge of the gravel, to the sagebrush where Adams had already made his break. How far would he get if he made a run for it now? How long did he have before Sergeant Crew Cut went through the contents of the glovebox and got suspicious? There was no way he was staying here, waiting for her to pull her gun and tell him to get on the ground. He kept going, expecting at each step to hear her ordering him to stop. One more step. Another. He was in the sagebrush, and then the trees of the copse closed their cool leaves behind him.

He heard her shout now, and the crunch of her boots as she came running. Felix broke into a jog. She'd run him down in a minute, but so be it. Had to wake up early if you were going to catch wily old Felix Callahan! He pushed through some sumac, wading fast and steady, all the while listening for the heavy tread of the policewoman behind him, bracing for the impact of her tackle. Man, it hurt to run!

But there, just to his left, hunkered down like a rattler, was Adams, and Felix almost yelped at the sight of him. He was holding a rock, and before Felix could say anything, he had already leapt at the officer. Her scream was cut off. There was a meaty thud and she collapsed. Adams held onto the rock. Some of her hair was on it, stuck there to the dark blood. Felix couldn't look at her, at what had happened to the little mole near her gaping mouth.

'Let's go,' Adams told him. He wasn't even breathing hard.

The two men kept their heads down as they emerged from the vegetation. There were eyes watching them from the cars on the road, but no one got out. No one opened a window and asked where the woman had gone. It was the sweater that did it, thought Felix. No man wearing a reindeer across his chest could be much of a threat.

They got into the car and Adams eased it along the circular track, past the black-ringed smears of ancient fires and back to the edge of the highway.

'Jesus! Was that some kind of test? Or did you actually just hang me out to dry?' Felix asked. Now that he was sitting down, his heart was hammering at his ribs.

'Well, either way, you got the job done, so no harm.'

'Not yet. But keep that shit up and it's just a matter of time.'

'Anyway, the traffic's moving. It ought to be safe to carry on,' said Adams. He edged the car over the lip of the asphalt and waved a cheery goodbye to a woman in the back seat of a Passat.

14

It was only after midday that Dyce and Vida both felt safe enough to fall asleep at the same time. Until then, the unspoken agreement was that one would stay awake so that the other didn't also have to worry as they watched the line of cars inch by. Still, the worry was unavoidable: the mind searched for rough spots and losses, and so Vida fretted feverishly about her mother, who could be anywhere, and Dyce in his turn worried about Vida. For the first time he wished Ruth was with them. He'd seen shallower wounds than the one on Vida's leg end in amputation. Buddy had done his best – cleaned it out with a stash of cotton swabs that had collected on the floor like bloody snowflakes, then squeezed two tubes of antibacterial cream into the filleted wound, trying to replace the lost flesh until it could grow back in its own time. He had tried to be gentle, but even so the sweat stood sharply in Vida's hairline and she hadn't been able to speak through the pain, her breath hissing in when the pressure got too intense. Then he had taken care to wrap the whole mess from ankle to thigh so tightly that she could hardly move. Maybe that was the idea. At least she could sleep – or maybe it was a kind of protective coma, Dyce thought when he woke up first.

The whole healing process was horrible to watch – how did parents stand the suffering of their children? – but it was also pretty weird. It was clear that whatever the mushrooms were doing to immunize them against the random viruses, they were also working to keep Vida's leg from turning green. It was still hard to believe, though it felt as if they'd lived this way forever. Against the evidence, he was always expecting her to collapse, but Vida was made of iron. No, that's wrong, Dyce thought. It was pure determination. She had some deep drive in her that other people lacked, and it was always going to save her life. Not like Bethie, or the other hundreds of thousands – millions? – of people who had given up and died during the War, and then in all the years after it. Vida was different. How did she ever end up with me? he wondered.

He turned over to look at her closely now that she was oblivious and he had her to himself. He wanted to stroke her curling eyelashes, the damp dimple of her upper lip. It made his heart hurt, and even in the moment he knew what it was: they loved each other, and they loved each other's bodies, whole or damaged, but after this, she wouldn't need him. Dyce sighed. There was no script for this one – no roses or dates or first fucking base. It was a love that had been made for the end of the world.

Vida opened one eye. 'Okay, Casanova. You know it's creepy to watch someone sleeping, right?'

'Now you tell me.'

She stuck out her tongue. 'No one's having sex today, buddy. Have mercy on the crippled lady. But you know what?'

'What?'

'I'll get better faster on my own.' She tried to smile. 'And then we'll make up for lost time, I promise.'

'I can get behind that.'

'That, my furry friend, is exactly what I was thinking. Go

and limber up outside somewhere. Gotta keep flexible.' She was smiling that crooked smile again, and he saw that it was costing her.

Dyce dropped a smooch on her lips and then got up. He'd just hang outside, close to the fuselage of the plane so no one saw him. It was enough just to be able to breathe freely. He still wasn't used to the air. It stank of carbon monoxide from the stalled engines on the road, but it was real, and it was clean enough to inhale without fear. Northern air. Those fuckers didn't know how lucky they were. He wondered if they knew what price had been paid by the South for that good air. He surveyed the land from horizon to horizon. There was something strange about everything, even the plants beneath his feet: they were more orderly here than back South. The same blue grama and buffalo grass fought for space, but here they seemed to draw their battle lines and grow in neat patches. Back South, even the grass would tussle, overcoming saplings, sending its seeds out to infiltrate and colonize not just bare patches but established shrubs.

Dyce decided that he preferred the South. There was something unnatural about the restraint that pulsed through the North – from Buddy's smile right down to the dirt.

When he came back inside, Vida was properly under and the afternoon was quiet, the voices of the people in the cars drifting back to them over the distance. He lay down back to back with her, the bad leg resting on the good, her spine touching his, like twins.

Buddy woke them an hour before sundown.

'Look,' he said, and pointed outside. 'It's two-way again. We're clear to get moving. Got about a ten-hour trip ahead of us, so if you need a pee – or worse – go get that done now.'

'Where we headed?' In his sleep, Dyce had turned to lie behind Vida, his arm resting across the curve of her stomach.

'It's a surprise,' Buddy replied.

'Look,' said Dyce, sitting up and leaving a cold spot where he had lain. 'You're not a leprechaun, Buddy. We're not searching for a pot of gold. Help me out here. There's a reason I'm asking. We weren't the only ones to make it across the Wall. We've got friends and relations somewhere up North. We got to know where we're headed so we can make a call, see who survived.'

'Ten hours' drive,' murmured Vida, 'and we're starting to turn east. What's ten hours east of here? That's clear through Nebraska, right?'

Buddy snorted. 'Not the way you remember it.'

'Iowa, then? Or whatever it is now? Blink if I'm getting warm.' Dyce faced him square-on. 'We need to know where we're going. Believe me, we're grateful for all your help, and we've seen no reason not to trust you, Buddy. You've been mighty kind. But.'

'I'm North and you're South, and never the twain shall meet?'

'That's about the stretch of it.'

'So? This ain't *Romeo and Juliet*, pal. You're not pretty enough.' Buddy took his cap off and blew air upward, nettled. 'The more people who know about the Resistance HQ, the more likely someone will tell, that's all. First thing they teach you.'

Dyce and Vida said nothing. Finally Buddy conceded.

'Okay, okay. Iowa. Des Moines, if you must know. The old Capitol Building. Happy now?'

'Ecstatic.'

Buddy shook his head. 'Hope I get a medal for this.' He turned to go and then came back. 'Those others, the Southerners: you want to know the best-case scenario? Maybe one of the other scouts found them, way they did with your man Felix Callahan, and if that's the case, they'll be heading where we're heading.'

'And worst-case?'

'Didn't your mama teach you not to ask questions when you already know the answers?'

They packed up, Vida moving stiffly and Dyce doing most of the work, but there wasn't much apart from the supplies that Buddy had left in the plane.

Back at the truck, they found it had sunk down in the water-logged prairie grass, and Dyce wasted minutes fetching stones and old bits of carpet from the cockpit to jam under the tires for grip. Buddy spun the wheels while Dyce leant on the tailgate, and the truck finally jumped forward.

They were all back in the vehicle, bumping over the soggy grassland to the road, and Vida was nestling against Dyce so he couldn't see the pain yanking at her mouth.

'I feel like such a fucking burden.'

'Well, that's because you are,' he said, and kissed the top of her head. 'But you're my burden. And I intend to get full value.'

Vida grimaced. For some reason her insides were sore: even against the steady complaint of her leg it felt like some tendon in her ovaries – did you even have tendons there? – was stretching. Quit whining, she told herself. That's what Ruth would have said. Burn that old bridge when you get to it.

The red sun went down somewhere behind the clouds, throwing shafts of light over the landscape, and the hundreds of cars were brushed with gold, the heads of their passengers fuzzed with light. After the initial thunk back onto the asphalt, and Buddy's grin and thumbs-up to the driver behind who had let him jump the queue, there was only the hum of the engine and the static of the wheels to lull Dyce and Vida to sleep.

They woke after a couple of hours in the dark somewhere on the flat face of Nebraska.

Buddy looked at them in the mirror when he noticed them stirring and turning their faces to the cold glass. 'You ain't missed much. Welcome to the good life.'

'Fuck,' said Dyce slowly, looking out at the desolation.

'Yup.' Buddy sighed and it turned into a yawn. 'Just wait till it gets light and you can see what you're up against.'

Dyce hadn't explained that he could see in the dark – that kind of secret was worth holding onto.

'Nebraska wasn't exactly easy on the eyes before the War,' Buddy went on. 'Wall-to-wall factory farms, but at least they were producing, you know? But now . . .' He shook his head, and the bill of the red baseball cap made him look like a watchful bird. 'Buildings are all caved in, the cages are empty. Just scrub and rusty barbed wire. You ever get a hankering for tetanus, you go for a stroll in old Nebraska. Out here's like the Wild West all over again.'

Vida's heart sank. She could see nothing, just the darkness spread flat on the landscape, and somewhere out there was her mother under the same sulky clouds and weak moon. Her leg was aching worse than it had before, rebelling against the attention, and her abdomen throbbed in time with it. Maybe her mama could fix all those things, but she was long ago and far away. Let her be there, Vida said to herself. At the Capitol Building, in Nebraska, anywhere in the North. I'll find her as soon this leg's fixed; just let her be there. But she had no idea where to direct her prayer.

15

When Kurt woke up, the highway beside the diner was bumper to bumper with Northerners heading home after the storm. He uncurled and slid out from under the booth table, looking around for Linus, but the creature was already up and about on cat business.

He felt for the pendant. Still there. He could lose everything else, but the ivory swan was the only thing he cared about, taken from Bethie after she'd died and couldn't stop him, nestled there between her breasts. She wanted him to have it. She had told him with her eyes.

His clothes were strung up on butcher's string behind the grill, where he'd left one plate on all night to warm the place and to draw the moisture from his jeans. He felt them. They were still wet along the waist, but he slid them on. Things to do.

He hadn't noticed before, but now when he looked, his shirt was cut up pretty bad along the back, from his struggle with the North Platte. That wouldn't do. No, sir. Callahans got standards. He went to search the cleaning cupboard, hoping for a change of clothes, overalls maybe, but found nothing he could use. He looked at Norma where she lay spread-eagled on the floor, her keys twinkling beside her like treasure. She still had on her floral blouse underneath that housecoat – and why wouldn't she? He wasn't some kind of pervert, but that might have to do. It was about three sizes too big for him and stank of her perfume, but he worked it off her sodden limbs anyway. He would have to rinse the blackened blood from the collar under the kitchen tap, but that was easy enough.

'Cold water for hot blood. That right, lady?'

He rubbed at the mapped stain, and it faded but wouldn't disappear entirely. He gave up and set himself to cutting the wet material to size with the diner's kitchen scissors. It wasn't the first time he'd adapted the oversized clothes of the grown-up dead: he'd taken one of his uncle's shirts too after the damn fool man got himself caught in the wind. Kurt had cut and crudely shaped it with a knife, then sewed it all back together in a smaller size with the unraveled thread from the hem of a ragged blanket. Now he would have to leave it hanging behind the grill like a corpse. He was sad to leave it: that shirt was the closest to an inheritance he was going to get.

When he was dressed, he went looking for the cat. It had to be somewhere, since he'd closed all the windows before bedtime to keep the warmth in from the stove. He finally found the tabby wedged between two chest freezers, their white sides rumbling, hot with electricity.

'Wake up, sleepyhead.'

He yanked Linus out by the back legs, the cat growling as his claws squeaked uselessly against the linoleum. Kurt held him tight under his arm while he made coffee with one hand. Linus dug his claws into Kurt's arm in token protest, but the boy didn't react except to watch his bright blood bead along the welting grooves.

'That's fair, Linus. Just let me know when you're done.'

He collected the last of the world's stalest donuts and went to sit himself down at a booth right against the diner window and stare out at the cars. Prime position. The cat had given up and resigned himself to being cradled. Kurt dipped a corner of his napkin into his coffee and wiped the blood away. It rose steadily to the skin's surface, and itched. Even if Linus had some dirt underneath his claws, Kurt still thought he was safe. Immune was immune. He wondered how long the dose in the syringe was active. He'd have to get a booster shot somewhere pretty soon, just to be safe.

When breakfast was done, he went around opening all the fridge and freezer doors wide and making sure the stove plates were on, as well as the vacuum cleaner, the portable air con and the radio, for luck. The cat sat on the floor, bristling.

'Every bit helps, old pal. It ain't exactly going to cripple the North to lose this electricity, but you got to keep chipping away. Rome wasn't destroyed in a day, right?'

He emptied out Norma's tote bag and went through her things, but there was nothing there of much use. Women. At least the bag was useful.

'It won't be for long,' he told Linus, lowering him into it, 'so just hold tight and don't make a fuss. When I'm famous, you can say you were there at the start. Ain't you never wanted to see the world?' He stuffed the tabby none too gently down into the tote and clicked the clips. There was enough air for the cat, and it could see out if it was so inclined. The bag bulged and spat as the cat struggled and scratched, and Kurt held it away from his body and shook it.

'Now you just settle and count your blessings while you're in there. I'll be honest with you. I ain't got no use for humans 'cept the smart ones. At least I know where we stand. And just so you know, I'll be calling the shots. That changes, I'll be wearing me a pair of tabby slippers come fall.'

The bag roiled and then fell still. Kurt picked Norma's keys up from the floor and hoisted the bag over his shoulder. He gave Norma a little wave and then locked up after himself.

'Leave it the way you want to find it, Linus.'

He crossed the parking lot and started his walk, keeping next to the highway alongside the cars. Nobody offered him a lift. Maybe they were all full up with their furniture and their kids – or maybe the blouse made him smell of crazy. Either way, it was a fair walk before he reached the suburbs of Saratoga, and Linus was getting restless.

'Not much longer, Puss in Boots.' He stuck a finger in the bag and tried to scratch Linus's head, but the cat ducked away from him.

Kurt made his slow patrol of the streets in a grid, marking the families as they returned – the adults stretching their backs as they stood on the remains of their front lawns, assessing the damage. It was the first look that was the hardest. After that, you knew what you were dealing with.

As he watched, jobs were allocated. The mothers were mostly set to unpacking and herding the children while the fathers busied themselves lifting branches off porches or standing on the sidewalk opposite for a better view of the destruction in the universal stance: hands on hips, heads shaking. No one commented on his makeshift shirt, cut and tied back together in tiny knots like boils. No one even noticed him at all, it seemed to Kurt, and there was some defiant, lonely part of him that was angered.

Outside the closest house – a two-storey red-brick, like an old-time insurance advert – was a white Toyota. Kurt stared.

Strapped to the bonnet was an adult pronghorn.

He crossed the street to get a better look. Yup. There it was.

Someone had done a little hunting on the way home. Waste not, want not.

He wandered up the drive and bent to examine the buck. It had been tied down with a black ratchet strap. The grille was bent in and the buck lay in the dent that it had made in the metal. As far as he could tell, it looked like a couple of legs were broken; the side of its skull was concave, and dried blood streaked the face like war paint, starting from the corner of one dull eye.

'Big one, isn't he, Blondie?' came a woman's croaky voice from the house. Kurt looked up and saw a dyed orange head leaning out of an upstairs window. She wanted to talk, the relief of surviving loosening her tongue. 'Hit it in the night on the way back from my sister's place. Came out of nowhere. We didn't know what to do, so my husband tied the thing on the bonnet, like we seen in movies. He's on the phone now to ask what to do with it.'

'Oh,' said Kurt. Then, 'I know what to do with it.'

'You do? What?'

'Eat it.'

The woman laughed. 'I'm sure that's against the law. He's on the phone right now, Derrick – that's my husband – so we'll figure it out. Should be some kind of ranger service? Where they take these things away? We couldn't just leave it there.'

Why the fuck not? Kurt wanted to say. It could have been you, lady. Don't you know this is a war?

He held his tongue and the ginger woman craned her neck, watching him walk around her car with the wild animal strapped to it like a satyr, some wartime hybrid of steel and flesh. He reached out and felt the buck's horns, like leather. Linus started his wriggling again; the smell of blood was making him antsy.

Kurt squeezed the bag hard. The struggle intensified and then the cat flopped back, panting.

'You know where Des Moines is? Or how to get there from here?' Kurt called back to the window.

'There's a map book in the car. Give me a second and I'll come get it for you.'

While he waited, he ran his fingers over the pronghorn's hair, then felt under the ribs for the organs. You could tell a lot about an animal by its interior. Most critters down South had swollen livers: that was something the body did in response to the airborne viruses, trying to get rid of toxins like alcoholics' insides fought the liquor. This buck, old as he was, seemed fine. If it hadn't been for the grille of the Toyota, he'd have been alive for another five years, Kurt guessed. Long road ahead of him, and then – pow – nothing. There was some kind of lesson there.

'*Carpe diem*, motherfucker,' he whispered, low in the buck's ear.

The woman had hurried out of the house in a pink toweling dressing gown, clutching it closed against the wind, the keys held up in her hand as if she was going into battle.

'Excuse me?'

'Just saying a little prayer for Bambi over here.'

'Oh. That's sweet of you. We never even thought about that – just drove home before the kids woke up and got scared. Do animals get last rites?'

Kurt shrugged. 'They deserve 'em more than a lot of humans I could name.'

The red-haired woman tittered. 'Well. You're a nice young man.'

She unlocked the car door and swiveled her knees to sit so that she could reach inside the glovebox. She took a dog-eared map book out and then wriggled out again in reverse, still clutching her gown at the throat.

'Now let's see how to get you home.' She opened the map book on the hood beside the pronghorn's blood-rimmed mouth and began to search the pages, yakking all the while.

'Des Moines, Des Moines. It scared the you-know-what out of me when we hit it. The buck, I mean. Jeepers creepers! I was driving too, which made it worse. Just a flash in the headlights and bang, right on the grille. Could've come through the windscreen! That would have been all she wrote for me and Derrick, and this old pronghorn too. Just shows that you never know when your time is up. Ah, Des Moines,' she said, holding her finger to a spot on the page.

Kurt peered at the paper roads and arteries, but he needed to get closer.

'You mind holding my cat for a second?'

She blinked at him, and then gawped in merriment. 'A cat!'

'Sure. He's no bother. Just here in the bag. Will you hold onto him for a sec? You're not allergic or anything, are you?'

She took Norma's tote and Linus thumped to the other side of it. The ginger woman held her eye against the opening.

'Don't get too close now.'

'Oh, he's darling! I used to have a tabby when I was a little girl. Don't you love that M mark they all have on their foreheads? Like they're solving the world's problems. If only they could speak!'

'Uh-huh.' Kurt studied the map.

'Kit-kit-kit!' said the woman. 'Mister Whiskers! You got a pen? Can't hurt to write down the directions. I know how muddled I get with all the 430s and 750s and 680s. You know what? You can use a page from the back. There's empty ones for notes that we're never going to use. Derrick is a pretty good navigator. Here, kitty, kitty!'

Kurt felt in his pocket for a pen, but his hand found the multi-tool instead.

And why the fuck not?

He drew it like a pistol and in one movement sank the blade into the woman's neck. He got the angle right this time, and she dropped to the ground without shrieking. The blood only started jetting when he pulled the blade back and wiped it on Norma's zombie blouse.

He grabbed the tote and flung it onto the passenger seat of the Toyota, ignoring the growl and squeal that came from it.

'The pen is mightier than the sword, Linus, but today it's every man for himself.'

He slid slickly into the seat and started the engine: what his uncle had taught him about cars had stuck.

As he rolled out of the drive, a skinny man emerged and stood on the porch, scratching his head dumbly. When he saw his wife's crumpled body, he shouted and broke into a run, but by then it was too late.

'Sayonara, Derrick.' Kurt banged the toe. 'Don't stop till we hit Des Moines, pardner. Yeehaw!' He swung the car onto the highway, only clipping the sidewalk an inch or so. 'And guess what? We got ourselves a packed lunch for a week.' He waved a hand at the pronghorn, whose cloudy dead eye locked on his. In the bag, Linus was quiet.

On the way out, they passed by the diner and its dead freight again. This time there was smoke rising from the building. Kurt didn't notice. He was driving! Not a Mustang or anything, but still. A real car! Take that, motherfuckers! Yeehaw!

16

Somewhere in the gloaming of old Nebraska, Adams pulled the De Luxe to the side of the road. The absence of movement was what woke Felix from his old man's doze.

Adams nudged him, the stale air recycled through the damaged passages of his nose. 'Your turn, partner. You know how to drive, right?'

Now that Felix had woken from his black, dreamless sleep, he saw a deeper blackness, lit only by a single weak headlight pointing down at the cracked asphalt in front of the car. He rubbed his scratchy eyes, unsure whether he'd opened them at all.

Adams persisted. 'You do remember how to drive, right?'

'Is it like riding a bicycle?' Felix said, and when Adams shot him a look, he answered himself. 'Sure. I can drive.'

Adams pulled the latch on his door and it popped open a crack.

'Ready? Got to be quick switching seats. Can't be sure what prowls the forgotten highways.' He'd made his voice horror-movie deep, but Felix knew he wasn't joking.

'Yup.'

Felix felt for the latch on his own door and opened it. The two men crossed in front of the lone headlight and then sat back down in the body-warmed seats, each prepared by the other.

'What do you reckon is out there?' Felix asked. He felt with his foot for the accelerator.

'You hear stories.'

Felix ran his hand down between the seats and found the cold metal of the handbrake lever. He dropped it and checked the highway, then turned back onto the road.

'You don't have to watch for traffic here,' commented Adams, already curling up against the passenger door.

Felix tried the brake, then pulled the car over to the side again.

'What's up?' Adams asked.

'Been waiting for a chance to get rid of that damn scented basketball ever since Saratoga. You reckon you can reach it back there?'

Adams twisted around and leant into the back, feeling for the ball in the dark. When he had it, he opened his window and tossed it out. It bounced a few times in the wake of the De Luxe as Felix pulled off.

'Any directions?' Felix asked.

'Keep on this road. I'll be awake before we get to the end of it.'

Felix let the De Luxe climb its slow gears and then held it steady, staring out at the circle of light that lit the way as Adams drifted off. The broken white lines flew under him like bullets, all aimed too low. For the first time since he'd woken on the banks of the North Platte, he thought about his exercise bike and the darkness held back by a machine – but only just. He was grateful that he didn't have to do any pedaling now. He felt with one hand across the central console of the car, searching for the open mouth of a tape deck. There wasn't one. Besides, his tapes were far away and probably lost to the floodwaters, along with everything else. But it was only the tapes that mattered to him at this moment. Felix tested himself, cuing the first one up in his mind and recalling the sound of his own rusty voice.

Felix, I hope you've still got the balls to have that gun on the table. Okay. Here we go. My name is Felix Callahan, but you know that, don't you? I was born in Norman, Oklahoma, back when it was still a place.

Was that how it went? He couldn't be sure. Maybe he was even now lying on the leeward slope of the hill behind his shack, slowly losing his mind to whatever contagion was in Stringbeard's blood and mucus. Surely that was more likely than this: driving a real-life working car across the giraffe-infested North, aiming for the defunct heart of Renard's America – the old Capitol Building.

Des Moines.

It was like talking about Mars. For a moment he wondered whether steering the De Luxe off the road into some deep-rooted tree or a ten-ton rock would jolt him awake, the Llama Danton heavy in his hand, ready to pull the trigger and end it all. His way, at least.

'My way,' he told himself. 'My way or the highway, mother-fuckers.'

Even as he spoke, part of him stood outside himself; eating those mushrooms back in Horse Head had made him healthy, but one of their side effects was a terrible clarity. Felix knew that he couldn't escape his here and now.

A sign appeared in the gloom and grew bigger until it whooshed past and into the darkness behind, white slashes on green like an olden-day lawn.

He turned his thoughts to Adams, who slept restlessly and breathed mostly through his mouth, held upright only by his seat belt. Why had he left him to deal with that butch police-woman at the rest stop? It was deliberate, Felix was pretty sure. Maybe it was safer to let a Southerner deal with a cop, rather than a member of the Resistance.

Or maybe Adams was a wanted man. But why not explain it after the fact? Why not come back to the car and say, 'Sorry, Gramps, but they know I'm Resistance'?

Felix glanced at Adams again. That craggy face, with its fissures and repairs.

Unless he was wanted for something else. The kind of thing you don't mention to a man you've just met.

Felix shook his head to clear his thoughts. Concentrate, asshole. He focused on the lines zipping past beneath the De Luxe. After a minute, he cued up the imaginary tape again and searched the faded rooms of his mind for the good words.

I had older brothers, once upon a time, and a mother and a father, the way it ought to be. I was the youngest by far. Not remembering it much probably means it was pretty smooth. There was milkshake vomit in footwells – that I remember – and broken arms from trampolines, and crackers in turds. The usual.

He'd made it all the way to his memory of Concession by the time Adams took over the driving duties for the last stretch into Des Moines. They were avoiding the populated suburbs, aiming the De Luxe in a roundabout way for the domes of the Capitol Building. There were makeshift blockades that looked deliberate – rubble in the middle of the road, or overturned cars. Adams noticed him looking.

'One way in; one way out.'

Felix couldn't quite believe his eyes as he stared out at the city, overlaying what he was seeing onto the blueprint of his ramshackle memories. A lot had changed. Des Moines, when he was last here, was the administrative capital of the North. Now all the infrastructure and development that had been injected into it lay unused or half finished, like Roman ruins. Renard must have been quick to leave the city. There was abandoned scaffolding on almost every structure – and cranes too, rusting away, all stopped like a clock.

It was, Felix thought, just a little too much like the broken cities of the South – the way they'd seized up as their inhabitants grew sicker. He'd stayed clear, mostly, but after a year being holed up in his shack, he'd taken a long trek out to see Denver. Most of his weather instruments had come from the university there, the kitty headphones for his tape deck from an electronics shop on South Pearl Street. If Denver was gone, it was all real.

In the event, the city was empty. On the road in there was an open manhole with orange cones in a ring around it, a last warning to the dazed and desperate few who might be walking the streets at night, searching for lost relatives. It was a simple civilian house that had made Felix understand how truly fucked everything was – nothing fancy, just completely and hopelessly final. The walls were half painted over a white base, but now they were flaking in sheets like sunburnt skin. A building jack held a door frame up while some long-dead soul planned to extend the lintel in perpetuity: the space for it had been cut into the bricks, and the concrete beam lay on the sidewalk, ready to be lifted into place. But Felix knew that the house was the wartime effort of a woman and her children – maybe a man too, exempt from fighting due to some disorder – the optimistic work of citizens convinced that they would win. This was the mighty South.

'Fuck Renard,' he murmured. It snapped him fully back into the present.

'Amen.'

Adams pulled the car up outside a deserted coffee shop and came to a stop. 'Can't just stroll up to the front door. Got to do some crawling before we're in the clear.'

17

In the night the car had stopped once. Vida slept through, but Dyce opened a slit eye to watch Buddy get out of the vehicle and hurry off into the darkness, coming back with a jerry can, retrieved like treasure from some hidey-hole only he knew. He poured the gas into the tank – his face twitchy, lit by the red glow of the rear lights – and then scurried back to his side and got in. He slid the can over onto the passenger seat and closed the door quickly. They rolled back onto the 680. He said nothing, but he didn't have to: they'd passed no gas stations since they'd left Wyoming. You didn't cross these plains without planning ahead. The rising sun revealed the flat expanse of the Iowa prairie, low grassed hills like ocean swell. The few trees looked foreign, the masts of scuttled ships.

'I was going to suggest waking her in a bit.' Buddy spoke without turning around, locked into his all-night long-distance gaze. Vida's head lolled heavy on Dyce's lap. He was just grateful she could sleep. Her leg must be less bothersome. 'As I said, Capitol Building's sealed up pretty tight – you only really know it's night in there by the shade of the dark. When you're in, you're in – there's no coming and going. No daily stroll around the parking lot out back. Resistance rules. But you adjust. Most of us jog every morning: ten circuits of the lower floor, hit the stairs and then ten more circuits upstairs. It's okay, but if you find yourself in there for as long as I've been, you'll start volunteering for whatever'll get you some fresh air – even driving the border in the storm of the century. I'll remember every minute I've had out here – even if it was in old Nebrasky.' Buddy smiled, but he kept his eyes on the road. 'So, if she's done sleeping, then maybe she'd like to see daylight for a bit. I know I would.'

'Sure,' replied Dyce. 'In a bit.'

Buddy leant down and tried to find a radio station. The signal had hissed gradually into static as they approached the edge of Wyoming and he'd turned the thing off: that was the way it had stayed all night.

'Lucky if I get anything this far out,' he said, twiddling the dial. 'If the wind's blowing right, it works.' Dyce watched the red bar move clean across the numbers, like a Ouija board, then Buddy brought it all the way back. Nothing. He gave up, and Dyce looked out of the window as they passed tall silos and then went over a bridge with the familiar foaming brown water rushing underneath. Would it never end, the mindless destruction? Everything he'd known had been washed away, and still it wouldn't stop.

'Capitol Building doesn't sound too bad,' said Dyce eventually. 'Being holed up is basically my life. When the wind blows we hunker down – or at least we used to. We'd be out in the open, my brother Garrett and me, and there'd be this change of pressure. I could feel it in my head. Garrett was pretty useless at knowing: he would've been dead long before if it wasn't for me. Same goes the other way round, I guess. Gotta look out for your people, right? When the wind's coming, the far-off trees start shaking, and if you're in a town, you get inside fast. But, man, if you're out in the open, you got to find a hole. Like hide-and-go-seek, except if it finds you, you don't get another turn. Some winds blow in and they blow out. But some blow for days, so you got to have all you need packed and ready in a bag: water and food and something to do. Something to do is the most important.'

He stopped talking. He wasn't sure why he was telling Buddy all of this, maybe to make up for almost stabbing him in the neck with a pair of sewing scissors. Maybe just to have someone hear it.

'You been with Vida long?'

'Not long.'

'You two gonna get married, or is it too early to tell?'

Dyce snorted a laugh and Vida stirred.

'What's funny about that?' Buddy asked.

'No one gets married down South.'

'Why not?'

'Because "Till death do us part" might be "Till next week Thursday".' Dyce smiled but Buddy's lips tightened.

'Jesus,' he said.

'Yeah. Fuck Renard, right?'

The two men sat in silence, and Dyce let Vida sleep until they could see the skyline of Des Moines.

'Getting close,' he finally said.

She sat up, taking it slow. Her leg was numb from sleep; it had taken the edge off the worst pain, but now it had stiffened and she'd have to walk like she was ninety. She wasn't sure if she could. Just try, said her stepdaddy's voice in her head. She closed her eyes again and she was back when Everett was whole and alive, tossing the old tennis ball to her over and over until she could face the baseball pitch. You gotta try, Veedles. Cain't win it if you ain't in it. In the long-ago evening light his face was seamed with kindness, and back in the pickup her heart squeezed with sorrow. It never went away.

'Let me give you the tour,' Buddy was saying. He waved a sarcastic hand like a magician.

There were no other cars and no people on foot – and there wouldn't be, either. Dyce whistled and shook his head, unsure what was worse.

'Mostly deserted, as you-all can tell. City's too big to be full, and most communities are south-side of the river.' They kept driving, and the endless empty parking lots and four-lane roads channeled the wind and the dirt northward.

The Capitol Building rose abruptly out of the ruined city. The blurry doors and windows that Vida could see were boarded up with plywood. Somehow the gold leaf on the domes was still shiny and intact, the way she imagined a Russian church or the Taj Mahal.

Or a mushroom.

The building stood proud above a coiled razor-wire fence that ranged ten-feet high and rusted. But who would want to get in anyway? The grass that had once grown in sloping ter-raced lawns had turned to rubble. Through it grew shrubs and the sapling children of the original oaks, sawn-off trunks poking through the mess in a warning to trespassers.

'You can see why it's a good headquarters,' said Buddy. 'Kind of looks like you'd be killed just for side-eyeing the thing. Des Moines folk don't come near it. Like it's cursed.' But he was puffed with pride even as he disparaged the place, and Vida understood how much it meant to him. For Buddy, the Resistance was everything.

'It's pretty, though,' she said, 'if you imagine it how it was.'

'Oh, she's a beauty for sure, even without her makeup on. Five domes. Count 'em. More than any other state building. How about that?' Now he was driving slowly right by the building.

He turned the truck into a side street so that the view of the domes was obscured. 'I'm overshooting by a few blocks and we'll walk back a little way. Hope that's okay with your leg and all.'

'We'll manage,' said Dyce. He had seen Vida's heaviness but called it sleep. She's tired, he told himself. We just got to get her inside. She'll get through it.

Buddy rolled the truck nose-first in front of a vandalized shop front and stopped beside a De Luxe, the soft top replaced with makeshift plywood and painted white. The glass from the Starbucks window still lay in diamonds on the floor. When they crossed over the wasteland, it crunched underfoot.

'Anyone want a latte?' Buddy asked.

'I already drank my own piss today,' said Dyce, looking up at the mermaid. Good old Mami Wata, taking care of her own.

18

Felix and Adams got out of the car slowly, then picked their way over shards of glass along the sidewalk toward the Capitol Building. At least there was no dog shit: you could say that for the apocalypse. Human – sure; dog – not so much.

Adams led Felix into a dead-end side alley, and then over to a dull green dumpster set on casters. He leant against the side and it rolled away to reveal a square sewer cover inscribed with PROPERTY OF THE CITY OF DES MOINES. He wedged his fingers along the edge and lifted it. Felix bent to help and they set the rusted plate beside the hole.

'Age before beauty,' said Adams. He had to hold his cheek when he smiled. 'Wait when you get to the bottom, okay?'

Felix sat himself down on the edge and groaned, his legs dangling into the black. 'Damn straight I'm waiting. Didn't get to be this old rushing in where angels fear to tread, sonny.'

He felt inside the hole for rungs and tested them for weight. They held. Then he turned his back on Adams. In seconds he had descended into the darkness like a miner down a shaft.

Adams waited until the old man's fingers were out of the way, and stepped onto the iron rungs. He leant forward and pulled the dumpster back in jerks until it was over the entrance.

'This is the home stretch,' he called down softly.

Felix expected him to pull a flashlight from his pocket or to light a match, but it looked like he'd done this trip enough times to feel that that was a waste. Adams kept low and moved fast, and Felix crept along behind him in the dimness under the city, listening to his heavy breathing and the scrape of his feet on the damp floor. No one would be flushing a toilet any time soon in the heart of Des Moines, so there was that, at least, and if there were any gators left in the sewers, they'd probably had to turn cannibal.

It wasn't long before Adams stopped and stood up straight. Felix did so too, aware of his own harsh panting. Adams seemed to check a map in his head and then made his way to another set of rungs – a different kind to the ones at the entrance. Felix saw a glowing halo of pinpricks at the top – some sort of drain, or a vent for a defunct air-conditioning system that had babied the lungs of fat-ass politicians as they sent the turning world to shit.

'You coming?'

Felix followed Adams upward, his old legs burning with each ponderous lift. When Adams reached the top, he knocked on the underside of the plate – some kind of code like you had when you shared a house with a roommate who couldn't keep his mitts off the sticky magazines under the bed.

'The others are coming,' he said. 'Takes a while.'

For a moment Felix felt his heart shrink. What if this was all some sort of set-up and he'd walked straight into a Northern trap? He swallowed, his throat thick with sudden doubt. Another minute of silence.

Then there was a scraping, and dusty second-hand sunlight poured down the hole, thick as honey, and a woman's face peered out.

Adams lifted himself up and out and then turned to give Felix a hand.

The woman was past her prime, but pretty. She stepped back as Felix emerged. Then she covered her mouth.

'Felix Callahan! Is that you?'

Felix looked at her to see whether he knew her, something he'd not done in years. But there was no spark of recognition in the slow lobes of his skull.

'You don't know me. I'm Edith, the one who spotted your phone call.'

He nodded. She nattered on, undeterred.

'We've been monitoring the phone numbers that belonged to Southerners for, what's it now, seven, eight years? Yours was the first one, you know. It's just hard to believe you're real! Oh, come here! Let me hug you!'

Felix didn't answer in time, because Edith stepped forward and squeezed him tight. It felt good to have a kindly woman's arms around him, and a younger Felix might have given plump Edith some prodding through old Mr Norma's hand-me-down trousers. But all thought of arousal evaporated when he looked over her shoulder at the room where they all stood.

'My God,' he said. He set Edith aside, none too gently.

'What's the matter?'

'Here? The same room? Really?'

Adams stepped between the old man and the woman, his hands spread in warning and surrender. 'Hey, now. What's up with you?'

'Ain't you got no shame?' Felix hissed. 'You using this room, where she died?' He pointed a scarred finger at the cubicle toilets.

One porcelain bowl was missing, the U-bend left decapitated. If they had tried, the three people in the room would have been able to peer down into the subterranean dankness of the crater the ill-starred bomb had made.

Oh, Felix knew this little room and its cracked white fixtures. How could he not? He had gone over its twin structure a dozen times with Tye McKenzie in the days of the Concession.

The ladies' room. The same one they had turned into a mausoleum for Renard's lovely lady wife.

19

The short walk to the dumpster made Vida sweat. It helped some that Dyce took care to wipe her face, but he had enough going on trying to hold her up. She knew her wounds were seeping through the bandage: the slurry of fresh blood and anti-bacterial cream kept creeping to the surface.

After that there was a descent, Dyce telling her where to place her feet on the rungs, Buddy asking questions about how come he could see so well in the dark. Oh, this? Dyce wanted to say. This is a little present I got for nearly dying in the South because of your fearless leader's fucking viruses. Well, I didn't die. I hung in there even though I shat my brains out and got Garrett killed into the bargain, because the trail of crap led the Callahans straight to us. But the bonus prize is being able to see real good in the dark. A war wound, I guess you could call it. Fair's fair, right, Buddy? Fair is fucking fair.

Vida couldn't tell whether the blackness was because they were travelling underground. Her eyes felt glued shut and she was giving herself over to the heat rising in her veins, the blood pounding in her brain until she thought she would pass clean out. She felt Dyce gripping her, keeping her on her feet. Then the temperature and the air pressure changed, and there were voices echoing like they were in a chamber. For a moment Vida felt panicky and deaf; they were in those dank, hopeless tunnels under the Mouth again, and this time Ed would never let them go. She and Dyce would join all those poor dead people who only wanted to be left in peace, but who would spend eternity choking on the mushrooms crowding their mouths.

But then her ears popped and she came back to herself. It wasn't the Mouth. It was somewhere like it – a place filled with noise and jostling bodies, a station of some kind. And there were some people she knew! That wasn't right. They belonged in the South. Why were they here? Maybe she hadn't recovered. Maybe her leg had been too bad, finally, the thing that had done her in after all this time thinking she was immune. Maybe none of it had happened – not Buddy, not the plane, not the perv with his hand in his pants. She was dead, wasn't she? She knew it because there was an angel who looked like her mother, peering anxiously into her face, her hair a springy backlit halo against the bathroom ceiling.

Vida opened her eyes properly. Ruth was still there. Oh, this felt good. This felt so good. She wanted to laugh.

'Hey, Mama. Where's Everett?'

'Oh!' Ruth put her hand over her mouth, and then recovered herself to grab Vida's hand again.

Don't hurt her, Dyce wanted to say, but he kept his mouth shut.

Ruth squeezed and squeezed the bones of her daughter's fingers. She leant in and rested her head on Vida's shoulder and sobbed.

'Get her some water.' She had to keep clearing her throat, but she wouldn't let go. Vida blinked, and Dyce faded out of her blurred circle of vision. 'She needs a proper place to lie down.'

Vida felt herself being jostled and lifted into what felt like a hammock. There were people at the corners – no, she told herself, more angels, and started to giggle. Matthew, Mark, Luke and John! Saddle the horse till I get on!

'Stop,' said the head angel. 'You're hurting her.' They thought she was crying!

Then they were carrying her in her sheet up a flight of stairs, into the vaults of heaven with its wooden paneling and gilded cornices and the mosaics of cherub-chubby wagon riders carrying wheat and grapes, all followed by flocks of cotton-ball sheep. Vida tried to rub her face, clear her mind of these hallucinations – but these were also real. Looky there! The frescoes on the walls of the Capitol Building lived in their glorious past. Look at all those families! And their *food*! Real soil-grown crops! No locusts they were catching – bright-eyed does and fat rabbits, ready for the skinning. Her stomach hitched and burnt at the thought.

There was music too, not trumpets but something earthly and kind, a guitar maybe, and a man's voice singing high and sweet. I wonder what happened to Dyce's mandolin heads, thought Vida. I hope he still has them. He's no good on the harp.

They had arrived in a room with a carpet that had a pattern of swirling autumn leaves. Vida wanted to lie down there with Dyce and cover herself in a dusty, crackling blanket of them on a cool forest floor; take off her stiff and sweaty clothes and give herself over to the comfort of his hands on her naked skin.

Instead the stretcher-bearers lifted her onto a bed and Ruth folded the sheet in around one corner of the mattress; the wounded leg they left open to the air. Ruth looked at it a long time. Then she made up her mind.

'Give her some space,' she said. 'You too, Dyce, please.'

Vida wanted to say: No. Let him stay. He's the one I want here with me. But there was no strength in her.

Dyce obliged, setting down the bottle of water. He took Vida's hand and squeezed it tight, then left.

Now Ruth was stroking her damp forehead. 'Close your eyes, baby girl,' she said, but Vida didn't want to.

'Are you real?'

'I hope so. Have a good look and tell me what you see. If this doesn't persuade you, nothing will.'

Vida opened her scratchy eyes all the way. Ruth was holding out a raggedy cloth-covered book to her, and Vida wrinkled her nose. The pages smelt of damp and fire and desperation.

'That damn recipe book! It's like your blankie, Mama. You never go anywhere without it.'

Ruth rested the medicine journal on the pillow beside Vida's head, as if its cures and collective history would seep into her head while she slept. And despite herself, Vida felt the death-less song of them all coming back to her in a great rush, as if the book was magic. Her whole childhood was in there, and her mama's, and all the women in her family back in South Africa, a hundred years of them at least, from the time they started to write down the things they knew. She wasn't alone.

And when she thought about it now, the burning in her leg was taking up a little less of her brain. She felt the sweat cold on her chest, and grew properly sober.

'Didn't think I'd see this book again, Mama. Or you.'

'We keep popping up when you need us. That's no accident, baby. But first things first. I need to talk hard to you now, and you need to listen. So brace yourself.'

Vida nodded. It felt strange to be lying on a clean pillow.

'You know it's bad, don't you, Vida? We got to make a

decision soon, one way or the other. We got to find a way to save that leg of yours. I don't want to scare you, you know that. I've seen some pretty terrible things in my time – and some of them I haven't told you yet – but cutting off my own daughter's leg is about the worst of them.'

'You think I don't know that, Mama? Besides, nobody's asking you to do it.' She hated the way just seeing her mother made her feel five years old. The lines of suffering written on her face!

'I'll do it if I got to.'

'That's not an option right now, Mama.'

'You taken a good look at it lately?'

Vida felt the tears begin to trickle sideways onto the pillow.

Ruth rubbed her daughter's hand. 'I meant it. I'm really not trying to scare you, honey. Don't cry. Not on the book.' She smiled weakly. 'We'll watch it for a day or so and see how bad it gets. That make sense?'

Vida nodded. She wanted to curl herself up into a tiny ball and creep back inside the warm circle of her mother, forget everything and start again, before everything had gone wrong and she had got stuck in the end of the world.

Instead Ruth sat back and started to peel the book's pages apart, trying not to inflict more damage than there already was. Passage in a backpack had rubbed some of the writing away, and the North Platte water had smudged the ink in places into Rorschach blots: those poultices and tinctures and tips were gone forever. Wrapping it in plastic had kept the worst of the wet out, but it hadn't worked all the way. Ruth's lips were pressed tightly together as she turned the pages.

Vida let her hand fall back on the sheet and listened to her mother's harsh breathing. She could practically hear the cogs whirring in Ruth's fierce brain.

'What are you looking for?'

'I remember stashing something here in the way-back. Kind of a cure-all for worst-case.'

Three quarters of the way through the book, Ruth stopped at a tiny home-made envelope pinned to a page. She pried it off carefully and opened it, like a letter from a dead lover.

'What I thought.' She shook the envelope gently at Vida, and there was a small, hopeful rustling. 'Mullein seeds. Supposed to use the flowers, but I reckon these will be as close as we'll get.'

Ruth took the bottle that Dyce had left, unscrewed its lid and dropped the rough brown seeds into the dregs of the water. Then she stood and searched the room for a pestle that would fit the mouth of the bottle. She measured the rubber-capped leg of the chair.

'No one is going to care about the chairs.'

The leg broke off easily. The rest of the furniture in the Capitol Building would give up the ghost over the next few years, and there would be nothing to replace it.

Ruth set herself to crushing the seeds. When she was done she presented the bottle to Vida.

'Here, now. Sit up and drink this, and try to get it all down. Could be the difference between one leg and two.'

'Thought you weren't trying to scare me.'

Vida sat up shakily and drank the medicine, then flopped back down, exhausted.

'You just rest now. We'll be right here. You know it.' Ruth ran her hand down Vida's side, then stood and covered her with a sheet. She took the medicine journal and propped it near a boarded-up window, where she hoped the faint breeze might dry it altogether. Then she turned and folded her arms, waiting for Vida to fall asleep so she could get a better look at her while she was unawares. There was another reason Ruth was dreading having to amputate her daughter's leg – and not only because Vida was in this terrible weakened state.

There. She was under.

Ruth leant closer to the girl on the bed and inspected her chest. Vida had always had a little extra flesh on her, but never like this. She should look thinner, if anything, considering what she'd been through. If she'd been swept through the gap in the Wall on the Platte the same way the other survivors had, then she ought to show more damage.

Ruth reached out and felt the weight of Vida's breast in her hand, the way she had for a hundred girls who had come to her for help in more ordinary times.

There it was: the dense, swelling tissue that could only mean one thing. Vida murmured, 'Dyce,' and moved in her sleep, and Ruth withdrew her hand. She sighed.

Heavy times were coming for her daughter.

She moved her hands gently over the sleeping girl's abdomen and palpated her. Yup. There it was. Not far along, but un-mistakable. Did Dyce know? Hell, did Vida herself even have a clue?

Dyce was still leaning back against the wall in the corridor outside, his hands dangling in between his knees. He stood up fast as Ruth emerged. They were never going to like each other. She was a bitch, thought Dyce. A hard woman. And he knew she probably thought he was a lightweight, a boy who didn't deserve her daughter, and who couldn't protect her. Maybe she was right.

'Is she going to be okay?'

'I think so,' said Ruth. 'But I'm not sure you are.'

'What do you mean?'

'Welcome to the family, Daddy.'

Dyce stared at her, confused.

She stated it as plainly as she could. 'Vida's pregnant.'

20

Vida slept on and her baby slept inside her. Above their heads, word spread through the Capitol Building of the meeting in the Senate Chamber. Dyce wandered aimlessly around the halls and passages, staring ahead into a blurry middle ground, fighting the time-traveling feeling, turning the mandolin machine heads over together in his pockets like a talisman. Without his night sight he'd have taken a while to figure out his way around in the gloom of the building, but the disorientation was more than that.

He was going to be a father!

It wasn't real. Think about something else, he told himself. You got time.

He wasn't the only one who was lost and weary. After the initial flurry of greetings, most of the Southerners had just sat, awed, staring at the portraits of stern Northern presidents in their rows on the wall. There was Renard, painted oversized, smack in the center, like an African dictator on a throne. All of the canvases except his had been torn up in their previous life, but someone had tried to tape them back together, the burnt scraps of one fixed in place by a pane of glass. They'd obviously not been welcome decoration during Renard's rule here: too much competition. Dyce wondered why they'd left Renard's portrait up at all. Maybe they used it for darts practice.

He set out, intent on making his way to the chamber, which was already humming with curiosity. Some kind of meeting was going to happen, and people were settling themselves on balconies and in little camps as they waited to know their future. It was easy to tell who was Northern and who was new. The guests kept craning their necks at the vault of the dome, with its four dusty chandeliers at the corners of the supports. It wasn't clear to any of them whether surviving as long as they had was a good or bad omen, but this was a kind of heaven, at least, and Dyce could almost hear their prayers of gratitude rising in the windless, opulent darkness.

The stale air was layered with more smoke, both ancient and newly risen, as if those prayers had thickened into ectoplasm. On every level surrounding the atrium there were small groups of Resistance members collected around empty oil drums, red hot with coals, adding their blue-gray smoke to the miasma. Here and there, while they waited, some women were holding damp washing close to the fires. There was food roasting too. The saliva ran under Dyce's tongue as he caught a whiff of the blistering meat – roadkill or bushmeat, as far as he could tell. It had been caught and skewered on wire. Someone with presence of mind had taken a spade to one of the walls and sliced air vents into the plaster; one or two people had positioned themselves and tried to read by the light. Now that was faith – that books still meant something. Dyce wasn't sure how they managed to see the words on the page.

But there was that same music in the air, soft at first, and then, as he gravitated toward it, the notes stinging and lingering as they were plucked. Mostly home-made instruments, Dyce saw, one square-cut from a Spam tin that his bad brother Garrett would have called a hamdolin.

But the voices hadn't changed. Those were the way Dyce still remembered them, from lullabies and campfire rounds. A lot of people still knew the words of the hymns and the country songs, the Southern songs, mournful and triumphant. They ran under the earth if they had to, but they always emerged, their gold thread sewn into the fabric of humanity.

'You play?' It was an old white guy in a leather waistcoat. He held out his ukulele.

'Not really,' said Dyce. 'Always wanted to learn, though.'

'You got an instrument?'

'Bits of one.' Dyce decided to trust him. He pulled the lumps of brass from his pocket and showed them to the man by the light of the brazier. The old guy took a couple and felt their weight in his palm.

'I can put these onto something for you, if you like.'

'Well, I would like,' said Dyce, 'but you ought to know I got nothing to trade you.'

'You're one of the Southerners, right? You're too new here to know how it works. But it's your lucky day, kid.' He spread his arms, and the leather waistcoat gaped. 'This place doesn't work on trade. It works on how-about-we-try-to-be-decent-human-beings. Things are as they are, so what if I just fix something for you and we can parley later about who owes what?'

The man took the rest of the machine heads out of Dyce's open hand and stuffed them in his own pocket. 'Give me a couple of days,' he said, and then he turned back to the fire and picked up a few notes that were already in the air.

Dyce wasn't sure whether he'd just been robbed, plain as day. He stayed and listened a bit longer, a woman's voice, low and sweet, singing that she'd shot poor Delia. It was the chorus that did it. Dyce decided to let the old man play his hand. Best case, he'd have some strings to learn on; worst case, he'd have to go looking for his machine heads and maybe blacken an eye for the inconvenience.

He walked on, trying not to think about the baby. He couldn't figure these Northerners out. It was clear even in his bemusement that there were stark divisions among the Resistance. Here there were men who looked as though they'd been released from prison, smoked with suffering; workers, slimmer and kinder-faced, who cooked or stoked fires or ran necessary errands that did not fall by the wayside even when the cities went down.

But there were also lots of people who did nothing at all except watch, wide-eyed. Lazy? wondered Dyce. Or just off-duty, like the shrewd man with the ukulele? He couldn't imagine how they organized the labor in the Capitol Building. Some were surely scouts and hunters and night-shift guards.

Or plumbers. Dyce didn't have the presence to guess or to ask, though it was clear that the building needed attention: the smell he caught passing the men's bathroom was worse than any death he'd attended. There was a sign on the door that said KEEP CLOSED AT ALL TIMES. As he had read it, a woman dashed out in front of him, holding a hand over her mouth and nose, and coughing so hard he thought she would retch. Maybe they kept the fires burning on purpose: the wood was a kind of incense, like the stuff that Ruth liked to burn – what was it? Maybe sage, except that she called it by its older name: imphepho, the dream herb. Whatever it was, it made him cough, just like this smoke now.

He screwed his eyes up against the dizzying smoke, and found himself following the stream of people headed for the Senate Chamber, pushing him along through the corridors with their

urgency – and under that a nerviness, a fear. Maybe living in
secret did that to a person.

By the time he reached the Senate Chamber, it was too full
to get a seat, so he sat flat with his back against the wall. How
had anyone survived here as long as they had? Men, women,
little kids, even.

Little kids. Christ! He was about to have one of his own.
Dyce thought of Bethie Callahan, how Garrett must have seen
her struggling in the dust under the hard hands of her kins-
women, clutching at the ivory swan pendant for the luck that
didn't come. It bothered him that the pendant was gone too.
His own creation alongside his brother's, the only carving he
had made that Garrett had ever liked. Dyce had felt the same
way about the baby in Bethie's belly – his niece or nephew.

And now there was another little Jackson due on this
fucked-up planet.

His baby.

Every woman old enough was pregnant – or maybe you
just saw whatever you were thinking about most. Vida was
in good company. Some waddled, others moved more easily.
For a moment Dyce's heart skipped back to the Mouth, and
Ester's harem of heartsick girls who had lost their babies. The
colostrum-makers.

Then a door opened, and with it came the sound of crying,
only one or two, but in that small space a cacophony of little
voices. Dyce looked in and saw babies on hips or laid down on
grimy mattresses. Too many for a holed-up population, but at
least they were here – alive and cared for.

He wiped his face. He realized that Ruth was sitting beside
him and looking at him with narrowed eyes, and he tried to pay
attention to the people who were gathering around him to take

stock of where they stood. He hadn't had a moment until now to make an inventory of who else known to him had made it across the Wall. Clear across Nebraska to Des Moines! That had to mean something. He looked around, dazed, and then was thrown sideways by a thin man who had hurled away his crutches and launched himself at him, throwing fierce arms around his neck.

'Sam!'

'My partner in crime!'

The man who had once saved his life at Horse Head camp grinned and grinned, and Dyce hugged him again. They thumped each other on the back, talking over one another as the other remnants of the Resistance began to assemble. Some of them were removing mattresses from the floor of the chamber: it had clearly been the warmest place to sleep. Strength in numbers, thought Dyce. More residents appeared, arranging themselves on the built-in desks and counters, and crowding the upstairs balconies like a Roman arena. There was a susurration like wheat as they talked behind their hands, and Dyce realized again that there was no wind to fear inside the Capitol Building.

Real-life Southerners! He felt the hot eyes on him.

He didn't care. They were here, weren't they? Vida and Ruth and Sam.

And the baby.

'How's Vida?' asked Sam. The hilarity was fading from his face.

'She got cut up pretty bad on the razor wire across the river. Infected.' Dyce shrugged and his mouth pulled down. Sam knew better than to say the worst.

'She's brave, man. She'll pull through.' He looked around, the real horror of what would happen if her leg didn't heal lying thick between them.

She could die, thought Dyce. It could kill her, either way: the baby or the hurt.

They sat down with Ruth and scanned the gathering audience for other Southerners. They were rewarded too, as familiar faces from Horse Head camp appeared, frightened, elated as they realized that Dyce had made it through. Here and there people were waving. Some began threading their way over the sloped carpet with its leafed pattern toward their fellows.

'Hey.' Sam nudged him. 'There's that old dude. The Weatherman. What's his name? Felix. Check him out. Did you know he was here too?'

Dyce shook his head.

Felix had come in alone. Now he looked them over and lifted his shaggy eyebrows in disbelief. Then he nodded slowly – I see you, motherfucker, said that nod – and sat down behind them. The smile on Dyce's face felt tight.

'He's a cockroach, man. There's something not right about that guy.'

It was the man in the leather jacket who got up on the senate bench first, the man who had Dyce's precious machine heads in his pocket. He held his makeshift ukulele in his hand and the crowd hushed at the sight of him. Dyce didn't recognize the song he sang, but it seemed like an old favorite here. The chorus rose with a hundred voices.

> *The fox came down from the hills one night.*
> *What a terrible smell and a terrible sight!*
> *And he found a length of the old chicken wire*
> *And he tied one end to a tractor tire.*
> *He rolled it out down the middle of the farm.*
> *Leave him to it, son, what's the harm?*

But now the rooster doesn't have his hen,
And the pig's locked out of his fa-vo-rite pen.
The cow's one side, the bull the other,
And six new lambs can't find their mother!

The applause was deafening – far more than the song itself
warranted. The ukulele man winked right at Dyce and got down.

Then Adams clambered onto the bench. He shushed the
expectant crowd, his hands raised like a Southern preacher,
inviting the spirit of God to come on down and baptize his
flock. The talking petered out and the Northerners focused on
Adams, unsurprised by his grizzled face with its sticking plaster,
high with expectation.

'You might have noticed something a little different here
today,' he began. His delivery reminded Dyce of Ed, the fat
slave-driver of the Mouth. There was something similar in the
meter of the two men's speech, a lilting that seemed to point
every sentence toward a grand revelation. 'We finally found us
some motherfucking Southerners!'

The hall thundered with applause. Ruth pulled a face at
Dyce: they were worried that the noise would wake Vida even
in her drugged state.

The remnants of Horse Head were smiling, uncertain but
pleased with their reception. It was friendly fire.

'We got to let our new guests have some rest pretty soon.
They've all been through more than you and I can imagine. But
I figured there ought to be some kind of formal introduction. So
from me and the rest of us here in Des Moines: welcome! This
is your home now.'

The audience clapped wildly, flushed with excitement and
the prospect of change.

A voice from the back, near Felix: 'Go on! Tell us about the South!'

'No, no.' Adams was holding up a placatory hand. 'We got lots of time for that later. I'm sure these folks need to clean up and then get some rest.'

There was a roar from the spectators, and Adams saw that his trophies wouldn't get away so lightly.

'Quiet down, please, and let's show some respect for our guests, who've traveled so far to be here.' He waited. There was shuffling and mumbling, but the Northerners let him speak.

'Now, I can tell you that I did have the good fortune to speak with one of the Southerners, and he was able to confirm some of what we've suspected about what goes on behind the Wall.'

Someone else shouted, 'Fuck Renard!' Other voices yelled, 'Yeah!'

'Well, it's worse down South than we'd thought. The whole place is a wasteland, plagued by viruses on the air. There's no one that side to send viruses our way – it's Renard himself who's poisoning the air. Some of us have suspected that for a long time, I know, but these folks bring confirmation. If their reports are true, then this handful of people here might be all the Southerners left in the whole wide world.'

Adams let his words sink in, gauging the mood.

'Of course, we're hoping – we're all hoping – that this group is all we need for our own work. Together we will bring down Renard! And the Wall! And end the stranglehold he has on us with his everlasting an-tee-dotes!' He could barely be heard over the cheering as he finished off, but he gave it a try. He pumped the air with his fist.

'America will be one free, diverse nation once again!'

The audience kept up the giddy applause, but Adams had

to hold his hand over the sticking plaster on his cheek. The speech had made him sweat. He paused to tamp down the covering.

'We're gonna let our new friends rest now, so please let them go to their rooms. Don't bug them with questions – like I been doing.' The crowd offered another, weaker laugh. 'And tomorrow we will set our plan in action. So all of you: get some sleep. Tomorrow is a big day for us all. Tomorrow is the day Renard will remember as the beginning of the end.'

There was something contagious about Adams's certainty, and when Dyce looked around at the people from Horse Head, they all had confused smiles on their faces. For most of them, up until now, the only certainty had been death.

He turned to check on how Felix was receiving the news that he was the instrument of Renard's defeat, but he was already leaving the chamber through the gigantic carved wooden doors. He was shaking his head. Maybe that one attempt on Renard's life all those years ago had been enough.

The rest of the Southerners stood too and filed out between the black leather chairs and the counters.

In the passageway outside, a woman was waiting for them, her wild gray hair tied ferociously back in a bun, her pregnant stomach bulging against the worn fabric of her dress. Surely she was too old!

She caught at Dyce's arm as he tried to pass the alcove where she stood.

'Lock your doors tonight,' she said in a stage whisper, and put a finger to her lips.

'Excuse me?' asked Dyce.

'At night. Lock your doors.'

'Why? What would want to get in here?'

'It's not about what can get in, silly,' said the woman. Message delivered, she set her wrinkled hands over her stomach and went scurrying away down into the darkness of the stairwell. Dyce only barely caught the rest of her warning. 'It's about what's already inside.'

21

In the late afternoon a dull siren sounded in the Capitol Building, and all the able-bodied men in the place seemed to know what to do. They came flying down the staircases and running breathless along the corridors. There was something frightening about how quiet they were. In a real emergency, you didn't scream.

Felix stood back against the wood paneling to let them pass. A few men had guns in their hands, and others had chosen baseball bats or iron pipes. The years in his shack had taught Felix exactly what was his business and what wasn't – and he'd thought until pretty recently that he had had the distinction clear in his head.

The black-and-white had shifted some now that the shack was gone and the South with it, but Felix found that the divide was still useful. A younger version of himself would at least have gone and taken a look. But a younger version of himself was the one who'd nearly met his maker, courtesy of Tye Callahan.

'Best way to get your head blown off is to stick your neck out,' Felix said to himself. Still, he was smarter than trying to ignore the world around him. That was the other way of getting yourself killed – faster, usually – and so when an elderly fighter passed, Felix asked what the fuss was all about. The old guy was panting, but his eyes were bright with disaster.

'One of ours, ole Otis, captured a border patrolman. Otis had to bring him in 'cause it was pretty clear he knew what he was looking for. We always knew it was just a matter of time before Renard figured out 'xactly what was in the Capitol. But the fucker escaped right before Otis could bring him up through the sewer. Kicked ole Otis right in the sniffer with his boot heel. Hey! Speak of the devil!'

Two men in white carried a stretcher through the groups of people, pushing against the tide. On the stretcher lay a dark-skinned man who was lights-out, knocked clean unconscious so that the blood was still pooling in his dark moustache and running in ribbons around his neck.

The old man waved an arm as he went past. 'Another fucking thing to do. Now we got to hunt that patrolman down before he has a chance to blab about what he's seen – otherwise we got to move headquarters. Don't need to tell you what a giant fuck-up that would be. Years of planning, down the toilet. But we'll get him. Not a lot of hidey-holes in Des Moines that we don't know about.'

Felix nodded. The man shrugged and limped away after the others, who were moving a lot faster. Felix thought of that old story about the piper and the rats – and then the piper and the kids.

It was still strange to talk to a man as old as himself. They didn't make old bones, down South, and Felix was all too aware that he was on borrowed time. How could he avoid thinking about it? With every friend that passed away over Felix's long life, and every stranger young enough to be his kid or grand-kid kicking the bucket, he felt the weight heavier around his scraggy shoulders. His time was coming: the Weatherman had already dodged too many bullets. Tye and Stringbeard had both missed him, but not by a whole lot. It had to mean something, didn't it? That some were saved, and some went to the devil?

Felix stayed back, watching the men as they dashed for the sewer system below the women's bathroom, the intent written plain and ugly as hate on their faces. Purpose. Fate. Whatever you wanted to call that motherfucker. You could make your maps and measure your weather and drink yourself blind every birthday, but it never went away. Felix discerned no divinity in it. No. This was good old-fashioned destiny: it came for you and you stood against the machine or you let it go over you. He was facing the engine that Renard had set in motion, and neither of them could stop until it had done what it was meant to do.

The stampede was over. When the hall was empty again and the echoes had settled, Felix decided that it was a good time to give himself the grand tour, undisturbed. He remembered the place as it was when he'd first visited, but if things had changed even half as much as he himself had, he needed to start from scratch.

In the foyer he passed his fingers over the numbers of the brass-plate map of the building. Had they taken the audio tour back in the day? Felix couldn't remember. He had also forgotten about the battle-flag collection in the first-floor atrium and he perused them now, comforted and dismayed by the arrogance of old-world prosperity. The greatest nation on earth. But the ruin was in the small things: the display case had been pulled away from the wall and the empty nylon plugs protruded like bullets.

The rooms were endless, and unoccupied. Human beings grouped together when they were afraid. Old offices were now storerooms for supplies, or dormitories where people slept in mild discomfort. Felix tried to tally against the map the rooms he'd seen and the ones he was yet to explore.

And then he was in familiar territory – the kitchen in the old canteen, and the library, with only a skeletal score of books. Burnt for warmth, in alphabetical fucking order, and that was the way of the world.

There was a war room too, the old Secretary of State's office, though he couldn't remember that from the concession talks. He padded along the carpet, peering into darkened rooms until he found it.

It was a coffin-shaped space halved by a desk, a whiteboard on one wall and a chalk board on the other: the statistics of battle. On the hand-drawn attack plans the lines of access were inked in ancient red, like cuts. Was this real? Were these still Renard's old scratchings?

'Well, a man's gotta start somewhere,' he said, and kept looking.

On the middle desk were maps, and he could tell from here that each was at different scale. These ones were new – the game plan of the Resistance, it looked like. The top one had a red-domed structure stuck onto it, blocking out the entire city of Chicago.

He paged slowly through them. Each layer revealed what came next; the size of the red dome shrank until it was just a single building on the outskirts of the city.

Was that it? Renard's virus factory? It looked pretty ordinary. Was that possible?

Felix thought it was. It was the Windy City, after all. Where else would that fucker build it? He shivered. The room was cold and airless, and the reindeer jumper was thinner than it looked.

But one building? It was crazy to put all your poisoned little eggs in one basket, wasn't it? Crazy *and* stupid. Warcraft 101. He kept staring, trying to work out the logic.

And here it was. On the last map, around the building in a neat circle, the zone colored blue.

No-man's-land.

No living man, anyway. Not anymore. Not after Renard had set up shop in plain view.

Fuck Renard.

But also fuck everyone else who had stood by and let it happen. How did something like this go unnoticed?

'The viruses are coming from the South, my friends and neighbors,' mocked Felix in a falsetto. 'Oh, and don't mind this fucking virus factory I've got going in Chicago.' He lapsed back into his growl. 'What is this? Dachau?'

Silence was consent. He wiped his eyes. 'It's *consent*, you assholes.' He thought of all the ruined and desolate cities, the waste and rot, the broken bonds between families and friends. Who among them deserved to live on the earth as it was now?

None of them, that was who, and he was including himself.

He scrubbed at his eyes. Evening was falling but there was more to see, and by God, he was in the mood to see it.

He tried to remember that when he arrived at the two rooms behind the terraced House of Representatives, the darkest part of the building. Now that he was here, he was kind of sorry that he'd forged ahead, because the rooms were being used for something bad: he knew it. It smelt like a prisoner-of-war camp. Each door had an extra gate covering it, welded together from scrap rebar, and he bet it was Adams's doing. That fucker had nothing to lose, him and his face that was caving in.

'Never trust a Northerner, right?' Felix whispered. 'And now we're backstage. That's where I am, isn't that so, you lying fuck?'

He got no answer from the filing cabinets and the low-slung, sick fluorescent tubes; the faint, dark smell of the sewer below was no comfort. His gaze traveled up.

My God. Shackles, bolted into the walls.

Fucking shackles! Like the ones you saw in abolition muse-ums! They were solid – so rusted that some links in the chains had fused.

The small noise alerted him and Felix reversed as fast as he could, but already a woman had appeared at the entrance to the chamber, carrying some washing in a woven-grass basket like a peasant in one of them Dutch paintings. Clearly the drill was over.

'I'm looking for the toilet,' croaked Felix.

'Oh, no-no-no-no-no,' she said, like Miss Brown who had marched him to the headmaster when he was in kindergarten a hundred years ago.

She set her basket down and took Felix by the arm, holding his meatless elbow too hard through the wool, then shoved him out along the passage. She pointed forcefully to the ground-floor toilets. Felix tipped an imaginary hat and followed the directions, putting on his best old-man's walk and looking up aimlessly at the ceiling as though he'd already forgotten where he was.

22

Kurt stopped to check the trunk of the car just outside Saratoga, hoping for a change of clothes. Norma's cheap old-lady perfume was making him gag and he couldn't bear it. He felt like it was getting stronger too.

No clothes. Instead, he found four sixty-gallon jerry cans of gas – two full, one halfway and the other empty, or as good as. He wanted to whoop. He'd never been in possession of the stuff before in his life. He dipped a finger in the gas and rubbed it on Norma's collar. It smelt like the future and the best parts of the past – sweet and full of power.

'The gods are smiling on us, Linus.' He got back in the car and took off east, the weather worsening as he went. He found the headlights and flicked them on. It was like magic, he thought. There were some things that men could be proud of, and cars was one of them.

He camped the night somewhere in old Nebraska. He hadn't heard the stories of wild men and the undead come alive in the open lands once night fell. They were Native American spirits, ancestors or gods, riding their ghost horses over the rise – not pale in the moonlight but dark and purposed, come to settle an eternal score.

He had heard nothing of the monsters, neither, the beasts spawned by the factory-farmed animals turned loose, six-legged chickens, cows grown square from their tight stalls, slack-jawed pigs that bayed but couldn't bite.

And there were the ghosts of the people too, of course: the unlucky ones caught out in the open and consumed, sprayed in bloody particles across the countryside they had loved, searching for their bodies.

Kurt saw none of it, or perhaps whatever lurked in the dark knew better than to cross the boy with the blouse stained with the blood of two good women, four dead at his hands in less than twenty-four hours. Now he approached the day-old pronghorn, the multi-tool open and ready.

'Got to know what you're looking for, Linus.' The cat was motionless in the car, curled up against the rear window so that he was as far away as he could get.

Kurt grunted and dug into the hide of the pronghorn, scoring the skin with the side of the flat-head screwdriver until it gave way and the old blood leaked, sluggish. When he'd ripped an opening big enough, he tore it further and then slid his naked arm inside, searching for the slippery liver. 'Got to get your hands dirty, kitty-cat. But don't cut into the poopstring. Then you gotta throw the whole thing away.'

He wrenched the liver out. Outside the cavity the organ flopped and glistened its deep purple. Kurt sawed at the nerves and veins that still connected it to the carcass. Linus lifted his head, sniffed, and then looked away.

'Don't be like that. I've not done any more nor any less than what's right. In fact . . .' he raised his voice, peering into the dim yellow interior of the Toyota and pointing the bloody multi-tool at Linus, 'I got a long way still to go before things are square. Eye for an eye, doesn't the Bible say? Well, there's a lot of eyes at stake here, cat. There's half a continent wiped out

– humans, animals, the works. Animals, my furry friend. Your people too. That's got to be worth something in St Peter's big book.'

He straightened up and slapped the wet liver on the roof. Then he set himself to collecting firewood and finding the dry grass among the wet. He stacked his finds neatly next to the body of the car, the way his daddy had taught him, along with a length of fencing wire that didn't look too rusted. Kurt had learnt all the ways of starting a fire; back South, there hadn't exactly been standard-issue cigarette lighters.

He opened the car door, anticipating the leap that Linus always made for his freedom, and caught the cat. He shoved him firmly back into the vehicle, shut the door, and slid over to the central console. He pushed the plunger of the lighter in, waiting for the pop. It smelt of burning plastic. Then: the click. He pulled it out and turned it over. Like an evil eye – a floating pupil in an iris filamented with rage.

'Looks a bit like you right now,' he told the cat where he sulked on his perch at the back. 'Tough luck, buddy.'

He backed out of the car again and turned his attention to the fire. The grass smoked against the lighter's coil, wet through from the storm and the relentless drizzle, but a minute later a small flame jumped to life. Kurt stuffed the driest of the grass into the wood pile and heard it sizzle.

He pushed the wire through the liver, the tissue tearing reluctantly. Then he bent it so that it could stand over the coals.

'Yes, sir. Plenty for everyone,' he said. 'Everyone who plays nice. You need to change your attitude, Mister Sulky Face.'

As the liver cooked, the juices dribbled out, and Kurt's taste buds tingled. He sliced the meat away, carving it down bit by bit. He took a long sliver and dropped it through the crack in the window he'd left open so Linus got some air. The cat crouched, waiting for Kurt to sit back down at the fire before he leapt down and deigned to eat it.

'Wasn't that good? Yeah. You're mad, but you're not stupid. You're gonna get real grateful as we go.'

When the meat was finished and the fire had burnt down, Kurt got back into the car, where he curled up on the back seat. Linus shrank into a tighter crouch. That cat had a bladder made of iron.

They slept.

23

It wouldn't stop. He knew he was safe for the moment, but every time Dyce closed his eyes, he saw the mushroom mines: their earthy catacombed walls housing the army of the innocent dead. All those children. Some babies, even, and – good God Almighty – here he was, he himself, about to be a father! The idea was terrible and thrilling. He could feel the spores blooming beneath his fingernails and rupturing the skin, cool and efficient as razor blades. Life found a way, even where it wasn't wanted. And did he want this baby? Could he be responsible for the life of a whole other human? He shuddered. An actual baby. Fuck. How was it possible?

He gave up trying to sleep, and sat up instead. He had chosen to sleep up here with Ruth, so they could take turns to keep an eye on Vida. As far as he could make out, the other Southerners had gathered downstairs in one place, like old-timers circling the wagons against whatever was hunting them when the sun went down. Only Felix had chosen to sleep apart from the rest of the survivors. He'd taken off with blankets and sheets and a pillow to find a hidey-hole of his own. Typical. He didn't care about anything but himself.

Dyce listened, imagining the sleeping bodies. Mostly restful. Except for Vida.

Her sleep was an effort and it showed on her face, her forehead lined with some interior struggle and flight, the sweat leaking through her skin, slick as oil. She was fighting for two now, and Ruth had been pretty clear about the risk: the fever couldn't go on too long without endangering the baby. Lips compressed, she had given Vida a time limit. If the fever hadn't broken by 10 p.m., they'd have to move on to the next step. When Dyce had asked whether amputation was really and truly the next step, Ruth had squeezed his arm so hard it hurt, and hissed, 'We're not baking cakes here, so don't be a baby.'

Then, just after everyone else had settled themselves downstairs on the army cots for the night, Dyce had caught her in the main kitchen. She was pawing through the drawers, head down, lips pressed tightly together.

Dyce felt his heart drop. 'You should be sleeping,' he told her.

'So should you,' Ruth replied. She ignored him and kept going.

'What are you looking for?'

'Cake mix.'

Dyce got the message.

But as it turned out, ten o'clock came and went. Ruth checked her daughter's forehead, then checked her again.

'The morning,' she said. 'If it's not over by morning.' She couldn't bring herself to say what it was they would have to do.

What had she found in the kitchen? He imagined her reaching over the side of her cot in the middle of the night while everyone else snored and dreamt of their old lives. Out of the bag she slid a meat cleaver and held it up, her small bicep flexing as she turned it over in her hands. She tested her index finger against the sharp edge and hissed in breath as it sliced into the thin, nerved pad. She sucked the cut finger and then hefted the cleaver a couple of times to get a sense of the weight of the thing in motion. Like a guillotine, thought Dyce.

Now he got up and walked to the boarded window, where Ears sat like a totem on the sill, watching the room with his seed-eyes. Dyce peeked out between the slats. It was deep night and there was no distant lifting of the dark along the horizon and no singing birds. There was still time for Vida. The small hairs of his ears shuddered, and in the quiet he was aware of footsteps in the hallway, cushioned as they were by the carpet like a funeral parlor.

He first thought of Felix, searching rooms for a place to throw his blanket down. But the steps were too swift. Plus there was something sinister in the deliberate quiet, the heel-toe padding. As though whoever it was was hoping to creep right into the room unnoticed, to be on top of them before they opened their eyes.

'Just the night watch,' Dyce whispered to himself, though he didn't believe it.

He moved to the wall and followed the progress of the feet. They slowed, then stopped at the door. There was a long silence, minutes passed. All the while Dyce watched the brass door handle, unable to stir in case there was an eye on the other side of the keyhole waiting for movement.

After ten minutes he had to wonder whether the person had moved on without his noticing. A minute more and he began to doubt whether he'd heard the steps at all. He'd had a lot to chew over these past few days; he was twitchy, and he had a fucking right to be. He was about to step back from the door and lie down again when the handle dipped. He stiffened against the icy pulse of adrenaline in his muscles.

There it came: the click of the deadbolt catching on the strike plate. Thank God he'd locked it. The handle lifted again in defeat and the footsteps retreated. It's about what's already inside, the woman with the wild hair had told him after the meeting. Be afraid of what's already inside.

Dyce was sure he wouldn't sleep after that, but it was already weak morning when the knocking woke him and Adams called through the door.

'Southern folk! Let's get this day started. Half an hour. Downstairs foyer.'

Dyce stood and went across to Ruth. She was leaning over Vida, trying to get her to drink from an oversized coffee mug, which said I HEART IOWA. Vida was gray. Dyce had known that human skin went ashy under stress, but this was a new and alien spectrum. She raised her colorless head and drank a few sips, then lay back down, almost without waking. Her eyes were bulbous under their lids, like a baby bird's. When Dyce looked at Ruth, she shook her head.

'Why don't you let me have a turn?' he said softly.

'No. I owe her. She did it for me. Besides,' and she actually smiled, 'I don't trust anyone else to do it right.' Her own eyes were puffy with exhaustion, the skunk streak in her hair bristling. 'This is the kind of thing that needs to be done right or not at all. You wouldn't want to screw it up and not be able to forgive yourself, would you?' Her tone sharpened. 'It's going to be a hard day for everyone, anyway. I hope you're ready. Midday, got it? That's the absolute longest we can wait. We're going to need all the light we can get.'

They let Vida sleep on, locking her safely in her room, while the rest of the yawning Southerners gathered downstairs.

It was good to be back with the others, with Pete and Sam;

even Ruth seemed happy to be there. Dyce felt his stomach untwist a little. He didn't know the names of most others, but he recognized their faces from that miracle day in the ghost colony – the day his blindness lifted like a veil. He'd never forget the hope with which they'd stared at him. Now a woman hugged him and asked after Vida.

'She's been better,' Dyce told her.

Adams, with a fresh dressing on his cheek, met them in the foyer where the old brass-plate map of the building was still displayed. It had been part of a pre-War audio tour or something, Dyce guessed, the kind with numbers that had once matched up to recordings of trivia about the building, the sort of thing made by people who'd loved it for what it was as well as what it stood for.

No one would be going on that tour now, though. Dyce imagined the new version playing through a set of grimy headphones.

This, ladies and gentlemen, is where we shit in a hole. And this is where we sleep in our flea-ridden piles. Over there is a woman hanging streaky diapers, and here's a man with a home-made guitar! Isn't that something?

Adams led the group along a passage, past the bathrooms to a windowless hall that must once have been used for staff meetings – the kind of place where the HR woman would've cut a communal birthday cake. Now the room was partitioned with untidy plastic sheeting, some panels transparent, some speckled with paint.

In each pocket made by the partitions there were Northerners. They were standing over desks with measuring spoons and egg whisks, the tables strewn with mortars and pestles, cups and bowls, like an alchemist's chamber or a science class. When the

NORTH ✿ ✿ ✿ 151

workers noticed the Southerners congregating, they put down their utensils and joined the meeting.

'Find a space to sit,' said Adams. He was rubbing at the pain in the bulbous joints in his hands.

Arthritis, thought Dyce. I guess that's coming too. But only for the lucky ones.

'Get ready to be blown away,' said Adams. 'I mean it. I'm going to let you all in on the grand plan to bring down Renard and every single asshole under him. Now I know you all can get behind that, right?'

There were murmurs of holy assent. These guys were ready to go without even a couple of warm-up hymns. Dyce half expected people to moan and faint as Adams worked himself up to a couple of rounds of can-you-give-me-a-hallelujahs, and then some frothing and writhing on the carpet.

His stomach gave a warning twinge, and he felt his neck tense up. Some fuckery was coming soon.

'So here's the thing,' said Adams. 'I'm gonna spell it out again, just so's everyone is on the same page. To get to Renard, we need immunity – and I mean to all those path-ee-gens he's sending out, and all the ones he's ever sent out. We need a blanket cure-all, and here's why. If we try to set up an attack on him or his factory, his men will simply wipe us out with some new virus while we're ten miles away. You want to know how we found this out? Happened once before. I can tell you about that another time when you feel like throwing up your Cheerios, but it was, as they say, a lesson. You can trust me on that. And we in the Resistance are quick learners.' He looked around, gauging the impact of his words on the raggedy group. Dyce wondered what it was, exactly, that had eaten his cheek. Noma? Leprosy? Good old-fashioned staph gone wild?

Adams went on. 'So, to get to Renard – the head honcho, the big kahuna, Baron Samedi, the man himself – we need immunity to every single thing they can throw at us. Every goddam virus imaginable. And the ones you can't imagine too. Once we have that in the bag, the plan is to knock his factory offline. Now, I know what you're thinking.'

Dyce raised his hand. 'How exactly?'

Adams shrugged. 'The usual way. Blow it up. But we need to cut the head off the snake, so to speak, else the whole system will start up again. This room you're in here, this is where we've been trying to manufacture our own antidotes. As you can see, I tested some of them myself.' He stuck a finger in the fabric dent of his cheek.

'You-all know this story, but for the benefit of our new friends, this was part of a little miracle that worked for three whole days. A long time in politics, as the man said. Anyhoo. I stopped drinking the water, the way we always start these things: control group, don't you know. There were some high-fives those first few days – then I just started to rot clean away. Took some months before I could walk again too. My missus didn't like that so much, but the cause is the cause, right?'

'Fuck Renard!' said someone. Dyce couldn't tell if it was the same person who had wanted to fuck Renard the day before.

'And I was lucky too.'

Dyce snorted, and Adams gave him the side-eye. 'Believe it, sunshine. Lots more folks volunteered too, but they ain't here to give you the history tour.' He hitched his thumbs into his belt loops. 'So this is where you-all come in. You know we been looking for Southerners, right? That was an idea that came right from one of our founders, a brave lady who did some of the early testing. It didn't turn out well for her, else she'd be the one standing here now, talking to you fine people.'

'What happened to her?' Dyce again.

'You got a lot of questions, son.'

'And you got the answers, right?'

'Look. A lot of us here in the North bought into the idea that the South was sending these viruses over the Wall. And why wouldn't we? It came straight from the horse's mouth. Horse named Renard, that is: the government, home of the free and land of the brave. But this lady, she saw it at the source. She was a nurse – used to work in one of Renard's labs. Said she saw things there that made what Mengele did at Auschwitz look like a round of flu shots. What she told the Resistance – and there were only a few of us back in the day – was that she knew for sure that it was Renard himself who was poisoning the South.'

'But why bother? Wasn't he winning the War anyway?'

'Son, your faith in the history books is touching, but let me tell you this: Renard was losing the War there, right at the end. You believe that? He didn't, either. That was round about the time the viruses got really out of hand. I guess it was his way of decimating the South so it couldn't rise again, but it also made sure that there would be no coup back home in the North. Divide and conquer, little buddy.'

'And now? What are you saying here?'

'I'm saying no one can get close to Renard, not as long as he has a hundred strains of poison on his side, and a bunch of dumb-bunny citizens afraid to ask the big questions.

'But that's not the end of my tale, friends. This lady, her plan, her idea, was to get back to basics. Find some Southerners. She figured that anyone who made it over the Wall would have to be some kind of superhuman. They'd have a kind of blanket immunity, you understand? And a handle on the truth. Otherwise they'd already be dead and buried.'

The Southerners traded looks with one another.

'You get it, don't you? You folks right here are getting something right, and I need to know how it works. You can see why.' He held up his palms, hectoring and supplicatory. 'I done enough talking now. It's your turn. Tell me about those magic mushrooms. Tell me about the boomers.'

Dyce's stomach cramped and he twitched guiltily. Adams caught the shudder.

'Jackson. 'Fess up. You gonna tell me how you two did it?'

Every Southern face was turning to scan the room. The myriad eyes settled on Dyce; he felt them like insects, crawling curiously over his surfaces.

'Son. These people are waiting. How do we reproduce them antiviral mushrooms till they're coming out of our ears?'

Out of our ears? Dyce wanted to laugh. Out of our eye sockets and nostrils too! Rupturing from our lungs, clean through our ribs!

But what the hell. What did he have to lose? The least he could do was explain why this was a shitty idea.

He hoisted himself up and began pushing his way through the group, wincing at the pins and needles in his leg. But it was his stomach that was really going to town. He had to find a bathroom right now.

He managed to make it inside the women's toilets before he vomited two days of rations down into the smashed U-bend that was all that remained of the original bombsite.

24

When Kurt stretched out his crooked spine in the morning, he saw the ruined silos not far from the road, strewn with graffiti at their bases. He bent closer to the damp ashes: they had had a visitor in the night. There were tiny footprints in the soft gray powder where a prairie critter had nibbled at the wire.

'You're a crap guard dog, Linus,' Kurt yawned.

Before he let the cat out, he tied a string around its neck, just like he'd done with Mason. Linus pulled back, yanking on the makeshift lead and growling.

Kurt shook his head. 'Got to be clean, kitty. This is your chance to do your business.'

The cat was trying to get the string off over its head. Kurt gave up. 'Fine. Have it your way.' He tied the end of the string onto the side mirror and went to get his own routine started.

'In days of old,' he called back to Linus. 'You know that one? In days of old, when knights were bold and paper uninvented, you wiped your ass with tufts of grass and went away contented.'

When he got back, he saw the telltale scrapes on the wet ground. Linus was still pawing at the string, growling low, the fur on his head furrowed and reversed. Kurt kept waiting for him to lose his shit completely and strangle himself, but the cat was only menacing and sullen, like he was biding his time. Maybe he was.

'Well done. Doesn't that feel better? Now let's hit the highway.'

The road was empty till he got near Des Moines. When a car passed, going the other way, Kurt waved at it and smiled.

'Even if no one deserves to live, you don't need to be a dick about it, right? Manners maketh the man, Linus. What my mama always said. You could do worse than take that to heart.'

At the limits of the city, he slowed the car and parked it in a daze, under the wiry shade of an elm with its top leaves flagging. For the first time Kurt Callahan doubted himself.

'Sure puts Glenvale to shame, I can tell you, Linus. How'm I gonna find Uncle Felix in all of this mess?'

The cat was silent, the string trailing from his collar over the seat.

'Come on. Time to hustle.' Kurt got out of the car, with Linus on his string, and they walked up the sidewalk.

'Thought there'd be more folks around,' he told the cat, looking left and right at an intersection. 'But you know what we really need right now? Elevation. One of the few things I liked about Uncle Tye was that bird of his. Now that's real elevation!'

Another block along he entered the foyer of a high-rise. They made their way up the endless stairwell, littered with rubble and the dried white shit of long-gone campers, both human and animal, so old it'd lost its stink.

Linus refused to climb after the fourth floor, and Kurt had to pick him up and hold him under his arm right the way to the top. It felt familiar.

They looked out. The city stretched away under them and the grid of roads was clear. One or two had been blocked by brick barricades from ancient protests. Far to the south-west there was activity, and Kurt wondered if he could really be hearing voices carrying over the straight-edged walls and lifting high on thin trails of smoke. He tried to memorize it all and place his car in relation to the path of the sun. He might not know how to find Felix, but he could sure fucking learn his way around.

He lay back and waited. Near mid-morning there were the sounds of engines, cars coming in a line from the other end of the city – the quiet end. He watched them cross a bridge, some turning off left, and others right. Far below he saw a battered Jeep stop beside an old man carrying a pole and two balanced buckets of water. He watched them talk, too distant to hear the actual words. Then the old man raised a finger, pointing up and up, the digit raising like the sight on a gun, until it came to rest on a window in the next building over. The men with guns streamed into the building, emerging minutes later dragging a prisoner behind them. Some kind of policeman or military man, judging from the badge sewn to his shirt. Kurt watched them load him into the Jeep and then the crowd dissipated, as though they were simply seeping into the ground.

'Those fellas have a home base somewhere, Linus, and it's top secret. Otherwise they wouldn't bother with the smoke and mirrors. And I'll take a bet – let's say the good pronghorn fillet for the winner – that Uncle Felix is with them. Now we just got to play it cool.'

He crouched down, out of sight.

25

Adams was kneeling beside Dyce as he retched, one hand on his shoulder, soothing him like a child with night terrors.

'Shh, shh. It's all right now. Take all the time you need.'

Dyce shrugged the hand off and kept kneeling over the maw of the toilet. There was no amount of time that would make things easier, or numb him to the last few days. Some people dealt with change easier than others: Hey, sure! This is how the world is now? No problem! Hand me that handkerchief!

He was not one of them. He felt another spasm coming and he hocked a string of bile down the open pipe. Some days he knew he wasn't all the way over the sickness he'd caught before he'd met Vida, there in the way-back; some days were just better than others. Were they really going to make him recount that nightmare time under the Mouth in front of all those hopeful Southern faces? He shook his head like a terrier with a toad, the foam flying.

Those minutes underground he counted among the worst of his life – and there was a fair amount of competition. He sat back on his haunches and tried to breathe, but the images stayed stubbornly in his head.

The pitiless, expanding death the boys had seen from Gracie's window as it approached, a miasma.

Bethie and Garrett's tiny baby, come too early from the

body of its sick mama, born lifeless under the sick sky and then discarded.

And Ester! A woman – only just a woman – bartering colostrum for a living, like her sisters were dairy cows. Even the ones who seemed to survive were the walking dead.

And between every scene: always the mushrooms. They sprouted, ever-living, in his memory, patient as cancer. Between his waking up and swinging his legs off the bed, they were there. In the quiet before sleep took him they rose up and swamped him. Behind his eyes the bright white buttons stared back from the black nursery of his brain, hungry for hosts. It felt, though Dyce wouldn't admit it, not even to Vida – especially not to her, and especially not now – that those fungal eyes shielded themselves behind his own, watching the world as it went by, seeing everything he saw. They were part of him now, and he was part of them.

And so was every other person who had died horribly down there in the mines, sacrificed in their making of this knobbly cannibal chain. They had laid their pitiful selves down in his bones, and he owed them.

'Easy, there,' said Adams. 'How about we talk man to man? No real need to put you up there in front of all those folk. That's not helping the jitters. It was just an idea. I like things out in the open and I can't resist a bit of a performance, I'll admit to that. How about you clean up and I'll take you somewhere to talk – somewhere we can get a little fresh air.'

Dyce coughed and heard the echo, hollow and wet, from the toilet's workings below. I'm a trophy. He wanted to show me off.

'Okay.'

He stood up, his knees complaining.

'Get some water on your face. You'll feel better.'

Dyce splashed his eyes and stared at his yellow features splintered in the mirror over the sink. How did he still look so normal from the outside?

Adams led him dumbly away from the bathroom, away from the gathered crowd, and they doubled back to the main foyer. He turned around, looking up, like a tourist in a church.

'We'll go there,' he said, pointing above his head. Dyce shrugged.

The two men climbed the stairs and then took a service entrance up to the base of the dome. The stairwell was narrow, and Dyce felt like the air there was thinner, barely enough for the both of them, as if everything, all the hopes and prayers and wishes – and experiments too, because what were those if not prayers to some other deity? – was directed up into the very top of the dome, closer to God.

It opened onto a landing, and he could see into the heart of the whole beehive structure.

And that was where the Weatherman was, right in the center of things, wrapped snug in his blankets like a Mexican, lying asleep against the pale curved wall. Always liked to be high up, didn't he? When the winds weren't keeping him camped underground, that is. Keep an eye on the goings-on. Don't have to be a weatherman to see which way the wind is blowing. He squinted when Dyce and Adams appeared, but didn't say anything about the intrusion. He rolled over, expecting them to pass by, like nurses on night duty.

But Adams stopped. Right above Felix's gray head was a window in the wall – locked, Dyce saw, because Adams had to lean over the old man where he lay in his cocoon and struggle with the corroded latch. It gave, and he opened it outward. The blast of fresh air and daylight was so pure it almost knocked Dyce off his feet.

Felix shielded his eyes. 'Hey,' he complained.

Adams ignored him. 'Keep up,' he said.

Outside the window was a set of iron rungs welded onto the dome. Dyce followed Adams as he ascended, rung after rung, half afraid to look out or down in case it triggered some residual queasiness in him: the bile still burnt in the back of his throat. They were aiming for the top of the golden dome, he saw now, a little round room like the crow's nest on a sailing ship.

No, he thought. Like a shrine in an old encyclopedia. He wasn't stupid. He knew what holy places ought to look like, even if he'd never been in one himself, like those towers in India where they set out the dead for the birds to feed on.

He watched his hands, his fingers gripping tight to the metal, his feet finding their way blindly to step after step until they reached the parapet. Adams hoisted himself over and then turned back to help Dyce, who swatted his hand away. He allowed himself to look out now while he caught his breath. It was like they'd climbed from the bowels of hell, through the crust of the earth with its dirt and its trees, then up through the clouds and into heaven. They looked down over the world with its rubble-strewn gardens. Old paths looped in bald patterns; dried fountains lay cracked, their shards being quietly smothered with creepers. The lonesome flagpoles rattled their halyards in the breeze, though no flag flew.

Stretching out behind the Capitol Building were parking lots, and the skeletons of buildings ransacked long ago for firewood, and for their piping and wiring. The lots were empty but for the leaves and branches blown there by the storm – and a single car, rusting gently on its bricks.

Adams swept his arm over the ruins. 'Can you believe there were ever enough cars to fill these? And enough gas to run them all?'

Dyce shook his head and peered into the distance, where among the high-rises of Des Moines city center there were a few lonely columns of smoke that gave away day-to-day lives. Some people were still there, holding out like bacteria, hardy and tenacious, trying to start again. A handful of tiny glows flickered, flame-orange. There were some electrical bulbs, Dyce gathered, and the phones seemed to work inside the Capitol itself. But there was no excess: bare-bones electrickery in the cables of Iowa, and none at all in the death-dark plains.

Dyce shivered. It wasn't just the breeze picking up. It was strange to be outside without checking the weather. The clouds were rolling in, though they seemed higher than before, dark only in the North, but it was okay. He and Adams had some-where to go if it all turned to shit.

Adams sat with his legs dangling through the grille of a flaking railing and Dyce sat down too. They looked out between the bars like prisoners.

'So,' Adams began.

Here it comes. He's going to try and sell me some bullshit about my responsibility and the good of the community. Truth, justice and the American fucking way.

'You're the guy who knows how we're going to win this thing. Think about that when you tell me the details. I know it's not easy. But with your help we can make a change. We want it as bad as you and that's the truth. Think about your family – the dead ones as well as the ones still alive. This is for them.'

For a second Dyce had forgotten that Garrett was dead. Now it came rushing back, the way it always fucking did. But this time the sick loss carried something else along with it: up at the top of the dome, Dyce understood that people like them were the end of a line – the last of a species, like you used to see in zoos.

That's not exactly true, little brother, Garrett drawled in his head. You ain't the last of the last.

True enough. Inside Vida's belly was a tiny creature with the whole of the Jackson family history in its veins. And it was fighting a fever so it could live.

'The mushrooms.' Dyce kept looking at the horizon, his head turned south toward where the Mouth had been. 'The thing is, they have to grow from dead bodies. That's the trick. And I know how that sounds.'

For once Adams was quiet.

'And I only saw the . . . the bodies at the end. I didn't see how it was done.'

'You know how long it lasts?' Adams searched. 'The antiviral effects, I mean.'

'Close to two weeks, so far. That's all the science I got.'

'We need to test that. Gotta be sure.'

Dyce nodded.

'One of you Southerners maybe drinks only rainwater from now on – none of Renard's magic from the tap. Then we can figure out the time frame of cover. We got a rain tank from the old tests. Gutter feeds in from the roof, clean and pure, the way the good Lord meant it.'

'That makes sense.' Might as well do something while Vida's lying there suffering, Dyce told himself. 'It ought to be me.'

Adams nodded. 'You happen to bring any of these mushrooms with you?'

Dyce nodded again. 'What's the plan?'

'We can salvage the spores, right?'

'Should be able to. I mean, they replicate themselves in the wild. You can take a few, not all. Pete still has a couple.' He stared hard at Adams. 'I want you to know, I brought out a bagful with me, and I paid a pretty high fucking price for the elixir of life. I haven't exactly slept much since then. Some days I think I shouldn't have taken them at all, considering the havoc they caused in the beginning. It was a total shit-show down there. And maybe I ought to be laying there too, keeping all them dead folks company.' His mouth twisted.

Adams grunted, careful not to interrupt now that Dyce had got going.

'Depending on what's on the other side, of course.'

'Son, that's our lot. We got no business wondering what's on the other side. It'll be there when we get there, one way or another, and I'm dead set on delaying the day I find out.'

'The thing is,' Dyce said, raising his voice now against the wind, 'if it was easy, I mean, if farming the antivirals was simply about finding some dead folks for compost, then Ed and his crew would've just gone out looking. I suppose there weren't a lot of people left down South – but even so. Why not shoot first and spread the spores later, like ordinary mushrooms?' He shook his head. 'No, I got a nasty feeling, Mister Adams, that these particular mushrooms – the super-special, antiviral, eternal-life motherfucking mushrooms we need – only work when they're first settled in living people. They're like fetuses. They have to feed.'

26

'You got to know where to look,' said Kurt, pulling Linus along behind him. 'We'll find where all those men disappeared to. How, you wonder? Well, young Linus, I'm a damn good tracker. Remember that on the day you try to make another escape.'

Kurt was at street level again. He'd marked in his mind where he'd seen the men go. But when he got to where he figured he'd find trace of them, there was nothing. He was quiet as he kicked through the ruins of a windowless laundromat, the red and white linoleum like a high-school corridor.

'I'm not going to lie. It's an off day for me, Linus,' he said. The truth was he had no idea what he would actually do if he found anyone. 'Play it as it lays, right?'

He wandered out to the street and into another shop – HOT BUNS BAKERY, if the peeling sign was anything to go by. But they hadn't stopped for coffee and croissants, the men who'd only minutes before been swarming the streets, hunting the other one. There was no sign of them. Kurt sat on a cinder block and held Linus up to his face.

'My mother always said not to make excuses. So this ain't an excuse, right? But back South I looked for the way grass had been stamped down, snapped branches, disturbed dew drops – that kind of thing. It's much harder here, is all I'm saying. Here it's just plastered walls and asphalt, and none of it is much good to me. Don't think less of me, cat.'

He stood and went back out onto the shattered sidewalk. He swept his gaze over the lines in the street: someone had made a spray-paint soccer field. Well, who was there to tell them to stop? No little old ladies were ever going to call the police to complain that someone had broken their windows. Kurt cocked an eye at the gray sky over his head, framed by the sharp angles of the buildings, and then he tucked Linus under his arm and walked out onto the center line, the string collar trailing. It wasn't like he had to worry about traffic.

The thumping of leather on the street made him jerk into alert mode, and Linus's claws dug into him. A boy his own age had appeared from a side street, chasing a soccer ball. Kurt watched him stop the ball with his foot, then pick it up. He had dark hair, black almost, and he was lean, with ears that stuck out like wings.

'That's a handball,' Kurt called across to him. 'That's cheating.'

The boy stared at Kurt, there on the center line with Linus under his arm. Then he smiled and came closer.

'You want to play?' he called.

His smile dropped.

'You like my blouse?' asked Kurt. 'I made it myself.' He plucked at the material with his free hand. The bloodstains were brown as iodine.

The boy shook his head.

'You any good at tag?'

The boy took a step backward, then he dropped the ball and ran, knowing he had to go faster than he ever had for soccer practice. But Kurt was on him with the multi-tool anyway, stabbing with one hand, the other holding Linus by his string lead as the cat groaned and howled and scrabbled to get away.

When the boy stopped twitching, Kurt stood up and yanked Linus back by his string.

'That was just in case you were still thinking of getting away,' he told the cat. 'What have we learnt today?' He shook the animal by its neck. 'Tracking in a city is mighty hard, but with all this open space, you know, the chasing is easy.'

27

The Northerners took shifts, working in pairs. Dyce thought if they got any closer they'd contaminate the spores, the way their faces were pressed up against the glass containers, like worshippers at a shrine poring over relics. At least they were properly dressed for it. Renard had probably looked the same way back in the day, pacing his laboratory like an evil overlord or a dad outside a delivery room.

Adams nudged him. 'What are you thinking?'

'Just thinking.'

'About what?'

'About how you guys look an awful lot like we did back South.'

Adams grunted. Then he held a hand across his nose and mouth. 'Those masks get saturated real quick, don't they?'

Dyce shrugged. 'Just another one of those things you never thought you'd have to find out.'

Pete's bag had held maybe twenty mushrooms, all kinds, fragmented and soaked by the mighty Platte, but good to go. That was the beauty of spores, wasn't it? They grew anywhere, on the things people thought weren't part of the system. The crew of Resistance scientists had been happy to get them at all, and they didn't seem deterred by their state.

As Dyce watched, another pair of frowning workers scraped

sterilized pins through the filaments, letting the motes drop onto cooked white rice. It was the method that worked best, Adams confided, boastful now that he was certain of his victory. From a library book, didn't you know, titled *Survival 101*.

'As long as it does what it says,' Dyce told him. 'My favorite was *Pickling, Salting and Drying*. You ever read that? My daddy loved that one. And a whole bunch of stuff on natural remedies and purifying water. You know. The usual.'

The two of them watched the careful hands of the scientists. The trick was to observe the spores grow and to isolate them before mold crept in. It would be a day or so until the first crop came on. And instead of wasting time and hoping that only these ones worked – the progeny of Dyce's original batch – the other scientists were experimenting. Who could blame them? Wasn't that how people found things out? Adams could testify to that.

The end of cities also meant that it hadn't been hard to find a range of lab rats. Actual rats: the buildings were overrun. There was the king rat, for sure, with outsize testicles and needling teeth, but along with him had come a gallinule, a rockdove chick and a red-eared slider. Dyce himself would have had trouble slicing open a live terrapin, but the Northerners had briskly set about preparing the flesh – 'Substrate, right?' said Adams – by opening the creatures and pinning them out like dissection specimens. 'We got to get these mushrooms growing on *something*.'

Like Vida, thought Dyce, as the scientists bent to their scraping. Like Vida, going under the knife.

28

Ruth looked at her hands. Steady as ever. She was ready to do it – wasn't she? She had the cleaver and the knives, all of which she'd made sure to sterilize, and which she was going to sterilize twice more, for safety, before she amputated Vida's rotting leg. She even had a thick-based frying pan for the cauterizing, bracing herself against even imagining the smell of burnt flesh. It was the only way to staunch the blood, though it wouldn't hold the femoral artery for long. For that she'd asked around for catgut, fine as thread, and a needle. She had found the right location, at least – there, where the library let the midday sun in. She had pried a board away to determine where it fell brightest. That was where they'd operate.

And the alcohol, of course, the cure-all. Enough for the patient as well as the wound. Fuck foetal alcohol syndrome, she thought, you got to be alive to get that.

And there was enough for her too, for after. Ruth was going to drink herself blind. Let Dyce change the weeping dressing and comfort the woman who was as good as his wife, the one who would never walk the same way. Let him pull his lame white-man's weight for a change.

Now Ruth sat with Vida, one hand resting on the slight curve of her daughter's belly, where the human seed had germinated. She was ready to take the leg off, sure, but she also wanted to explain, to herself and to her child – and to her child's child, who had the most to lose. What chance did an unborn baby have if its mother underwent an amputation? Surely the shock would kill it.

Yes, Ruth told herself. Do you think I don't know that?

One of the scientists was knocking on the open door, polite and persistent: she meant to have her way. Ruth saw it in her high ponytail and the wide angle of her jaw.

'Sorry to disturb you.'

She didn't look sorry, but Ruth was too gracious to say it. She nodded at the woman in the lab coat. Where had they found those things anyway? Robbing a hospital? Or did Renard still have labs somewhere close by? Never trust anyone in a white coat, thought Ruth. The needle is never far behind.

The woman was waiting, angling herself over the threshold. Ruth had seen her before but they had had no cause to speak. She judged her unthreatening and motioned her in, raising a finger to her lips while the woman got close enough to look Vida over where she still slept, sweating.

She sat down beside Ruth.

'I'm Jill. I work downstairs. How is she?'

'Not good,' Ruth replied in a low voice.

Jill frowned and moved her lower jaw until something clicked. There was something unpleasant about her, thought Ruth, now that she had her up close. Jill was the sort of girl who would cheat at golf.

'You know Vida?' Ruth asked. 'I mean, from before?'

'Not really.'

'Are you a doctor?'

'No.'

'Then may I ask why you are here?'

'I'm concerned,' said Jill and stretched a smile over her face. 'I just want to know how she is.'

'Oh, just tell me the fucking truth. No one gives two shits about us. All they want is the mushrooms.'

'That's not true.' Jill went into her spiel, as if she was reading from a cue card. 'You know, we're all in this together. And we both got just as much reason to see Renard dead.'

'Now that's not true, missy. Pardon my saying. We might both have reason, but you don't have nearly as much of it as we do. Not even close. They send you in here to talk to me?'

'Ruth . . . Can I call you Ruth?' Jill didn't wait for Ruth to answer. 'We're on the same team. We want the same things, even if it seems like we're getting there in roundabout ways.'

'Now what does that mean? And I mean specifically, what does it mean?'

Jill turned to face her, as if they were on an old-time talk show, glowing, earnest. 'Look. I want your daughter to make a full recovery. We all do, of course. But if it's worst-case scenario and her leg has to come off, well, we could make good use of it.'

'Of her leg?'

'Think of it as organ donation, you know? The substrate . . .'

'Substrate? For what?' Then it dawned on Ruth. 'To grow mushrooms on? My child's leg? Are you fucking crazy?'

'I'm just saying that if it's coming off anyway, don't . . . don't bury it out back.'

'Now you listen to me, and listen good,' hissed Ruth. 'I would sooner burn my own daughter up on a funeral pyre than let you vultures touch her. Just get out.'

Jill got to the door in record time, and just as well. Ruth unclenched her hands and looked at her palms, where the nails had dug crescents into the paler flesh. That fool girl with her bouncy ponytail and her white lab coat and her lack of basic feeling!

Adams. Ruth bet it was that asshole. All holy-roller on the outside, but every now and again you got a look at the real man underneath. She had seen his kind before – in Renard. She shuddered. How had she ever loved him? Let him touch her? And worse than that. Much worse.

But the past was the past, and for better or worse – mostly worse, when it came to Renard, and that was no lie – here they were. Ruth couldn't afford to let her old lives swallow her up. What was she supposed to do about it all? Cry? It was what it was. She took a deep breath to steady herself. Vida was hers: blood of her blood, flesh of her flesh. She would have to fight the infection. She would. There was no other option now. No way the leg was coming off. No way she and Dyce were creeping out in the darkness and burying it only for Jill to come sniffing, shovel in hand.

Ruth grabbed her daughter's hand again and squeezed gently, willing her energy to cross over the lines of her body into Vida's, as if they were still joined by the umbilical cord. Maybe it never snapped, Ruth thought. Maybe your children really were bound to you by a fine silver ribbon of suffering and care for ever and ever.

In the caul of her sickness Vida slept, and inside her limp body the struggle went on.

Near midday Dyce came in, face set in an older man's lines, ready to confront the operation. He had decided he could do it – hold her down – if that was what would save her, but his shirt was ringed with sweat at the armpits and neck like a hanged man.

He raised his eyebrows as Ruth prepared to redo the rough tacking sutures, neat and thin as embroidery this go-round – the kind you don't waste time doing right before an amputation; the kind that was meant to last.

'It's staying on,' she said. She kept her head down to hide her eyes, and she kept stitching.

Dyce slumped into a chair, his thighs shaking. 'Thank you,' he said. Ruth still wouldn't look at him.

'She won't come round. I dosed her up good.'

'Any left for me?' Dyce asked, eyeing the bottles of hooch on the floor.

'Touch it and die,' Ruth said. 'I mean it. I'm going to get real drunk now, Dyce, so you make sure you're the one who's clear enough to change the dressing in a couple of hours. Specially if the smell changes. You do your duty. You're the man of the house. You got that?'

He nodded, the responsibility and the relief settling on him like a cloak. He didn't care how bad it got.

'I'm staying for a spell first,' Ruth told him. 'You go on and get some rest, because you're going to need it when she comes round. But me and Vida, right now we got some catching up to do.'

He saw how she was tying off the thread, as proud of her handiwork as a fine lady in a turret, proud as Gracie had been of the testifying samplers she'd had up on her walls when the plague came.

'You still here, boy?'

'All right, all right. I'm going.'

And he did. Ruth sat down again and sighed. She examined the homebrew – what was it? Bourbon? Men couldn't brew worth a damn. No creativity – and then took a sip. The rotgut was milky and smelt of damp, but it was strong and that was all that counted. She let it rinse her tongue and throat like mouth-wash, burning and cleansing as it went.

'Ugh. You taste as bad as you look. But as long as you get the job done. Just like Renard used to say. Now. My turn to talk while you sleep, Vida,' she told her daughter softly. 'Just like Horse Head.' She looked at her own hands and thought of the work they had done in her lifetime, the small, defiant bodies they had cupped while their injured mothers writhed. 'It's time to talk about babies.'

29

For the second night in a row, Felix didn't sleep in the same room as the other Southerners. That first night he'd curled up and slept high in his crow's nest, safe and removed, his body craving the rest. Now he had found a forgotten stairwell and set up his bed at the top – blankets and a few cushions he'd taken from one of the rooms. Somebody would be pissed about that.

When he woke to pee, he fumbled for an old army canteen he'd found in the kitchen. There was no way he was stumbling around this place in the dark, not with those shackles on the walls, like some torture chamber. He pissed into the canteen and tried to be quiet, his ancient prostate making the urine spurt and judder when it came at last. It had smelt strong – like wet clothes and chemicals – ever since he'd had those mushrooms.

'Like an evil genie,' he whispered. He closed the lid of the canteen tight. 'Now just remember what's in there when you wake up looking for a drink, you old fart.'

He lay down, but he couldn't get back to sleep. He'd slept in worse places, but there were solitary noises every now and again that reminded him just how many people there were in the building. Like lab rats, Felix thought. He turned over.

All that commotion in the early evening – the siren and the men with guns funneling down to the basement – had definitely meant something, and he had a bad feeling about it. They'd captured one guy, the patrolman, he figured, and he'd looked pretty beat up already. Right now he'd be in one of those horrible little rooms, for sure. Maybe even shackled. Because that was what the shackles were for, right? Keeping people in their place.

It was no good. He had to go and see who it was, whether it was his business or not.

'Better to find out both sides of the story, right? Ain't that what the Wall's taught us?' he muttered.

There were people asleep in all the chambers now, rolled up in a dirty rainbow of sleeping bags and wedged together for warmth. Felix could remember a time when camping gear was designed for blending in rather than standing out.

He crept past them and some mumbled in their sleep, but no one, he figured, had seen him. And even if they had, he could just tell them he was looking for the john. It was almost true. All the way there he kept his ears tuned for guards or a watchman of some kind, but Adams's people were either arrogant or stupid, because he found no one on duty.

The doors of both prison rooms were shut and locked, the deadbolts running parallel down the edges of the doors, all in place. Felix began with the room on the left. He bent to bring his eye close to the keyhole to see if there was anything discernible, but as he leant in, something hairy slammed against the door from the other side and he fell back in fright. Then the shouting began.

'I'll kill you! I'll kill you!' The heavy chains clinked.

Christ, that was weird! What the fuck was going on there?

There was something else, as well, that was ringing little bells in the back of Felix's brain – a familiar smell, some trace he had caught over the ordinary stench of urine, something that reminded him of stale cakes.

Vanilla.

Mother of God. It was the basketball car freshener from the De Luxe. Or something very much like it. Was it coming from him? He held out his own shirt and sniffed, but the scent was wafting from whatever had thrown itself in rage against the door.

There was another bang on the door and Felix flinched. He was spooked. That shouting had been loud enough to raise the dead. Why was he still hanging around?

He scurried all the way back to his nest of blankets, and found after all that he did need to piss again. Old age and fear. Man, it was a bad combination. The canteen was too full to pee into without risk of overflow, so he took it with him down to the rest room.

In the toilet he emptied the canteen down the drain and tried to wash his hands quietly, but they were shaking and he splashed his clothes.

There were two rooms, weren't there? Two sets of shackles. One for the patrolman, but who besides him was being held captive? They had only gone out to catch one man, and they had returned with him.

But somehow the other cell was occupied now, occupied by someone from within the building. Someone who was part of the Resistance.

The same impossible name kept circling back. The smell from that fucking car freshener, sweet as marijuana, was only on the clothes of two men that he knew.

His own, of course.

And Adams's.

30

Ruth felt Vida's forehead. Hot. She checked the room once more to see whether they really were alone. It was an old habit, to keep checking. Things changed down South faster than Ruth was comfortable with. You just never knew. Then she settled her back against an ageing chair and told her daughter everything. There was relief in knowing that Vida was only half aware. If she remembered nothing of this, at least Ruth could say she tried. More than once, in fact.

'On the banks of the North Platte, right before we rode our horses into that fierce water, I tried to tell you everything. I got further than I ever managed before, but I missed some things. I'll blame it on the timing, that we were pressed for time and hunkered down, pinned below that storm. But the truth is that for me to tell you everything, I'm going to need to numb the pain some. And maybe more than some.' Ruth sipped the hooch and swallowed hard. 'You know there are some things I never told you. You're going to ask me why that is, so I'm going to do my best to explain. I was scared. Believe it. Your scary, tough-as-nails mama was scared of what you'd think of her. But there was something else too. I was scared of what you'd think of yourself.

'You asked me a couple of times why you never caught any

of those viruses that came on the air. And it's true. You weren't sick a day in your life while everyone else coughed their lungs out and the world went to shit.' Ruth drank and winced, drank again. 'Well, brace yourself, because here it comes.

'You always knew I worked North-side before the War, didn't you, baby? You knew I was a nurse at the same hospital as Big Bad Renard: I made no secret of that.' A fit of coughing overcame her as she spoke, as if even his name was enough to choke her.

'Excuse me. I thought I would be able to tell it all straight, but now it's time, there isn't an easy way to say it. Okay. What you don't know is that we had . . . an affair, I suppose it was. It sounds ridiculous now, hindsight being twenty-twenty and all that. But you have to understand. I was new to the place, young and out of my depth, and what we were working on in that hospital felt important, like we could actually save the world. He was doing government work, secret work, engineering viruses to live airborne for months, then engineering the antivirals. He had real power back then. And he was . . . charismatic. Drew people to him, wherever he went. He could be charming, Vida, in his own way. Isn't that the real horror? Like the snake in the garden who just wanted some company. Tired of being alone, tired of being the only one sliding on his belly through the dirt.

'But Renard didn't even have that excuse. He was already married. You believe that? Someone had married him. I pity that poor woman. Queenie, they called her. People talk about that bomb like it was the worst thing that could have happened to her, but I'm telling you here it was a mercy. Saved her years of suffering under his hand. Something wrong with her insides: that was the rumor. She couldn't have children. So Renard, he

felt free to be spreading his seed around, and I guess . . .' Ruth
paused again, closing her eyes tight against what she was about
to say next, 'I got lucky.

'Don't judge me, baby. I was engaged too – that publisher
man I told you about, the one who was the reason I ended up
in the US of A at all. It wasn't his fault, either. Renard, he just
had this power over me. Neither of us sinners was free, and I'm
truly glad I wasn't the one who ended up with him for richer,
for poorer, because I know which side of that vow she got.

'Does it sound like I'm sidestepping my responsibility? Maybe
I am. But being young and confused is bad, and it makes a
person do strange things. You know that as well I do, Vida.'
Ruth leant into her daughter's side. 'I want you to know: back
then I was a kind of lonely I never want to feel again. And I
won't. But in a way Renard saved me.

'I was pregnant. Pregnant! By Renard himself! Having a baby
in my belly, the way you have in yours right now – well, that
made things clear for me. I started thinking about what we were
really doing in those labs, and I knew it was just wrong. People
change, baby. Never forget that. At the beginning of the War,
long before the Wall went up, back when the North figured
they'd win the usual way, with guns and men and God on their
side, I could live with it. I always knew what those viruses were
for, what they would do to little babies like the one I was carrying myself.

'Once you find yourself in charge of a real human life, there's
a kind of hope and terror that can suffocate you, Vida. Some
nights I'd wake up and the panic would send your little legs
kicking against my ribs like another heart. So I made up my
mind to run away – to make myself unfindable. I would leave
everything. I would leave it all and just go and there'd be

nothing anyone could do to find me. Even Renard. When he found out that I had taken his one precious baby, he was going to look under every stone in America until he could hunt me down.

'So I took out some insurance. I stole one of his precious goddam syringes. Worth a thousand years' salary in dollars and more because of what it could do. He called it the cure-all, the bastard. For all the viruses there ever were, or ever would be. You believe that?

'And I took one, baby! Me. Little low-down Ruthie, all the way from Africa, stealing fire from the gods. And it wasn't even difficult. I took it the night I left and I kept it until the morning you were born. I injected you the same day, and the way you cried – well, I've delivered hundreds in my time, but I never heard a baby cry that way, and I hope never to hear it again. Vida, you cried like I broke your newborn heart. Your arm swelled up like a balloon, and it was shiny and purple for two weeks. People were going to think I was beating you. It went back to normal eventually, but you never cried after that – like the reservoir was empty. I don't think you ever trusted me again. But you know what? It was worth it. I'm not sorry, Vida. You are alive and you are here with me.'

Ruth sighed again. She had thought she would feel lighter after her confession. She stroked her daughter's arm where it lay, smooth and cooling, on the sheet.

'Sometimes I see your father in you, baby. I see him. Renard. It doesn't scare me. It just tells me that you're going to be fine. You're going to be okay. You're too smart and too strong to give up. You got the best of both of us. That's why I called you Vida. I called you Life. And you've still got a lot of living in you. Isn't that right?'

She didn't wait for an answer. She lifted the bottle and watched a couple of bubbles springing to the surface like a hypodermic. She swallowed a mouthful, and then another.

When she set the bottle back down, Vida's eyelids were flickering.

31

In the morning, there were mushrooms. The new growths drew everyone in the Capitol Building to the makeshift labs, where people stood shoulder to shoulder, Northern and Southern, and exclaimed over the animal remains with their precious cargo. Like a cookery lesson they were laid out in the hosts: the red-eared slider, pared open like fruit, its shell the bowl in which the mushrooms had budded.

Next to it was the splayed rat, its mouth a rictus, polka-dotted with spheres.

And a jar of plain rice, topped with fresh white golf balls – all of them the offspring of those mushrooms below the Mouth.

There were already volunteers – two young men and a woman, the one who'd greeted Felix when he'd crawled up the ladder. So where was Adams? Why was he not around to offici-ate at the most important part?

Word spread that something was happening, and the members of the Resistance began to gather in the House of Represent-atives, crowding the central stage as though it were a concert or a revival. Then the three volunteers came up, each carefully carrying a cup of water.

Ah. Felix saw that it was Buddy who would take command in Adams's absence.

Still wearing his baseball cap, the little man went up on stage and stood behind the bench. On it were three plates from the kitchen, and on each was a single mushroom, one from each substrate donor. He positioned the volunteers in front of the bench and they copied his gestures, like it was a marriage ceremony or a play.

'Don't drink the Kool-Aid,' muttered Felix, but the audience was too intent to pay him any notice.

One by one the volunteers stepped forward and poured their cups of water out onto the floor. Over the dark stains at their feet, they repeated after Buddy: 'By this action, I declare that I volunteer for this test. It is out of my own free will that I risk my health and life, for the good of us all.'

Slowly, ceremoniously, Buddy took a mushroom and placed it in each set of cupped hands. It had been a while since Felix had considered himself a believer, but even he saw the thread of church running through it all, them with their self-help Eucharist.

But maybe that was how it all started, in the way-back. Maybe this was something people had been doing since the beginning. You had to eat to live. It started out as cannibalism and turned into vampirism; it was co-opted and transformed, and a man found himself sitting at a table with his twelve good friends, partaking of their last communal supper.

Well, He'd risen again, hadn't He? 'Praise Jesus and pass the fungus,' said Felix, and smiled at his neighbor. What sad-asses they all were! Why would anyone want to survive? There was no way life would ever be anything like the way it had been even twenty years ago – and this was the side that had won!

The volunteers held their mushrooms like apples and took a small, symbolic bite. The mushrooms were tiny, and they were soon done, the crowd clapping and whooping its satisfaction and relief. Approval was thick in the air, and Felix needed to get out to escape the suffocation. It was like this building had some sort of fucking power, and it made his head feel light. All that energy had to go somewhere, right? Wasn't that why humans had first built ziggurats, and pyramids, and domes? Renard's cult had been displaced and another had arisen within its walls, and as he pushed his way through the happy, sweating people, Felix was still making his mind up about which would do more damage. You couldn't just coop people up this way like chickens and expect them not to start pecking each other's eyes out. Some cataclysm was due – the Weatherman could feel it – and he wasn't waiting around for it to happen.

Dyce caught the old man by the arm at the top of the stairwell – always the same arm! – and Felix flinched at the pain.

'Where've you been?'

'Looking around. Getting my bearings. Seeing which way the wind's blowing.'

'You get any answers?'

'Just more fucking questions. This place is just plain wrong. You seen Adams anywhere around?'

Dyce pursed his lips and shrugged, but he let Felix go.

At the women's bathroom, Felix turned in. He expected a guard to stop him from lifting the drain plate and climbing down, but security didn't seem as high a priority as it had been the day before, when the prisoner was taken.

His back twinged as he slid the metal disk aside. 'You hang in there,' he told the vertebrae. 'Someone around here's gotta have a spine.'

Then he descended into the darkness.

32

'Vida. Vida, baby, come and sit out here with us.'

Vida knew it was a dream right away, but knowing what it was and doing something about it were not the same thing. She watched it play out, helpless.

Ruth was in sunglasses, holding a glass of white wine like liquid sunshine. Vida watched the light catch and strobe, and she couldn't look away. She rubbed her eyes, but the entoptics refused to fade. They overlaid Renard where he sat and beamed at her from his fold-up chair, as if they'd been together all her life.

And oh, she knew him for her father, though she'd never seen his face. His name, that she'd seen and heard – written on walls in black paint, and yelled out: Fuck Renard! She stared, wanting to eat him with her eyes, notice everything about him, consume the hidden histories.

For someone who ran the world as she knew it, he was fuzzy and shrunken, not much taller than she was, dark in the same way. In her dream Vida touched her own face, searching for clues, and knew it for his mirror image.

Renard.

He was smiling intently at her, as if he was trying to convince her of his kind intentions, but those eyes! Vida shivered in the even sunshine of the dreamland beach. Flat and greedy, the

way monsters looked in the old movies, assessing you for lush-
ness and riches.

Someone tugged at her other hand, breaking the spell, and
Vida looked down. The girl standing barefoot in the sand beside
her was her daughter, wasn't she? She had Dyce's soft eyes and
eyelashes, that smoky sweep that hid what he was thinking. But
the Afro-puffs – those are mine, thought Vida, and her heart
squeezed with love. I gave them to her, the same way my mama
gave them to me. My little girl.

'Come on, Mama. I want to swim.'

Vida turned and saw the sea, the smooth green welcome of
it, the new start, and knew she couldn't let the waters close over
her head. Not after the river; not after the flood.

'Later, baby, okay? Let's just sit here a while. You want to
make a mermaid? That's what your daddy liked to do.'

The two of them sat down on the damp ground and swept the
gritty sand over their legs until they were buried in its coolness
to their waists. Vida felt Renard's eyes always on their backs,
avid, calculating.

'Finish the story,' the girl told Ruth.

'Hmm. Where were we?'

'"Why have not we an immortal soul?" asked the little
mermaid. Like that. And don't leave anything out.'

'Yes, boss lady. "Why have not we an immortal soul?" asked
the little mermaid. "I would give gladly all the hundreds of years
that I have to live, to be a human being only for one day, and to
have the hope of knowing the happiness of that glorious world
above the stars."'

Vida scooped and patted the sand, but there was something
of the graveyard about it, and the sun was getting weaker. They
would have to go in soon. For the moment she was content to

listen. She had heard the story dozens of times when she was little, and Ruth still told it exactly the same way.

'Look at us, Grampa! Look at us!'

Oh, don't, Vida thought suddenly. Don't look at my baby with those hungry eyes.

'"But if you take away my voice," said the little mermaid, "what is left for me?"'

Vida began to struggle out of the sand so that she could turn around and watch Renard, but it was slow going.

He hadn't moved out of the chair. Instead, he seemed to have slumped back, and something gluey was dripping through the mesh fabric of the seat, leaking into the sand.

Vida stood up, whole and unblemished, the sand of her mermaid's tail pattering like dust in a demolished castle. The ground underneath Renard was stained black now, like oil and blood. No one else had noticed. Ruth was still smiling calmly as she told the story, and the little girl was patting small white shells onto her tail. Vida bent closer.

Those weren't shells.

They were fingernails.

She sucked in her breath and turned back to face whatever Renard was becoming. His hot eyeballs had gone and Vida looked through the holes they'd left in his skull. The bone man stood creakily, streaming blood and stinking of rot, and tried to take a step toward the girl. In the second that Vida had, she saw that he was hollow: he had been filleted like a deer, strips of flesh flapping around the empty cavity like surgery gone wrong.

She threw herself at the child and wrestled her from the earth.

'Let's swim! Let's swim!' She tried to turn the girl's head so she wouldn't see the thing shambling behind them.

The sea was a couple of feet away, and they would make it to the water, but Renard kept coming, staggering and determined, powered now by some other evil engine. Ruth stayed in her chair, frozen but for her lips, which kept moving as if she was mouthing an incantation or a recipe. Vida heard the words even as they left her behind.

'Every step she took was as the witch had said it would be. She felt as if she were treading upon the points of needles or sharp knives.' And then they were in the water up to the girl's chest, her small round face upturned in worry and delight, their hands held tight against loss as they breasted the growing waves.

Everything is against us, thought Vida. Where has the sun gone?

Renard kept coming, the trails of blood spilling into the sea around his legs and then washing out fast toward them like tendrils. He would never let them go.

It was too deep to stand. 'Swim!' Vida said, and she didn't care now if she sounded panicked. 'Get on my back, but don't choke me.' And they did, the two of them turning and swimming into the sea, ducking the breakers that eventually became swell in the vast and open ocean.

Vida went on until she couldn't, and they bobbed in the brine, treading water. Her lungs were on fire and her eyes were blurry and burning. There was no sight of land.

Exhausted, she flipped them onto their backs. 'Take deep breaths,' she told the girl. 'That way, you float.' Every now and again she tried to hold the girl up so that her small arms could rest, but it was no good.

She felt the cold, bloodless water wash over her face. It would be so nice just to let go, she thought. Just to sink to the bottom of the sea. On the ocean floor she would finally see the little mermaid and all her sisters in their gardens of coral, their flowers red as sunset. There she would find the white statue of the prince, and it would be Dyce, and she would kiss his undead face.

Her little girl would be fine. Wouldn't she? Didn't the mermaids have to turn into foam and become daughters of the air?

She sucked in the salt water until she coughed and began to sink. She tried to push the girl up toward the sunlight.

And then there came a pale hand diving down through the water.

It gripped Vida and the girl, and pulled them both up into the good, dry air. Not Renard – this hand still had all its fingernails, even if they had been bitten to the quick. It collared her and hauled her waterlogged weight onto a fiber-glass fishing dinghy, and then went back to retrieve the little girl, who rolled and coughed across her mother.

It was Garrett, with his goofy smile and his acne scars. It had to be him.

And Dyce, right there beside him, just as he was always meant to be. Behind them both, perched on the edge, was a scrawny woman who must be Bethie. She was cradling a baby. When she saw Vida studying her, she held the bundle out for approval.

'Vida.' Dyce smiled at her, and even in her half-dead state, Vida felt the lift of her heart at the warm sound of his voice. 'It's finally happening. We're off across the ocean to see what's on the other side. What do you think of that? You coming?'

But when she tried to speak, only water rushed out of her mouth, endlessly.

☠

Vida woke, spluttering. She lay and coughed and coughed, as if she was trying to rid herself of the thing in her chest that wanted to take her down with it.

It was dark here. She sat up and felt something in her stomach twinge. She pulled the sheet away so she could get a look at her leg, but there was no light. It felt tight – laced up, like a boot. She ran a hand down from her thigh to her ankle and felt the prickle of tied-off sutures like cactus spines. The flesh on either side was hot and raised, but that death smell – the smell of Renard, the secret smell that had attended her since they were in the plane's fuselage – was gone.

Ruth had fixed her, hadn't she? Her mother had sewn her, stitched her back into the story of her life. It hurt like nothing she had ever known before, and tomorrow it would start to itch like a brainworm, but for now, the bone-deep pain was receding like the tide.

She shuddered. That weird dream, with all of them on the sand, untying the blood knots of family.

She lay back down and tried to separate the dreams from the hard truth. She'd heard everything Ruth had said, but the words had drifted into her mind and settled in a messy heap that muddled space and time. Now she tried to sort them, picking up each sentence to examine the science of it.

One. She was pregnant.

That she could live with: she had chosen it for herself whether she had known it or not at the time.

Two. Renard was her father.

And she couldn't live with that.

33

Felix was exhausted by the time he was up and out of the sewer. He sat for a moment with his back against the dumpster and caught his breath, staring up at the rectangle of gray sky. It was cold out here and he'd had no time to go back for his jacket; inside, the dome buzzed with its own paranoid warmth, and it made a man forget what conditions were like outside.

He stood slowly and retraced his steps to where the old De Luxe was parked, its guilty vanilla stink still strong. He wanted to get out of the city, back to where there were trees and grass, something real enough to touch.

The keys were still there. Maybe leaving keys in ignitions was a sign of the trust and timidity of the Northerners, Felix thought. Or maybe the police were just quick and brutal. It didn't matter. He pumped the gas a few times before he turned the key. The car coughed but the engine rumbled. He backed it away from the building and headed back in the direction he thought was westward, looking for a road that would take him away from the shattered glass and sheer cliffs of concrete.

It wasn't easy. Some roads were blocked by rubble, others by the shells of cars. It was clear that these had been deliberately placed. The Resistance was making sure there was only a single route in and out: no one could happen upon the Capitol Building by chance. He tried to remember the way Adams had come in – the road signs and the buildings – and he found it, the maze that allowed a car-wide gap between burnt-out buses and chunks of concrete. He stopped the car a moment to memorize his position. He looked up at the broken spire of a church, and a billboard hanging askew from the side of a block of shops: IMPROVED FORMU, the writing said before it bled into the hair of a grinning woman. The left part of her face had peeled off, like she'd been scalped.

Felix drove on again, swerving around debris, searching for a sign that would point him to a bigger road, but straight away he had to jam on the brakes.

Up ahead was a white car, with a pronghorn buck strapped to the bonnet.

It looked abandoned.

He eased the De Luxe forward cautiously and parked parallel to the buck, then got out. It was a few days dead, its leg bones shattered, probably hit on a highway. That happened a lot. Road sense wasn't big either side of the Wall.

But despite its age, someone had been eating from it. There was a ragged cut along its stomach where the deep organs had been raided.

'Now that don't seem like a real Northern thing to do, does it?' Felix muttered. He inspected it from all sides and then scanned the streets.

He was rewarded. Out from a foyer ambled a white-haired boy, with a scraggly tabby cat on a piece of string. And Felix knew that face, despite the bloodied blouse and the dirt-caked trousers. He'd seen this boy before – outside his shack with a posse – and thought even then that the kid had seemed a little young to be out with a band of killers. When he got closer, the old man would see the killing eyes of the Callahans: Viking eyes, ice-blue. He would bet on it.

'Uncle Felix!' called the boy from across the street. He was waving.

34

By lunch all three volunteers were bleeding from their ears. Adams had reappeared with a fresh plaster on his cheek. He kept fingering the edges, like a boy irritating a scab. But he was back with a vengeance, briskly resuming captaincy so that Buddy had to step down, disgruntled. Adams's first order was to forbid the three volunteers to drink anything before one o'clock, so it was no surprise to the Southerners in the Capitol Building when the vomiting began.

When one of the tasters blacked out, Ruth was sent to insert some surgical tubing directly into his stomach, and they pumped in the tap water as fast as the cramps allowed. The two others gulped at water bottles. It was a kind of magic, thought Dyce, to watch their symptoms start easing immediately. There would be weeks of recovery now, but they would probably survive. Wouldn't they?

Just after lunchtime, Adams asked all three of them – Dyce, Ruth and Vida – to meet him in the war room.

'Really? He calls it the war room?'

'Oh, Mama. Just hear him out.'

'You aren't ready.'

Vida licked her cracked lips. 'I need to test my new leg, don't I? If I don't start using the muscles pretty soon, they're going to wither. Then I'll never walk down the aisle.'

Ruth grimaced at the joke. She knew she wasn't going to win. She fussed around her daughter, re-bandaging Vida's leg as tightly as she could. Then she went scrounging for crutches.

They limped crossways down the corridors. The pain made her sweat at first, but Vida kept telling herself to send her mind away. The building obliged with distraction. The heavenly scenes she'd glimpsed on her way in were real – frescos painted across the walls back when the Capitol Building was first built. White pioneers, rosy-cheeked and smiling, plowing the land and holding bushels of wheat, surrounded by the plenty that is industry's godly reward. Even the dogs that peered out from behind the wagons seemed happy. But Vida looked closer. The only people not smiling in the frescos were the Native Americans, offering food to the newcomers for the blankets that would spell their end.

Not a lot different, Vida thought as she shuffled down the hallway. America was built on viral warfare. The seeds of it lay dormant in the history: Renard had just given them a dark, moist place to sprout. And if they did manage to get rid of that fucker, another – worse – one might spring up in his place. What is wrong with us? she wondered. This is just the latest cycle. It's never, ever going to end. She felt the small being inside her womb like a stone.

When they got to the room, Adams had positioned himself like a magnate in his swivel chair, staring as though looking at the view, though the window was boarded up like all the others.

Dyce felt his chest tighten. This wasn't good. The man was gearing up to tell them something important, and that something looked to be unpleasant.

He helped Vida onto the leatherette sofa and then stood behind her, pretending to study the maps on the wall.

'First thing,' said Adams. 'I been away for a bit.'

'We noticed,' said Dyce.

'Sometimes I got to get away for a while. Do some strate-gizing. I need peace and quiet every now and again. Got me a room back there where I do my thinking.'

Dyce thought of madwomen in attics and lunatics chained in cellars. He watched Adams carefully.

'But enough about me. Dyce, boy, how're you feeling? You been drinking only the rainwater, right? Those mushrooms still doing their work?'

'The water tastes like birdshit. All good so far, but I got some insurance in case that changes.' Dyce patted the mushrooms in his pocket.

'Amen to that! Vida, I see you're hale and hearty. And Ruth, you are your usual charming self. So now, to business,' said Adams. 'We've all been waiting a long time now, you know that?'

'For what?' Vida asked. 'The Second Coming?'

Adams sighed. 'For the cure, my fighting friend. To put into action all the plans that we've worked so hard on for so long.' He waved a discolored hand at the maps. 'Don't you want to bring an end to all this? I do. And I'm going to be frank with you. It's confession time.'

This guy, thought Dyce, not for the first time, is not all there.

Adams stood up, untucked his shirt from his trousers and lifted it off over his head without undoing the buttons. Ruth folded her arms.

On Adams's bumpy hip was a series of tattoos, dark against his skin, a long row of them. Next to that was a cut that looked fresh, the edges rubbed black with ink.

'You seen these on anyone else yet?' he asked.

'No,' Dyce said carefully. He stepped closer to get a better look. 'What do they mean?'

'These are my sin stripes, buddy boy. Like boy-scout badges. Old and new, side by side.'

'Sins?'

'We're all sinners, I know, I know. But these are my special sins – the ones that I committed not because I chose them, but because of Renard and his dirty water. I drank his poison, people, day after day. He did this to me.' He smiled crookedly, and the plaster moved.

'I have other sins, ones from before the War, and those are mine alone. But these ones I kept track of, because I needed reminding. You get a good long look now, because each one of these came from a virus Renard gave me. A different one every time, because that was how he did it. I was one of the unlucky ones.'

Adams tapped his temple, and Vida caught herself beginning to feel sorry for him.

'You mean brain sickness? You one of those who get the crazies?'

Adams looked at her with his sad eyes. 'Even at the beginning I knew something was going bad. Other people didn't understand. The water helped cure them of whatever they were suffering – the fevers, the bleeding.

'But it didn't work for me. I guess some of us are resistant. You know a bit about that, I'll warrant. I drank that water the way they did – religiously, you might say – and still I could feel something changing. It wasn't fair. It was like things were crawling over my brain and I couldn't scratch them, you know? Inside my skull. Under the bone.'

'Are you saying it was the water, not the viruses?'

'I'm saying the water cures the viruses – mostly – but it also drives some people crazy. A side effect. Some say Renard meant it that way. When the population dips, like it did after the War, then sexual assaults go up. No coincidence, I'm telling you.

'So I want you to know how it worked out, and how I know what I know about ole Renard. Me, I did some things to try to make the brain stuff go away. Some pretty terrible things.'

Looks like he's just fine now, thought Vida. Looks like he's proud of some of those things.

'Now this one here,' Adams pointed a black-tipped finger at the first stripe on his hip, 'that's where I set my parents' house on fire. They didn't die in the blaze, though. This next one, I beat this guy who came to my door selling bags of dried peaches. He lived, so it's just a stripe. The next one, I stabbed a girl in my office in the eye with her pen: she didn't want to go out with me. I liked the taste of that one. Next, I raped my landlady one day when she returned my spare key.'

Vida's eyes were dry and sore. He was so matter-of-fact.

'And this fresh one here is from last night. While you all were sleeping, I was swinging a baseball bat at one of the scientists. I broke her arm in four places – just shattered it, like glass.'

Hope it was Jill, thought Ruth, and then washed the wish away.

Adams was spreading his hands across his flesh. There were stars like asterisks on that row. 'This last line is for murders. There's twelve. The first two are my parents, because they survived the fire but I shot them about a month after that. The itch, it came back, but at least they got to go together, right? The next bunch are strangers: that all happened around about the same time. It was a bad day. Then three policemen, soon after that, with a tire iron.

'But I want you to know, most are from a few years back. I can recognize the symptoms now, before it comes down real bad. I'm used to it. When I feel it coming on, I've got a place to go. They lock me up. I asked them to. But all these – I gotta own them, or else it will mean nothing.'

Dyce understood with a jolt that Adams was asking their permission, pleading with them. He wanted them to understand! He held Vida's hand tightly, ready to jump if they had to. But Adams was just staring off into space again, picking at the edge of the sticking plaster on his cheek. A corner came away and he grimaced with satisfaction as it peeled off.

Vida cleared her throat. 'Does it stop?'

'Does what stop?'

'The itch. When you . . . you know, hurt people.'

'Isn't that the most terrible thing? It does. It helps a lot. For a while there's just quiet – like white noise.' Adams shrugged.

They were all silent, listening for it.

'I got something else to show you.' He pointed to his face. The skin where the plaster had fallen away was curling like a leaf. 'You see this?' He stretched his jaw and they saw it very clearly – the ragged hole clean through his cheek. They could see the jagged line of his teeth clenched in an everlasting grin. When he spoke again, he whistled, the air being sucked through the gap like a man with a tracheotomy.

'That's what I got for fighting against the system. Hole in my head. Poetic justice, you might say. Soon as I knew it was the water, I stopped drinking it. And I was better for a while. I really was. But the thing was, then my body started to fall apart on me, the way everyone's is going to if they don't have the antidote. My flesh began to flake off my bones, in itty-bitty bits, like a . . . like a leper.'

'And now?'

'Now, it's a non-stop fight to build my resistance: both kinds. Don't get me wrong, I'm not afraid to die – but I'm sure as hell not going without Renard. We're both going to the hot place, but I'm just warming the seat for him.'

'Was there anyone else? Like you, I mean?' asked Vida.

'You mean hardcore bonko? What do you think? It affects people differently. Men, mostly. The testosterone starts talking. It never shuts up. Maybe it just takes what's already there and amplifies it.'

Vida thought of the man who had come sniffing around the plane when the traffic had dammed the highway.

'At least here in the building we can keep tabs on it. Folks go straight to the shackles if they start acting weird. Kind of like werewolves at that time of the month. Teaches you not to trust anyone. And that goes double for yourself. Still, shit happens, as the Good Book says. And it's going to keep happening if we don't do what needs to get done.'

Dyce knew where this was going, but Vida was still curious.

'What do you mean, "what needs to get done"?'

'Those donor substrates aren't working. You saw that, clear as day. Bottom line: what we need is some human tissue. Supply and demand. We got a lot of people to save.'

35

When the boy threw an arm around Felix, the old man stiffened, but then returned the embrace. It would have been heartbreaking not to: the kid was covered in scratches.

'Someone pull you through a bush backward?'

'Just about.' He thumbed at the scraggly tabby cat on the length of string. 'This is Linus.'

'Well, look at that. Linus. Feisty, ain't he? I used to have a cat. Dallas. Big old tuxedo.' Felix bent down and called the cat, but it stayed back, tight at the end of its leash. He stood again.

Kurt nodded. He looked keen and fit, despite the ridiculous blouse he was wearing, and Felix suddenly felt every hinge and knob of his ancient skeleton. Goddam! The boy reminded him of himself, going off to New York all those years ago with nothing but attitude.

'Uncle Felix, do you really remember me?'

'Kurt, ain't it? You were running with that Callahan posse.'

'Well, are you surprised to see me?'

'I've had a lot of surprises, kid. The way things have been shaping up, I might've guessed you'd be here, where the action is. You just happen to be passing through Des Moines?'

He knew the answer, but he wanted to see what story the kid would spin. From what he recalled, he had a tongue on him.

Whip-smart too, which set him a couple of rungs above the rest of his godforsaken family.

'Came looking. Heard news of you from a nice fat lady in a diner in Saratoga.' Kurt grinned and plucked at the blouse.

Felix suddenly realized why the tabby looked familiar. It was Norma's cat. He felt his stomach subside slowly. He swallowed his disapproval. 'I don't think I want to know the rest of that story, son.' There were a whole lot of bloodstains on that blouse, and they weren't Kurt's.

'Last two Callahans on the continent, you and me. Gotta stick together, right? I figured together we might do more damage than either of us alone.'

'That right? Well, right now I'm in need of a bit of nature. I been holed up in that there building too long, so I'm going to get some air. You care to join me?'

'Your car or mine?' Kurt asked, beaming.

Felix couldn't help smiling back at him. There was something wholesome about the boy, something blond and corn-fed and American that you didn't see a lot of these days. And who was to say how he'd really come by that cat? Maybe old Norma had been in a generous mood. That swan pendant wasn't hers, not that he could remember.

'How about we take a walk?'

The old Callahan and the young one set off in silence, the cat pulling now and again at the string, graceless and unwilling, but Kurt just yanked at the creature's throat and cursed until it got moving again. They passed boarded-up buildings, gutted fridges, mattresses vomiting stuffing. Felix was still getting used to the idea of privation in the North; all the housing concrete had got siphoned off into the Wall, and the rest of the infra-structure had sure suffered. The earlier buildings were mostly intact; it was the newer, shoddier ones that were crumbling. Oldies are goodies, he thought. Ain't that always the way?

They had reached the river.

'Here's as good a place as any.'

He eased himself down, and they sat with their legs dangling off the edge of a concrete platform – the foundation of a new bridge that would never be. The moss was encroaching. Felix looked out, wondering where to start. Sometimes it was all too much. A man lived with it best if he didn't think too hard. What would Kurt think of the tapes? Maybe if you were born into this world, there was no telling what was the old you and what the new. Like being born with a brain virus.

They stared at the water. In places the surface of the river was smooth, but in others it twisted and knotted – the brown and the gray blending – and it was hard to tell exactly where it first happened. A mess of sticks and plastic bags had caught on a submerged rock and a great blue heron stood on top of it, surveying the new world.

'That sad pronghorn your doing?'

'Found it like that.'

'You know much about them?'

'I know how they taste. I know where the liver is.'

Felix snorted. 'Good on you, son.' He studied the boy. Sometimes he forgot how smart the younger ones were, and that was a mistake that was going to cost him one of these days. He wasn't the only person in the South who had studied and watched and figured out how to survive. The truth was that the end of the world had a way of culling the slowest people; they were long dead. And they hadn't burnt all the books yet back at the Callahan place, Felix wagered. Maybe they weren't read a whole lot by the others, but Kurt looked like the kind of kid who'd had a lonely time of it. Felix knew how that was. Maybe that was what they had in common: they were loners. Books were trustworthy. You knew where you stood with them. They never changed, and they never got sick and left you to fend for yourself.

Kurt clocked the attention and shrugged. He was proud of his portable pantry.

'Pronghorns,' said Felix. It was the prelude to something. Kurt scrunched up his face and Felix knew what he was thinking: ninety per cent of everything anyone ever said was to hear their own voice. Did it matter? The kid didn't have to take it to heart. But it had to be said.

'You know, people reckon the way things are right now is the way they were always meant to be. It helps them to feel okay about what they did to get here. What do you think of that?'

Kurt couldn't give a shit either way, but he respected Felix enough to watch him carefully.

'Well, I don't think it's true,' said the old man. 'Take that pronghorn on your car. I had a book on them. A whole book all about them in my shack.'

'Was it a recipe book?' Kurt asked, and Felix smiled, then continued.

'Recipe for disaster, maybe. People showed up on this continent from fucking Italy, Columbus and his crew, and they look out at this new land and there's a goddam pronghorn running like the wind across the prairie. It's a fucking blur.' Felix raised his arm and shot a finger in a great arc. 'So these Eye-talians look behind it to see what's coming – because if something's running, then something's chasing – but there's nothing. There's nothing chasing it. Anyway, if you discover a new world, you expect some crazy shit. There's no need for explanation.

'Then comes Lincoln and Jefferson and everyone else, and then it's the twentieth century, and the scientists, the ones who wrote my book, they want to explain why the pronghorn runs away from nothing. For them, well, there's got to be a reason. So they set up their cameras. They see a mountain lion stalking down the talus, slinking low, getting close, then – wham! – it jumps and they're off. The chase, right. But compared to the pronghorn, the lion is treading water – slow as a turtle on crutches – and it gives up. The pronghorns are jumpy fuckers, so they keep running at top speed. Nothing on the continent can come close to catching them.

'But the scientists aren't satisfied. Why would the pronghorn have evolved to run twice as fast as the predators they're trying to escape from? They don't need that kind of speed to survive. But the scientists, they're thinking about the present. They think that right now is what counts.

'Then one guy has an idea: maybe they're running from something that used to exist, long ago. So they look in the fossil records, and sure as shit, there's an American cheetah – used to be, anyways. Bigger than the African kind, and fuckin' faster than greased lightning. How about that? Turns out the pronghorn's been outrunning a ghost for thousands of years.'

'Neat,' Kurt offered. The wind was blowing in off the water, and he reached out for Linus to hold the cat against his body.

'Son, what I'm saying is that sometimes things take the wrong path and we all just go on along with it. Instead of standing up, we say, "This is how it is, so this is how it was meant to be." All the while we're exactly like the pronghorns. You get what I'm saying?'

Again the shrug.

'What if Columbus arriving was that point, the place where

we left our proper path?' Felix waved his hand through the air, at the invisible pathogens that rode the currents. 'You know what that means? We're doing all of this to ourselves. We're running from the ghosts of things that stopped existing a long time ago. Know what I think? Maybe it's time to stop running and to start acting again.'

With his free hand Kurt peeled back a finger of moss that had grown in a crack. There were small, grayish beetles underneath. He flicked one out into the water.

Felix was done. He lay back and looked up at the sky, taking the air deep into his lungs. He was still not used to it.

'Okay, but what are you saying exactly?'

'I'm saying that seeing you today has cleared up some things. It was meant to be. Maybe it's time for us to put things right. Get back on track.' Felix paused. 'In that building back there, the one with the fancy domes' – he thumbed over his shoulder and Kurt craned his neck to get a look – 'there's a group of Northerners who're going to attack Renard and get rid of the viruses, once and for all. You'd be a good addition. What do you say?'

'Old man, I say what I always say: Fuck Renard!'

'That's what I figured. Now, I got something to show you.'

36

Dyce flinched. Supply and demand. Where had he heard that before? The fat guy. Ed. Down under the Mouth, in the tunnels where they farmed the mushrooms, forcing them back from death into life. Look how that had turned out.

Adams pressed on. 'There's no more time for trial-and-error with the mushroom production. We do it like you saw it in your caverns. Just like that. Seed the spores in someone while they're still alive, then harvest from the body.'

Ruth shook her head. 'I think you need some more time in the shackles.'

'But who's going to volunteer?' Dyce spoke up.

'We got us a compulsory volunteer yesterday. Northern patrolman who learnt our location. Hank Someone. There's no way we can let him go and there's no point in keeping him. Manna from heaven.'

They took a moment to digest the news.

'All's fair in love and war, right?' Adams wasn't really asking: he was explaining what he was going to do, and there was no avoiding it. They were technical consultants, and that was all. 'Now, I just need you to tell me again, without missing a single detail, about what you saw down in those mines so we can do this. We get one good shot. One batch should do it. We can end this now.'

Dyce looked over at Vida. She was touching her flaking lips with the tips of her fingers, the way people did when they were about to tell a lie.

'I can't be part of that,' he said, and she looked at him in surprise. Two days ago he'd have given anything for a shot at Renard.

Fuck. Was it the baby? Was this shit happening already? For Vida it was working the other way around. The idea of her child made her more willing than before to do whatever had to be done. One Northern death, when so many Southerners had already given up their lives, seemed like a good deal. Sacrifices. They all had to make them, right? And with a new generation to think about, she was doubly prepared to make them.

She tried to speak softly, but she knew Adams would hear everything anyway. It was like he was part of the building: nothing happened within its walls without his knowledge.

'Dyce? Can we just talk about this?'

He looked her straight in the eyes, fierce. 'You didn't see them, down there in the mines. The way they were lying. They'd been slaughtered. They died screaming, Vida. The kids too. That's on me, burnt in here.' He put a finger to his head and twisted it against his temple, as though he was trying to bore his own hole. 'And I can't let that happen again – to anyone.'

She shook her head, but she also felt herself softening.

Ah, fuck.

'But, Dyce, what else is there?'

'We'll think of something,' Ruth said. 'Don't we always?'

Adams cleared his throat. 'I appreciate the, ah, sentiment, but we don't have time for pussyfooting. This is the only way. Believe me – I've given it a lot of thought.'

Vida tried to intervene. 'Look. Isn't this patrolman good for information, at least? In the meantime, you could try growing the mushrooms from a . . . a corpse. That's their natural state, right? There must be cemeteries everywhere in Des Moines. If you're that desperate, you could dig up a body.'

'I look like a resurrection man to you? You're going to need to do some heavy persuading before ole Grizzly Adams reaches for the torch and the spade.'

Vida and Ruth exchanged a long look. Vida took a deep breath. 'Okay. Well, how about this? I have something that Renard would be very interested in getting his hands on. We could lure him out. And then, blammo. The end of Mister Fox.'

Ruth was nodding. 'We'd need a way of sending him the message, letting him know what it is. Like a carrier pigeon.'

It was Dyce's turn to be shocked. 'What the fuck? Lure Renard out? Are you serious? What do we have that he would possibly want?'

Adams's eyes shot from one to the other, traveled down Vida's body to her stomach, and then back up again. He smiled slowly.

'I see you have something to discuss among yourselves,' he said. His eyes were narrowed, but that permanent grin was in place. 'I'll give you five minutes, and then I'm coming back inside.' He got up and left the room, his shirt tucked neatly back into his pants, as if the revelation of his tattooed belly had never happened.

'You need to sit down,' said Dyce to Vida. 'You need to sit down right now and tell me what the fuck is going on with the two of you.'

'Vida, you want me to stay?' asked Ruth.

'Of course I want you to stay. It's your fault we're in this almighty fuck-up in the first place! In fact, how about you start, and I'll jump in?'

Ruth pursed her lips and turned to face Dyce full on. 'Maybe it's you who's going to need that chair, Allerdyce.'

'We're wasting time. Just tell me.'

37

Ruth lifted her chin. 'All right. You asked for it. Dyce, you know I used to work up North before the War. In the labs.'

'Vida told me all that stuff when we met. I don't hold it against you.'

'I'm not asking for your forgiveness. I've had a long life. When you have the same, you'll find out how it is.'

'Get on with it.' Dyce couldn't help himself. He knew this wasn't the way he ought to be speaking to Ruth. The worm turns, he kept thinking. The worm fucking turns, lady!

'I had an affair with Renard.'

'You what?'

'You heard me. We were lovers. He was married. That woman who got blown up in the toilets by one of the Callahans. Queenie.'

'Fuck. Me.'

She went smoothly on, and Dyce let her. 'I got pregnant, Dyce. I got pregnant by Renard and I stole some of the antidote he was working on: the panacea, he called it, like he hadn't been responsible for the viruses in the first place. I ran down South and I had the baby. Then I met Everett. The rest you know. I have spent my life waiting for Renard to track me down, but I'm not sorry I went.'

'Wait, wait, wait. Just wait one cotton-picking minute. What happened to the baby? Does Vida have a brother or a sister?'

Ruth shook her head slowly, watching Dyce in case he did something he couldn't come back from.

'Dyce.' Vida's voice was a whisper. She cleared her throat.

And then he did have to sit down. The seat was still warm where Adams had left it.

'My Christ. My sweet motherfucking Savior.'

'Dyce!'

'It's you, isn't it? It's you. You're Renard's daughter. Oh, my sweet, sweet jumped-up Jesus!'

Vida got over to him quite quickly in spite of the crutches. She set them aside and tried to take his face in her hands. Dyce kept turning away from her, but she wouldn't let him.

'Dyce. It's me. It's still me. Don't you think it was a terrible thing for me to find out too?'

'How long have you known? When did she tell you?'

'I'm standing right here,' Ruth snapped. 'I told her when she first arrived. When she was under. I couldn't let her go without her knowing. She could have died.'

'You think this is news to me? I fucking know she could have died! I was there!'

'Enough,' said Vida. 'It is what it is, Dyce, and we can't change it. But you know what? We can use it. We can use it to lure Renard into a meeting. It might be the only thing in the world that he still wants.'

'Lure? Lure? You have any idea what we're putting on that hook?'

Vida nodded, exasperated. 'Dyce. This is what we've been talking about since the beginning. What do you think "Fuck Renard" really means?' She held his arms. 'You've got your mushroom nightmares, and I've got mine. Well, I'm tired of being scared to fall asleep. And I'm tired of waking up to this shit too. What'll life be like with Renard still in charge? Just think about it. No reward without risk, right? This is the risk. He can't refuse!'

Adams had stuck his head around the door.

'All clear?' His eyes darted among them, calculating, and they all heard his breath hissing in and out through the hole in his cheek. 'Okay,' he said. 'What's the buzz? What have you got that Renard can't refuse?'

Vida let Dyce's arm go and pointed at her belly. Dyce felt the blood rushing away from his face.

38

Hank lay on his side on the floor in the dark. After the beating, they hadn't bothered to shackle him, though he saw there were rings attached to the wall, like old-time slavers'. There'd been screaming in the night – shrill, so that he couldn't decide whether it was a man's voice or a woman's. 'I'll kill you!' it kept saying, over and over. And then there was the thumping – a body slamming against a door, he guessed. It seemed to him as though it was just a matter of time before the wood of that barrier broke and the monster would be at his door – and then on him: a worse monster than the ones who had beaten him.

But patrolmen were chosen for their grit. And also, the screaming had stopped. In the blessed, quiet dark, Hank had given in to his concussion. You sent your mind away, he knew that, when it was in danger of being broken or lost forever. It wasn't weakness.

'Live to fight another day,' he murmured.

And Hank knew it was another day when he was woken by the sounds of industry that carried through the building – the metered vibrations of footfalls, the mutter of distant voices. The normality of it reminded him of the patrol station, and he was buffeted by homesickness. He even missed that bitch who was always screaming at them to close the door. By God, his head hurt!

Now the latches clunked open one by one, and Hank felt his heartbeat speed up in protest. When the door opened, four people came in. The one in front carried a hurricane lamp that made their shadows dance on the walls like demons until they closed the door behind them.

Hank knew what happened behind closed doors.

He sat up fast, his head ringing.

The little group that was inspecting him wasn't in much better shape than their shadows. The leader was a grisly white man with a hole clean through his cheek. Behind him was a dark-skinned girl on crutches, her leg bandaged and outsized, like someone had stuffed the thing to make it look normal again but had failed. Now and again she leant against a guy, young and pale and so tired he was rocking on his feet. The smudged growth of stubble gave his age away. He was the kind one, Hank marked. The weak link. The last one was a tiny woman with fierce lines around her mouth. Hank had seen enough in his years as a patrolman to know not to fuck with someone who looked that way, woman or man, old or young. You earned those lines; they didn't come free.

The leader began, his voice hollow. 'Hank Simmons? That you?'

There was no sense in lying. They'd find out, and then they'd lay into him again. Shatter something this time. And who was he being loyal to anyway? Hank sniffed.

'Yeah,' he said, and Vida saw how bad the recent hammering had been. Blood from Hank's nose had turned to scabs, and they clung to his moustache like ticks.

'Let me fill you in, then. When you escaped, you got our guy real good. Because of you, one of my best men, my best marks- man too, Otis, got eight stitches in his tongue – and enough alcohol to float the *Titanic*. He's bandaged up like a mummy. He worked with you at your precinct, undercover Resistance, and you didn't even know. He's still out now, otherwise he'd have been here too. And you're lucky he's not.

'But it's not Otis I'm interested in right now. It's you, my fine friend. Sit up and take note of these good people. On the crutches here is Vida, and over there is Dyce.' The leader gestured theatrically, and the others nodded, silent. 'But most important for our purposes is this lady here: Ruth. Say hello to Ruth, Hank Simmons.'

Hank edged his back against the wall properly, so he could sit up straight to face whatever was coming. He hadn't known that he'd pissed himself at some point in the night, and now his trousers clung cold and heavy on the backs of his legs.

'Now, I 'spect you're wondering why I dragged them all down here when we got so much to do. Well, these kind folks just had an idea that might save your sorry life. How does that sound? Am I selling it right?'

'Depends,' Hank said. His voice was a nasal snuffle through the damage.

'Well, keep an open mind and don't go anywhere. That's all we're asking.'

Ruth came closer, impatient with Adams's grandstanding. Men. They loved the sound of their own voices.

'Actually, Mister Simmons – that's not all we're asking. We have something that Renard would be very interested in. And we need to set up a meeting with him – in person. You reckon you can do that?'

Hank snorted, then winced. It hurt like hell.

'A face-to-face with Renard? No way. That never happens. Doesn't matter who you talk to. He knows better than that.'

'Look.' She was trying to make her voice kind, but Hank heard the iron in it. 'We're a hundred per cent sure that what we have is something he wants. He'll meet us – that part is none of your business – but we need to know whether you can pass the message along to him. Put us in touch.'

Hank coughed into his fist and cleared his throat of the blood and phlegm. 'What is it? What have you got?'

'It's none of your concern right now,' Dyce echoed. Though his vision was still blurry and the lantern swung, Hank saw that he didn't have the same fire as the others. The boy sounded like he was just going through the motions. A coward. If Hank had been planning his second escape, that was the guy he would have gone through first.

'You'll have to tell me what it is if you really want me to do this. How am I supposed to pass on a message if you won't tell me?'

'Whiny motherfucker,' commented Adams mildly to Ruth. Bad cop.

'Give him a chance,' she said. Good cop.

Adams shrugged and sighed. 'Okay, then. How about this? We have his daughter. And his grandchild.'

Hank snorted a laugh, then coughed again and held his ribs. They had probably been cracked, but there was nothing a person could do about that except strap them up and pray.

'Grandchild? Now you're shitting me. Old man doesn't have kids. It's kind of his thing – you know, like that song?' Hank hummed through his nose. 'Hitler only had one ball. The War was the only time Renard didn't shoot blanks – you never heard that one?'

'Well, he got one shot off. So tell me: what do you need to set this up?'

'Renard didn't get where he is by being stupid. I'm not sure he'll bite.'

'It's not a trick,' said Vida, quick and intense. 'It's real.'

'As I mentioned,' said Adams, looking at her until she was quiet, and then turning back to focus on Hank, 'you can set it up, or you can find out what being buried alive feels like. I know which I'd prefer. You going to do it or not?'

Hank thought. Live to fight another day, he said to himself. 'I'll need a phone.'

'Good,' said Adams. 'It's settled, then.' Hank watched in fascination as the lantern light glinted off his exposed molars. 'Be ready. And now we will leave you to your beauty sleep.'

He led the others out and the bolts were shot again, leaving Hank alone with the perennial darkness.

He slid back down flat on the floor. His head didn't hurt so bad when he lay still. He stared up at the low ceiling, trying to force his eyes to see the shadows – and then trying to force his eyes to stop seeing them.

39

Adams was patting the deadbolts on the door of the holding cell, checking them methodically.

'You win this one. Luring Renard out was the one thing we wouldn't ever have a handle on. So high-fives to you for that. If it works.'

Dyce smiled, but Adams was shaking his head. 'I'm still not waiting around for the antivirals, though. Digging up corpses is bullshit. But now that I think about it . . .' He stopped with his hand on a bolt. 'You know, I've just had an idea.'

Vida swapped a look with Dyce.

Adams grinned. 'Let's go and talk to the nice folks about sacrifice and commitment and all-for-one, shall we? Come and watch how it's done.'

Ruth stopped, then turned to Vida. 'I'm going to lie down,' she said, and Dyce was sure she was lying. She climbed a staircase and was gone.

Dyce tried to help Vida along, but she shook him off and leant on the crutches. 'I have to practice.'

Adams was leading them down to the central atrium. 'This isn't a speech for the podium. I need to be close. Find me something to stand on.'

Dyce looked around. 'Like that?'

There was a Budweiser crate that the Southerners had been using as a table.

'Thank you,' said Adams.

He spun the crate around like a gunslinger and turned it upside down in the very center of the floor. Above him the clouds and sky painted on the inside of the dome had been steadily blackened by the smoke.

He looks like he has a message from the devil, thought Vida. Damn, he actually likes this stuff! She glanced around. How many of the Northern Resistance were people who'd been on the sidelines in their old lives? Fighting Renard had given them a purpose.

Adams heaved himself up on the crate like a circus bear and began talking.

'This is not a meeting,' he called out. He was making sure that his voice rang up and out, into the three empty stories of the vault above, like the word of God. 'We all know meetings are for official Resistance purposes – but this is not official. I just have a question for you all. Go and get your friends and bring them here.'

The passers-by hurried to spread the news, and people began to crowd the banisters a floor above and to feed into the foyer to sit cross-legged around him. It was not long before the place was full. People wanted a distraction: they left their daily chores, some still wearing their aprons. Others were covered in dust, wiping their faces. A row of women held babies to their breasts – the next generation, thought Vida, like my baby. If they survive.

'The Sermon on the Mount,' she said to Dyce. 'Brace yourself.'

He nodded. Here it came.

'I'm going to tell you all the truth, because I think you deserve it,' Adams began. 'Our first round of mushrooms failed, as I'm sure you have all heard by now.' There was a hum of acquiescence.

'So we're moving on to Plan B, and it's not pretty – but it is necessary. I want you to know that there are people right now digging in the Des Moines Cemetery.' He held up a hand to forestall any comment, but there was a definite underground hum.

'That's a lie,' whispered Vida. 'He hasn't sent anyone out to the cemetery.'

'Now, I know how that sounds,' Adams went on. 'This isn't fun for anyone. But we need something closer to the human, uh, form.' He waited for the persistent murmuring to die back.

'And there is no guarantee that this will work either. In fact, I'm going to go out on a limb here and say that it probably won't.'

Vida caught a ponytailed woman still in her lab coat nudging the man who stood next to her. Bullshit, her face said.

'What I'm asking for is not going to be easy. People: we need a live volunteer,' Adams said. 'In the Bible days they had a name for someone who was willing to die for the cause. A martyr.' He lifted his arms and raised his voice over the horrified commentary that was emerging more loudly from the crowd.

That hole in his cheek wasn't bothering him none now, thought Dyce.

'This is not something I ask lightly. Believe me when I say I didn't get a lot of sleep last night. But just hear me out. A single living person will allow us to have enough antiviral mushrooms in about two days from now. Guaranteed. I don't know about you all, but I'm sick of waiting. I know some of you will be saying, "We can wait and we must wait. We have discovered this holy grail and we must not be ungrateful. We must not be greedy or hasty or impatient." But haven't we all been patient long enough? Too long?'

Vida expected someone to shout: Preach! But now there was only silence.

'We have shown that we can be patient. We will wait while Renard increases his strength. Maybe the next round of mushrooms will work – or the next!

'But maybe' – Adams lowered his voice, soothing now instead of operatic – 'that won't work either. And then I will be up here asking this same question. But the next time it will out of desperation. And whoever volunteers then might feel forced by the weight of the moment instead of the goodness of their heart.' His voice dipped still lower, intimate and confiding. I feel your pain, said that voice. Why not make it stop?

The crowd swayed a little. Even Vida felt the tidal pull. What was it all for, anyway, this stubborn clinging to life? She hadn't ever really considered why she wanted to live in a place that had been gutted like a skeleton of all the things that made existence comfortable, or rich, or various. There was just some fierce urge, like blue-green algae on the floor of the ocean – or like spores on the membranes of a dying man.

Adams was getting to the good bit. It was weird, but his words were completely clear now that he was worked up. 'But there might be someone special among you, someone who is ready, someone who hears my words as a calling, as an answer to a life that has trickled away in disappointment and loss. A life without loving family or meaningful work. Maybe you have lost your true love; maybe you have lost your dog.' The audience tittered, but it had hit home, as it was meant to. Pets belonged in a softer, more indulgent universe, and Adams was doing more than tugging on people's clammy heartstrings. He was raising their childhood ghosts – calling them up and parading them so that all the things buried in the overgrown recesses of memory were held blinking up to the light.

Pavlov, thought Dyce, and looked at Vida, knowing she was thinking the same thing. Adams was a resurrection man, though you wouldn't catch him with his own hands in the graveyard dirt. No 'bout-a-doubt it.

Adams was shaking his head in sorrow at what he was being forced to do, the parent who must discipline his wayward children for their own good, out of love. This hurts me more than it hurts you, Dyce thought, and snorted.

'People, if I don't ask now, the opportunity will be gone. And so I lay it here before you. I expect you all to leave this gathering now and go back to your tasks. But do as you think fit, my friends. Think long and hard about it. Remember that each small action is part of a much greater reaction against Renard, and we must all make sacrifices.'

'Except you,' whispered Dyce. 'I don't see you making no sacrifices, asshole.'

Vida shushed him.

'The day is near. I promise you that. Go, now, and savor the anticipation.'

The crowd didn't move. The words had struck deep.

'Go on!' said Adams, pretending to shoo them like chickens. 'Go on now!'

And there it was – a hand had shot up in the crowd. Vida saw the smile flickering across Adams's face, a benediction. Every head in the room turned to see who it belonged to – someone obscured by the mess of bodies.

'I'll do it,' a voice called, and there was a cheer.

Vida spotted the baseball cap as Buddy was lifted off his feet on a sea of hands. She gripped Dyce's arm.

Shit. What was really going on here?

'All right!' called Adams over the applause. 'Let's give Buddy another round!'

It rolled around the room, the relief and the joy.

Adams calculated how long it ought to last, and then he said, 'Thank you, everyone. I hope you all feel proud of what we've achieved here today. You can go back to your work now. Those who are off duty are to go to the ammunition room. We'll start cleaning and oiling. It's the beginning of the end, people. T minus two days, and counting.'

The crowd dispersed quickly, a new sense of purpose sending them marching to their duties. Buddy's back was repeatedly clapped, his cap tapped; people wanted to touch him for luck.

40

Adams got down at last from the crate and put his arm around Buddy's shoulders, the man hot and flushed with excitement. Adams leant in and spoke the words against his reddish ear. 'Meet me here in an hour. Go get a smoke; ask someone for a blow job. Right now the world is your fucking oyster.'

He turned and left, and Buddy was alone, his mouth turning down like a child's. He touched his baseball cap for luck, and Dyce saw that his hand was shaking.

'Need some company?' Dyce asked him. Buddy nodded, and they followed him as he moved up the stairs and along the plush corridor. The crutches were clunky, and Dyce propped Vida up as they went. This time she let him.

Buddy was outpacing them pretty rapidly, a man with a purpose. It looked as if he was making his way to one of about a hundred broom closets behind the buff-colored doors. Then he seemed to choose one at random and dodged inside.

When they caught up with him, he was already drinking homebrew straight from a bottle, and the stench of alcohol made the flesh on Vida's leg shrink in surgical memory. The air vent gaped in the dimness: he'd hidden a stash there.

'You don't have to do this,' Vida said. She was breathing hard against the pain in her leg, and she couldn't see clearly in the gloaming of the closet. She'd have to use Dyce's eyes again.

Buddy stopped drinking for a second without lowering the bottle. Then he closed his eyes and swallowed another mouthful. When he spoke, his teeth were stained maroon, like a vampire's. 'You come to give me my free blow job? Because if not, you can fuck off,' he said.

'Jesus, man,' said Dyce. 'We're concerned. What are you doing?'

'Don't take the Lord's name in vain,' said Buddy, and leant against the wall. At least he'd stopped chugging that disgusting brew. 'And guess what, travelers? I don't fucking want to talk about it. It's too late for any of that.' He reached his hand into the vent and produced a carton of cigarettes still wrapped in cellophane. He punctured it like a lung, and wiggled out a cigarette. 'Now get out of here. You're killing my buzz.'

'Buddy,' said Vida. 'Adams is bluffing. You must know that. He's not going around digging up bodies, for Christ's sake.'

'I said no more blasphemy. Not now. And I know that. He knows that I know that. So just leave it alone.'

'But I don't think you know what you're doing,' Dyce pleaded, and his voice broke a little, the way it used to with Garrett. 'I saw the way those people died. There were mushrooms growing out of their eyes, Buddy. Exploding from their chests. It was pain like you've never seen. Torment. That's what you'll go through.'

'Good.'

'Good?'

'You're the one who doesn't understand. You and your little lady here. You want to understand? You want to know my reasoning? All right.' Buddy clamped the cigarette between his lips and started unbuttoning his shirt, bottom to top so that they saw his stomach first.

'Ah, Christ.'

'What did I tell you about the Lord's name?'

'Oh, Buddy.'

Fuck.

So many tattoos: a myriad stripes and crosses and asterisks, like the cross-hatched shadows of the comics Vida used to read. And they'd thought that Adams's tattoos were bad. The idea that they had traveled with this man for days – slept near him in the plane's fuselage, let him into their personal space – made the spit dry up in her mouth.

'I'm the reason you lock your doors,' said Buddy. He wasn't boasting. It was a fact.

He wasn't finished, either. At the top button, he pulled his shirt off. Vida was squinting in the closet's dimness, but Dyce could see plain as day.

Every inch of Buddy's skin below his neck was covered with marks, some freshly scabbed, some old and faded.

Then he reached up and took his cap off.

Across his bald scalp were more etchings. Hundreds of them, Dyce saw. Maybe thousands.

41

Felix groaned as he climbed out of the sewer, feeling the squeeze of Kurt Callahan hot on his heels. In and out, he said to himself. In and out the dusty bluebells – wasn't that how it went? You will be my darling.

Yup, he wasn't the man he used to be, but it was good pain, the kind that came with knowing what you were doing next. And Kurt had a lot to do with that. Felix chuckled to himself. I am about to blow your cotton-picking mind, Sonny Jim.

They worked their way out of the shattered bathroom and up into the atrium, like they were minor demons ascending the circles of hell. It was too quiet, though. Felix wondered whether the place was deserted – had the revolution happened without him? – but then there was the clang of pans from the kitchen. When he stood still and listened, trying not to show Kurt how much his chest was heaving, there was also the hum of people moving.

He didn't have to worry. The boy was transfixed. He'd never seen anything like it before in his short life, had he? Callahans got no time for fancy woodwork and portraits on the walls. They had never been high and mighty, and they sure weren't about to start. The structures in Glenvale were cottages at best; the whitewashed church was probably the finest piece of architecture Kurt had laid his young eyes on.

But this monument to prosperity, with its murals and gilt and arching stairways, must be making the boy think he'd died and gone to heaven.

Felix nudged Kurt's boot with his foot. 'Come on. You're catching flies.' He led the way up the plush staircase. Kurt bent down and scooped up the cat, who had for once consented to lie still for the ascent, ears laid back, but who now needed to be back on his string.

The two Callahans joined the back of a snake of people, and as Felix peered further along the corridors, he saw that they were lined with Northerners.

'Whoa, now.' He dropped back and held a hand across Kurt's chest to make him stop. 'Looks like we got ourselves mixed up in some kind of Mardi Gras here, buckaroo.'

There was a line of scientists making their way to the prison cells, carrying trays of mushrooms under the domes of old Pyrex dishes like bell jars. Some kind of procession: they were walking quietly but looking mighty pleased with themselves, Felix thought.

He nudged a woman. 'What's going on?'

She ignored him and kept following, her eyes never leaving the groups in their lab coats. It was a little too much like an old-time lynching, Felix thought. He shrugged.

'Looks like we're going to have to do our own detective work.'

He scanned the passage. They weren't hard to see, the Southerners – Vida on crutches, Dyce with his worried puppy eyes. He couldn't see leathery old Ruth with the mouth that always turned down, but Pete and Sam were there, and other faces Felix recognized.

Felix made his way over, trying not to limp, aware of how old the boy made him seem in comparison, with his jerky energy and his white bullet head and that frigging zombie cat of plump old donut-serving Norma's. Jesus. Why hadn't it died of fright yet?

Felix led Kurt to where Dyce and Vida rested against a wall, then stood before them and puffed his chest out. 'Look,' he announced, 'this is Kurt Callahan. Found him out in the city. Can you believe it? One of our own. He's come to join us. Any objections?'

Dyce eyed the boy. He didn't look right around the eyes. There were plenty of people these days without the human light in them, but Kurt's gaze was completely flat. Like something from the swamp, thought Dyce. That's it. A big old daddy gator, snout above the surface, bulletproof, greedy, and cruising for a kill.

Then Dyce spotted the pendant around Kurt's skinny neck. It looked real familiar. For a moment he thought it was the swan pendant he'd carved and given to Garrett, who in turn had given it to Bethie as a love token.

It couldn't be, though, could it?

Kurt noticed him looking and tucked the necklace inside his makeshift shirt. He looked steadily at Dyce and then blew him a kiss.

42

A crew of men was checking the cell, making sure the walls and windows were airtight. As Dyce watched, they searched and stuffed, wedged torn strips like burial cloths into the gaps in the boarded windows, and rubbed lard over the places they felt the breath of cold air. It made him dizzy with déjà vu: this was exactly what he and his family had done when the bad sicknesses blew in. He shuddered. Poor Gracie, pale and dead on the sidewalk, her knees up and her panties on display for all to see, the bag of ground beef bleeding out beside her.

Vida leant on him. I'm here, that shoulder said. Ruth was back standing near him too, the three of them on the same side for once. He thought if he ever fell that she would probably catch him. Or at least not let him smash his brains out on the ground. She was his family now, by blood but also by choice.

Dyce shook his head to clear his memory and put his arm around Vida so she wouldn't have to lean on the crutches. Those people – Gracie, Garrett, every person he had ever known – were all gone. It had happened, and there was nothing he could do about it now. If you wanted to be free you had to walk past those things you'd hoped never to see again. Dyce waited. It was Buddy he was curious about. How did other people live with themselves?

'Talk of the devil,' he said softly, and Vida nudged him.

'Blasphemy. Remember how tight-ass he was about that stuff?'

But Buddy made a sorry devil. Adams had gone to meet him in the foyer, and it was clear that he was drunk enough to sway, the stink of cigarettes clinging to him like a censer. Adams said something quiet and deliberate in his ear, and the little man nodded. Adams backed away. Buddy balanced on one unsteady foot and began to undress. The red HARRIERS cap came off first. Vida realized she was going to miss him: the ready chatter but also the protection he had offered. He was the only person in this building who cared about what happened to her.

It was really happening. He was really going to die here. Not today, maybe, but soon.

Buddy stood naked. He didn't even try to hide his privates. He was beyond embarrassment now. Beyond shame, even. It was the quietest Vida had ever heard the Capitol Building: people were transfixed as he stripped, as if the tattoos were Bible verses, and Buddy was the Word made flesh.

The etchings ranged wider than she and Dyce had been allowed to see, as if they'd spread like blood poisoning in the dark – not pictures, but an alphabet of pain. The record marks crawled down his thighs and around to his buttocks, and she had to blink them away when they made her eyes blur. It was as if they had taken on a life of their own – or taken on Buddy's life in exchange for the terrible things he'd done.

Yet this was still the same gentle man who'd rescued them, mild and calm in the face of their agony and distress. Wasn't it?

She looked around at the other witnesses from where she'd hobbled into a small space, guarding her leg against the shoving. There must be some people here who had been at the receiving end of some of his atrocities. Vida studied the faces in view, but they were blank, expectant. Relieved, maybe? Was Buddy right? Maybe they weren't his own sins: they were Renard's, and Buddy had been a vector, the way the viruses needed carriers to replicate and spread.

No, Vida decided, and there was a tiny flutter under her navel, as if the fetus was pleased. We all decide what to do with the hand we're dealt. You get what you get, and you don't get upset.

The cell was ready. Now Adams was leading Buddy up the staircase, around the muffled atrium and through the Senate Chamber. Here and there hands reached out to touch Buddy as he went past, like there was magic that might rub off. When he passed Dyce, he didn't look up, but they saw the dark splashes on the floor where his sweat or tears had dripped. Dyce thought again of the bag of mince, and Gracie flopped next to it. FEAR NOT, her sampler had said. FEAR NOT, FOR I AM WITH YOU.

'You don't have to do it,' Dyce blurted, but Buddy was streaming tears, being urged on by Adams, and he staggered past. The rest of the Northerners peeled away from the walls as he went, a growing throng as well as an armed guard, making sure he would see his promise through. They didn't really care if it worked, Vida thought. They just wanted someone to do something. It felt like action; it felt like progress.

At the door to the cell, Adams stopped and held Buddy by the shoulders. 'We've done our best to think of everything. Take a look. There's even a couch.'

The little man shook his head, but he looked Adams in the eyes.

Adams went on. 'You're a good man, Buddy. You're a better man than me. Now the end has come, and it is your chance to end the suffering for us all, to put things right, to restore the order of things.' He paused, his voice changing from death-row priest to old friend and conspirator. 'There is no more to fear.'

Buddy blurted a sob and a rope of mucus dangled suddenly from his stricken face. Vida thought of Stringbeard, the woman who had spent her last days looking for her ghost dog, all the lost people, the ones driven mad by the hopelessness of their new world, their bonds to the people who loved them worn through by Renard. He had a lot to answer for, that fucker. He didn't know how much – questions about her own life, and questions about the way the world had turned out. And she was going to get the chance to ask them.

Adams was wiping Buddy's face with a frayed handkerchief. He stuffed it back in his pocket and held the little man by the shoulders.

'This is where we must part ways, my friend. It's time for you to go in there. We're real proud of you. And we're counting on you. All of us, we're counting on you. Now listen carefully. When the door is locked, feel around for the bowls. We set out as many mushrooms as we could find. We've covered them to keep the spores from floating around. Lucky they grow so fast! What you got to do, you got to uncover those mushrooms like it's a fancy restaurant and you've ordered the steak tartare. Then you just sit back and breathe deep. They'll come to you.'

Like a gas chamber at the dog pound, thought Dyce. Like a fucking gas chamber! Who volunteers for that? It was just plain wrong.

Buddy sniffed and Adams added quickly, 'There'll be air and everything now, but you won't be getting the water tomorrow. We can't prolong it. You won't suffer. It'll be like going to sleep. Wouldn't you like that?' He squeezed Buddy's shoulder again, but now that the man was calmer, he seemed to have nothing to say. Vida had heard about it happening with snakes and rabbits: a kind of death dance where the victim accepted its fate and waited, quivering, for the end. But this: she didn't buy it. Surely a person should fight until they couldn't? Wasn't that what Ruth had taught her? Buddy wasn't even saying goodbye, like his mind was already somewhere else where it couldn't be touched. He crossed over the threshold and was swallowed by the dimness of the cell.

'I'll see you on the other side, my brother,' Adams announced, as if the scene called for some coda, and then he closed the door, fast. Vida saw how he used his full weight on the deadbolts so there was no way that Buddy could change his mind at the last moment. He beckoned some helpers – had they also been there all along? – and they busily began to seal the door with grease, pressing it into the breathing cracks.

While they were working, Adams turned to the crowd; he was the reverend again.

'Today he breathes spores. Tomorrow he breathes a virus. The next day we will be ready. Go now and prepare yourselves!'

'Amen! On the third day, our Savior shall rise!' whispered Vida into Dyce's ear. He grimaced behind the head of the person in front of him, careful not to let Adams see him do it. The guy was as bad as Renard – as ruthlessly single-minded.

Or worse, maybe. If you wiped out everything in the world, you only had to do it once. But redemption: that needed repeating.

The halls emptied as the residents of the Capitol Building went back to their work, mildly stunned. Vida watched them at their tasks, waiting for the flow of human traffic to ease. Most people were filling gas tanks or packing rations or checking weapons for rust. They worked shoulder to shoulder, but no one spoke beyond what was necessary in order to get things done. There was something sickening about it, thought Vida, that reverence and relief that came when someone else told you what to do, when everyone was working for one purpose.

They made their way back in a daze to their quarters, and Ruth made Vida lie down so that her dressing could be changed. The wound was crusty and yellowing, but there was no sign of septicemia.

Vida lay staring at the cherrywood ceiling, imagining what they were all imagining: Buddy alone in that cell, the dish lids removed from the mushrooms, the spores escaping to fill the air till it grew thick as soup. They listened in the quiet for the distant coughing.

It would be like drowning, Dyce thought. Just like that.

43

'Good day. Secretary to the President's office.' The woman who answered had clearly been trained to smile when she talked.

Hank had to clear his throat. 'Hello, ma'am. I know how this is going to sound, but I have a very important message for Renard. I mean, for President Renard.'

'How did you get this number, sir?'

'No, no. Sorry. I'm not a . . . a civilian. I'm a patrolman. Badge number 7798-RG. You can check that if you want. I got it from the head of policing at the Casper station – Jules Priory? Badge 4498-RH. This is, uh, of the highest priority. Top secret and really, really urgent. Can I speak with him?'

'I'm sorry, sir. What you're looking for is public relations. I'll give you the number. Do you have a piece of paper?'

'Ma'am? You don't understand. It's a personal matter. Of a highly personal nature. Life-and-death-type situation.'

'Patrolman, you should know that no one speaks directly to the President. But if you call the public relations department and leave your name and number . . .'

Hank was rubbing his forehead, over and over. 'Can I at least tell you the message?'

'Sir—'

He blurted out, 'He has a daughter! President Renard, I mean.' The secretary was silent. Hank tried again. 'And that's not the end of it. She's pregnant now – all grown up, of course – and he needs to know he's going to be a grandfather!'

'Sir, how did you come by this information?'

'Just tell him the name. Will you do that? Ruth Vambane. She was a sister in the labs. Just tell him the name.'

'Sir, I—'

'Lady, there's no protocol for this. I realize that, but it's true. And I wouldn't be taking this chance if I thought that information was untrustworthy. The President needs to know!' He lowered his voice – not a threat, exactly, but close. 'If you don't pass this along, well, I don't see him being too happy about it.'

The secretary was silent. Hank tried to imagine what she looked like, but the smile in her voice was long gone, and there were no other clues.

'Come on,' he wheedled. 'Just take my number down. If she turns out to be a screwball he needs to know that too. Take it down and then tell him that name and just see what he says. Deal?'

She sighed, and Hank felt his heart swell with relief. 'What's the number?'

'0339714895. And it's Ruth Vambane.'

'Is that all you want to say?'

'That's it, I think. And thank you. Thank you so much! You're doing the right thing.'

Hank hung up the phone, his hands wet with nerves. They were all staring at him from the other side of the desk: Adams, Ruth, Dyce and Vida, the crutches leaning against the wall.

'I did it, all right?'

'Okay, Hank,' said Adams. 'Good job. Ruth, you're up next. When this phone rings – and Hank better hope it does – you're answering. You remember where and when you're going to meet?'

'Yes,' Ruth said. They watched her swallowing hard, readying herself to go toe-to-toe with her guilty past. Not a lot of people got that chance, did they? she told herself as she patted her hair. 'Don't be stupid. Of course I remember.'

Adams called out for someone to take Hank back to his cell. Luck or planning meant that it was Otis who arrived, Native American heritage strong in his veins, his dark face set in its hatchet lines. He was going to walk stiffly for a couple of days, and the bandages wrapped under his chin and around his head weren't coming off any time soon. His dark hair was still matted with dried blood.

'Go easy on him, Otis,' said Adams. 'We might still need him. Life is unpredictable, isn't it, Hank? And try not to let him go this time. Shame on me and all of that.'

Silently Otis took Hank by the arm and the two of them went out together, companions in injury and resentment.

'Now we wait,' said Adams. He moved around the table and took up the seat where Hank had been. He lifted a leg and rested it on the corner of the table, master of his domain.

It must have been about fifteen minutes by Dyce's reckoning, but it felt longer. The phone shrilled. By the second ring Adams had jumped up out of his seat, offering it to Ruth with an exaggerated bow.

She grimaced and reached for the receiver, and for a moment it felt too heavy to lift. She forced her fingers to grip the handset and press it to her ear, where Renard's breath rasped against her head like the sea. Her voice was weak and she hated herself for it.

'Hello.'

'Ruth?'

It was him. Of course it was. His voice hadn't changed, even after all these years. She'd heard it in her secret, violent dreams – and they were all nightmares, Renard had seen to that. She'd run as far as she could and yet here she was – trapped into par-leying with him again.

'Speaking.'

'Is it true? About the girl?' His voice was shaky, and that was worse.

'It's true.'

'Ruthie, you ran away. You took her away from me.' He sounded like he was going to cry, and Ruth didn't know if she would be able to bear it.

She twisted her finger in the phone cord and made her voice cold. 'I did what I thought was best for her.'

'So why call me now?'

'It wasn't my idea. She wants to meet you. She's all grown up and, Didier, she's pregnant. She wants to meet the grandfather of her child. Try and put her family back together.'

'Ruth. Ruthie.' He was crooning at her, a man trying to make a little girl sit on his knee. 'What have you told her about me?'

'Nothing. She didn't know about you until a few days ago. You think I'm proud of it? She wants to meet you. I can't stop her. I told her how I feel, but she wants to make her own mind up.'

'Clever girl.'

'It would be best for everyone if you just said you didn't want to meet her. I promised I'd call you and ask, but I don't want any part of this.' Reverse psychology. She looked over at Adams, who was giving her a big thumbs-up sign. She waved him away.

Renard's voice hardened. 'Listen carefully. I want to meet her. She's my daughter. She's mine as well as yours, and that counts for something in my book. Oh, yes, it does.'

His fear's gone, thought Ruth. He thinks he's entitled to her! Same old Didier Renard.

She looked at her hand in her lap and clenched it into a fist to stop herself hurling the phone down and grabbing Vida, making off with her somewhere safe as soon as she could. Now that he knew she existed, they would never have another moment's peace.

What had they done?

'Ruth-ie,' sang Renard. 'Are you still there?'

'We'll be in Chicago in three days' time, and I'll tell you the terms. You come alone, or it's not going to happen. Maple Lake Overlook – you'll find it on a map. Eight a.m., three days from now. I mean it. If you're not alone, we're not coming.'

'I'll be there. And Ruthie, if I invite my little girl back for a sleepover at her daddy's house, will you let her go?'

'I'm hanging up now.'

'Ruth, wait. What's her name?'

Ruth paused. She didn't want to hear the name come out of his mouth. 'It's Vida.'

'Vida. That's lovely. To life!'

'Fuck you,' said Ruth, and she hurled the phone down.

44

Kurt stared at Otis, and tried not to look like he was staring. This was what the revolution was about! He had liked the previous instructors: a pretty-faced man named Farrow, who gave a lesson in carrying weapons – how to run with them, where to keep a handgun, how best to access ammo – and a woman, Gabby, with a greasy bob of brunette hair, who had lectured them about what to do if they were captured. She spoke about the time frame during which all information would be sensitive, how to withstand torture – and what kind they might expect. Old Norma could have done with a little of that, Kurt thought.

But it was Otis who really fascinated him. He was so quiet about it – so matter-of-fact. The man was silent, thanks to the bandages around his chin, even as he led the class in the A–Z of weaponry. He had started by demonstrating how weapons were all around them – shards of glass or stones or dirt. But Kurt had already known that, hadn't he? He smoothed Norma's blouse over his sides, nicely washed but still testifying to her sticky end. It was going to bring him good luck. Besides, it was the other stuff he was keen on: the handguns and the rifles with scopes, the ones that could put a hole in the moon if he wanted.

Kurt was sorry now that he had found out that the old couple he'd sent down the North Platte were Resistance. He'd figured it out when Gabby was talking about the threats out there in the wild world – she mentioned them, murdered and thrown in the river while they were driving the banks looking for Southern survivors. She was quiet for a moment when she was done, as though she had a closer connection to them than simply fellow fighters. But why hadn't the old man and his wife been more wary, more vigilant? That was stupid. Trust no one.

These guys, though! They really knew what they were doing. Kurt decided immediately that he wouldn't let on that it was he who'd killed the two old people. No sense in that. Now Adams was talking. Kurt willed even the little hairs inside his ears to pay attention. This was his big chance.

D-Day would start with a mushroom dinner at ten thirty in the evening, and then a long drive along the back roads to Chicago. The cars would split off at intersections and rejoin down the line so that they didn't look to outsiders like a convoy. Heads nodded in agreement, and Adams went on. Weapons were to be stashed in ice-hockey bags – 'I know no one here is Wayne Gretzky,' he chuckled – or in specially crafted compartments in the upholstery. If a cop pulled a car over, and if the driver couldn't talk his or her way out of a search, then the officer would get a bullet. Adams shrugged, and no one disagreed. This was war. Each car would have one executioner. Another passenger would put the body into the boot of the cop car and it too would join the procession. Bloodstains on the interstate would be covered with sand. Bullet shells would be collected.

Kurt was impressed. They really had thought of everything. He looked across at Felix to gauge his reaction. His whole life he'd heard stories about the legendary Weatherman from the rest of the Callahans, but so far he was completely different to the rumors. They'd said he was a grumpy hermit, lived like a gopher in a hole under an old dam; how he was Callahan only by blood – and pussy through and through.

But even Kurt could tell that Felix was everything Tye had never been, him with his reluctant bird. Felix was smart, for starters, and he was tough too. Here he was, volunteering himself for action. And the Resistance had trusted him with a stash of guns – an AK-47 that he'd showed Kurt, then an M9 handgun and an M14 rifle with enough ammunition to keep all of them humming for days. Kurt liked the heft of them, the bone-deep cold of the mechanisms. It was nothing personal, with guns. Even though it really was, all of this. He knew he had a lot more killing to do before he felt the weight of guilt. That was a long way off still.

Kurt had taken to spending his evenings elbow to elbow with Felix, the two of them quiet as they cleaned and oiled the guns, practicing loading and unloading. Afterward, Felix would tell Kurt about the plans he'd seen on the walls of the rooms he'd sneaked into – maps of Chicago, the virus factory, the route there – as well as all he'd learnt from Adams about viruses and how the antiviral water worked. Kurt was eager to listen and to learn, and it made Felix proud to have such a dedicated apprentice. The talking also helped him to set things straight in his brain, like the tapes used to do, where he'd listen to the recordings he'd made of his old life and line them up with what he still remembered. He'd started that to keep track of brain viruses, to know when one had settled in – but it had quickly turned into a kind of therapy. This was the same. Felix wasn't shy to repeat things he'd said before, and Kurt was always watching, absorbing.

They slept close by in the Senate Chamber, two Callahans where they belonged, though they took care to mingle just enough with the Northerners who would be their comrades in arms. Linus had got shot of Kurt almost as soon as the boy put him down in the Capitol Building, but Kurt was bearing no grudges. He had Felix now – an old cat for an old cat; fair's fair. And Linus was smart: any feline worth the name would find his place among the hard women who worked the kitchen, the ones who had lost something and remembered the ache. What else were animals for, if not comfort and company? Let Linus hunt all the rats he could find. Kurt had bigger things to occupy his mind.

The target of the Resistance's attack was the virus factory – a single building ringed like Saturn with razor wire and concrete walls. A sequence of RPGs and mortars would create a path of access, according to Adams. Once the guards got wind of an attack, they'd deploy the airborne viruses – each one new and deadly.

'HQ. Just like old times,' said Felix.

'You better hope it isn't,' Adams told him. 'You better hope it isn't like the first time we went in.' He went on to detail that attack, from before the Resistance was the Resistance. Those rebels had been careful to drink their morning dose, but the new viruses were strangely undeterred. 'People melted clean away.' Adams drew a hand over his face as if he was wiping out his features.

Kurt shivered. Man, he would've liked to see that!

This time around, if Buddy's mushrooms did their good work, the Resistance army could keep going, impervious to sickness. C-4 would blow a hole in the side of the building.

'And then we hope for flashover.' Adams grinned.

Goddam, thought Felix. This fucker is enjoying the explanation.

'And then what?'

'Then lots more C-4.'

Adams was making triple sure. There were two teams dedicated to planting the bombs, and two more teams as backup. On top of that there had been a couple of extra classes, mandatory for everyone in the Capitol Building, which covered the basics of carrying, placing and arming the explosives.

'This ain't kindergarten,' warned Adams. 'That shit may look like Play-Doh, but we're not fucking around here. If this sounds simple, then you got the wrong end of it.' He paused and looked around, scanning for faces that appeared unsure, the weak links that would break the whole careful, deadly chain.

'Those mushrooms are miracles: ain't no mistaking that. We ought to take a moment now to think about Buddy and his sacrifice, but we also need to remember that they aren't going to make us immune to bullets or grenades or shrapnel. This is a battlefield, people. We can't say how quickly Renard's forces will rally, but you can bet your bottom dollar that they're ready for anything. We may have to deal with armored cars and whole squads of soldiers. But the beauty of it is, if we can knock that virus plant offline, then the whole shebang will be open to attack. We have the chance to make sure it's an even fight again. And we need to grab onto that!

'Now listen close. I have good news. Pay attention now! Something most of you don't know is that the Resistance isn't just the people under this roof. I've kept it secret for good reason, to keep the organization safe, but there are a lot of sleepers who are part of the Resistance. People working in police stations and coffee shops, plumbers and housewives and nannies and fucking hairdressers, all of whom are going to mobilize as soon as that factory comes down.' A cheer went up and the crowd clapped.

'And, my friends, that's when the hard work will begin: the real fighting, the kind that sorts the heroes from the zeroes. Wheat and chaff, isn't that what the Good Book says? What happens after that depends on our stamina and our determination. But, folks, I know you got that in spades. Heck, what am I saying? If it comes down to willpower, I know – goddam it, I know down to my pinky toe – that we got truckloads more of it than those motherfuckers!'

More cheering. Felix cleared his throat and started to say something to Kurt, but he was drowned out by the people around him. Kurt caught his eye and shook his head slowly, his eyes shining as he focused again on Otis, who stood grimly behind Adams. Felix gave up. He owed Kurt family loyalty. One chance, he thought. One loner to another. See if he's the good kind of Callahan or the bad kind.

And if he was the bad kind, Felix figured that was okay. There were worse ways to meet your maker. So maybe the kid was right to be excited. It would be over soon enough.

45

It was midnight when the plane flew high over the Capitol Building. Its engines whined as it banked and then turned north-west. Adams heard it only because he'd been listening for it for years. He sat up and pulled on the essentials, and then he willed the blood back into his sleep-heavy legs so that he could get up to where Felix had first laid out his bed.

Adams opened the window and climbed out. The plane was circling, a distant flashing red light, and then it was gone behind the scudding moonlit clouds. But he knew what it meant. The Northmen knew where they were. They'd probably traced the call Hank had been forced to make to Renard. Or – and it made Adams pant harder to think it – the patrolman had already got his message out by the time they'd even found him. It could have been something as simple as an old lady awake in the night with her weak bladder, looking out of her window at the desolate city, thinking over her past and how long it had been since the quiet time had come.

Shee-yit. Adams sat down to get his breath back. That they hadn't been bombed outright, or sprayed with pathogens from a crop duster, was probably because of Vida and Ruth.

'Don't spoil the merchandise,' Adams said to himself. His finger crept to the hole in his cheek, as it always did in times of stress.

There was no more time to guess. He made up his mind, cupped his hands around his mouth to make a megaphone and started shouting down inside the dome at the sleeping Resistance. His voice echoed off the walls.

The guards on duty took up the call as soon as they realized what it was. 'Spotter plane! We're a go! We're a go!'

Alarms were sounding as Adams made his way quickly down the staircase before it became impassable, and joined the swarm of Resistance running to get their gear.

'No one stays!' he shouted, but he'd created a monster. No one could hear him. He reached out and grabbed a bearded man in pajama pants. 'Everyone gets out of here. Everyone packs up. Women and children – everyone. No one stays in the building. I don't care where they go. Make sure the word gets out.' The man nodded dumbly. 'You understand what I'm saying? We're burning this place to the ground!'

Shit. The mushrooms. Adams had planned to wait at least another half a day for them to take and multiply, but he would have to work with whatever was there now. He didn't think about Buddy: he forced his mind away from what he would find there. There had been shrieks, and then whimpers, and then nothing, quite early on. What was done was done.

In the kitchen he searched the drawers for a paring knife and a colander. Then he raced back through the Senate Chamber, clambering over people and their piles of belongings. They had packed fast, but they were still too laden with their worldly goods.

'Take only what you need, folks!' They shook their heads and kept packing. He hoped to Christ that Felix was in the armory.

At Buddy's cell he stopped to breathe. Then he braced himself and banged on the door.

'Buddy!'

No response. Why would there be, if it all had happened the way it was supposed to? Better to be sure, though.

'Buddy! You in there?'

He drew the deadbolts back as quickly as he could, then grabbed the handle, held his breath and pulled.

The grease around the door gave way with a sucking sound, and the baptismal air from the cell spilt out, wet with humidity. Adams had expected the graveyard and the sewer, but instead it made him want to weep with memory. He couldn't see much, but the little room smelt like grass cuttings and compost heaps and battery acid. He stepped backward and pulled his shirt up to cover his mouth.

He let the air dissipate for a minute, and then he stepped over the threshold, cursing himself for forgetting the lantern. But it would waste too much time to go back for a light: the Capitol Building would be choked with people scurrying for their lives. He would have to try and find the silky, sticky mushrooms by feel in the darkness. He inhaled again, trying to make his other senses do the work of his useless eyes.

This time there was some other smell underlying the mushrooms: a heavy, pheromonal stink that made him think of armpits and skunks.

That was human, wasn't it, that smell? Buddy was dead, right?

He inched his foot forward and began to search the room, expecting at each skating stroke to come up against a cold leg or an arm. He took care to move without crushing anything that might be growing in the murk.

But there was only, now and again, the maddening clink of the mushroom bowls as he blundered against them. Adams realized that his hands were damp. His heart was tickering away under his shirt with the kind of fear he hadn't felt since he was a small boy, certain that the shape on the back of his bedroom door was the Hat Man, come to smother him.

At the couch, he reached his arms out, terrified of what he might touch. But the seat was empty. The sacrifice had chosen somewhere else to settle. He suddenly had the idea that Buddy was a bat suspended from the ceiling, lying in wait to enfold him in his furry black wings.

Adams pressed the foam stuffing with his fingers. The fabric had been stripped off it. He backed away, confused – and collided with the body standing upright in the center of the room. His throat seized. He was trying to scream, but the muscles wouldn't let him. He turned to where he thought the door was and ran.

In the Senate Chamber he found the closest lantern: a woman was carrying it, guiding her children through the congregation. Adams took it from her without a word. When she saw who'd snatched it, she let it go without complaint. He was pale as milk except for his fevered spots, and she knew better than to argue.

He was still shaking when he approached the cell door again, half expecting to see Buddy standing there framed by the yawning blackness of the room, back from the dead and ready for vengeance.

But there was no sign of anything strange. Adams held the lamp out in front of him. Every fiber of his body resisted going back inside, but he had to have the mushrooms. Had to. Otherwise it was all for nothing.

He held his breath again, though he was pretty sure the spores that had dispersed were gone. He stepped inside the cell.

And there Buddy was, a man standing ready to face his future with all its torments.

No. Not standing.

What was left of him was hanging. The body and its hungry passengers swayed a little, or maybe it was the lantern in Adams's hand that shook.

Adams felt his stomach lurch. Soon after they had left him in the cell, the little man must have fashioned a rope out of the couch fabric, and knotted it for strength into a noose. It looped, taut, over a rafter now, attaching him to heaven. Around his feet on the floor the Pyrex dishes were scattered. It looked like he'd balanced on them. Yep, that was it. Adams sighed, and the yellow light wavered again. Then he must have settled himself into the noose and kicked the crockery over. Buddy's eyes were open, rolled back into his shaven head. Adams wasn't stupid. He knew what color they ought to be: black, turned demonic with the burst blood vessels. Still they looked down at him in judgment, the flesh around them seeming to move and gibber.

He put the lantern down and pushed the couch away from the wall until it was below the corpse. He climbed up onto the seat and balanced carefully on the back so that he could reach the rope. He made sure Buddy's head was turned away from him, and then he hacked at the fibers, but the paring knife needed more persistent use and eventually he had to saw through them, the wrongness of the weight thrown against him all the while.

And the smell! That earthy, sewery stink, like someone had dropped a load in his khakis.

Christ.

He had, hadn't he? Buddy had shat himself.

Adams turned his head and tried to vomit, but there was nothing in him willing to come out. He had to be up close for his work, and he had to get on with it.

It was just that the dirty orbs in the sockets were not Buddy's eyes.

The mushrooms. They'd started there, seeking out all the wet membranes.

And then, oh God, they had spread.

Buddy's whole face was leprous now, bulging, the mushrooms colonizing the flesh as he watched, like maggots.

Adams jerked back and nearly slipped as Buddy fell at last, toppling over onto the bowls so that some shattered.

He was quick to follow after. He steeled himself, and positioned the lamp on the eviscerated seat of the couch for better light. Get it over with, he told himself. Like a surgeon. That's all I am. Cutting out the bits that can give other people life. Yes. That's what Buddy is: an organ donor.

He began trimming the mushrooms away from his friend's body, starting with the eyes – he had to stop that accusing look, for God's sake. Fingers streaked with gore, he set the fungi in the colander for safe keeping, and from then on he couldn't say which were the mushrooms and which his fingers. If he cut himself, he wouldn't be able to tell.

The bottoms of the stems were drenched with Buddy's blood, and this time Adams had to fight the urge to vomit. The man's nostrils had split: from the crevasses grew the longest, thinnest filaments, like hairs. His mouth was also stuffed with mushrooms – not big ones, those caught halfway to full-grown, but they'd have to do. Adams slid the knife in through Buddy's cheek and severed the stalks that reached down into his throat. The brown and yellow caps fell out like broken teeth – each precious one placed carefully into the colander.

The tattooed chest was swollen with the growths, and Adams hesitated. There was something especially terrible about that: he was doing a sort of autopsy. But he said a quick prayer and then he went ahead and cut into the skin below Buddy's sternum.

The ribs held firm. Adams had to dig in deep and then reach a hand in to find the lungs, knobbly and tight with their fruit. They split as he touched them. He pulled out mushroom after mushroom until the colander was full. Blood had already collected at the perforations in its base. He would drip as he went, like a murderer.

When he emerged from the cell with the colander, Otis was there, as if he'd been waiting.

'Take them,' said Adams. He wiped his face and left smudges of Buddy's blood across his dented cheeks, like camouflage. 'Everyone who's fighting today has to get some. You got that?'

Otis gave him a withering look, but he took the colander and was gone.

Adams turned back to the cell and closed the door. He slid every lock closed. He found that he was crying as he did it.

46

'You go. Then come back and tell me what's going on,' Vida told Dyce. She wasn't exactly ready to run up mountains, but as long as sleep was doing its good work, she would be all right.

'Sure, baby,' said Dyce. He wouldn't tell her, but his throat was feeling scratchy, in the same way it had been right in the beginning, when he was on the run with Garrett. This time it could be anything – love, grief, heartache, revenge: they'd all been circulating inside him for years. Wasn't that what the immune system was, when you got down to it?

But it could be something else too – something nasty and specific – especially if they had all miscalculated and the mushroom dose had been too low, or Renard's latest gift was settling in. By now Dyce knew his way around the sicknesses. He had marked his own immunity at about a fortnight now, maybe nearer three weeks. And of those days some had raced; others had dragged. Just to be sure, he felt in his pocket and found the wrinkled, giving mound of a mushroom, and popped it in his mouth. Gagging on the earthy bitterness, he thought that if Adams needed more hard science, he could run the fucking tests on himself.

'You ready?' Ruth was motioning at the people gathering below.

They went to watch from the atrium as the soldiers lined up, their hands cupped like supplicants. Otis had sliced the new mushrooms as fine as he could make them, and he was handing the wafers out to each man and woman. There was something festive about the scene. Felix and Kurt stood side by side, grinning like children.

'My Lord,' said Ruth, soft and low: it was a prayer. 'How do they know it'll work?'

'They don't.'

'Faith, then.'

'For sure. Same as the church kind. You can call it whatever you want. It doesn't matter.'

Dyce watched the procession. There were all sorts – tall and short, ragged and neat. He kept thinking of those Depression posters of the food lines. So many of us, he thought. If he thought about it too much it would get the better of him, and so he concentrated on one or two people. That was the way to do it: focus; get specific; keep your eyes on the prize.

Like this guy here. He'd seen better days, that was for fucking sure. His arms dangled by his sides like a sleepwalker, and he hadn't washed them in a while. Adams would shit when he saw that: he couldn't allow his precious mushrooms to be cross-contaminated.

The man kept wavering. Now he was trying to make his way against the people in the line, as if he was coming up the staircase. Dyce was fascinated. The man's arms, from his fingers to his elbows, were stained brown. As he got closer, Dyce saw that his clothes were none too clean neither, speckled with something black; his flesh hung sallow on his cheekbones.

And his torn cheek.

Christ. It was Adams.

Dyce's stomach clenched. The man had lost ten pounds and gained ten years overnight. He stopped when he got to them.

'In case you hadn't figured, we're moving house,' he said. As he talked, his hands kept moving, wiping themselves against his trousers, over and over. Dyce was pretty sure he didn't know he was doing it. 'How're we doing on those boomers, Dyce? You seeing stars yet?' He grinned, and it was awful, a death's head. Dyce was gentle with him.

'Took another dose of mushrooms a few minutes back, when I got something in the throat that wasn't going away. I'd say they gave me about three weeks' immunity. Give or take.'

'Good. Good,' said Adams, still wiping, still grinning. 'Man's gotta be able to talk, don't he? To parley? Three weeks! That's more than we need. Much more. It's good!'

'Are you sure we been spotted here? I mean, are you sure the whole building is at risk?' Ruth asked carefully. Adams shrugged. She had seen this kind of dissociation before in the ghost colony. Folks let their minds wander when they came up against something truly terrible, and you never knew how it was going to manifest. Here Adams was, out of his mind and betrayed by his busy hands, but still the bold leader of his troops.

'We've been seen. I can't say they know what it is they've seen. But we can't wait for them to put two and two together.' Wiping, turning the palms over, wiping again. 'We'll hold off on our attack as long as we can, but we could be forced to pull the trigger early. Maybe Renard will bail on the meeting. Maybe he won't. That's out of our control.

'But I wanted to come by and wish you luck. And I got a present for you, a thank you for all your doctoring work with us here. Buddy's truck is yours. It's gassed up. You'll find it where you left it.'

'That's kind of you,' Ruth answered.

Adams leant forward, and for the first time they got the butchery smell off him. Here was a man who'd been slaughtering things.

'There is a condition.'

Ruth tried not to lean away. 'Say it.'

'When you find Renard, you make him suffer.'

She didn't hesitate. 'You can rely on me.'

'Now there's only one more thing I'm going to ask you. We're going to move now, but I'm not one for loose ends. And this whole building?' He waved one bloodstained hand and then looked at it in surprise. He dragged his attention back. 'This is a loose end. Our plans of attack are pinned to the walls, that sort of thing. Too much of us still in it if anyone comes sniffing around for the wrong reasons.'

Ruth nodded. This was easy. Maybe they'd given Adams what he wanted: the mushrooms.

Adams permitted himself a smile. 'I want you to burn the place down when you leave. Last one out, whoosh! There's gasoline and matches in the store. Won't be much left, so I don't have to tell you to use it wisely. I'm kind of sorry I won't be doing it myself, but they'll need me on the front lines.' He drifted off, seeing other things than the people in front of him. Then he snapped back and gave his hands some final, decisive wipes.

'We will,' said Ruth. 'I promise.' She didn't care, even if it was a trap. She just wanted to be clean and free. To be done with everything, once and for all – the half-truths and the struggle and the blind allegiances to who-knew-what.

Adams nodded and moved dreamily away, following some ghostly voice. 'Look after yourselves,' he called when he reached the top of the stairs. 'And the friendly fungus.'

Then he descended.

Ruth stared after him. 'You know, sometimes I kind of feel sorry for that guy. He's so hot with the idea that he's going to set himself alight if he's not careful. Then other times I think he's two hooves and two horns away from being the devil.'

'It would be easier if he was just plain bad, wouldn't it?'

'Young man, sometimes your insight surprises me.' Dyce bowed and Ruth went on. 'Right. Let's get going. I'll check on Vida.'

'I'll hunt down the gasoline.'

47

Everyone was moving in a different direction and it took Dyce a few minutes to work his way down. When he reached the floor of the atrium, Felix and Kurt had already received their rations. Dyce made his way closer. They were standing side by side, the slices of mushroom lying on their palms. Dyce wanted to shake the old man.

'Hey. What's up with you?' he asked.

Felix turned to him and the smile dropped off his face. 'What do you mean by that?'

'That day I saw you, after the meeting, you'd had enough of this place. Saw you head for the ladies' room and I figured that'd be the last we'd see of you. Felix Callahan, the one I met down South, he'd have cleared out of here long ago. Probably have gone to find some open ground – one of them silos in the middle of Nebraska, maybe. Then you come back with this kid,' Dyce pointed a finger at Kurt, 'and suddenly you're a team player?'

Felix eyed him and popped the mushroom onto his tongue. He spoke through the chewing. 'Time's come, I suppose. That's the only way I can explain it. Got me some family in young Kurt, so we're going to see how that pans out. Us loners got to stick together. Besides, settling a silo in Nebraska is going to be more days' work than I got left in me. This is good. This is the way it ends for me.'

Now people were beginning to get noisier, working on the wave of elation that would turn them into an army. The shouting and whooping grew louder around them, and Dyce wasn't sure he caught the last of what Felix had to say.

Felix shook Dyce's hand – he'd never been this genial – and then he and Kurt were gone.

When Dyce got back to the room, Vida was holding an instrument, plucking curiously at the strings and listening to the notes linger.

'What's that? A hamdolin?'

'Some guy in a waistcoat left it for you. He said he wasn't quite done sanding and painting it but that things are as they are.' She cocked an eyebrow at him and held it out. Dyce took it and turned it over. 'Looks like a cross between a mandolin and a ukulele, doesn't it?'

The body was an old cookie tin with the paint scraped off down to the rust-spotted silver. The machine heads sat polished and proud, jewels in a crown. Dyce set himself down on the bed and felt the strings under his fingers.

'You know the reason I never learnt to play an instrument?' he asked.

'No talent?'

He ignored the joke. 'It's the same reason Southerners don't get married.' He kept his black eyes fixed on the instrument. 'Why start, you know? Long-term isn't exactly something we can count on. But this: I got a good feeling about this. Like maybe I'm a natural. I'll *get* good. I'll teach myself.'

Vida smiled. 'So what's your first song, troubadour?'

'First I reckon I'm going to get the hang of the lullabies.'

48

The troops were lined up along either side of the passages, some winding up the stairs, ready as they'd ever be. The plan was to pass through the bowels of the Capitol Building and emerge, Adams kept saying, like a shadow army from beneath the dumpster, and then – pow!

Felix shook his head, out of breath. He knew what usually came out of bowels. He held onto the back of Kurt's shirt – they'd offered him a new one, but he had kept the blouse in defiance – and said, 'Don't know whether I'll make it up and down those rungs one more time. You know that story about the boy in the well?'

Kurt said nothing. He knew Felix was talking to hear himself talk. The boy patted the handgun he'd shoved in the waistband of his pants, and adjusted the rifle slung across his back. Now that it was really going to happen, he was jumpy. He tried to stand up straighter, to be worthy of those weapons.

Felix stopped. There was something warm pressing against his shin: Linus. The stripy tail curled around his leg.

'Boy. Looks like your cat came home. Didn't think he'd want to play Happy Families.'

'He's not here for me,' Kurt said. 'That cat hates me and I guess he's got a right.'

'Goodbyes are not only for friends, son,' said Felix. He bent down to stroke Linus, craving the forgiving fur, but the tabby ducked out of reach and then didn't stop, skittering back into the building. 'Hope he's smart enough to get himself out when he needs to.'

'You seen how fat he is already? He's gonna survive us all. King of the castle.'

'Cats. They tell it how it is.' Felix sighed. Dallas. Was it stupid to mourn a creature lost as long as you could remember?

Of course it was. But still.

'I was always more of a dog person,' said Kurt.

Did that kid feel anything at all? Maybe not all cats were as special as his old Dallas had been, back in the day. Felix looked at Kurt again, wondering if it was the boy himself that was cold, or if all teenagers were another species. He had thought he was getting a handle on him.

There was a thud and a crash behind them, then the crack of splintering wood.

'What's that?' Kurt asked.

'You know what, runt? It don't matter,' Felix told him. 'But whyn't you go take a look? Make yourself useful.'

Kurt left his place and walked back toward the commotion. It soon became obvious. Four men were pulling boarding from the frame of the Capitol Building's grand entrance, clearing a way out, groundhogs out of their hole to face the weather. Kurt could feel the difference in the air already: fresh and cold, the scent of the new order – or of the old one being smashed like a matchstick ship.

He reported back. When word spread about the door, the lines of armed men and women did an about-turn, and those who'd been last in line found themselves first. Best of all, Kurt and Felix were automatically bumped up to the front, or near enough. Still they waited, quiet with nerves, for Adams to give the go-ahead – his final command, if Felix knew anything about old men.

And now he appeared, aged and filthy, a homelessness to him that hadn't been there the day before. His voice was giving way, and he looked like he was going to keel over any minute right where he stood.

He made his way down the middle of the corridor, sweating the dirt into streaks, through the guard of honor the army made for him. Or maybe it was just that they stood back because they didn't want to be contaminated by whatever he had. People hushed and stood to attention as he passed. When he got to the doorway, it was mostly clear of debris. He stopped and faced them.

'I thought you-all'd like this new exit. Better than crawling out the toilet. Been a while since we used the door, hasn't it?'

Titters. Nerves, thought Kurt. But also people wanted to please him.

Adams didn't need to go over the plan again. He'd been through it a thousand times himself, and at least a dozen more times with the whole of the Resistance. So he just stood front and center, lifted a fist into the air and yelled, 'Fuck . . . !' His voice was hoarse and wet – hardly a voice to instill courage – and Kurt thought: What he needs is me. I could help him.

Instead Adams gathered himself, rubbed hard at his throat with his red right hand and said, 'Forgive me. I've had a hard night.'

He cleared his throat and tried again.

'Fuck Renard!'

This time the message got through the way he had meant it, and the soldiers responded with their own shout of consent.

Then he stepped to one side and the army took his lead, filing past him. Felix wondered how long they'd been in the Capitol Building. Years, some of them. Goddam! He found his own throat clogged with unexpected tears. There weren't a whole lot of times in a man's life that he came to a clear choice and understood it for what it was.

'Two roads in the wood,' he said to himself, and swallowed against the lump.

He felt Kurt's hard eyes looking him over for signs of weakness, signs of failure. He pretended to be busy, checking his bag for the hard little apples he'd taken from the kitchen. Still there. When he raised his head again on his wobbly neck, Kurt was looking elsewhere.

One man and one woman, each with a torch, were leading the exit march. Some soldiers cursed as they clambered over the rubble like an obstacle race; they were making for the hole that had been cut in the razor wire. They went on without looking at the headless statues and the sawn-off trees, the gaping fountains with their long-dead fish. It made Felix heartsick for some other time when he'd sprinted down the night streets of Norman, Oklahoma with his brothers, ringing doorbells and running away, laughing their buzz-cut heads off, high with drink and daring.

One by one now the soldiers emerged into the streets of Des Moines, the cloudless Northern sky above sprinkled with innocent stars. When they judged enough time had passed for orientation, the leaders motioned them onward, and they spread out like spores to find the cars parked in the ruins of the city.

Kurt was through the razor wire; Felix had to hobble after him. It was first come, first served with the cars and the trucks, and it made Adams's change to the exit strategy all the more

telling. The last first, all right. Here were the stragglers, the
bone-thin men, the pre-teen girls, the sick and lowly and dis-
enfranchised – the ones who had the most to lose were the
ones who had the pick of the vehicles. There was something
dishonest but honorable in that. Typical Adams.

Felix tried to follow close, but Kurt loped on along the streets,
past the four-by-fours and the double cabs and the luxury sedans
that had once had seat-warmers and fancy speakers. Those didn't
interest him one bit; he'd seen something else that called him
on. Felix stopped and shouted after him, but it was impossible to
hear anything. He took off again, puffing hard, the rifle slapping
against his bony back hard enough almost to wind him.

Kurt had stopped. The car he was after was parked trunk-first
in a deserted clothing store. It was the white Toyota, brought in
by a recce squad, maybe: too good to pass up. He went around
the front. The pronghorn had been removed and the bonnet
wiped clean, but he recognized the bent bumper, the squint
headlight.

'That your car?' Felix asked between breaths. 'Don't recognize it without the butchery.'

'Hey. Look what they did. You think that was Buddy?' Kurt
was running his hand along the bonnet to where the pronghorn's
cleaned horns had been secured to the grille. The figurehead
had been cut roughly from the animal's skull and secured with
wire.

'Nice,' said Felix. He didn't approve of the posturing, but
Kurt did, and he was in no position to disagree. He felt some
balance in the world tip slowly against him.

Kurt hoisted himself into the driver's seat and felt for the keys.
Without asking, Felix stashed his rifle under the foam bench at
the back. He kept the handgun tucked into his trousers.

'Now what?' said Kurt.

'You know what the man said. Gotta have every car full.'

They waited. People streamed by them, and then one person didn't. A tousled red head shoved itself in the back window.

'This seat taken?'

Felix jutted his chin at the back seat, but it was Kurt who wanted to speak yet couldn't. Bethie. That was who she looked like. He felt at once the flustered weight of his fifteen years and the ancient sadness that descended whenever he thought of his lost girl in her grave.

She slid into the passenger seat and exhaled. 'Whew. I'm Danni.' She reached for Felix's hand and then Kurt's. 'Nice blouse. And nice swan necklace. They really go.'

Afterward he folded the touch into his fist. They must have met before in passing – maybe at one of the explosives lectures. Kurt watched her in the rear-view mirror. She had Beth's ears, sculptured and exact, delicate as seashells.

They didn't have long. Two men arrived, real GI Joes, their shirts too tight and their hair cut close, their aggression making brothers out of them. They were pissed off that Adams had turned the line back to front. Felix was sure he'd seen them near the women's bathroom, preparing to slide down into the sewers and come up first. They sat either side of Danni.

'Mario, and that's Sy. Why're you sitting with your dick out? Go already.' They were wriggling to get comfortable on the guns. Kurt turned the key in the ignition and rolled the car into the street. He followed the line of vehicles.

'I hope you can drive, kid, 'cause me, I am itching,' said Mario.

'You get a cream for that,' said Danni. She said it softly, but she meant it, and Felix snorted his appreciation.

'Hardy-har-har,' said the tough man. 'If you weren't sitting down, you'd be a stand-up comedian. Jesus, what car is this anyway? A fucking Toyota? We'll all probably die today, you know that, right? And here we are driving a motherfucking thirteen-hundred Toyota. And what the hell's that strapped to the grille?'

'The last thing that fucked with me,' muttered Kurt.

'Woo! Well, isn't that just going to make Renard shit himself? Here we come, big man, ready to tear you a new one: Team Pronghorn!'

'Save it,' said Danni, and Kurt threw her a grateful glance in the mirror. 'It doesn't matter how we get to Chicago. Let's just get there without killing each other first.'

49

The Capitol Building was quiet for the first time. All the other Southerners were gone to be God's army, said Adams. Even Pete and Sam had said their goodbyes. There'd been no tears. Now Dyce sat at the window of Vida's room, free at last of its boards, and looked out at the final cars leaving the ravaged city. Ruth was silent, keeping herself busy, flipping through her medicine book and then getting up to mix some herbs in a chipped mug – just for something to do, Dyce thought. The spoon clattered against the sides because her hands were shaking.

In the bed Vida tried to rest, but she was done with sleep. There was too much space in her head for the meeting with Renard. She looked over to her mother and tried to decide what she'd inherited from her, and what her father had gifted her with. Some things were easy, like her ears. Those were different to Ruth's: hers clung close to her skull, while Vida's lobes hung down, unrepentant.

But the other stuff, that was on the inside, and you never knew what you were getting until it was too late.

Vida closed her eyes and attempted to fit the pieces together, trying to forget the images of Renard she'd saved over the years: posters, but also nightmares. She chose faces for the man, tweaking them and swapping parts, until his features melted and ran and she saw his skull for what it was: the incarnation of creeping, tittering death.

At least Dyce would be there. She hadn't had to ask: she'd felt him, hot-eyed and loyal, at her bedside, like one of those guardian angels. Adams had given special permission for him to choose whatever gun he'd wanted from the armory. Vida knew Dyce had agonized over it. He'd first chosen a handgun – something up close and personal; something to hold against Renard's temple and the cold rage it contained, that incurable brain a prison just as much as the cell where the patrolman, Hank, paced, or the bed where Vida had lain for days, sweating out her injury and sickness.

But a rifle would be more effective, wouldn't it? A long-range shot might be all he could hope to get, and then a handgun would be a waste. Dyce held the gun now, turning it over and over in his hands – a rifle with a scope. He untucked a corner of his shirt to clean the lens and peered through the telescope at the cars. He could see a white Toyota with something attached to the grille, but even with his night-lit eyes he couldn't make out what it was. Maybe a buck's head, but that seemed unlikely.

'Dyce,' Vida called softly.

'You're awake.' He rested the rifle against the wall beside his new mandolin and came over. He sat on the bed and planted a hand on either side of her shoulders, then dropped a deliberate kiss on her forehead. The skin was cool. Ruth raised an eyebrow but said nothing.

Vida took hold of his hand and he felt the electric throb of her pulse. 'I'm not going to get any more sleep. Let's go now.'

'Are you sure?'

'We'll be early, but I want to work out the geography. Adams chose it because it was secluded. Because it's away from the city. But what's there that's going to help us? Is secluded good or bad?'

'Okay, but before we go . . .' He leant over again and kissed her on the lips, the soft give and parting of hers as she kissed him back. Ruth made a small sound, something between a growl and a sigh, and kept stirring her potion.

'Come with me,' Dyce said. 'I want to show you something.'

He took Vida properly by the hands and eased her off the bed.

'You need those?' Ruth nodded at the crutches.

'No, Mama. I'm fine. I really am.' The two women grinned at one another, the first time in days.

'Okay. But be careful.' Wild horses, Ruth thought. That's my girl. If Everett was here asking me the same, I'd go too – bad leg or not. It might be the last time they enjoy each other, free and clear.

Dyce led Vida slowly down the staircase. 'I feel like one of them grand ladies making an entrance at the ball,' she said, but then the words were blown away from her in the cold, fresh air at the cleared entrance. They held each other's arms and shivered, with delight and with desire. Even in the face of the coming battle – or because of it – they felt it: the itching of life.

The darkened city was laid out before them, speckled with the tiny lights of far-off fires.

He felt her eyes on his face. 'That smell,' he murmured. 'Like old times. But also like anything could happen.'

'You look like a deer.'

'Don't spoil it.'

Vida leant into his side. 'Your eyes are something that I really like about you. That I love about you. You're terrible at hiding your feelings. It's all there in those baby-deer eyes.'

'Okay, so what am I feeling right now?'

'You're feeling like it's the end of the world – for real, this time. And you're feeling horny, and you're wondering if we have time.'

'I knew there was a reason I let you tag along.'

She wiggled her hand free and stroked his jaw, felt the stubble there, the muscle jumping underneath the skin. 'But, Dyce, seriously. You know what I want?'

'What?'

'To feel normal. Like myself again. To feel good. Just for a bit. Before it all goes to shit. You can help me with that.'

'Right now? Here?'

'No one's left. And when else will we get another chance?'

'Are you sure? What about your leg? I don't want to hurt you.'

'You won't. You lie down first. And for God's sake, stop talking. It's not sexy.'

She gestured at the steps, and then breathed once and looked up at the faithful sky with its high clouds racing north, as if all the earth was coming to meet them.

'Okay, but you've got to give me a moment.'

He was smiling, unbuckling his trousers and dragging them off, hopping as he lost his balance, his hair flopping in his face.

'Should have brought the crutches.'

'Stop mocking me, woman, and get down here and help.'

And she did, taking off her own clothes and then settling her weight over his body, moving on him until he was hard. She held his dick, the silk and heft of it, until he moaned. Then she relented, sliding him slowly inside her, and he gasped at the squeezing heat.

'God, Vida. I missed you.'

She moved and saw the pale straining tendons of his throat where the sun had never touched him, his clenching animal teeth, the O of his mouth as he fell into the long bliss and wonder of recognition. She rocked on him; their hip bones clashed at the thrusts. Then Dyce was muttering, and Vida bent her ear to his mouth to catch the warm, panting breath.

'Never. Never. Never,' he was saying.

'Never what, baby?'

'Never let me go.'

They lay side by side on the cold stone of the steps, their bodies humming in time, and the stars turned above, floating as though in deep water.

'The sky,' she said.

'I know.'

Vida lifted her head from Dyce's shoulder and he pulled her back.

'Where do you think you're going? We're not done.'

'I was just thinking.'

'That's always bad news.'

'Shut up. I was thinking that if the world wasn't this fucked up, we'd never have met. And even if we had, we'd never have got together. We've been lucky.'

'Was it all worth it?' He was smiling again; he knew the answer.

'Of course not. I'd trade you away in a heartbeat if things could be normal. You would too.'

'Ouch.'

'No offence, but no one's love is worth what happened to the South.'

'Renard thought it was. His wife dying? That was like Hitler not getting into art school.'

'He didn't love her, Dyce. But she belonged to him. A possession, and she was taken away before he was ready to let go. He wanted revenge. That's what all this is. The South fucked with him, and he couldn't stand it.'

'Maybe. But there doesn't always have to be an explanation. Some people are just born without that feeling gene: it's not because something went wrong for them. And here we are.'

'Here we are.'

'I don't believe in destiny, Vida.' He was serious. 'All there is is what we have here. This thing. The universe didn't align so that we could be together. But it did align anyway. And we are together. It doesn't make the love less real.'

In the silence the lonely dogs barked in the city below and the wind buffeted the building, insistent at the boarded windows.

Dyce finished pulling on his boots. 'So if I asked you to marry me, would you say yes?' He sounded as if he was talking to himself.

She laughed and kept dressing. 'Barefoot, pregnant and in the kitchen?'

'Gotta find a kitchen first.'

'Why not? Now that I got two bare feet to stand on. Plus I got the other thing covered too. You're getting a twofer.'

He grabbed her hand to his mouth. She felt the hot words against her skin. 'Do you know that you are everything I ever wanted?'

She felt the blood rising in her, her mouth swollen with his little bites and long kisses. 'Then show me again.'

But Dyce was standing up. He knelt like a knight on the step below her.

'Vida Washington, will you marry me?'

'And be stepmama to Ears McCreedy? I can't wait.'

'Be serious.'

'You want serious? How about: if we live through tomorrow, you'll be stuck with me till I'm old and gray?'

'That's exactly what I was hoping.'

'Then yes, Mister Jackson. You and me and baby makes three.'

50

'I'll go get our things. You're packed up, right?'

Vida nodded.

'*Adios.*'

Dyce left her on the steps. As he walked away, his legs sang with the spent adrenaline; there was more coming, and soon. He hadn't fully realized it until now. More of everything. The end of Renard was the beginning of family again for him. What would Garrett have thought of that?

Vida was calling after him. 'Don't forget your mother-in-law!'

He shook his head. No one with half a brain had ever forgotten Ruth. She wouldn't let them.

The gasoline was where Adams had said it would be – a red jerry can, maybe half full, sitting bang in the center of the storeroom, a box of Diamond matches balanced on top. Torching the place would be easy enough with all the wood paneling and those velvet curtains: the Senate Chamber and the House of Representatives would go up in seconds. He would be lucky to get out of there himself. If anyone was left behind, they'd be toast.

Not toast. Roasted. Dyce shuddered, thinking of all the critters he'd gutted in his lifetime, their tiny carcasses on a hundred spits, making the juices spring in his mouth. He picked up the canister and went to do a final check.

When he found Ruth, she was packing the last of her things.

She must know I've just fucked her daughter, Dyce thought. She can see it on my face, or smell it on my fingers. It ought to be more awkward. But she stood and faced him, the recipe book held tight against her chest.

'This is it, isn't it? The end.'

Dyce nodded. 'Vida's waiting outside.' He lifted the can. 'It's time.' She just looked steadily at him, calculating his ability to protect the things she held dear.

'Ruth. Are you ready?'

'I've made something,' she said. She picked up a sports-drink bottle. A couple of milliliters of liquid sloshed at the bottom. 'You know, I thought I'd lost the seeds. But they were there in the book, all along, safe in their little envelope. Meant to be, wouldn't you say?'

'What is it?'

'Bushman's poison.'

'Whoa.'

'Get over yourself, white boy. That's its proper name. I've been waiting a long time to put it to its proper use. You ever heard of the Kalahari?'

'The desert.'

Ruth nodded. 'In the old days it was used on the end of arrows. It could bring down an eland in under a minute. Every part of the plant is poisonous, except maybe the fruit – but no one's exactly gagging to give that a try. So this is a risk: the seeds have been sitting for a long time.'

'For Renard?'

She nodded again. 'Poetic justice. If the poison doesn't work fast enough, I'll tell him it's already inside him, and that it'll sear his organs like broken glass until he bleeds from every hole in his body. Give him a heart attack.'

Dyce didn't know whether she was being serious. But it happened. People died of fright: he nearly had himself, twice over – once in the river when Ester had tried to take him under, and once in the tunnels below the Mouth, when he was running for his life. It was possible.

'Are you done preparing it? I mean, is it ready?'

'You better believe it.' Ruth stowed the bottle and then slowly shouldered her bag, as well as Vida's. The way she moved made her look old, and Dyce watched her as she went, to make sure she was going the right way. It wasn't like her to be distracted.

He couldn't deal with that right now. He unscrewed the cap on the jerry can and gave it a cautious sniff: sweet and strong, with an instant headache, just the way it ought to be. He replaced the cap and picked up his bag, first making sure Ears was safe inside, then his gun and the makeshift instrument.

He looked around the way people used to do before checking out of a hotel room. He trotted down the staircase. 'Goodbye, chandeliers: I kind of feel sorry about you. Goodbye, portraits: you're long overdue for the bonfire, you and your shifty mother-fucking eyes.'

The thirsty curtains in the Senate Chamber soaked up the gasoline, and the jerry can was soon dry. Dyce began to light the matches and fling them into the fabric, length by length, and there was something holy about that. The flames leapt up the red velvet, racing toward the vaulted ceiling. The room was filled with light for the first time in years. It would all go fast. The whole place, and its fleas – whoosh! He wished Garrett was here to see it.

'Back to the Stone Age, bro. Back to Eden.'

He looked around the room, its agreeable heat licking his face. Soon he wouldn't be able to breathe, and wouldn't that be ridiculous? The arsonist, overcome by his own smoke. He pictured Garrett, doubled over from laughing so hard.

What was that?

Somewhere, a man was laughing.

Wait. Not laughing. Shouting; coughing. Screaming for help.

Oh, fuck. The patrolman. Hank.

No one had thought to release him, had they? He'd be roasted like a chicken in his cell if the smoke inhalation didn't get him first. Dyce rubbed his sore eyes and hurried through to the rooms at the back. He had no personal affection for the man, but he didn't deserve to be burnt to death like a medieval witch.

Both cells were closed and bolted and, more ominously, both had fallen quiet.

Dyce slid the bolts back with a careful hand, but didn't open the unlocked door. If Hank was alive enough to scream, he was alive enough to punch.

He didn't stay to check. Let Hank fend for himself. Dyce didn't need another burden. 'I got plenty of things to carry, man,' he told the invisible patrolman. 'Sorry. You're on your own.'

He hurried for the exit, holding his shirt over his mouth and nose. The curtains were mostly gone, and now the furniture had taken – all that wood! A couch had been pushed up against paneling in one place, and all the braziers had been toppled. Black smoke was engulfing the atrium and the dome, turning the lofty heaven into roaring hell.

Ruth and Vida were already at the bottom of the staircase, thank God, and moving fast. Dyce settled an arm around Vida and helped her along. Ruth brought the bags and they exited the Capitol Building for the last time. They could hear the fire crackling behind them, and the blast of heat pushing them out like the breath of the devil.

With the three of them together, it was simple enough to follow the path hammered out for them by the troops through the razor wire and out into the moldering city. Even so, it took a few wrong turns before they found their bearings, the heat behind them a constant reminder of how little time they had to get it right.

And there it was: Buddy's truck, still standing where it had been left for them. Adams had been as good as his word.

'Ain't no place like home,' Vida said. She was trying to be funny but it came out with a hiccup, and she scrubbed at her sweaty face.

'Hey,' Dyce said. He turned around and hugged her quickly. They were all orange in the light of the blaze, and he had to shout to make himself heard. 'You're fine. We're all fine, okay? Let's just get this day done.' She nodded. 'You want to wipe your nose on my shirt?'

'Ugh. No.'

'Right. We got everyone?'

'Spoken like a dad,' called Ruth.

Dyce grimaced. 'Just keep the windows closed until we're clear.'

The truck had a full tank. Since they had last been there, it had been cleaned, inside and out. An open map book sat on the driver's seat, set deliberately to the correct page. Dyce studied it briefly, rubbed his eyes, and then started the engine.

They worked their way through the rubble-strewn streets, Vida's head lolling on the back of the passenger seat.

'We did that,' Dyce said in wonder, looking in the rear-view mirror. 'Will you look at that!'

The windows of the Capitol Building were lit up, the flames licking inside the frame like a Halloween lantern.

51

Hank woke to the sound of a curtain rail hitting the carpet outside his door. He listened. The place was quiet – none of the usual sounds of voices and footsteps or the constant banging of pots and pans from those cack-handed workers in the canteen.

But there was a sound. He strained to hear it. Some underlying white noise, like the breathing of the great beast at the heart of the maze.

Another hiss.

And the smell of smoke too – quickly hot and acrid in his nostrils. Hank coughed.

He was familiar with this. He stayed where he was, on the floor, and sent up a sort of prayer.

'Oh, shit. Oh, mighty fuck. Make a space for me, Lord. Here I come.'

He stood creakily and went over to the door, mindful of his bruises and his abused muscles. He banged on the wood. 'Hey! Hey! I'm still in here! Someone!' It was locked. He shouted again, pleading for someone to hear him over the growing moan of the folding structure.

'Please, God, open this door! Please!'

He tried the door again, expecting the same immovable result, but to his surprise it opened, pushing outward against the unlatched security gate. He stood in shock for a second, then crossed his heart and ran.

The ceiling of the Senate Chamber was billowing with fire. Bubbles of hot resin and melted plastic fell like God's judgment from the ceiling. Hank pulled his shirt over his head and fought against the wall of heat. Still the smoke found its way into his struggling lungs and seared them like steak. As far as he could make out, the carpet was already gooey, halfway to melted, a nightmare. Clumps of it clung to his shoes and he slipped and skidded, but kept his balance in the end. He raced on out of the chamber, then paused, trying to remember where the exit was. He knew he had to get down a flight of stairs.

He went left. The air was clearer that way. And there, high up, perched on a ledge below a painted fresco, was a bundle of striped fur, trying to make itself as small as possible. When Linus saw Hank, he yowled.

Hank took a breath of the least fouled air, and it cost him. He grabbed a leather-padded chair and leant it against the wall, then climbed up and reached for the cat. He didn't have time for the coaxing and the gentle voice. He grabbed Linus, expecting to be clawed, but the cat just huddled, exhausted, and let Hank tuck him under his arm like a football. There. One small thing that didn't have to be destroyed.

The patrolman made an ungainly hop to the floor and kept on down the first flight of stairs he found. Suddenly it was clear to him what he was looking for. He had to find the women's bathroom, the same way he'd come in.

He would have got there too, but he saw that the main entrance was wide open. Strong gusts of cold wind were blasting in now as the heat of the fire forced the air up and out of the building.

Hank headed into that wind, out of the doorway and down the steps.

But there was only rubble and a razor-wire fence. The building would come down at some point, and by then he needed to be far away. He paused, panting, then stumbled over the rocky perimeter, feeling along the wire until he found the gap.

He got onto all fours and crawled, still hugging the cat to his chest. At last he came out into the open street and straightened up, made human again. He hobbled along the asphalt, down and away from the building, as tongues of flame ringed the domes.

He chose a place to sit and rest overlooking the Des Moines river so he could watch the burning building. It was too impressive to turn his back on. He set the cat down beside him, but it didn't move, the way rabbits were supposed to freeze when they stared into the eyes of a snake.

He reached over and dragged the tabby onto his lap, and the two of them watched the Capitol burn, the heat scorching the little hairs on Hank's arms. Whatever it was, it meant the end of something.

'Pleased to meet you, cat. My name's Hank.' The tabby shook, bones sharp and fragile against its fur. 'You know that song, kitty? "The times they are a-changin'."' Now the domes were collapsing like vaults in a bank heist, sending choking powdery dust to merge with the flames. Hank took another breath of careful air into his damaged lungs.

'All right,' he said. 'I think that's about enough of that. Let's figure out how we're going to get ourselves home.'

52

It was barely morning when Kurt rolled the Toyota off West Plainfield Road and down the ramp into the decaying underground garage. He found the others and parked. Mario and Sy were quick to escape, as if just being close to an old man, a boy and a woman was sapping their strength. Felix smiled as they ran off to join the rest of the marines, high-fiving them, full to the ears with bravado. Fuckers. That was not a North-versus-South thing; that was people being assholes. Felix had always hated the macho guys. They reminded him of Tye Callahan.

But you couldn't choose your fellows, could you? A man had to make do with what he had. Being born Callahan had taught him some things, at least.

Felix looked around. The parking garage was damaged the way everything was up North, the columns swollen where the metal reinforcing had oxidized. Chunks of concrete lay scattered across the floor, fallen from the low ceiling. The place practically reeked of anxiety and collapse. Perfect.

It wasn't full yet. Some drivers had taken the back roads, and Kurt's team was among the first arrivals waiting for everyone to assemble. A few people sat in groups and examined their weapons, adjusting the straps on their bags, fingering the plastic explosives, feeling the weight of grenades. Felix thought of old-time airports and suicide bombers, the limbo of intention, the way everyone had had to migrate when the United America movement forced the census and everyone had to pack up and head home, whether they liked it or not.

As far as he could gather, there had been no major hitches during the night journey – just a little mechanical trouble with a Passat, and that had been fixed in fifteen minutes, the driver said. Adams had done his homework, but the cars were old even for the North: a single breakdown was a minor miracle. Felix knew that it helped people to know that they were capable in a real-life situation instead of the dummy runs they'd been doing. Gave a man a purpose.

The sun was up when the last car arrived. No one besides Adams did a head count. If they had, they'd have discovered one car fewer than had left Des Moines, and one man missing. Adams was banking on them being too preoccupied to notice, and he was right. A leader had to have a plan that not everyone owned, just as he'd kept secret the real size of the Resistance. He figured it was best to keep this secret too. Insurance was what Dyce called the leftover mushrooms in his pocket, and insurance was the word Adams had used in his one-on-one discussion with Otis two days ago.

Even after the last of the convoy arrived, there was waiting to do. Vida's meeting with Renard was scheduled to happen at the same time as the Resistance went over the top – eight a.m., so as not to spook anyone, Adams kept saying.

Felix alternated between keeping an eye on the rising wind outside and watching the man. Sometime during the journey Adams had lost his preacherly gait – or maybe it was seeing the end of Buddy that had eroded him. He was tense now, humming with nerves. Felix counted: Adams had managed to hold off for forty minutes, but he was plainly dying to get it all over with.

Felix felt a flicker of sympathy for the guy. As a group they were cornered underground like rabbits in a warren. If Renard really was on to them – and it seemed only a fool wouldn't have tracked the convoy through the night – all he had to do was toss a grenade in and bring the whole place down on their scheming heads. That would be it.

'Kaput,' whispered Felix. Years of planning up in a cloud of dust, like Pompeii or one of those Scando volcanoes. And who knew when they would next get a chance? Would there even be any survivors?

Now Adams was clearing his throat, and Felix focused.

'Right. It's time. Everybody listening? This is how it goes from now on in. You'll come up onto the street and the factory will be right in front of you. You couldn't see it in the dark, but I promise you it's right there.' Adams drew a square with his hands, and Felix saw the trembling. 'Big square building, gray, razor wire every-fuckin'-where. I don't have to tell you what to look out for; God knows we've practiced enough.'

Felix expected some kind of rallying speech to follow, but it didn't come. For the first time since he'd met Adams, the man seemed to be out of words. Adams nodded at Mario and Sy. They looked to Felix like fighting dogs, primed and bristling, straining against the leash.

I sure hope you two assholes get the chance to scratch that itch, he thought. It's now or fucking never.

And it was only then that the impact of what they were doing rolled over Felix's head. Adams wasn't kidding. This *was* it. No more hiding underground; no more checking the maps and weather boxes; no more jerky; no more whiskey; no more tapes. What had that bought him anyway, except more days to hide away? The pronghorn lived in fear of ghosts, and so did he. And Felix was done being skittish. It was time to turn and act.

He felt a great calm descend on him. He looked over to the boy. The Weatherman wasn't any further along the human tree than fifteen-year-old Kurt, with his guns and his blouse and his slow burn for his cousin Bethie. Neither of them had found their place in the world. Lying low and waiting in hope for better times was a shitty way to live. And now here they both were at the gates of the toxic citadel, the poisonous Garden of Eden. There could be no better way to go. He hoped he had lived with as much dignity as he could muster, and he sure as hell planned on dying the same way.

Felix had no more time to settle his score with the Almighty. He watched from underground as the mortar men went in first, setting their weapons in place along the sidewalk, weighting them, calibrating for the stiff wind. There were no pedestrians in this industrial corner, but still two Resistance soldiers patrolled, on the watch for windows opening in distant apartment blocks, or curious early-morning workers.

When the mortars were in place, the RPG squad filed up and out into the street. They would take out the innermost walls, the lines of defense beyond the reach of the mortar shells. Now they ran, heads down as they'd been trained, for the outermost rim of razor wire, trusting that it would be gone in the seconds it took for them to reach it.

There was a hollow thud as the first mortar went up, and then the others followed in quick succession.

So fast, thought Felix, dazed in the silence that blanketed the city and spread into the parking garage. No one else dared to breathe either. The canals inside his ears protested: they felt blocked. He shook his head from side to side, trying to make the sound come back. But there wasn't any. Not until the next one.

And then down they came, mortar after mortar, popping and burning, shaking the concrete columns so that flakes of stone and rust rained down like a plague.

Adams had his arm raised. When the last of the mortars hit, he dropped it and the Resistance army emerged like cockroaches from under the city, silent but for the pounding of their boots on the thin asphalt.

The RPG squad moved into place. One after the other they tore holes in the walls that blocked their advance.

How single-minded they all were! Felix knew that they would wear faces like robots, bleached of all human feeling. The wrongness of it made his heart hammer harder. He was sure he would pass out.

53

With every step, they fell further behind. Felix watched the soldiers run ahead: Adams and Sy and Mario in the front line, then Pete and Sam and hundreds more, guns tucked neatly against their backs, focused on what was in front of them.

At the lip of the ramp, Kurt stopped and grabbed at Felix's arm to hold him back. Felix shook free and ran on a few paces, then turned back in frustration.

'What's going on, kid?' he asked. The boy's face was flushed, his cheeks pink and his eyes bright.

'You smell that?' Kurt asked.

Something acrid. Felix had known no airborne virus that smelt, but then he'd never been this close to the source. It was coming from inside the building.

As the bombs detonated, the factory was defending itself.

Why hadn't Adams planned for that? Felix's stomach clenched.

Kurt was nodding, trying to play it cool, but his heaving chest gave him away. At every explosion he jumped a little, and then tried to hide it. The army had come and gone, and the two Callahans looked across the street at the men and women running hard through the strands of wire, trying to cover their faces as they went even as they breathed the toxic air. Adams must be praying that the mushrooms were doing their miracle work deep inside each human cell.

'Do you trust me?' Kurt asked. He was still panting a little.

'Not one little bit. Why?'

'Just stay here with me a minute.'

Was he scared? Felix looked out into the morning light, the low clouds moving in over the city and the rising plumes of smoke over the fires. Kurt was still twitching at every explosion, narrowing his eyes to look tough. He has a heart in there somewhere, thought Felix.

'I hear you. Sometimes it helps to hang back a little and get a bit of perspective. Big picture.' There was real gunfire now, Renard's men taking aim from their fortress.

'Uncle Felix, what if there was another way? Another option?'

Felix screwed up his face in confusion.

'Like, it's not just them or us now, North or South. You see what I mean?' Kurt ducked as an RPG hit the side of the groaning factory, and Felix half pulled away from his grip to watch it.

'Son, I don't. Come on, now. Don't you want to get in there, at least? See what all the hoo-ha is about? This is your big chance.'

Kurt shook his head, the white hair flopping. 'Who are you fighting for, anyway?'

'I'm fighting Renard,' said Felix. He looked at Kurt carefully. The boy was losing it. I should have seen it, he thought. He never sat right with me from the beginning.

Around them Resistance soldiers were falling – shot, mostly, by Renard's snipers from inside the factory. They were always going to have the territorial advantage.

Kurt was insistent, the hand on Felix's shoulder hard enough to hurt. 'I'm serious. Those pronghorns. How about we don't choose a side? What do you think of that? We're not Southerners anymore really, not since it's gone to dust, and the North can go fuck itself. Or are you just fighting because that's all you know how to do?'

'I'm fighting like I used to. Because my whole life I've been hanging back and letting bad things happen. I've got to take a stand now, Kurt.'

'Me too. Absolutely. Fuck Renard. Fuck him. But fuck Adams too. And fuck you, Uncle Felix. Hell! Fuck me as well! I heard what you said about those pronghorns and about how we all took a wrong turn a long time ago. And you're right, Uncle Felix!' Kurt's eyes were bright; Felix had never seen him this passionate about anything.

'We can get inside that factory. We can get whatever machines are in there to turn the air to poison. And better than that. We can shut down Renard's magic. With the air gone to shit and no immunity in the tap water, it'll all be over soon as the mushrooms wear off! The end! Everybody out of the pool! A clean start, like the Great Flood in the Bible. Do you know that story?'

Felix nodded slowly. Sometimes he forgot that Kurt had never been to Sunday school, never seen a Gideon's bible in a hotel room, never heard a sermon on the radio.

'Sure. A million times. It always fascinated me. Every *useful* animal.'

'That's it! You get it! Only the useful ones, Uncle Felix. This is our chance, right here. It's not God looking down and judging us, or anything like Adams wants you to think. It's just you and me. We can decide. Us. The clearest thinkers. The most quali-fied.' He thumbed his chest.

As they watched, a bullet ripped clean through the back of Farrow's skull near them, as if he'd planned it himself.

'See?' said Kurt. He was shaking with both fear and elation.

'No more lessons. He lived by the sword, man.' Farrow fell face down, silent and professional, his gun tucked neatly against his back.

'You see that? It's a sign. Let the pronghorns and the giraffes have America. They're not going to fuck it up,' said Kurt.

'You're messed up, son. You know that?'

'I know it. But so what? Who isn't? Are you with me or not?'

The old man felt around in his ammunition bag and found the pair of patchy apples he'd stolen from the canteen. Wordlessly he offered one to Kurt.

The boy's shoulders sagged. He took the apple and turned it around: one side was green, the other red. He stared right into Felix's eyes, then he bit into the heart of it, and spat it out.

54

Dyce was still getting to grips with driving, and the thrill of it. He'd spent years dreaming of horses, the way that they could shrink geography and stretch the known world out to beyond the horizon. But cars! Cars, man. That was real-life time travel. A city that was weeks' worth of journeying on foot became a couple of hours away. Time and distance got fuzzy in a car. But he couldn't afford that: not when they were going to meet the man himself.

He toyed with the upper limits of the truck's speedometer, watching the miles tick past faster and faster. He had given up on the radio. Sometime late in the night he had tried it, searching for a station he could stand. So far the music was wrong – heavy beats that sounded the same whichever way he heard them, and singers who needed lessons they weren't getting. He had switched it off. There was a time for music and this wasn't it. Even if there'd been some decent song on, there was already too much floating around in the air inside the truck's cabin: thoughts and fears and expectations.

The women were paying him no attention, lulled into the rhythm that driving allowed. They were close together but did not speak, each occupied with their destination and what would happen there.

The end, Ruth was thinking. The end of every known thing.

She sat straight in her seat, the map book open on her lap, though Dyce hadn't asked for directions yet. It felt strange to be holding something other than the recipe book, but she'd brought that along too. It was all she had, wasn't it? Her legacy. Vida's too. The only real, physical link to the country she had left behind. She stared at the thickening foliage through the window, trying to remember what the trees looked like in South Africa. Were there any maples back home? She tried to conjure up the species she knew, trees transplanted by people who moved on afterward or stayed and put down pale roots of their own: pin oak, blue gum, jacaranda.

She racked her brain, trying to recall what she'd told Vida about Renard in the way-back, before she'd said he was her father, when it was just a story about her old life up North, like her old life back in South Africa: foreign; too far back to hurt anyone in the present. Had she even mentioned what he looked like? Had she ever said any tender thing about him? Had Vida had any idea of the suffering motherhood had been for Ruth, the terrible mixed blessing of that paternity? It was Everett she missed now, Ruth thought. She always would. The love that came after the blistering damage of youth: that was the most precious kind, because it was clear-eyed and knew its own worth.

She shifted and sighed, and Vida watched her mother from the back seat, where she lay against the door handle. She had fished Ears McCreedy out of the bag and was using him as cushioning against the bumps in the road. There was some primitive scent to the creature that appealed to her, some memory connected to the thing. As he traveled with them, Ears had started looking less and less like the squirrel he had been; now he was a bean-bag totem holding the grit and gravel of the South that

Garrett had so lovingly stuffed inside him. Vida thought: He'll probably be the baby's first toy.

Not toy.

Ancestral spirit. Guardian angel.

She thought about her own time with Everett: the days they had spent moving between settlements, and then the days in the old house. Once Vida had come back after a strange man had blundered into their yard, screaming wordlessly at the sky. There was blood trickling from his ears so that his shoulders were cloaked. It was Everett she wanted, Everett who would keep her safe. She must have been little, but she'd slammed the door against the bleeding man and shouted, 'Fuck Renard!' Had her mother echoed the sentiment about her old-time lover? Had she ever said 'Fuck Renard'? Vida couldn't remember. It was too wrapped up with all the other things she felt about Ruth: the love, and the resentment, and the guilt.

Dyce clicked his back and yawned. The lights of towns were flecking the horizon, more than they'd seen closer back to the Wall. Wyoming had been okay, but Nebraska and their whip through Iowa had smelt of decline. Des Moines, now that Dyce saw the true lights of other cities racing past, had been une-lectrified in whole sections, rot on a body that hadn't spread yet but would. Here, further east, the night-covered landscape twinkled with street lights and back-lit shop signs. The further they drove and the faster they went – Iowa City; Davenport; Ottawa – the closer modernity came, eating history even as they made it, until at last they crested a hill and the rising sun revealed the outskirts of distant Chicago.

'Now that,' said Dyce, 'is a metropolis.'

And then time speeded up again, the way cars made it, and they were close to Maple Lake. Every now and again Dyce asked

Ruth to match the road signs with the map, translating them from paper into the language of tree and rock and road. She held fast to her sports bottle all the while, the sparse green-brown fibers swilling.

They passed a white clapboard church in the encroaching forest, the cemetery choked with dandelions and the palisades pushed over in places by fallen branches. They went on, along a road flanked by more maples until it forked right at a bright yellow triangle that said NO PASSING ZONE.

The road climbed slightly and the foliage seemed to grow thicker, crowding the road until the canopy reached over them, the trees touching to form a tunnel that felt ominous, as though they were being funneled into a trap. Dyce and Garrett had watched trapdoor spiders at work, before they began the game with the pins, fascinated by the way the little critters dug and spun and crafted their tunnels. Nothing that went in there ever came out – no wings or legs or crispy carapace leftovers. Those doors were all one-way for the visitors. He hoped like hell that he and Ruth and Vida were the spiders.

'We're almost there,' he said in a tight voice, and Vida sat up properly and looked out at the closeness of the leaves and the sparse yellow chevrons that marked their passage.

Then, too fast, at another fork, there was suddenly water beyond an edging of trees and another sign that pointed them left around a grassy triangle.

'So this is Maple Lake,' murmured Vida. 'It's pretty.'

'Nice place for a showdown,' said Dyce.

They slowly skirted the lake and came to the overlook: a parking lot with a low wall and oil-drum bins – the same kind, Vida noticed, they had used as braziers in the Capitol Building. She imagined it now, its burnt-out shell. Somewhere in there were the fatty, scorched remains of Buddy and his red baseball cap. She fought the nausea down. You just help me now, she told the baby. This is all for you. So behave.

Ever law-abiding, Dyce turned the truck into a bay and cut the engine.

When they opened the car doors, the air was cold outside. They climbed out, taking stock of the place as Vida stretched her aching leg. On the opposite bank were more maple trees, crowding the edge to make a thin shore. There was an early-morning haze over the water, clinging to the surface in tendrils. Two geese flew overhead, honking damply, silhouetted against the orange sky.

'It's lovely here,' said Ruth. She was still holding the bottle. 'So quiet.' For some reason it made her want to cry.

'Maybe we'll come back,' Dyce lied, and he put his arm around her. To his surprise, she let him. They stood and contemplated the path that led out along a spit of land reaching into the lake, ending with a rusting jetty. On the sand was a picnic table. Some parks-and-recreation man had once coated it with bitumen, and the smell made Vida long again for Everett.

'I just need to know why we're meeting here,' she said, turning around to take it all in.

'At least it's quiet. We'll be able to tell whether Renard comes alone or not,' Dyce said. He wasn't sure.

'And if he doesn't?'

'We make a run for it.' He shrugged. 'What else are we going to do? But that won't happen. He's expecting you and Ruth, right? Not me.'

'Yeah.' Vida wasn't sure where he was going with this.

'If he sees me, that'll be the deal blown. But I could take the rifle and hide somewhere out of sight with a clear line. In case something goes wrong, you know? In case it's not just him that shows up. He's not exactly known for his fair dealings.'

Vida shivered. 'That would make me feel better.'

'I was thinking about that in the car. I could take him out. I could shoot him. I'd do it happily. He's your father. I know that.'

'Stop,' said Vida. She took his hand and squeezed it. 'I have to do it myself, okay?'

'You're just going to kill him?'

'I've thought about it.' She was matter-of-fact, and in that moment Dyce was afraid of her. 'I'll drown him. I will. I'll push him into the water and I'll hold onto him until there isn't one fucking bubble left. Like Mami Wata.'

Dyce didn't have to look at Ruth to know that she was shaking her head. 'You don't have to.'

'I know that. But it's personal, Dyce. I want him to suffer. I don't believe in all that heaven-and-hell shit. You know that. He has to know what he's done. If you shoot him, then he won't get it. Does that make sense? He's killed millions of people, far away, in a place he can't see because he forced his own people to build a wall to hide it. He couldn't even watch. He's a fucking coward. He's not my father in any way that actually counts. Renard doesn't get long-distance death or turn-the-other-cheek. He gets me. With my hands around his neck.'

'Jesus, Vida.'

'What did you think was going to happen, Dyce?'

'I just didn't imagine you would enjoy it.'

She clicked her tongue. 'Don't shoot him unless something goes wrong.'

'All right,' said Dyce.

'Promise me.'

'Fuck! I promise!'

Ruth spoke up. 'You need to get going now. Vida and me, we'll sit at the bench. It'll give you a clear view.'

Dyce turned Vida to face him. He angled his head to kiss her and she pulled him fiercely to her. Ruth looked away, and made a show of searching for somewhere to hide the bottle where it would be safe.

'I love you,' said Dyce. 'I fucking love you and I hope you know that.'

He walked off up the road and Vida watched him go. It was the pearly light and the lope of his stride, but she thought of Garrett. A little way along he turned back to blow her a kiss.

It was Dyce, all right. There was no mistaking that. But he'd changed. She turned the idea over in her head.

He didn't look young anymore, or meek. That was it.

Then, in his new skin, he turned off the path into the forest and was gone.

55

The virus factory, lit orange by the early sun, looked as though it had been designed to mimic a Norman castle or a monastery. At the base, behind all those barriers and barbed wires, Felix could make out a gray patchwork on the wall – he'd seen it plenty in New York, where someone had covered over graffiti that disagreed with them. There was hope in that – for one, it meant the building's security wasn't watertight, but also it meant there were people here willing to risk their lives to send a message. It gave Felix a warm feeling and it made him wonder just how many Resistance fighters there were up North.

What if it was half the Northern population? What if it was more than that?

The main structure was square and at least ten stories high, the walls smooth and windowless – except for a panel of blackened glass just below the lip of the precipice. Felix scaled the wall with his gaze and settled on the windows, that row of sightless eyes, gleaming reinforced glass. If there was a control center, it'd be up there, he was sure. He glanced over at Kurt and saw that he had made the same deduction. Was the kid serious when he said he wanted to end it all? Did he think that by simply waiting and watching, he could walk right into the heart of the beast and turn it all back on itself?

Felix pictured the building sprouting legs and arms and

standing up, its fists clenched like Godzilla. But of course it didn't have to: it brought more destruction in its permanence, spewing viruses out into the sky and letting nature take its course, strangling the South and controlling the North.

Above the glass windows along the roof were four galvanized pipes, each big enough to swallow a small plane. Those, Felix bet, were the faucets for the airborne diseases. Somewhere behind and deep below them were the labs where the viruses and their matching antivirals were manufactured, like test-tube twins.

Beneath it all was the waterworks that ensured that the good citizens got their daily dose. Felix wondered if there was something else in the water apart from the antivirals. Something that made people relaxed, less likely to fight, like that stuff they used in the soldiers' canteens during the world wars: bluestone.

But real blood-and-guts fighting was happening right in front of him. Even from across the street it felt to Felix as though he was watching a battle on one of his old televisions – the really big ones, the ones that cost a fortune to keep in stock, heavy as hell, but worth it for colors that vivid, the sound effects ringing in your ears long after, so that a man's dream life bled into his daytime. The clash and roar rose and fell in waves around them, but still Felix held back. He'd finally decided to fight, and now he couldn't. Whatever he did, he couldn't let the boy out of his sight or something terrible would happen.

Kurt sat and watched too, his face expressionless – and it made Felix wonder again what he'd done to Norma. Kind, dumb old Norma. It was her blood and her blouse he wore, like trophies of war.

The Resistance army had desperation on its side, and it was making good ground. It was pretty obvious that the guards up in the factory weren't trained for a full-on assault once a virus had already been released. Felix reckoned it was likely a one-off, a unique strain designed for the purpose – and that meant no antiviral to turn it toothless. None, at least, that would make it into the water supply.

The Resistance just kept coming. If Felix hadn't been there to see it with his own eyes, he wouldn't have believed it. Adams's people were nothing short of miraculous, pushing on through the mist of deadly pathogens. With each wave of attack another perimeter wall fell: the explosions were sowing the havoc that they were always meant to.

At last the factory guards emerged along the rooftop between the huge pipes with their guns and their masks, lying low against the structure to make themselves more slender targets. It was a fuck-up, that was for sure. The soldiers were distant specks of black against the gray wall, but it was clear enough to any-one watching. If reinforcements were coming, they were taking their time. Had the North planned another, later attack on the Capitol Building? Or had they really just not seen the convoy leaving Des Moines? Perhaps Renard's men and Adams's army had passed in opposite directions on the open highway. Felix snorted at the idea.

'Great minds,' he told himself. It happened.

As far as he could tell, the Resistance was suffering. The fac-tory guards, once they were in place, recovered themselves and began to do serious damage to the army. Where the mortars had blasted holes in the perimeter walls there were bottlenecks of Resistance soldiers, pushing and shoving: they made soft targets for the men on the roof, like peasants storming the castle.

An RPG hit the front wall and set the Northern guards back. Felix could tell they were assessing the damage before they crept to the edge again. While they did, the Resistance men and women crouched and sprinted, crouched and sprinted. He was glad not to be in the thick of it now – not especially because of the bullets, but because he didn't think his calceous spine could have stood it.

Surely they were within reach now. The first tattered explosives crew touched the base of the factory wall and began setting up, their compatriots covering their activities with distracting fire. Still the factory guards aimed over the edge, their bullets boring holes straight through the tops of two Resistance skulls. Felix felt each one.

The rest didn't stop their work, bolstered as they were by the arrival of the reserve crew. Even at this distance it was easy to tell when the bomb was armed. That determined wave of attack against the building stopped abruptly, and the Resistance army peeled off left and right to get some distance from the explosion's impact.

He and Kurt saw the ball of fire erupt. When the explosion came, a moment later, the earth actually shook. It felt as though someone had punched Felix in the chest. He coughed up a piece of apple and doubled over.

When he could breathe again, Kurt was holding his hands over his ears like a little kid who didn't want to hear an insult. Felix grabbed his arm so the boy looked at him, and mouthed, 'You okay there?'

'That's our cue,' shouted Kurt. He had that look again. 'Every Northern soldier is probably on his way now, thanks to that little alarm bell. So if you're good to go, let's move!'

Felix nodded as if it was his idea, and straightened up all the way, grasping at the old authority of adulthood. They made their way quickly across the street, but once they were on the opposite sidewalk, Kurt broke into a jog and it hurt Felix to keep up. His knees were twanging like a banjo – his hips too – and with each jolt there was a sharp pain in his neck. I'm the fucking Tin Man, he thought sourly.

What kept him going, measured his pace close to Kurt's, was knowing that this was the last time he'd feel this terrible. His body telling him how old it was, how ready it was for the end of all suffering. Wasn't that what they said about torture? That you could stand the worst kind if you just knew there would be an end?

He kept his head down, tallying up the bodies as he passed them. There they were: Pete and Sam from Horse Head, bleeding out into the cold dirt; Gabby the torture expert, caught upright on a coil of razor wire and shot through a dozen times because she couldn't fall; Sy and Mario side by side, their faces frozen in snarls of death under the Northern sky, gone the way they would have wanted; dozens more Felix recognized but whose names he'd never known.

But it was Adams he was looking for among the twisted heads and twisted limbs. Adams was the only one who counted. And there was no sign of him, was there?

He and Kurt forced their way through the corpses, dodging the craters and the fragments of razor coils that sat like cottonmouths in the grass. He wanted to apologize, and then he didn't, because there were too many for it to mean anything. They still smelt human, that was the worst of it: of shit and blood and some dirty, wet stink that underlay it all and seared his nostrils. It was only now that he recognized it for what it was, though he'd inhaled it every time he'd peed since he'd eaten Dyce's fucking miracle cure.

It was the smell of the mushrooms, here among these new

bodies: the stench of Buddy's ghost. It turned the recent dead as dank and earthen as the guilty caverns under the Mouth; it stole their decent particular names. Felix tried to wave the stink away and kept on, his lungs burning, for the last stretch.

The hole in the building looked like a mouth too, with the sharp points of reinforcing pointing down like teeth. The ground was still warm, moist where the soil had melted into muddy globs like it was the first day of Creation.

Kurt was unfazed and he scuttled through. Felix followed him.

And then they were in the basement of the factory, dizzying and stagnant as a nightmare. Somewhere a man was shouting, and Felix turned his head as if he could identify the voice.

Adams. It had to be. He was somewhere ahead of them. Felix would bet everything he had that the man hadn't seen any bullets up close. Through the maze of the mezzanine stairs and the curve of the outsize pipes, the Resistance was setting the final bomb – the one that would paralyze the factory for keeps. The allies, however many there were – and all right-thinking people – were about to get word that Big Daddy was gone: Renard's control of everything they drank and breathed no longer meant a thing.

Kurt led Felix on, deeper into the factory's innards.

He was rewarded. There was Adams, standing over a crew of three people, each of them pressing explosives up against the biggest pipes running straight up through the ceiling like a cathedral organ. When he saw Kurt, he jerked his gun up and away.

The boy made his way forward, Felix lurking behind, trying to hold down a fit of coughing. Kurt was as calm as if he were approaching cows or sheep.

'Hellfire, son! What are you doing? I nearly sent you to kingdom come!' Adams lowered his weapon. 'Felix's young friend. Kenny, right? I almost put one between your eyes! Ah, and the old man himself! Felix. Good to see you.' He had to raise his voice against the clanging and shouting of the battle in the building.

Kurt was holding up his hands in surrender. 'Friendly fire. Isn't that what they call it? It's Kurt, by the way.' Felix bent over, hands on his knees, trying to catch his breath.

'Well, I'm glad to see you anyhow. Can you watch over these three? They just need a couple more minutes to set the bomb. If anyone else comes through there,' Adams pointed his gun at a couple of gray metal doors, 'you make sure it's the last thing they do.'

'Sir, I am *happy* to help,' replied Kurt. He unholstered his pistol.

'I got to get some elevation,' Adams explained. 'Rule of war, right? We need to see what we're dealing with on the way out. *If* there's a way out.' He grinned. 'Kidding.'

He turned his attention to the grimy explosives crew, each twisting wires and setting dials. 'If I'm not back in five minutes, you go ahead and let her rip.'

One of them nodded, intent on her work.

'Good,' said Adams. He limped to the exit, passing Felix. 'That kid of yours is the real deal. I hope you're proud of him.'

The old man wanted to protest, but with his breath came the coughing.

With Adams gone, Kurt put the pistol in his belt and looked around, playing guard. He felt in his pocket for the multi-tool. It was where it always was.

He took it out idly and examined the hinges, where blood

had congealed. That would make it hard to open: that was bad. He cleaned it off with his fingernails and wiped the tool down.

It had to go. All of it. The building and the bomb – and the bombers too. It would just be the two of them: Callahans together, as it was always meant to be. They could remake the world the way it should have been in the first place.

Kurt moved, fast and quiet, his lips drawn back over his teeth. He set about butchering the explosives crew: one fast, hard blow to the neck each time.

There. That was for his asshole family.

There. That was for Bethie, who never loved him.

And *there.* That was for the stupid fucking cat.

He was done and bloody to the elbows before Felix could stop him.

56

Vida and Ruth sat at the bench, trying not to seem as though they were looking. Dyce would be somewhere not far along the bank, directly behind Ruth.

After a minute of scanning the leaves, Ruth said suddenly, 'We shouldn't look, in case someone's watching us.' She turned her head to stare out over the water.

'I keep expecting jets,' said Vida. 'A big roar and then napalm or something raining down. The end of the world ought to be like that. You ought to know it's happening.' If she was looking for reassurance, Ruth was the wrong place for it. Another trio of geese passed over and Vida wished for their wings and their certitude.

'If we were here for anything else, this would be pretty idyllic,' Ruth said mildly. It was costing her to look casual, Vida thought. Ruth was holding tightly to the edge of the table. The bottle was hidden somewhere Vida hadn't seen. Where was it?

'How are you feeling, Vida?'

'I'm okay, Mama. If it changes, I'll let you know. Don't worry so much.' She paused. 'Actually, there's something I want to know.' Ruth tensed. 'I never asked you how you got to the Capitol Building. You would've told me already if you'd felt inclined, right?'

'We were busy.'

'A little distracted,' Vida agreed. The women smiled the same smile at each other.

'Well, now. In the river,' Ruth began, 'I tried real hard to swim back to you but the water took me. It wasn't so deep, was it? But it was strong as the devil. I woke up staring at the ceiling of an ambulance, a nurse over me, holding my IV. Took me right back. For a while I thought she was me and I was out of my body, floating somewhere near the roof of the ambulance. I didn't know how close I was to drowning for real.' Her mouth turned down and a tear slid out. Vida held her hand tight across the table.

'Well, it turned out that she was me, in a way. The way I used to be, I mean. I used to work with her mother back in the day. Angela. How's that for coincidence? I knew that face. When we worked it out, she told her mother, and she came to the hospital right away. Middle of the night! All those years later and she hadn't forgotten me, Vida. All those people I left behind in the North too.' Ruth sighed.

'She wheeled me right out the front door, sat me in her Mazda, and drove me straight to the Capitol Building. They told me that if you were alive, you'd get there too. So I waited, and you came. I knew you would. You are my whole life, given back to me. The only thing. You'll know how that feels real soon.'

'God, Mama.' Vida was crying too: the last few minutes they had before everything changed. They looked out to the water to let the air cool their faces.

'It's strange, isn't it?' said Ruth finally. 'Carrying a baby. No one can tell you how it really is. You're an incubator for this life that comes from somewhere else. A carrier for the little human seed.'

'I'm a regular old recipe book, Mama.'

'But you are. You really are.'

After that there was time for less intense but more loving words, and Vida felt the air between them thicken with the bond of tenderness again, the way it had been when she was little.

Forty minutes later, around what must have been eight o'clock, a maroon Jaguar rolled along the road that skirted Maple Lake. The invisible driver parked it beside Buddy's pickup.

'E-Type,' said Ruth as the door opened. 'Typical. It's him.'

Even from a hundred yards away, Renard was not the man Vida had imagined. He was smaller, for starters, barely taller than the roof of the car when he stood straight to set the jazzy panama hat properly on his head. He was darker than she had expected too. In her imaginings he'd always been white: cold and dazzling, powered by some diseased internal light, or the monster of her nightmares.

But there he was instead, like a hundred people Vida had known in her old life, an ordinary man in a summer-weight suit, old and stiff enough to move carefully. Vida saw Ruth's knuckles whiten, but her mother's face stayed the same.

He looked right at them on the bench, then waved and smiled as if they were paparazzi. They didn't wave back. He moved to the trunk of his car, popped it open and searched inside it for something.

'What's he getting?' Vida whispered. 'A machine gun?'

Christ. Renard was pulling out a wicker basket.

'I don't believe it,' she murmured. 'Mama. Look at the check-ered cloth!'

He settled it on his arm like an upmarket waiter, and made his way over the low wall to the lake shore, strolling along the water's edge toward them. His white suit flashed in the morning sun, and Ruth thought of all the baptisms she had seen back home, the billowing vestments of the newly adopted being swallowed by the gray-green water. He was holding the basket away from his body so that it didn't bump against his thigh at each step, and Vida felt a dangerous bubble of laughter rising from her throat. All along she'd thought he was the wicked wolf, but here he was in Grandma's nightgown.

Stop it, she told herself sternly. You just stop it. You know how rotten he is on the inside, like the nested electrics in a condemned building that sparked and burnt anyone who touched them. She made herself think of all those walls with 'Fuck Renard' scribbled on their crumbling concrete or scratched into their cladding, easily more powerful than 'God bless us, every one'. Each one had been sincere, and each one had been born of some terrible act Renard had designed. It didn't matter what he looked like, did it? He might as well be the snake-headed man or the giant with the fists like mallets or the hooded man with the devil's eyes. It was what was on the inside that counted.

The pendulum weight of the picnic basket connected with his leg and he hopped away from the pain, the basket swinging back – but now Vida wasn't smiling, not even to herself. And then he was there. He stopped and cocked his neat head to the side.

'Ruthie!' he cooed, fond and familiar.

Vida felt her mother draw herself up with something beyond outrage and revulsion. She had a pretty good idea of what it was. Self-loathing. Ruth wouldn't even say his name now except to curse it. She felt a burst of pride for her mother. It wasn't the mess you made that was important. Wasn't that what Ruth had always told her? It was how you cleaned it up afterward. Reparation.

Renard had stopped fussing with the basket; now he was dusting the crease back into his white trousers. He held out a hand to Ruth, supplicatory, theatrical. 'You are more beautiful than the day you left me.'

Ruth stared him coldly in the eye.

'I don't blame you,' he confided. He winked at Vida, as if they were co-conspirators.

Then he offered his hand to her. Surprised into manners, Vida took it, only to feel its bony undead weight, an exhibit in an abandoned museum.

'Baron Samedi.'

She drew back in shock.

'A little joke! Didier Renard, of course. My slave name, but I kept it.' He looked her over with flat, metallic eyes. 'And you are Vida. Vida. Vida! You can't understand how happy I am to finally meet you! And so healthy! You're blooming! Is it indelicate to comment on your condition? I am just so happy, and so very, very proud.'

Vida found herself at a loss. She wanted to wipe her hand on her shirt, thinking of that story of the woman whose arm had been paralyzed when she touched a convicted murderer through the bars of his cell. She crossed her arms low over her stomach.

'Hello.'

'I've hoped for you for so long! You do know that? I've looked and looked for you. And now you're here and my only prayer has been answered – that I'd meet my daughter before I die.' Renard set his hand over his heart.

He's mocking us, Vida thought. He's making a show of being

polite because he knows it's making Mama furious. Renard beamed, and she thought of Adams, with his sticking plaster and his steamy rhetoric that other people breathed right in, the rhetoric that sent them to their deaths. Why couldn't people just say what they meant? Why did they want to do evil but cloak it with pretense? It made no sense.

He waved an expansive arm. 'I came alone. I hope you noticed that. A show of goodwill. If you are going to make an attempt on my life' – he smiled, as if this was beyond the bounds of all good sense – 'then I must take my chances, no?' They stared at him. He shrugged. 'So now let us break bread together to celebrate our reunion. We are a family, after all.'

Vida shuddered at the words, echoes of the way Ruth sometimes spoke, signs of a long-ago co-mingling of this man and her mother. It wasn't just sex: thoughts and feelings and conversations, a long-enough time together so that he'd gleaned some of her language. Or had it been the other way around? Vida couldn't tell, but it chilled her. Had Ruth been echoing his phrases all this time? And did she know she was doing it? Or was Renard just part of her, seeded deep and invisible into her flesh as mushroom spores – just as he was for Vida?

And beyond Vida too. For her baby, and everyone who came after them, for ever more.

Renard picked the basket up and set it on the table, chattering in a kind of relief. 'I hope it's not too soon for a family picnic? I've brought coffee and wine and pork sausages.' He smiled at them, sure of himself. 'They say you should never peer into the factory where the sausages are made – backstage, as it were; otherwise you would never eat them again.'

He began to unpack the contents of the basket onto the table: willow-pattern plates; heavy silver cutlery with someone else's family crest on it; glasses that Ruth was pretty sure were crystal. He even set out a little vase, and into it put a single stem with an unopened rosebud topping it.

'I dethorned it myself,' he said softly. He put the basket on the ground and sat down beside Ruth on the bench. 'May I?' he asked, after the fact. 'And now, to business.

'As I think I mentioned, you're welcome to do your best to kill me. I don't have many more natural years left in me. Better here with the geese and the sunrise than home in my lonely bed. But I'm going to make one request.'

'You can ask anything you like,' Vida burst out, the enchantment worn off. 'But we'll decide. There's been enough of that. Enough of you getting your own way. Do you have any idea how many people you've hurt? How many families you've shattered? Homes burnt? Lives lost? Have you ever even been down South?'

'You are a resilient girl,' said Renard. 'You remind me of someone I used to know.'

Ruth was quiet. Vida wondered if it was the silence of consent, a dog returning belly-first to its master. She felt her own stomach flop with despair and dread. Ruth would be no help at all. Why had she ever thought that her mother would stand up to her tormentor? She was probably still half in love with him! The nausea rippled up from Vida's gut. Look at him. How normal he was, how eager to please. She wouldn't be able to kill him, frail and small in his clean white suit and that silly panama hat. Why had she told Dyce to hold off on the shot? She wanted Renard dead now, before he could say anything else to charm her boneless mother back into the circle of his arms, the maiden in the grip of the vampire.

Renard paused, pouring a cup of coffee for himself and one

for Ruth. 'None for you, young lady,' he said playfully. 'Not with that cargo on-board. Do you know, the night your mother ran away, I knew she was pregnant. The happiest and the saddest day of my life! A child would have been everything. Everything. I looked through the things she left, searching for clues, but your mother could be cruel. She'd left everything except her ridiculous comics and that recipe book. You remember that old thing?' He was smiling at Ruth, who nodded slowly.

'Every single other item of value she left behind. She knew I'd have eyes watching when her gold watch turned up, or that bracelet with the diamonds. But she took one other thing that I was very pleased about. She was always clever, weren't you, Ruthie? To take that syringe from the lab? Oh, it was before the chemical warfare the South brought down on their own heads, but the nurses had seen up close what we were doing in the labs. Insurance, eh, Ruth? If it ever seemed as though we might be losing the War, why, then the viruses would save everyone in the North. Everyone who had chosen the right side. And if God is with us, who can stand against us? Isn't that what they say?' He broke off and hummed a few holy bars. Vida made out 'Emmanuel' and 'Come To Us' but she knew he was mocking them again. Renard, like Adams, had no use for the Almighty; men like that created the earth from scratch in their backyards, blowing their own sick breath into men made of mud.

'Ah, Ruthie. You knew we'd use the viruses, and you knew when. Back then there was only one vial to take, and so you took it. You know, I'm proud of you for that master stroke. But your mother didn't use it on herself, Vida. She waited for your arrival, like Mary waited for Little Baby Jesus. Such sacrifice. It was your birthright, the only gift your father ever gave you.'

I don't believe this, Vida thought. He's comparing himself

to God. She wanted to see if Ruth understood, but her mother kept her head down.

'I know all of this,' Vida said slowly. As she spoke, she saw her mother's wrists twisting gently under the table while Renard was still busy dishing up food they couldn't eat. Ruth was wringing her hands.

No. Not wringing at all.

She was unscrewing the lid of the bottle! Her show of quiet submission was a decoy. If Vida could manage to keep the old guy talking, they'd poison him like Rasputin. She tried not to let the relief show. Ask him something, she told herself. Anything. He wants to talk. So let him.

'Why are you really here?'

Renard poured cream into his coffee, then stirred it. 'It's a long story.'

'We have time.'

He cocked one eyebrow. 'Do we? Yes, I think we do. Well. Let me think back now. I want to get it absolutely right.

'You know I had a wife? Queenie. A lovely woman. Soft-hearted. Too soft-hearted. When she found out about the viruses, she tried to persuade me against using them to win the War. Imagine! Every cause must have its martyrs, I suppose. Along with a fellow from the South, well, I made a martyr out of her. And it turned out well, didn't it? Two birds, as the saying goes. One stone. It was a great time. A time without interference. I could send anything I wanted over that border, and I could make sure that the South would never rise again. And also, Vida,' Renard turned his great unblinking eyes on her, 'I could find you.'

'How?' asked Vida, keeping her attention from drifting to her mother's hands.

'Thanks to your mother's light fingers, thanks to that vial of immunity, you'd be the only girl left alive. The whole of the South would be a wasteland, and just you standing. Can you picture it? The jewel in the center of it all.' He smiled fondly.

Vida stood, and then had to sit down again quickly when her bandage scraped against the picnic table. She winced and bent down to repair it.

'Are you all right?' Ruth asked. But how could she be? Renard had started the War because he was a madman, but he'd kept going, kept grinding the South into the dirt just so that he could find *her*! All those lives lost, all those families turned to bones, just so that there'd be one last survivor, sticking out of the scrubland like a sore thumb. God! Was it really true?

She nodded, lips compressed.

'Shall I go on? Well, then. I have always had allies in the South. They formed what you might call a task force. I didn't say that I was looking for my daughter – never let the enemy know your soft spot! – but I told them to keep an eye out for anyone special. Anyone immune. And would you believe it? I actually had some promising reports from my man Tye Callahan, just before the storm hit.

'Oh, Vida, it was a mixed blessing! I knew that a storm that big would unearth every dormant virus I'd sent over the years. Imagine my distress! I wasn't sure that your single dose would hold out against our history of illness. The system had never been designed for that – one at a time, yes, maybe two, but not hundreds.

'So when that storm came and went, I thought I'd lost my chance. I'd lost you. I'll be honest with you, Vida. I nearly gave you up for dead.' Renard shook his head, and Vida expected him to produce a spotted handkerchief from one of those white pockets and honk discreetly into it.

'But fortune was on our side! I got the call, like a message from heaven. Come and sit back down, Vida. Come and sit with your old Papa Lazarus.'

Vida had stood again as if to stretch her leg. Now she coughed, then fell forward onto her hands and knees and pretended to retch. Renard sprang up, hobbling and concerned. Do it now, Vida told Ruth in her head. Do it now while he's helping me. Poison this devil! Give him a taste of his own vicious medicine!

Renard took hold of her arm with his bloodless hands, his grip a vice. He'll never let me go, she thought as she wiped her mouth. Never, ever.

He helped her to sit back down and regarded her with those silvery eyes. She cleared her throat. 'I just want to know why.'

'Why what?'

'Why any of it?'

He frowned. 'There is no why. Why does anyone do anything? Why did people build the Hanging Gardens or the Colossus of Rhodes or the Empire State Building? And why did other people try to tear them down? I did it because I could.'

'But all those thousands – millions – of people are gone.'

'And even I cannot bring them back. Have something to eat,' he said, and began buttering a slice of bread for her. 'Your baby needs more than it's getting. Come, come. The bread's good.' He put it on a plate, then forked two pork sausages from the bowl and set them on top. Vida felt the nausea, real this time, and reached for her mother's cold coffee. She took a sip to rinse her mouth and spat it out onto the grass, along with a coil of bile.

'There's no shame in it,' said Renard. 'Get it all out.'

She sipped from the cup again, hoping that Renard would do the same. He did, then peered into his cup.

'What's this?' He fished a fragment from the liquid and wiped it on the table.

'A maple leaf,' said Vida.

The first bullet arrived before the sound of its shot. It hit Ruth side-on, entering her left breast and punching a hole all the way through her. Vida shrieked and the geese honked their alarm too late and skittered up into the air over the lake. What was Dyce doing?

Ruth slumped forward and Vida scrambled to her, trying to duck whatever was coming next. 'Mama. Mama. Mama. Please be okay. Please.' The plastic bottle rolled away from them into the water, where it bobbed and then filled.

The second shot hit Renard as he jumped back, slamming into his left shoulder and staying there. He fell to the sound of his own high screaming.

It took Vida a second to realize that it wasn't Dyce who'd fired. The shots were coming from across the lake. Dyce was nearer to them, behind Ruth's bleeding back.

The realization hit her with almost as much force as a bullet. This was the reason Adams had chosen the open water of Maple Lake as the meeting place: it made a clear line of sight for a man with a rifle and a scope. Not a shrub or a leaf or a blade of fucking grass in the way – a clear line to make sure Renard was dead.

And his family too. Every single one of them.

Renard wasn't dead yet, though he had quit screaming. He was stumbling, holding his bloody shoulder, Ruth's poison in his veins. But he was upright, determined as one of the machines in his factory. He was a few paces away already by the time Vida collected her thoughts and ran him down into the shallows.

Another shot whizzed by, missing them both. Then, holding as tight to Renard as a little girl to her daddy's neck, Vida took a deep breath and swam down as far as she could under the water.

57

'Kurt! No!' Felix yelled. 'What are you doing?'

The boy turned to face him, the new blood pinned to him like roses, and a small spray in his hair.

'I'm doing what we spoke about, Uncle Felix. I'm ending it all.'

Felix made a lunge for the boy, but he hopped back out of his reach.

'It'll all be okay, just stay out of my way,' Kurt said. 'This will help.' He punched Felix in the face hard enough to set him on his backside. Then he made for the door Adams had disappeared through.

Kurt climbed up and up, his multi-tool back in his pocket and his gun lodged in one fist. The metal staircase groaned under his weight as if it was adjusting to the shock that had loosened it from the walls of the building.

It held fast. And he was ready, wasn't he? For guards to come thundering down the stairs from above. But perhaps there weren't as many of them as Adams had figured. Why would the factory need more than the bare minimum of controllers, there in among the machines and the piping? Still, it paid to be cautious, and so Kurt held his gun ahead of him, pointing up the stairs for the first sign of trouble.

At each landing he passed another gray door with a tiny window in the center, portholes into the inner workings of the

decimated factory. The place was mostly labs, he saw now, and
Renard had gone for clean design: everything was covered in
plastic or painted white to show the dirt. The knobbly red lights
throbbed like pimples on every wall as he climbed, but no one
came to stop him. The signs attached to each flat surface went
unread, and there was some pleasure in not obeying the com-
mands to CLEAN HANDS TWICE and REMEMBER YOUR
MASK. There were other less hysterical but more ominous
warnings too, with their death's-head graphics: ENTER AT
OWN RISK and KEEP DOOR CLOSED AT ALL TIMES!

'I like skulls too,' Kurt murmured. The ear-splitting alarms
he had anticipated were malfunctioning or had never been
installed in the first place.

Where the staircase stopped was a final door labeled
CONTROL ROOM. Renard had no sense of humor, did he?

Kurt took hold of the handle and pulled. It wasn't locked,
but it had jammed against the bent frame and he had to yank
it a couple of times before it opened.

'There goes the elephant of surprise,' he said, pointing his
gun into the room. The reinforced windows had been blown
out and a fresh breeze circulated inside, its own weather system.
The sinking ship had been abandoned.

Kurt crunched over the glass to a high-backed chair that
faced a panel of dials and gauges and tiny clocks. He sat and
stared at the buttons and levers. They were divided down the
middle. As far as he could make out, the left-hand side was dedicated to the release of viruses into the air. The right controlled
the antivirals in the water.

'Light and dark,' said Kurt. Even a kid could do it. 'Easy
peasy. Now let's see. If I was Renard, what would piss me off?'

It was obvious. 'First step,' Kurt told himself, and pulled every lever on the right side down to zero, 'is to stop the miracle water supply.'

The lights on that side of the meridian flickered out. Kurt waited. He had expected something more dramatic. Out there, far below, behind the walls of the houses and apartments, people would begin to die. A hundred different ways to go, triggered by the terrible things that already lay dormant in their bodies, had lain there sleeping ever since they were born – before birth, even, written into their genetic code when man swung down from the trees.

But he wouldn't be there to see it, would he? Kurt turned his attention to the other side.

'Tricky.'

He began cranking the dials up as far as they would go, throwing needles into the red zone wherever he could manage it. He felt the building hum underneath him, a rhythmic pulse, but he couldn't tell if it had only just started, or if he simply hadn't noticed it before. Was this it? Armageddon? Were the viruses spilling out into the air right now?

He turned to look out the window. Then he stood and went to the empty frames. There was that weird smell again, the smell he'd caught when the building had tried to defend itself: some viral substrate on the air.

It was much stronger. Kurt coughed. If he was Renard, he would have booby-trapped the shit out of this place.

Adams appeared in the doorway. So that was what the rhythm had been! The sound of an angry man thumping up the metal staircase.

'Kenny?' he said, bustling closer. His face was slack with disbelief, the plaster on his cheek dragging. 'That you, boy? What's going on?'

'Howdy. And it's still Kurt.'

'What are you doing in here? We've got two minutes, you know that? The building's coming down in two minutes!' He raced to the window and squinted out. 'They're here. Christ. They're finally here.'

Renard's forces were mobilized at last. They both marveled at the arrangement in the Chicago streets, a tide of tiny vehicles like army ants.

'Let's move!' Adams barked. 'That way.' He pointed east to a patch of open ground. 'We'll make it to the treeline.'

'No one's doing any running,' said Kurt.

Adams gaped. 'Are you nuts? *They're here*. You know what that means?'

Kurt raised the gun and Adams held out his hands, palms spread.

'Are you retarded? Did you fuck with the machines? Whose side are you on?'

'Sir, I am done with sides.'

Adams shook his head. 'I don't know what you're on, son, but it's fucking with your head. I'm going to go on over to the window, now, because I hear something bad is happening out there.'

Kurt gave him credit: Adams was as good as his word.

'What the holy fuck!'

Kurt nodded. That was about the size of it. He had pumped every single virus in storage, old and new, out into the atmosphere, and Renard's soldiers had no protective gear. They were still too far away for Adams to see the blood and the vomit and the shit that covered the street, but he could tell that the army had stopped. The living were scurrying like ants under a magnifying glass – then they each curled up, twitching. Some of them lay still already; the rest would follow soonish.

'You did this? You're *crazy*.' Adams's voice broke. He sounded as if he was going to cry, and for a moment Kurt pitied him.

'I did it for the pronghorns.'

'You've gone absolutely insane! This wasn't the plan!'

'Who cares?' Kurt said. 'I'm glad I did. One day maybe someone will write FUCK KURT on a wall. But I hope not. I hope that no one remembers me. And I really hope no one remembers Renard. Let everything he wanted die with him. He'll hate that, won't he? Being forgotten. Whoever arrives next, when the air is clear again – I hope they do better than we did.'

'You fucking moron! There were good people out there. You think you can just kill everyone and start again?'

'Listen carefully now, because I am getting a little tired of the yapping.' Kurt beckoned. 'Come in close. That's right. Now hear me: *There are not enough good people*. No one did a fucking thing to stop Renard at any step of the way. And it was a long road, old man. You know it. Your Resistance just fucked it up for everybody else *because you waited too long*. If you're really looking for someone to blame, blame yourself. You did this.'

Adams stepped even closer and gripped Kurt's free arm, ignoring the gun.

'But we could still stop this, right? We could pump the . . . the anti-viral shit right into the water, same as he did. These folk here are done, but maybe the people out on the west coast . . . we could save some.'

'You're right,' Kurt said. 'It's possible. And that's why I got to shoot you.'

Adams smiled, and it hurt him. 'You got another think coming, my friend. You ever actually fire that gun we gave you?'

Kurt narrowed his eyes, and Adams went on. 'I'm pretty sure

you were supposed to go into battle with a dud weapon and be shot early on in the action. We never trusted you. You or your Uncle Fuckwad. Turns out we were right on the money.'

Kurt pulled the trigger and it clicked, but there was no satisfying report.

Adams raised his own arm. There was a gun in his hand now.

'This one works,' he said.

But the boy was too quick for him. Trained in the Callahan wasteland of the South, he was more animal than human as he leapt and brought Adams down. He drew back the multi-tool and managed to puncture Adams in the chest three times before the man twisted away from him.

Kurt went for the windpipe next, but Adams had lived a long time. He turned his head to the side and Kurt grabbed at his face, his fingers sliding in through the plaster, deep into the man's mouth.

Adams gurgled and bit down. The bones in Kurt's fingers crunched between the rotting molars. Kurt howled and brought the multi-tool down one last time, straight into Adams's skull. The preacher shook in his death throes as if he was trying to buck the boy, and then he lay still. The blood seeped thick and slow from the tool protruding from his forehead.

Kurt pulled his hand back out of Adams's mouth. His ring finger had stayed behind, but he was never going to need it. The pinky and middle fingers hung limp and bloody; he wiped them absently on his blouse.

58

Dyce had found a hiding place just along the lake shore, where he'd crashed in through the foliage. He lay down in the mild maple leaves and edged forward until he had a distinct view of Ruth and Vida sitting on the bench. They were craning their necks to see where he'd set up camp, and he hoped they stopped that pretty soon. What they didn't know was that their voices carried across the still water.

Dyce tried to line them up in the cross-hairs. The angle was too low: the slope of the bank had him pointing at the water weed. He thought about Ester and her drowning, weeks back now but always with him, the bleeding evil she took with her. He shook his head to clear it. The leaves he lay on were damper and colder than he'd guessed, and the slow seep of dew rose to meet his clammy skin. It didn't matter. This was it. Today was the day.

He wriggled, searching for a likely stick or stone, and found a black rock, rounded on one side and flat on the other. He balanced it in front of him and tried the gun again. Perfect. While he had time to kill, he ran the scope over Vida. He watched her fingers moving on the table as she talked; the breaths that made her breasts push against her shirt. He focused them between the cross-hairs and felt his dick harden beneath him against the mulch.

'Focus, jerkwad,' he whispered. 'That's no lady; that's my wife-to-be.' He was hysterical, it was true. For some reason he kept thinking of a silly little ditty he'd heard some Northerners singing in the way-back – Northerners, or Southern traitors, or maybe even Garrett, because it was the sort of thing his big blond brother was given to saying before he found true love.

Here's to the girl with the bright red SHOES!
She smokes your cigarettes and drinks your BOOZE.
She's got no cherry but that's no SIN,
'Cause she's still got the BOX that the cherry came IN!

Let it run, Dyce told himself. Get it out of your head so you can fucking focus on what you're supposed to be doing here.

It worked, up to a point: he was spared more earworms. A car was coming, something expensive if he was guessing right, because the engine purred. He wanted to look, but he didn't dare move. It was Renard, he was sure. It had to be. He waited.

Christ! Was that him? That gimpy little guy with a picnic basket? Really? Dyce lined up the panama hat, just in case. Even if he missed, he'd have another shot in less than two seconds. The motion had become second nature after all that practice loading and unloading. The first shot, if it missed, would just be a marker, that was all. The second, well, it was up to him to bury it deep in Renard's sick skull. And he could do it. Garrett's small voice in Dyce was surprised, but it was also pleased. He heard it less now than he used to, but it wasn't going away.

From the moment Renard sat down, Dyce wanted to shoot him. Every second that passed, it felt as though he might have missed his only opportunity, that Renard's invisible men would come up from behind him and kill him where he lay, a moth on a pin. His back crawled with anticipation. But he held off on the shot, watching the man's red mouth moving, his chuckles and terms of endearment, a slave master gloating over a purchase.

The wave of revulsion rose in Dyce's chest. He really wanted to kill Renard, he realized: not just for Ruth and Vida and all the slaughtered innocents. It was a clean, slicing, energizing hatred that would only be relieved by the erasure of this man from the earth.

Then Ruth slumped suddenly forward and Dyce heard the shot a moment later. His rifle jerked up in surprise, battering his cheekbone, but he hauled it back down as another shot hit Renard in the chest of his white linen suit. Dyce used his scope to retrace the trajectory. On the opposite shore a blue-gray puff of smoke was still rising from the undergrowth, up toward the low branches of the maples.

He forced himself to breathe through his nose and homed in on the spot. There! A man crouched on one knee, the rifle now aimed at Vida. Dyce strained to make out his face in the shifting dappled light. The man adjusted his position and Dyce saw the cream-colored bandage around his chin, like a cowboy with toothache. It was the man who'd brought the patrolman to the Capitol Building and gotten knocked out for his troubles – silent, invisible, everywhere and nowhere: the Santee henchman who'd sold his soul. Otis.

'Fucking Adams,' hissed Dyce. 'I knew it!' He looked back desperately at Vida, but she was still fine. There was nothing he could do for the others. Even as he watched, Renard was trying to move, standing to limp away from the picnic table where Ruth lay doubled in on herself.

More puffs of smoke; more shots – all missed their targets.

His strike rate was low because he was going too fast, thought Dyce. He was rattled, and it was counting against him. Dyce couldn't make the same mistake himself.

He set Otis in the center of the scope and, compensating for the distance, lifted the rifle so that he was training it on a clump of old-man's-beard that hung above the marksman. He fired and watched the bullet strike to his left in a splatter of bark, close to Otis but not a hit. The man jumped in alarm, then raised his own gun and scanned the shore for the phantom shooter. Dyce already had another bullet in the chamber just as Otis found him, his hair dark against the green.

Dyce fired first, and this time Otis fell – injured or dead, he couldn't tell. He loaded twice more and sent those bullets into the leaves where he figured the man had dropped, just to be sure. Then he stood and ran back along the shore to the spit of land, out to the bench where Ruth lay. She wasn't moving. He looked for Vida and for Renard, but they had disappeared while he was busy with Otis.

There was something white on the water. A panama hat.

Fuck.

He forced himself to drop the rifle and ran in, wading into the deep water until he could no longer stand. Then he took a lungful of air and dived down into the weedy murk.

As he swam, he realized there was no panic, no flashback to Garrett holding him under the water at camp. That Dyce was dead along with his brother. There was only room for one thought: Vida and the baby, struggling at the bottom of the lake, eyes popping as they were choked in Renard's tentacles.

Dyce's damaged eyes found their bodies down there on the lake floor. How long had she been under? She still had enough air in her to struggle against her father. Dyce already felt the

burn in his chest, but Vida concentrated, unconcerned. Dyce
saw her holding Renard around the neck. With the other hand
she clawed for grip on the bed of the lake, slipping on rocks
and tangling in strands of water weed like hair. The old man
was demonic, writhing against her grip. Dyce saw the filaments
of blood wafting from his wound into the water, his lips drawn
back in a grimace of pain and rage.

They scrabbled at each other, she determined to hold him
down until he drowned, he just as determined to escape – as he
always had. Like Mami Wata she would keep him there, down
in the depths of the lake, where he belonged.

With each kick and lunge upward, Renard released a bubble
of air, one after the other, his lungs emptying. But Vida had
sealed her lips as though she didn't need to breathe, as though
she'd been born underwater. There was a terrible calm focus
on her face, the kind Dyce had seen when they'd lain together
side by side in the locomotive museum, sweating and entwined.

When Dyce reached them, the old man was limp, his silvery
eyes rolled back. Vida still didn't know Dyce was there: she
couldn't see him in the dark river. He hovered close, ready to
help her struggle back to the clean air of the surface, but he
hung back to see where he would be most use. Vida was facing
the unconscious Renard, her lips drawn back in a snarl that
Dyce had never seen before. She was terrifying. And she didn't
need his help. As Dyce watched in dread, she dug her strong
thumbs into her father's eye sockets as if she would split his
head open with her bare hands, let his venom be diluted and
swallowed by the water.

Renard's eyeballs burst and the pulp lolled and stuck to his
cheeks. He looked like he was crying, thought Dyce, before the
jelly fragmented in the water and Vida loosened her grip. The

optic nerves trailed, swaying with their movements. Renard had been turned into a desperate rock-clinging creature at the mercy of a small, greedy fish: reduced to beak and arms and tentacles, the lights ripped out of his skull.

Dyce couldn't stay to watch. His throat was on fire and his own eyes were tight in their sockets. Vida would keep going without him, rip Renard limb from limb, dismantle their history piece by flailing piece. All in a place she was sure no one could see. He abandoned her to her grisly work and kicked up, panicked. Air!

He turned his head to stare straight up at where he thought the morning sun was, but even with his eyesight the water above stayed murky with plumes of silt. He was further down than he had thought. He had no choice.

Just when he thought his lungs would implode, he tried to rear up above the waterline and suck in the sweet air, but he had misjudged where he was. The underside of the jetty was hard and ungiving, and the girder, rusted to a jagged point, smashed hard against his head. Dyce heard the click of his neck and thought: Is that really me?

He floated face-down in Maple Lake, unable to move his limbs. It was kind of funny, he thought, and he would have laughed. Even the idea of being in the water used to paralyze him. And then the universe had sent him Vida. He'd loved her enough to brave the water three times: after the tunnels under the Mouth, in the river at the Wall between North and South, and here in the lake, where his body bobbed gently on the surface. If only he could roll over!

But then the urge drained away, replaced by a bright sweetness. It's amazing, Dyce thought. He felt his eyes rolling up in his head. I can see everything now. All the stories are here: the one about the little mermaid, and the one about Mami Wata, and the one Ruth told me about the underwater villages back home, where the herd boys take their cattle up and down the riverbed, and their drowned bells ring.

He could hear those bells now. He smiled. He wasn't alone, because here was his mother, who had given up too easily the first time. She had come to find her own true boy. Under the water she held out her thin arms to him, rocked by the current, her hair spreading out around her face. Behind her his father stood nodding, yes, yes, they would go climbing between the rocks again and his dad would catch him if he fell.

And Garrett! There he was, his skin made miraculously smooth, standing proud next to Bethie, who was unstitched and whole – and their baby, the boy with the golden hair. Around his fat childish neck he wore the swan pendant.

The last person who came to welcome Dyce was the mermaid herself. She rose from the water, or from below that, somewhere more ancient than the water. She was a carving made in a cave, a cold-blooded creature with pins for teeth, and she flashed her kindly scales like coins. They covered her from head to toe, those scales, and they also covered the hand that held aloft the faceless, scoured head of Papa Renard.

'Mami Wata,' murmured Dyce. She had come for him at last.

59

When Felix came around, he pushed himself to his feet. The explosives team was dead, heaped together in a pile. One of them, he recognized, was Danni. He'd figured from their exchange in the car that Kurt had liked her some, but still she lay dead, punctured. Felix wobbled there a second, then got his bearing and limped through the doorway and up. His head hurt like hell; he was sure his nose was broken. But it didn't stop him from peering in through doorways as he went. He saw beakers and vials and long curling tubes covering the tables – not unlike the Capitol Building, now that he thought on it, only cleaner, newer and more hi-tech.

For a moment he missed his old shack down South in the worst way. He paused and clung to the ladder until the bout of pain and homesickness passed. Funny thing was, while he'd lived there all those years, he'd longed for his apartment in New York with its populated view out over the city, the apartment block opposite and the people in it staring back at you, everyone trying to get a look at the buildings beyond, knowing that together they meant something more than the architecture. He missed Dallas and the drug store across the street. He'd bought a big bottle of kids' cough syrup there once when the liquor store was too far away. Those were dark days, the ones after his wife left.

Not as dark as these, though, by Christ!

In comparison even his old life down South was a little slice of paradise he'd called up from nothing, at the base of that derelict dam wall in godforsaken Colorado. And so what if he'd put his head down and ignored the world around him? Wasn't that his due? He'd tried to kill Renard once; wasn't that more than most? It was unbelievable now to imagine his stand of almond trees, and good water five minutes' walk. He'd even had whiskey and maps and his old exercise bike, the entire place his own, where he could sleep or think or whack off.

He'd had something real to do too, hadn't he? Real enough, anyway. When last had someone called him Weatherman? That was one thing Renard had given him, at least. Waking up early to check the weather stations, plotting the next wind – he'd got it down to an art. There were more times than he could count when he'd scampered inside the old shack, closed the door and not a minute later heard the rattle of gravel against the wood and the creak of the roof bolts holding tight to the four walls. They could have just left him alone, couldn't they? Vida and Dyce and that asshole Garrett. The big storm would have come and he would have gone out to dance naked in the rain until it crushed him and washed his remains downriver, amen. That would have been the way to go. He'd been prepared for that. And yet here he was, thanks to Dyce's brother, who'd stuck his dick where he shouldn't have.

'Ain't that how all trouble starts?' Felix told himself. From Adam in the Garden, all the way down.

When Felix stepped into the control room, it didn't take him long to gauge the situation.

'What have you done?' he said, but he knew already.

Kurt had gone and done what he'd said he would. He'd

poisoned the whole world – or at least as far as he could reach. Adams lay there too, dead and bled out, the gun still in his hand.

As Felix watched, the boy picked up a brick and smashed it into the control panel, sending knobs and switches and splashes of blood from his mangled fingers flying – making sure there'd be no way to undo his handiwork. When he turned to see Felix, it was the old man who got the bigger fright: Kurt was crying, and now that it was too late, Felix finally understood.

Kurt had no idea why he did the things he did. He was doing only what he had been programmed to do from the day he came out squalling between his mama's bloodied thighs. Some people were just born that way: empty of feeling. They spent their lives trying to make everyone around them the same way – to drive the humanity from them by force.

And some started out all right and then turned bad, made that way by the things they saw when they were too small to know better. Kurt hadn't stood a chance in that fucked-up family. He was a virus, thought Felix, and there was only one cure.

And you know what that makes you, don't you, you motherfucker?

The host.

Felix had held and protected the boy, ushered him right into the heart of the Resistance. So now he had to live with what he had let happen.

Evil grows, he thought. No. It flourishes – that was the word. Evil flourishes when good men do nothing.

And I wasn't even a very good man.

Kurt came and threw his arms around him, and Felix had no choice but to hug him back. The swan pendant on its cord was slung over the boy's shoulder. It was a beautiful thing, Felix thought, delicately carved. Upside-down, if you looked at it the right way, it was a mermaid too.

He took it gently between his fingers and felt the strength of it. It would hold. He could strangle the boy with it. He could grip it and twist it and pin Kurt down. He could end the sickness. He held onto the cord.

But if he was ever going to do it, he should've done it an hour ago – outside the factory, there on the lip of the parking garage. There was no point now. When the mushrooms wore off in a few weeks, they'd all be dead anyway.

He let the necklace go and watched his own tears plink down onto Norma's blouse. They were stuck with one another.

Kurt stayed close to him and helped him down the rickety stairwell again. All the while Felix tried to find some place for the blame – someone to take responsibility for the dead world they'd walk out into in a minute. It wasn't just Kurt. They had all bartered the smallpox blankets.

The two survivors stepped out of the factory through the hole that the bomb had made, into the combat zone. The fighting was over, but the earth it had covered was still hot. Felix sniffed the air. There were no ghosts, not the way there were down South: every battlefield there was still soaked with the blood of the fallen, and it would never evaporate. Here there was only silence. The high Northern clouds raced across the sky, but the sun was warm when it shone through.

'You have any idea where you're headed?' Felix asked Kurt.

'Not really,' said Kurt. The flash and rigidity had gone out of him, Felix saw. Purged. He had let his mangled hand dangle down. The fingers dripped a dotted line of blood in a boundary. 'Thought I might tag along with you, Uncle Felix. Ain't you beholden to me? Family duty and all that?'

Felix frowned. 'I just want to say, so as you know, that the mushrooms are gone. All of them.' He didn't know if it was true or not, but he didn't want the boy going looking. 'So if that's the reason you're hanging around, get rid of that notion. We each got two, maybe three weeks till they wear off. Not a bang. A whimper, as the man said. 'Sides, you don't want to spend your last days following after an old fart like me. You should take a car, see the Grand Canyon, see New York – try to imagine it the way it once was. All I'm doing is heading back South. I'm going to find my old shack and then get very, very drunk. See if I can stay that way until the Lord calls my name. Call it my retirement plan.' He grinned, and Kurt looked at his old dog's teeth, the skin tight over his bones.

They walked on together, past the bodies and the razor wire and the chunks of concrete, slow enough to understand, but fast enough not to care too deeply. At the road, they stopped. A stranger lay across the center line like a drunken watchman, his cheek against the asphalt. Some time ago the blood had leaked out of him through his mouth. Kurt bent down and tore a strip from his T-shirt, and wrapped his hand in it, tight as he could.

'You know the story of Job? That's us, right there,' said Felix, jutting his chin at the man's forlorn corpse. 'That's us in three weeks. Maybe even less 'cause of how many viruses are up in the air right this minute. Thanks to you. Hell, that might be us tomorrow morning. You even know what I'm saying?'

'I think so.'

'Don't you have no dreams at all?'

The only reliable dream Kurt could call up was the one where he and Bethie were walking down beside the stream, near where he'd killed the good dog Mason. It was fall, and the leaves were stirring in the breeze. Some, shaken loose, were coming down like confetti all around them. She'd stopped and taken his hand and held it against her breast. Then she'd let it go and snaked her hand down into his trousers. It was him she wanted: only him and all of him, and that made Kurt feel just fine.

He wasn't going to find her in New York or the Grand Canyon, he knew that. Bethie was gone and soon there'd be no one else around either, if the viruses did what they were supposed to do. Felix was all he had.

'I think I'll hang around, if that's okay. I'm real sorry about hitting you in the nose,' he said. 'Maybe we could stop past Des Moines on the way.'

'Son, why d'you want to go back to that shithole?'

Kurt shrugged, defensive. 'The cat. He's mine, in a roundabout way. Not a lot of things I can say that about. He belongs with me.'

Felix frowned but said nothing. He knew how it was. Dallas.

'Okay. But I'm warning you: when we get back to the shack, you're sleeping upstairs, unless the downstairs has been washed away. If that's happened, then I'll sleep upstairs and you'll sleep in a bush somewhere. I got a nice stand of almond trees, boy. You better believe it. But before that, we're going to stop for some booze – enough to kill us. And not that rotgut we used to drink down South, neither. I'm talking old-school booze. Proper bourbon, with a label and an honest list of ingredients, and a nice picture of a bird. There'll be a couple of liquor stores between here and home, and we're going to clean them out.'

Kurt nodded. He didn't much care one way or the other. Drinking was what old men did to forget, and he wanted to remember. Bethie, mostly.

'Also, we're going to take that shitty Toyota of yours into

Chicago and we'll find the best car there is – a Porsche or a
Ferrari or something – and you're going to drive it till its nose
is right up against Renard's motherfucking Wall. And then we'll
plough through it. We'll find a way. We got in, didn't we? We
can find a way out. And, Kurt: one more thing.'

'What?'

'You drive too slow I'll goddam shoot you, you got that? I
don't care who your daddy was.'

Kurt hiccuped a laugh. 'Deal.'

The two Callahans found the Toyota, the pronghorn trophy
lopsided but still attached. They drove up and out of the underground parking, and into the city. Chicago was lined with
bodies laid out where they had collapsed, puppets with their
strings snipped. They had to roll up the windows because the
smell was starting again, but this time it only made Felix tired.
There was a finite measure of horror in him, and that cup had
been sipped dry. Kurt drove slowly through the city and the old
man made himself remember what it looked like, the landscape
of the ruined, though they'd seen it all before. This was the
end of something that had begun long ago, wasn't it? For every
dead Northern man, woman and child, there was a grave the
same size down South. Not retribution, he thought. There was
no such thing, anyway. A clean slate, rather. Anything could
happen now. Any fucking thing at all.

They swapped cars in Chicago, for a canary-yellow VW cabriolet, and headed south-west on the 630. It was almost evening
when Felix suddenly sat straight up in the passenger seat and
yelled for Kurt to stop.

'Jiminy Cricket!' The boy slammed on the brakes and the car
skidded in slow motion across the blacktop. Felix was yanking
at the door handle, trying to get out even before the car had

come to a stop. Kurt hit the steering wheel. 'You nearly gave me a heart attack! What is it?'

Felix had climbed out and was standing on the road, shading his eyes against the last shafts of gold on the horizon, straining to see clear across the field.

'I don't fucking believe it,' he said to himself.

'What now?'

'What's that look like to you?'

Kurt squinted across the top of the car. 'Uncle Felix, that looks like a giraffe.'

60

Vida rested. She was trying to pull Dyce back to shore, but his body was waterlogged. It felt as if something had got hold of him under Maple Lake and would pull him back down into its depths. She couldn't leave him there with Renard for eternity. She knew she had done her father some damage, though she hadn't been able to see what. Clawed at his face, mostly, and she hoped it had been enough to drown him properly. She scanned the water but her vision was too blurry. She coughed another mouthful of dirty lake water out of her lungs.

Oh, Dyce. She knew he was dead. She'd sure as shit carried him enough to know how he felt alive, hadn't she? She'd carried him out of Felix's shack and all the way across the little river and up that goddam mountain. And then known the heft of his body moving over hers, the thrust and meat and sigh of him, over all the nights that came after. Why would she give up now?

But this body in the water: it wasn't a person anymore. Dyce had become a log, a branch blown from one of the maples into the lake. When she tugged at him again, his shirt billowed up around his face, his arms trailing, but he shifted. She kept dragging his corpse in little bursts, trying not to think of the slime on the back of him. She had to get him back to Ruth – lay them both out neatly together so they could dry and she could look at them properly, her dead, and think what to do.

I can do this, she told herself. I am the recipe book.

When she could stand, she tried to take his weight over her shoulders, but he was heavier by double than she remembered. Dyce had changed: grown up or just got fattened up on the Northern diet like a boy in a witch's cage. There was her ruined leg too. In the water it had been weightless, but here on the flat earth there was no way she could move with speed or dexterity.

She flopped him down on the patchy ryegrass like a prize fish. He was pale, the color bleached out of him by the violence of his passing. His mouth gaped, his jaw slack. Why did people compare death and sleep? Vida wondered. They were nowhere near the same. It was only then that she saw the gash in his head. There was no blood, just meat cleaved cleanly open, then shards of bone and the pink-gray jelly of his brain. Around the lips of the wound were hair and splinters and rust mixed together, like someone was making a new man from the leftover parts.

She couldn't bear that. She leant in and arranged a clump of Dyce's wet hair over the wound. The hair hardly covered the split, but he looked better. More familiar. She could get closer to kiss him now, one last time on the lips.

The smell drove her back. The mushrooms! Would she ever be free of them? Instead of his sweat and sweetness, Dyce smelt of caves deep under the earth, of dirt in a predator's claws. Vida breathed through her mouth and lay down next to him, determined to stay with him until she was certain the last warmth from his core had risen to his skin's surface and floated over them both into the air. Then he was truly cold, and Vida felt the heat from her own insides being drawn into him, and the clouds move over the sun. She got up slowly, favoring her good leg, and made her way to the table where the picnic basket still gaped. Ruth was lying with her head on the wood like a drowsy schoolgirl on a Friday afternoon. Vida sat beside her and held the stiffening hand between her own. She could allow herself this.

'I'm so sorry, Mama. You know that, don't you? For everything. But especially for this. Even now you were helping me, weren't you? The way you always do. I couldn't have held him under, not if you hadn't dosed him with that poison first. He was strong, wasn't he, Mama? He was old, but he was wily and so damn strong. He was always too strong. I see it. You couldn't fight him on your own, and I couldn't, either. It was always going to take two of us.'

Ruth didn't answer. Her eyes were rolled up in their sockets like a holy painting of a saint at the stake. Vida felt her own tears burning stripes down her cheeks. She watched them plop neatly onto the table and then mingle with the drizzle that was moving in over Maple Lake.

'But I can't do this next bit on my own, Mama. It's too hard. I'm not ready.' She waited for some acknowledging kick from her abdomen, but the baby lay quiet. 'I thought I would have you to help me, the way you did all those girls who came to you over the years. All the lost ones. But now it's me who's too far gone, Mama. I need you now. I don't know what to do. And it's not fair!'

The rain was coming in harder now. As Vida wept with frustration, she felt it cool as grief on her face. Everywhere the leaves and shoots and grasses were drinking, taking in their fill, as if she hadn't lost everyone she had ever loved.

'Mama, you know what else? You were right. You remember at the beginning? You said he wasn't the one. Now I wish I'd never met him.'

The rage was slow to kindle, but it moved in increments up to her chest, and by the time it got to her gullet, the tears had dried up.

'I know what you're going to say, Mama. You get what you get, and you don't get upset. But it's true. None of this would have happened if I'd said no to his dumb brother, and to him, and to everything that came after that. Maybe then you'd still be here, and it would just be us two, same as it ever was.'

The anger was delicious. Vida felt its hot metal against her palate, and it made her legs move so that she was able, at last, to think clearly.

She got up and went back to the truck, Renard's fancy Jaguar parked beside it. How had Buddy done it? She tried to send her mind back to all those hours in the pickup, and then Dyce's careful explanations on the way to the lake too, but the memory kept clouding over with pain and loss; it was as if her brain was partitioned, and she had to peer over the walls that divided its parts.

She got in and started the truck's engine. She managed to reverse it out slowly, trundling along the stone wall to a gap in line with the boat ramp. The truck bucked a little over the uneven slipway, and for a sick moment she thought she had driven over Dyce's body.

Impossible. But she got out to check, just in case. Stranger things had happened. She got back in and eased the vehicle off and along the riverbank, parking it right between the two bodies. She turned the engine off and wiped her palms on her thighs. Her hands kept slipping.

She began with Ruth, in a kind of fireman's lift half over her shoulder, and limped with her in bursts over to the truck bed. Her mother's feet dragged as if she was drunk, reluctant to make the journey up the greasy slope. Vida rested and wiped the sweat and the rain from her forehead. The drizzle wasn't letting up. At least if anyone was watching, they would have a hard time making out what she was doing.

Vida froze.

The sniper. She didn't know if he was really gone, did she? Would he hang around?

Slowly she laid Ruth all the way down, then stretched and got her breath back. So be it. She had no choice. Out here she was a clear target. If anyone really wanted to pick her off, they had had enough time to do it already. Her heart was thudding in her ears, her blood drumming so that she wanted to pass out. She still had to go back for Dyce. She was dreading it.

Dyce was more difficult to maneuver than Ruth had been: it was incredible how much healthy flesh he'd managed to pack back on in the short time she'd known him. She took a deep breath, then hooked her hands under his armpits and tried to drag him up the greasy slope. She managed it in small, dismaying stretches, her leg one long, hollow ache. The stitches kept feeling as though they would pull loose with the strain, until she stood, panting and shaking with effort, and regarded her dead family.

She had heaved them onto the truck bed, but they looked uncomfortable, twisted back against the corrugated metal. She rearranged them so that they lay neatly, but even as she was moving their limbs she thought of Stringbeard and his cursed family back in Fieldstone. They had lain together so tidily, the dead woman and all her little ones in their eternal beds. Vida hurried back to fetch Renard's checked cloth. She unfurled it and let it fall damply over them, and then she tucked the edges in under their bodies so it wouldn't blow loose when she drove away. There. Now she was ready.

Still shivering, she got back into the driver's seat and turned the truck around to follow her own slick tracks back to the parking lot. It didn't matter if she hit a tree, as long as it was gentle. She'd be able to recover from that. She drove at a snail's pace around the entire rim of the lake – past the grass triangle and the low-slung trees, past the white clapboard church with its crooked gravestones like rotten teeth, a one-woman funeral cortège – and then on toward the highway. Luck was on her side.

She tilted the rear-view mirror, pointing it backward and down. She could only just see Dyce's foot through the tiny rear windows.

'Dyce,' she said, 'I got something to tell you. Don't laugh, but I've never seen the sea. But it sounded good when Garrett said it, didn't it? It'll be the right place to lay you down, both of you, so you can keep each other company, up on a hill with a view of the water. You might even run into ole Garrett there, come to think of it. He'll be cursing and setting up his boat, ready to sail off for somewhere new.' She wiped her nose on her shirt. 'Sounds like a good idea. A new start. Me, I'm thinking I'll head east. Mama, maybe I'll find the same coast that looks across to where you came from. Africa. Wouldn't that be a blast? I can taste the coconuts already. Pineapples. Melons. All of it. From one fruit salad to another. What do you say?'

She listened to the inhuman voice of the engine. Go on, it seemed to say, just get away from here. It doesn't matter where, as long as you hit the coast before they start to smell.

She shivered again. She searched the dashboard for the heater and found the knob that showed waves of heat like water. It still worked. She turned it up and set the fan to high speed. Her toes and ankles tingled and ached as the numbness began to lift. The ventilation in the car was mixing with the warmer air that was filtering in from outside now that the rain had stopped. She hung her head outside the window as she drove the slippery roads, sniffing at the freshness like a dog. She would never get tired of doing it: the freedom was too new to take for granted.

When she finally rolled the pickup into Lemont, it was the smell that first told her that something was wrong. She came to a stop on the outskirts before she gathered herself enough to go on through.

The bodies were strewn everywhere, surprised by their own endings: in the streets, on the lawns, some lying heavy on the railway track that ran parallel with the main road. She stopped the car beside a woman lying in the gutter, her face rotted in like a Halloween pumpkin forgotten on a porch.

'It's happening,' Vida said, but there was no one to hear her. 'It's fucking happening again.'

The engine stalled.

61

Kurt turned off to Des Moines, retracing the route from the night before. Even at the outskirts they saw the dirty smoke lazily twisting. The Capitol Building was ruined, the dome collapsed in on itself in jagged black shards against the haze. Kurt parked the cabriolet as close as he could.

'Don't be long,' Felix said. 'We ain't got all day. And you don't know what's still in there. What's infectious.'

Dumbass boy wasn't even going to find the cat, was he? If Linus was under there he would be a small charred skeleton. Kurt would smell him by the singed fur, like a voodoo poppet. Was he going to bring that little kitty corpse out with him? Felix hoped not.

'We'll burn that bridge when we get to it,' he told himself. Damn. It was times like these he wished he still smoked.

He waited in the car and Kurt kept looking over the hot clumps of rubble. He should have worn gloves, he told himself, but he only stopped when his hands sizzled.

'Give it up,' Felix called from the car window.

He was right, but that didn't make it hurt less. Kurt picked his way back to the car and got in. He turned his boot over. 'See that?'

'Whoa.'

'Rubber's melting.'

'You happy now? No cat survived that.'

Kurt said nothing. He turned on the engine and they drove across the Des Moines river bridge, the struts rattling. You just couldn't tell with this little fucker, Felix thought, and not for the first time. Other people, you knew when they were pissed off or sad or celebrating. But with Kurt, the highs and lows were hard to tell apart. He was a Callahan all right. And more.

'Hey, now. Wait a minute. Stop the car.'

He had quick reflexes, at least. The body of a man was laid out on a concrete piling where there was a nice view of the water. And beside it was a striped furry bundle. Alive. Felix nudged Kurt.

The boy got out as fast as he could. He jumped the roadside barrier and jogged over. Then he crouched down, trying to make himself unthreatening.

'Hey there. Hey, kitty. Hey, Linus. It's me, boy.'

The scraggly tabby wasn't going to come to him: Felix saw that right away. Instead it hissed and backed away, spine arched and ears flat. In frustration Kurt lunged, his bloody left hand out, trying to scare it into his right. But Linus had been here before, and cats learn their lessons. He tried to jump cleanly, but his back claws pedaled and ripped the skin of Kurt's arm before he leapt from the piling into the fescue. Kurt hunched over and cursed the pain and Felix saw himself; in the early days of the War he'd thought often enough of getting back North-side to search the alleys behind his old block. Dallas, in his dreams, would see him and come running. Felix would have a can of sardines with him and Dallas would sit still to pick them out. Afterwards they would go back to the apartment and he would lick the smell of home back onto his fishy paws.

Kurt wasn't giving up. Felix had had enough. It was himself he was angry with. 'No means no,' he yelled through the window.

The boy, empty-handed, turned to him and gave him a look of silvery hate. The old man's heart dipped. That was stupid. He shouldn't have said anything.

Kurt dropped off the platform and set off through the grass, swift as a deer – a pronghorn, thought Felix. He was gone from sight for almost half an hour. Felix settled back to doze in the seat. Fuck it. If today was his day to die, then so be it. He was done trying to set people straight.

At last Kurt came loping back, defeat in the skew set of his shoulders. Linus was gone for good and Felix felt a surge of joy for the animal. Linus would join up with the other cats of Des Moines, and if he'd learnt anything from Kurt at all, he'd be king of them all.

The boy swung himself back behind the wheel. 'He didn't recognize me,' he said.

Felix wanted to tell him straight: Kid, that cat recognized the hell out of you. That's why he ran like his tail was on fire. But he held himself back.

'He scratched me up pretty bad,' Kurt went on, showing Felix the blood on his arms.

'Who's the dead guy?' Felix asked instead as Kurt started the car.

'That border patrolman – the one who was in the cell. You know,' said Kurt thoughtfully, 'there was blood coming out of his skin.' Felix nodded. 'No, I mean it was coming out of his pores, like he was sweating. And his teeth were all fallen out. Like popcorn.'

Felix felt his guts heave. 'Huh,' he said.

Kurt had done that.

Not Renard. Kurt. The viruses that he'd released were spreading fast and far. Depending on the wind, they might have hit the west coast already. The east coast he was sure was already given over. There might not be a single person alive on the whole continent besides him and the boy. It would take two canny bullets to bring an end to the era of Columbus. Imagine that.

'You ever learn that Columbus song?'

Kurt shook his head. Felix warbled the song. He'd not sung nor heard it for decades, but the words were still there.

> *In fourteen hundred and ninety-two*
> *Columbus sailed the ocean blue.*
> *It was a courageous thing to do*
> *But someone was already here:*
> *The Inuit and Cherokee,*
> *The Aztec and Menominee,*
> *Onondaga and the Cree.*
> *Columbus sailed across the sea*
> *But someone was already here.*

'Does the radio work?' Kurt asked. Without waiting for a reply, he leant forward and turned it on. The car was filled with the hiss of static as he searched for a surviving station.

'What? You don't like my singing?'

Kurt kept fiddling with the dial, his twisted, bloodied fingers poking out of the makeshift bandage.

'You know there's no one there now? No deejays or anything. You're gonna get pre-recorded stuff.'

'I know,' said Kurt. 'I just want the weather report.'

The static stopped. 'Tomorrow,' the woman on the radio said, clear and earnest and friendly, 'will be mild and sunny.'

62

Vida got the engine going again, and after that it got easier, because she was leaving the despairing towns behind. She drove and drove, the road endless and flat before her as she headed east through Indiana, coughing and dry-eyed, making for the coast as the sun dropped behind her. It was as good a plan as any, and there was no one else to consult. There were no more tears to cry, either, and her throat was rough with ill use.

The drive was endless and the weather wasn't helping. It seemed to turn bad and then clear up some, as if it couldn't make up its mind. The viruses must be affecting the cloud cover, she thought. She didn't know how it worked, and she didn't know if rain made it better or worse. If Felix was here, he could tell her. What she did know was that she didn't want Dyce and Ruth lying there on the truck bed in the wet and the cold. She knew it wasn't rational.

'But rational,' she told the baby as she turned the wheel, 'isn't high on my list right now.' She had gone past sleep, into some grainy, shadowed place that made her brain itch.

Fort Wayne turned out to be the worst-hit. Against her wishes, Vida was forced to slow down: the place was a mess of bodies. The viruses unleashed from the factory must have been more ferocious than the ones that had just drifted south on the wind over Indiana. There must have been survivors somewhere down there, the way there were everywhere, against the odds, but here, hours after whatever had happened, every single person was dead, the hand of God smiting a citadel.

She cursed as she maneuvered the truck. People had been taken while they were driving, even, making the roads nearly impassable. Cars had crashed left and right off the street, into shop fronts and street lights and bus shelters, and it couldn't have been too long ago, either. That was the most terrible part. Engines were still ticking. There were piles of them, Vida realized as she wove her way through the wrecks, trying not to throw up: heaps of people. The Lincoln Bank Tower looked like the long-promised city of Atlantis, rising bone-white from a sea of corpses. They had fallen where they'd been walking, the commuters who had been getting off a double-decker spilt like dominoes out of the bus's doors, which kept trying to close on them, opening over and over with a steady pneumatic hiss in the stillness. If she got out and touched their faces, they would still be warm.

The rain was soaking her cargo now, and Vida had to stop to think properly. She needed covers. Shrouds. Something to protect Ruth and Dyce from the elements. She drove on slowly, the idea ticking over, until she came to a Home Depot. She parked the truck.

The electrics were still working; it was always weird to see what survived after the humans that operated them had gone. As Vida limped close to the glass doors, the sensors kicked in and they opened for her. She walked the aisles, massaging the muscles in her thigh, thinking back to the first place they'd stopped when Buddy had picked them up, all that time ago – back when she and Dyce had thought the North was paradise instead of purgatory. She had learnt a thing or two about freedom since then. It meant deciding what you could take responsibility for.

Like her family. That she was prepared to do. Fuck everything else.

There. Those curtains would do it. That felt right. Velvet drapes, heavy and creamy-white. To reach them she had to step back over a dead couple who'd been looking at shower curtains they would never take home. The man's face was pressed down against the linoleum, but the woman looked up into the lights in the roof, her dead eyes reflecting the strip tubes, her handbag spewing lipstick and tissues and furred sticks of gum like space garbage.

Vida nodded. 'You're right,' she told them. 'I'll be needing those too. They're perfect. Thank you.' She bundled the drapes and the couple's plastic curtains up into her arms. She had hobbled halfway across the store before she made her way back. 'I'm sorry for your loss,' she told the couple, and coughed. They hadn't moved.

Back at the truck, Vida threw both sets of curtains onto the flatbed and hauled herself up after them, ignoring her complaining leg. It would stiffen soon, and then she'd really be fucked. She still had a lot of work to do.

She bent to wrap Ruth, beginning with the creamy velvet, and then laying the plastic shower curtain over the cocoon.

She moved on to Dyce, swaddling him in the thick drape. She was tucking it neatly around his ruptured head when she saw the little black speckles dotting his chin like stubble.

'Oh, look at that. I'm so sorry, baby,' she told him. 'I'll try to go slower over the muddy bits, but there's only so much I can do, what with the rain and everything. You understand, don't you?' She licked a thumb and tried to wipe the black dots away.

They wouldn't budge.

She peered at them, but they clung, obstinate, as if they were splinters embedded in his flesh. Another weirdness in a day of weirdness, on top of weird weeks and months and years.

But she had to get going. She wasn't feeling great herself. Her throat was definitely worse, and the cough was persistent. She dragged the velvet over Dyce's peppery skin and covered him. Then she did the same with the shower curtain. There was such relief in keeping them both warm and waterproof.

'Shit. I forgot some things.'

She made her way back through the Home Depot doors that didn't know it was the end of the world. When she came back, she was carrying a green-handled spade and a coil of thin, whippy rope – and she'd found a pen in the pocket of a uniformed employee, and a ledger from a stocktake.

She got back up on the truck bed, groaning, and started to tie Dyce and her mother down so that they wouldn't slide out. She was tired of checking whether they were still there as she drove.

Then she nosed the pickup out toward the edge of the city again. There was a gas station on the fringes, and she pulled onto the cool blue forecourt. MARATHON said the sign, and she murmured the word to herself as she filled the truck with gas.

'That sounds about right.'

She drove along the empty roads until it got dark. I don't want to stop, she told herself, coughing. There is nothing for us here in any of these towns. They are just places to get through before we reach the end. There were still lights on in some of the neighborhoods, but she thought they would burn out soon enough and there would be no one to replace the bulbs. Some were flickering even now, flooding living rooms and front porches with useless light. These were the last illuminated moments of America, and Vida knew them for what they were.

63

By the time she reached Pittsburgh, Vida had decided to drive on instead of finding somewhere to sleep; she didn't know if she could take seeing another Fort Wayne, with its pity and horror. But some miles east of the city, her body was aching too much to drive further, stretched and bunched with exhaustion, and the coughing wouldn't let up. It felt as though she was finally getting sick, for the first time in her life. Her bulletproof armor was wearing thin. She drove back a way along the 22 and, at a sign showing a man in a bed, turned off the road and through a set of enormous metal gates. The front windows were frosted with age and neglect, and the topiary that guarded the entrance had grown woolly a long time ago.

'Okay, Chestnut Ridge Golf Resort,' she yawned. 'Show me what you got.'

Once she was inside the hotel, Vida walked the passages with impunity. No clerk in a button-down shirt or woman in a gray housedress was going to ask her what she was doing here. Chestnut Ridge was closed for business. Or maybe – and this thought made her shiver even worse than she already was – the rooms were occupied: it was just that the guests were embalmed in their rooms forever, lying on a hundred beds like funeral biers.

She tried a few doors before she found an empty beige room with a view of her pickup in the parking lot, where she could see Ruth and Dyce lying on the truck bed like mummies. She was too tired even to pee. She curled up under the pastel sheets and closed her eyes.

But it was Renard's bloodied face she saw against the black, and she kept dozing and coughing, waking to find herself battling the damp bedding. She sat up, shaky, and looked at her fingers. She was certain there were still chunks of his flesh lodged under her nails. She couldn't see them, but she could feel that they were there.

She got up and limped to the shower. At least the water was still warm. The water heater would keep cycling on and off until the next doomsday came. She squeezed out the whole tube of shower gel – why wait? – and rubbed at herself until she was foaming white, all the while trying to keep her bad leg out of the blast.

She inspected the wound casually when she was drying herself. It looked okay. Not great, but the stitches were still holding.

She looked more closely.

'Fuck.'

She had judged it too quickly. Up close there were faint spidery lines of infection running up from the wound. Blood poisoning.

Renard had said that her immunity wouldn't stand up to multiple viruses, and by now the mushrooms had probably worn off. When last had she eaten a dose anyway? Back in Horse Head? That long ago? Shit. No wonder she was feeling sick. She was at zero protection apart from Ruth's syringe in the way-back – and who knew how long that would hold out? And Dyce – generous, stupid, dead Dyce – had given the last of their precious, precious mushrooms away.

Vida got dressed, covering up her leg so she didn't have to

look at it. She couldn't think about all that right now. She just had to press on until she couldn't press on any longer.

'You get what you get, and you don't get upset, right, Mama?'

She looked out of the window. The body in the parking lot was silent.

She made a brief tour of the resort's kitchen, and got the makings of a couple of cheese sandwiches together, along with some coffee. She took a stash that would last her a week and made herself a cup as well.

She raised the paper cup in a toast to herself. 'Cheers to the queers. Applause to the whores. May prostitutes flourish and fuck be a household word.' She sipped and then muttered, 'Gone but not forgotten, Stringbeard, you asshole.'

There wasn't a whole lot to pack up. Back in the room, Vida made sure the recipe book was safe in her bag, where she always kept it, nestled up beside Ears McCreedy, then went out to the pickup. She couldn't bring herself to eat just yet, but the coffee was going down a treat as she reversed the truck out of the parking lot and in a big loop back onto the highway. The coughing even seemed to relent some, though her leg was feeling heavier and heavier as she drove, hot and prosthetic with infection. She knew it was going to be bad.

As the long, lonely night came on, she felt the landscape change. The nose of the truck began dipping down and the signs in her headlights told her that she was crossing the Appalachians, dropping toward the sea. But as for the scenery itself, she saw none of it. The passing city lights were flickering out. All of the world that mattered was in her headlights. She drove on in a half-sleep, automatically turning the wheel to keep aligned with the painted road, occasionally shifting lanes to pass cars, stopped dead. The sun must have been rising, because she felt its warmth creeping over her forearms and settling on the hairs there. The world she saw in the new light was not one she recognized. The plants and trees she was used to were replaced by others, shorter mostly, with darker leaves. The air had a new taste here too, thick with moisture and the hint of salt. It was the smell of progress. She took a bite of a sandwich and cracked a window to let the fresh air wake her. It worked some.

The sun was full over the horizon when Vida wiped her nose and noticed that the back of her hand was smeared crimson. She looked in the rear-view mirror and saw the line of blood trickling from her nose: she had smeared it across her cheek. She swallowed. The soft walls of her throat were like pincushions.

She wiped her hand and her face on her shirt and drove on, faster, fully awake for the first time since she had lain on the cold steps of the Capitol Building with Dyce. She'd been planning on digging two graves, but maybe she'd have to make three. That was okay, wasn't it? She'd put herself in the middle one. Lie down, because she was tired. That was just fine. They'd all be together, at last. Ruth and Dyce and Vida and the baby. They could all go looking for Garrett and Bethie and their little one, and Everett. A family vacation: yours, mine and ours.

She raced eastward, hardly noticing that the landscape was turning sandy and scrubby. She knew by the number of boats parked in driveways that she was approaching the coast. She was so close! In her imaginings it was always a pristine, powdery stretch of sand and sea, but now that she was really here, she found that it was disappointingly ordinary, built up, house beyond house until the roads simply gave way to the thin strip of sand. What was the point of that?

She slowed the truck. There were blurry signs that ordered NO CARS BEYOND THIS POINT. It took a minute for Vida to understand that the signs were clear. It was she who was blurry. She drove on. Warning signs were for a different time. For yesterday and all the days before it. The truck bucked over a concrete lip and the tires spun in the dry sand.

But there it was, finally.

The sea.

64

She turned off the engine. Of course she'd seen pictures, and she'd been told what it looked like, but still, it was nothing like she'd imagined. It was just water – endless gray-blue water, restless with waves. It cared nothing for her and her hundred troubles, and those weren't going away just because she had arrived at her destination.

Far out there was a fishing boat, taken by the current – its captain and crew long dead now. It looked so very tiny against the vast depths. It rose and fell behind distant walls of swell, and then it was gone.

Vida got out and felt the sand with her palm. The air was thick here, wet through and heavy with salt and spray. She thought it would be bracing and restorative, salve for her ragged throat, but it was just making her cough even more.

'We're here,' she said to the bodies in the back. 'The weather could be better, but we're here. Now, I'm going to do what I came here to do, and I hope that's okay. I want you to know that I'm going to do my best for you. If you have any preferences, now is the time to tell me.'

She coughed into her fist again and began to drive the truck along the beach, looking for a sand dune that would give her a view far across the water. There was only one, and that was distant, a pyramid above the flat expanse of sand. She drove slowly, her chest hurting when she breathed, coaxing the pickup along. 'Don't want to get stuck now, do we? We've come this far.'

At the dune, she backed the truck up the slope as far as she could. She got out and took the spade with her, and then made her way slowly to the top, sliding back a couple of inches with each step, her leg pulsing with sick pain whenever she put weight on it. A few more yards, then she could rest.

When she got to the top, she sat down, her breath harsh in the damp air. Digging would be difficult. Where the sand met the thick undergrowth, the plants were all twisted secretly together: goldenrod, bladdernut, white doll's daisy, panic grass.

But here she was. She began to scoop the soft, dry sand away, pushing her fingers between the roots.

Even when she took up the spade, the ground kept working against her. She sweated, struggling to sever the plants that kept the dune from washing down into the endless sea. She was going too slowly. The first grave, the one she figured would be for her mother, was going to take more than an hour. She sat down again to rest her dumb leg, panting and trying to fight the nausea.

'Not the first grave I dug for you, Mama,' she called down to the body on the truck. 'Just think how lucky you are. Someone loves you enough to bury you twice. Remember that? The one that fooled Dyce and Garrett into taking me along? I sure hope this is the last one. That was a nicer grave, but this one has a better view.'

Even as she rested, the sweat kept coming. Her attention kept dragging back to her leg, where she was sure the poison was radiating under her skin: she could feel it colonizing her flesh. She rolled up her pants leg. The skin's surface was discolored in patches, red and black pockmarks with jagged edges that itched even as they spread between inspections. She drew back in disgust. It was like her body didn't belong to her anymore. But she didn't have time to work out what was happening to her. She had to finish digging before she was too weak to do anything at all.

She made herself get up again. 'Small bites,' she said. 'That's how you eat an elephant, right?' She started on Dyce's grave, but the effort only made the nausea worse, as if her body was trying to turn itself inside out. Eventually she gave in to it, leaning over the handle of the spade and letting the acid chunks jerk up from her guts. The little blobs of rancid cheese spattered on the gravesite, gone to waste.

'Happy now?' she asked the baby. 'That was for you. How are we going to save our strength if you won't let me eat?' She wiped her mouth and her hand came away dirt-streaked and bloody again. Her nose was back to bleeding, the thin walls of her arteries blasted through by the sickness and the hard work and the pregnancy.

How deep did the graves have to be anyway? What predators would there be on the beach? A couple of little critters, maybe. Vida had no idea. There were predators everywhere in latitudes they didn't belong: the end of the world had turned out to be pretty good for some. Things were out of whack for everyone, furred or horned or feathered. Even the plants had seen opportunity and shifted beyond their natural zones, ready to take up the spaces that the people left behind.

She felt a bit better. Emptying her stomach seemed to have helped, or maybe she was getting used to the work. Her head seemed clearer, and when she started again, Dyce's grave went quicker. It helped when she breathed in time with the ocean, its soft, insistent roar erasing some of the throttling sadness and regret. It was the sort of thing she'd have to teach herself for later, for when the baby came.

Oh God! Even if she lived, she would be by herself for that too!

'Small bites, I said,' she reprimanded herself, before the bad feeling overwhelmed her. 'Just fucking do what needs to be done, and save the wailing for later.'

Now the midday sun was making her dizzy, but she kept digging. The blood from her nose dripped softly, endlessly onto the thirsty sand as she made a start on her own resting place. When she wanted to stop, she told herself that it wasn't about her. They were all waiting. That third hole would be for her and her baby – but only after everyone else had their own shelter. It wasn't as deep as the others, but that was too bad. Let whatever came snuffling around the graves take her first.

When the holes were dug – three side by side, just as she'd imagined – she jammed the spade into the sand and slid, boneless, down the dune.

'Ladies first, Mama.'

She went backward up the dune in increments, yanking Ruth by her wrapped feet. She stopped to cough in between her efforts; her lungs ached. The plastic of the shroud rustled, and Vida thought of crickets, of the beetles that would soon be making their own families in her mother's slick orifices. She spoke to Ruth so that the unfairness didn't blind her with its terror.

'Don't look yet, Mama. Save yourself for when we get to the top. I know I should have made some headstones, but I didn't have the time. If it's worth doing, it's worth doing properly, isn't that what you always said? But I'm trying. I hope you know that.'

And they were there. Vida pulled the plastic off the body until the creamy velvet was exposed. She had been right to choose it: Ruth looked like the queen she might once have been.

She tumbled her wrapped mother into the hole. She would undo the curtain and cover her over later: that was the easy part. But for now she had to press on. One last trip. Get it done.

Back down by the truck she tried to rest in its small noonday shade, leaning against the tire until she had the energy to handle Dyce. It was somehow worse to put her hands on his dead body – he who had always been flushed and feverish, with sickness or with desire, throbbing with blood and eagerness.

She hauled his flopping corpse off the flatbed, and that was all right, but then he was impossible to move – so heavy that if she didn't hold onto him he slid all the way back down.

'Please, Dyce,' she panted. 'Please. I need your help right now. Just help me, one last time.' She could hear her own voice rising, and she knew she was on the edge of something that would undo her for good. She tried to force herself to calm down, to breathe through her damaged nose and ignore the spatters that sprayed with each exhalation. But the sweats were back too now, and there was some kind of fever inside her again. Maybe it had never really gone away. Could sickness do that? Lie dormant?

When she looked up from her struggle, Dyce was on the sand and the sun had moved. She couldn't tell if she had passed out. She made her way on weak legs to the cab of the truck and found the dregs of her cold coffee.

When she could begin again, she did. It was easier to grab hold of him under the arms, the same way she had done before, keeping the most substantial part of him closest to her. The sun blazed down on them as they ascended by degrees.

'Maybe it's your heart, Dyce,' she told him as they went. 'That's what's so big in there, baby.'

And then they were up at last and he was lying beside his grave. Vida hunkered down, her biceps burning, and removed the outer plastic sheeting. Then she rolled him, still sheathed in the cream curtain, into the hole as gently as she could. Her legs were shaking too much to support her, so she lay down, thinking of the way the sand had already trickled in over the velvet.

65

The sun was sinking when Vida came around. She sat up, the sweat drying on her back, her eyes dry in their sockets. She looked over at the graves but they were both as they should have been, the white-shrouded bodies regal and still.

'One more trip,' Vida told the baby. 'The last one. This time I mean it. Help your mama go and get the grave goods for your daddy and your grandmama. Send them off the way they deserve.'

She slid down to the pickup one last time. She found the objects she was looking for exactly where she had left them – beside her bag in one of the rear footwells.

She took them back with her up the slope, a prophet with an offering on a mountain.

She sat for a while beside the two graves that already had bodies lying in them, trying to drum up the words. Then it was time. She reached inside the bag and held up a book, bloated and stained, all the paltry human knowledge of the world sustained between its pages.

'Look, Mama. You know what this is? That's right. Your recipe book. I was thinking about what a waste it would be just to bury it with you – all the useful things in it down there in the dark. Who's going to come along and page through it there? Nobody.

'But it's yours, so you should get to keep it. I figure all those seeds in it will grow right here. You'll be a garden, Mama, a medicine garden, with half the plants from home and half from here. There'll be proteas and baobabs and lucky bean trees growing right here on this dune, and between their stems will be all the useful plants this continent ever produced – goose-grass and alumroot and dogwoods. You'll be a drugstore, Mama, a one-stop oasis, just like you were for me.'

Vida waited. Then she leant forward and placed the book on her mother's chest and kissed the shroud over the place she thought Ruth's lips were most likely to be. The velvet was animal-furry, unscarred.

'It's time to go.' She scooped the sand, slow and determined, over her mother's face. 'Think of me, Mama. The love was always real. You taught me everything I know. And everything I didn't know, I found out, because of the way you made me. You taught me not to be afraid, Mama. Or maybe to know that I was afraid, but to do it anyway. I will see you soon, and I'll have your grandbaby with me.'

Vida turned to Dyce. 'It's your turn now.'

She reached for the small, strange instrument that Dyce had been given in the Capitol Building, its brass machine heads shining bright and incorruptible.

'Baby, I'm really, really sorry you never got to learn to play. You owe me those lullabies. I know you can't take this where you're going, but maybe you'll get a harp up there, huh? And eternity is long enough to get the hang of playing, even if you don't have the natural-born skill.' She laughed, and then sniffed. The blood was watery now, as if her arteries were exhausted, weakening and shutting down.

'I considered putting Ears in there beside you. But you know what? He wants to stay with me. So I'm keeping him for the baby. My mind's made up now, so don't argue.'

She set the mandolin beside Dyce in the grave, then leant closer over him and lowered her voice. This was only for them, for man and woman, the way it would have been if they had lived in some other, peaceful century.

'You know,' she whispered, 'I told my ma that I wished I'd never met you. But it's not true. You were the one thing that made me want things to be better. Before I met you, I never wanted to live a normal life: have a house and a car and a kid – that kind of normal. But I wanted that with you, Dyce. You were everything. And I had part of that – something my mama never had: a baby that was stitched together out of love and passion. I wanted to see this baby's face, Dyce. I really did.' She realized she was crying, but she didn't think he would mind. 'I'm so sorry I didn't love you better. But sorry gave up, oh, a whole long time ago.' She coughed hard into her fist and the slick wetness there was clotted red. 'I'm glad I had you, Dyce. Save a space for me.'

She wanted to see him one last time. She had to. She had to look at his face now; she had to see his lips and his nose and his hair. She searched for the loose end of the curtain and began unwrapping Dyce's body where he lay. His head was sticky against the white velvet and she had to peel the material back as if it was their wedding night. But she didn't stop. She would kiss him on the lips one last time, and then she would be spent. It was the right way to go.

But the Dyce she saw was not the Dyce she remembered. From his mouth and nose the mushrooms had sprouted, their tiny, eager heads pressing against her hand. She stroked them and tried to weep, but no more tears came. He must have carried those spores in his lungs all the way from the Mouth, the same way that she was carrying his softly burgeoning button in her own body.

She leant over him and inhaled the scent from where the life-giving fungi were most tightly clustered – around the terrible wound in his head. The mushrooms smelt as they always did, and the scent made her shudder in recognition: mold, and mistakes, and the return of the good earth – but also, this time, the beginning. She would see her baby; it was Dyce's last gift to her.

She pressed her face into the mushrooms as if they were flowers.

66

The mushrooms did their work quickly, the spidery rot in Vida's leg retreating until it faded into the red boundary around the slash. The sea air must have been good for the linings of her lungs: the cough got drier, and then it stopped altogether, though the muscles in her sternum ached.

Now she sat in the truck as night fell, with her view of the fading sea. She had set Ears McCreedy on the dash for company. From the set of her mouth, it was clear that she was thinking.

She switched on the cabin light and found the ledger and the pen she'd taken from Home Depot. There were a lot of decisions to make, and a lot of work to do too – but there was one thing she needed to get done before the restless waves of time washed over her memories, to leave her smooth and featureless.

'My child will know where she comes from,' she said. 'Ain't that right, Mama?'

She thought a while, the pen hovering over the lined paper, before she started.

You're not even born yet, but if I don't set this down, I'm afraid that I'll forget exactly how it was. Ma had her recipe book, but you're going to have your own history written plain and clear.

Baby, I want you to understand some things about the people you came from, how they fought and struggled so that you could be alive and here and with me. The world is going to be different by the time you're grown up in it, and for that I can only be grateful.

It was bad. And the War was only the beginning.